FROM THE CA...
STEVE ROCKFISH - 3

A BAD BOUT OF THE YIPS

KEN HARRIS

ISBN: 978-1-68513-153-1
PUBLISHED BY BLACK ROSE WRITING
www.blackrosewriting.com

Printed in the United States of America
Suggested Retail Price (SRP) $23.95

A Bad Bout of the Yips is printed in Baskerville

*As a planet-friendly publisher, Black Rose Writing does its best to eliminate unnecessary waste to reduce paper usage and energy costs, while never compromising the reading experience. As a result, the final word count vs. page count may not meet common expectations.

Books by
KEN HARRIS

The From the Case Files of Steve Rockfish Series:

THE PINE BARRENS STRATAGEM

SEE YOU NEXT TUESDAY

DEDICATION

For my Labs, Shady McCoy and Chalupa Batman and the endless hours of joy they bring

For James Rockford, Barnaby Jones, David Addison, Dr. R. Quincy, M.E., and the writers that brought these characters to life fueling my love and interest in the genre growing up

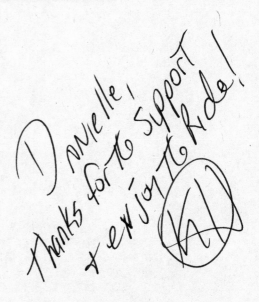

Danielle,
Thanks for the support
+ enjoy the Ride!

A Bad Bout of the Yips

PROLOGUE - RECONNECTING

Ninety days after the crime scene cleaners scraped the last pieces of Earl Porbeagle's brains off Steve Rockfish's front lawn, the July heat played havoc with the new grass. Rockfish & McGee - Investigative Specialists were back to working the type of cases that guaranteed an uneventful day. The kind that always closed with a win for the good guys and prompt payment by their clients. No doomsday cult members looked to separate any employee or their family members from their savings accounts, and two-thirds of the office was perfectly fine with it.

Jawnie McGee almost no longer itched for the adrenaline rush brought on by dangerous field work. She now enjoyed the monotony of infidelity, insurance fraud, and the occasional missing person. The work kept her busy moving forward and prevented her PTSD from cutting the line. But there were times her work outside the office against the cultists, or as the rest of the world learned through the media, the Church of the Universal Nurturing II, rushed to the forefront of her brain. A small part of the thrill of the chase tugged at her.

When those memories forced her to look back, she'd pull out her favorite hoodie, the one with the bullet hole through the side, and give in as thoughts flooded her consciousness. Then, it would be days before she felt herself again. Jawnie's therapist had said there was no way she'd mentally overcome all she had been through in only a matter of months and a handful of sessions.

Jawnie hoped moving forward there would be good days where she's a stronger person, mentally, and a shrinking number of bad ones.

The firm's only hire to date, Lynn Hurricane-Tesla, proved to be more than either partner imagined. Lynn excelled at running the day-to-day administrative duties of the office. She kept all the appointments running consecutively in the morning hours, leaving the two investigators free to handle casework in the afternoons and some evenings. Lynn, too, suffered her share of the all too often bad flashback from her kidnapping and time on the run with Earl Porbeagle. Three months wasn't an expected timeframe for her to stop flinching with the occasional scream when she'd see a white pickup truck, hear a loud noise, or even walk past a piece of white trash with a beard in the produce aisle of the grocery store.

Lynn needed to move on from those days of bondage and subjugation. She had moved out of the Motel 8 and back with her sister. Karen's heavy-handed approach and need to provide input on every decision Lynn made, only caused Lynn to recede further into the back of her brain. It didn't take long before Lynn fled and moved into Jawnie's condo. She, much like Jawnie, was happier behind a desk and typing away on her computer. It would be a long time before she played the role of confidential informant again.

Raphael "Raffi" Pérez, Rockfish's long-time friend, part-time confidential informant and full-time scam artist, had not missed a beat after Mack shot Porbeagle only inches from his own head. Raffi had picked himself off the front lawn, dusted off his suit and forged ahead toward his next sketchy, money-making venture. Needless to say, he did not show up for the initial therapy appointment made in his name.

As for the firm's founding partner, Steve Rockfish, he was in a full out effort to repair his relationship with friend and now Baltimore Police Department Captain Dan Decker. Decker received a much-deserved promotion over the hot mess that was the Porbeagle case. Close to a million dollars in asset forfeiture and the prevention of a WMD event was how the politicians spun it. The bump to Captain also helped take some of the sting out of his beef with Rockfish.

Rockfish was the one-third itching for something exciting to work. A case with large enough white caps to excite him, but small enough so the rest of his team wouldn't need to be chased down by the men with butterfly nets.

The office phones hadn't stopped ringing. Calls from potential clients continued to keep Lynn busy setting up meetings, but none of them gave Rockfish reason to pause, swallow hard, and feel the excitement meter rise. He wasn't looking forward to the upcoming meeting with Angel Davenport. Davenport, the producer of NikolaTV's streaming hit *The Pine Barrens Stratagem*, the docuseries detailing Rockfish and Jawnie's first case, was flying in shortly to discuss a second season covering the Porbeagle case. Not even the thought of another bountiful Hollywood paycheck could get him worked up about the meeting.

And finally, there was Mack, Rockfish's dad, and the man who pulled the trigger, sending Porbeagle's brain matter across the Kentucky bluegrass. Nothing phased him after he attained his revenge on the man who orchestrated the scam that temporarily separated the old man from seventeen thousand of his retirement dollars. He had handed the long gun over to the first officer on the scene, answered all their questions and slipped back inside to catch the final fifteen minutes of Homicide Hunter: Lt. Joe Kenda on DiscoveryID. Zippy the silver Labrador curled up at his feet.

CHAPTER ONE

You've reached Rockfish & McGee, Investigative Specialists. At the tone, leave your name and message. Someone will get back to you. [Beep]

Jawnie stared down at her phone, annoyed. She hung up the call after the office's message ended and slid the phone into her messenger bag. *With a proper receptionist comes a proper voicemail message. It's about time. Where the heck is everyone? Rockfish could be out doing God knows what, but what about Lynn? Maybe she's in the can after an extra spicy lunch?* Jawnie laughed to herself. *There were a thousand and one reasons Lynn couldn't get to the phone. Don't go all Rockfish at once.*

The sun had slipped behind the clouds on a mid-Thursday afternoon when Jawnie walked down the endless row of marble steps in front of the Baltimore County Government building. She had submitted her final report regarding former county employee Harvey Henderson, who had been sitting at home on disability from a leg injury suffered while on the job. Henderson ran a bulldozer at the county landfill. That was until he fell off the equipment and reportedly injured his leg.

Jawnie loved this type of case. She conducted a couple of surveillances to find out Henderson's daily schedule and then one final, quick outing to snap a few pictures from a safe distance. Jawnie followed Harvey and his mistress down to the town of Laurel and out on the Rocky Gorge Reservoir, where the couple spent the day attempting to wake-board. The day served as a twofer and the future ex-Mrs. Henderson would gain the information needed to win her freedom without spending a dime.

At the bottom of the steps, she pulled her phone back out, and double checked the time. Five after two and still no notifications. Apparently, nothing of importance had transpired while she was in the meeting with the County Commissioners. Her car was across the street in the paid lot, and she glanced up from the screen. Jawnie felt flush and concern filled her brain. The green Kia Soul remained parked at the corner, blocking a hydrant. Her heart kicked it up a notch.

The damn thing hadn't moved in the hour and a half while I was inside. Jesus Christ, I don't need this shit today. Or any day. Fuck.

Three times today since leaving her condo, the Kia coincidently found itself parked nearby, always within eyesight. The odd shaped vehicle and the color stood out. *Amateur hour or someone who clearly wants me to notice.* Jawnie gritted her teeth, glanced both ways, and then kept her head down as she jogged across the street. She walked through the small lot until she found her Subaru and slid behind the wheel. She pulled around to the exit gate and paid the attendant. A second later, the arm rose, but the car didn't move. Thoughts of the Kia had Jawnie lost deep in her mind.

What Would Rockfish Do? Probably tell me to go on the offensive, concern be damned. Well, I'm definitely not going to pull sideways in front of this guy, jump out and confront him, that's for sure. People are crazy these days and with my luck I'd end up TikTok famous #KarensGoneWild. Okay, let's see if I'm imagining things. Maybe give him a little I see you action instead.

Jawnie turned left onto Pennsylvania Ave and sped up. At the end of the block, when she was right alongside the Kia, she held her breath and cut the wheel. The Subaru hung a hard right onto Baltimore Ave and missed the Kia's left front fender by only a foot. *Enough to make him take notice.* She straightened the wheel and exhaled. Her eyes shot to the rearview mirror. The Kia followed suit but was losing ground as she pressed down on the accelerator. The car remained a block back when Jawnie turned right again. Her eyes flickered from the front windshield to the rearview, expecting to see the Kia at any second, but it never appeared. Or at least that she noticed. Her grip on the steering wheel grew tighter.

Did I lose him? Was he some civilian who flew into road rage when I almost hit him and then gave up once his blood pressure came down? No. I definitely saw that car multiple times today.

Half an hour later and back in Anne Arundel County, Jawnie received an answer to her question. She spotted the Kia two cars back at a traffic light. *Alright McGee, you aren't imagining things. Let's figure out who this driver is.*

"Hey Siri. New note."

"What do you want it to say?"

"Dark green Kia Soul Maryland Plate 555-RJ4K."

"Ok, I've created your note. It's called Dark green Kia Soul Maryland plate 555-RJ4K."

I'll call Michelle at DMV to run it as soon as I get back to the office. The favor may cost me a drink or an actual date, but it will be worth it to know who he is. Hopefully, the name will ring a bell. The last thing I need is a fresh surprise.

Jawnie was only a mile from the office but took the Kia on a short sight-seeing tour of Linthicum Heights. See exactly how dedicated the driver was to their mission. First stop was Fairway Car Wash. Jawnie got in line behind the others and when it was her turn, she lined up the front left tire to the guide and selected the Supreme.

A tapping on the driver's side glass caught her attention.

"Hands off the wheel, ma'am."

Jawnie looked down. White knuckles. Her hands slid off the wheel and fell to her lap as the car jerked forward. She tried to relax and think calmly as the conveyor pulled her forward. Each stage coated the windshield with a different chemical and blocked the view. *Because you don't see him, it doesn't mean he's gone. Maybe he's hiding behind that iHop, but with a simple line of sight as you exit the car wash? What's next? Mario's?* She had dry cleaning that was overdue to be picked up. *Big ass empty lot there, nowhere to hide and nowhere to street park.* As she exited the car wash, the track gave way. Her hands returned to the wheel. Jawnie waved off the man, wanting to finish drying the Subaru with an armful of hand towels. *I'm good, no thank you*, she mouthed as she cracked the window and slid out a five-dollar bill.

Mario's was four lights further down the road and by the third red light, the Kia emerged from the background. Jawnie could feel the sweat building on her lower back. A single drop formed on the side of her face. She lifted her arm and wiped away the drop with her sleeve. Mario's came up on the left and Jawnie put on her blinker. *No need to attempt some big ruse at this point.*

Five minutes later, she exited Mario's with her dry cleaning hung over her left shoulder and iPhone held in her right, ready to capture the moment for posterity's sake. Jawnie took the picture before the guy could raise his newspaper in a piss poor effort to hide his identity. She unlocked the Subaru and hung her clothes on the back hook. She got in and slammed the door. A combination of the force and noise caused her to jump.

Goddamnit! WWRD? I should have done something proactive after the meeting back at the county building. Jawnie reached into the center console. She chose her weapon of choice and speed walked to the Kia. *Deep breath, deep breath. Look and act like you belong here.*

The man was blond, with very short hair. Maybe balding. She couldn't tell with the slight window tint. When he spotted her approaching, the newspaper went back up. Jawnie snapped another picture before sliding the phone into her back pocket. She tapped on the window. The early edition of the Baltimore Sun didn't move.

She rapped her knuckles a second time. Harder, louder. This time the paper came down and the man's eyebrows went up. He reached over and lowered the window, roughly two inches, before speaking.

"Can I help—"

The mace streamed through the opening as if she was an Olympic crack shot. The creeper didn't see it coming and Jawnie didn't stick around to see the after-effects. She could hear his screams, interlaced with every curse word in the book by the time she slid behind the wheel. Her death grip returned, and she rocketed out of Mario's parking lot without a clear destination in mind and a little less rubber on her tires.

The Subaru ended up in the parking lot of a Wawa, a good half mile down the road. Jawnie parked behind the convenience store. She pulled up the note she made earlier with the Kia's license plate and added the photos. At the bottom of the note, she dictated the man's description in two sentences and returned her phone to the cup holder.

Jawnie exhaled and didn't move. *How long had it been? Three months? Maybe a little longer. Well, kid, it was an enjoyable ride. I look forward to the next extended period of calm. Maybe today showed I'm not built for this line of work.* Her mind went back to the night on Rockfish's front lawn. Porbeagle's gun. The sound of the shot. The smell of burning cotton as the bullet passed through the material of her oversized sweatshirt. *Fixing middle school laptops out of my garage doesn't sound so bad now. Granted, no one's launching a streaming network based on that show, but then again, I don't have to look over my shoulder every time I leave the goddamn house.* Jawnie stopped rubbing her hands and dropped her head into them. The tears flowed freely.

She didn't remember how long she remained parked next to the dumpster, but when she felt she could make it back to the office without having a complete emotional meltdown, she shifted into drive.

****

Rockfish and Lynn sat in the open bullpen area of the office. He preferred to meet here as a group, as opposed to squeezing into his own small private office. The partners recognized that the open area led to better collaboration and furnished it to accommodate those needs. A large sofa, two recliners and a small conference table facing a retractable screen for presentations filled the space. The sofa was a sleeper for those late nights when a case or one too many Jamesons kept Rockfish there overnight. A partially stocked bar lined the wall behind the recliners with a small refrigerator for cold drinks and DoorDash leftovers.

"It's not like her to be late," Lynn said.

Rockfish noticed Lynn had looked down at her phone every couple of minutes since the meeting started. This after-hours meeting had become a reoccurring routine on Thursday evenings. All agreed. This time was best spent strategizing about pending cases and brainstorming to confirm no one had overlooked any minor detail. No matter how small or routine. Also, Lynn would take the floor and discuss potential clients, upcoming meetings recently added to the office calendar and any administrative housekeeping issues.

Rockfish didn't want to sound any more alarms, so he quietly worried about Jawnie to himself. *It wasn't like her at all. I wonder if she—*

He didn't complete the thought before the front door swung open and in she walked. Jawnie power walked past reception and appeared to be headed for the short back hallway that led to their private offices. An apology flew over her shoulder before she disappeared.

"I'm so sorry. Gimme five, I'll be right back out," Jawnie said.

Lynn stood up and walked over to the front door, locked it, flipped the sign and pulled the shade.

Rockfish raised his eyebrows and tilted his head. He gave Lynn a look when she returned to the couch.

"Looks as if she's running on no sleep for the last seventy-two hours. Remind me again, Henderson was the guy at the dump, right? Nothing exciting there, nothing to cause her to look like she parachuted into North Vietnam and single-handedly rescued half a dozen POWs?"

"Rambo?" Lynn said.

"Nice. You're getting better at this game. But seriously, that dump case was a piece of cake, right?"

"Yeah, wrapped up with a big red bow and she was dropping it off and answering questions the county commissioners might have had."

"Just what I thought," Rockfish said and stood to pour himself another drink. *Red bow or not, something's under her skin. I'll cut Lynn loose after this and see what I can pry out of the kid.*

Jawnie didn't emerge from her office for another fifteen minutes. When she came out, she took up a seat next to Lynn on the couch.

"You all good?" Rockfish said.

"Totally. Let's do this," Jawnie replied.

Rockfish could see she had failed at putting up a good front, but didn't let on.

"Okay, I'll take the lead tonight," Rockfish said. "A few things off the top of my head on what is becoming an extremely vanilla case load for the firm." Rockfish chose his words carefully and looked over at Jawnie for any kind of reaction. Her head was down, buried in her laptop. He couldn't get a read on her reaction. "I think I've got everything I need to close out Stankovich. It's cases like this that I can work from the comfort of my seven-hundred-and-fifty-dollar ergonomic office chair that's gonna be the death of me. I know, I know, they pay the bills. Lynn, I'm going to need you to book some more exciting potential client meetings." *Hmm, still no reaction.* He looked at Lynn and she shrugged.

"The only other point I have tonight is for everyone to remember Davenport is flying in a week from tomorrow on Friday, the thirteenth. Quite ominous. Lynn, I know you were a big part of that case, but I don't want you to feel you have to take part. Only if you're up to it." Rockfish stood up and stepped closer to Lynn on the couch. "If any of it strikes a nerve or gets too hectic, don't feel the need to stick around. It's only a proposal meeting, nothing on a second season is in stone. To be honest, I'd like it not to be and for us to continue doing good investigations, with some hot sauce sprinkled on a few from time to time. I'm looking at you, Hurricane-Tesla."

"Thanks, Steve, trying my best. I'm all over Angel's visit. I made his reservation for The Sagamore Pendry Hotel."

"We paying for that?" Rockford said, hoping to get a rise out of his partner. It did not. "That's like eight fifty a night."

"No, we're not. I only made the reservation," Lynn said. "The studio is covering all his expenses for the trip."

Rockfish nodded. It did not thrill him to deal with all the headaches another season of reality TV would bring, but the money from NikolaTV more than made up for the pain. He and Mack would be closer to docking their dream boat behind the house.

"Floor's yours, Jawnie. I mean, if you have anything?"

Jawnie's eyes remained firmly on her laptop, and it took a tap on the shoulder from Lynn to bring her back to the meeting space.

Rockfish watched his partner. She put her laptop to the side and stood. *My guess is she's ready to pitch something. She always stands when she does. Is this what's got her wound around the axle? Fuck, she's got as much say in what cases we take as I do, so no need for the dramatics.*

Jawnie paced back and forth between the large conference table and the more informal bullpen area and detailed a potential case brought to her by two friends and partners, Pilar and Kara. The women had purchased Chesapeake Mini-Golf from the previous owners of forty-years with plans to refurbish the entire course and rechristen it Little Golf Big Tees.

"... Since they closed on the property, there have been vague online threats and some vandalism to their contractor's equipment and supplies. The cops claim it is nothing more than the actions of bored kids and suggested purchasing some security cameras."

"Sounds like your friends think it's more," Rockfish said.

"Pilar didn't buy the local kid angle from the get go. A company, Fulsome Commercial Realty Group, actually outbid Kara and Pilar. But the previous owners of Chesapeake Mini-Golf didn't accept the company's offer. They chose the lesser if only for the thought that the course would continue to bring joy to the community and keep the memories of the past 40 years alive. Even after settlement, Fulsome continues to reach out to Pilar and Kara with alternating threats or way over the top offers."

"So, in a nutshell, we're being asked to confirm Fulsome is behind all of this and help these women with making a case the police cannot drive away from?" Rockfish looked across at Jawnie. *She still looks like absolute shit, but made her pitch for that case, like a pro. But this can't be what's bothering her. I also have a nagging feeling about those clients being her crunchy granola friends. Would they be able to meet our rates, or is every cent tied up in the purchase and renovation of this mini-golf money pit?*

"And I know what you're thinking, Steve. No, they can't meet our rates, but sometimes you need to give back to the community," Jawnie said. "These two are trying to salvage a historical landmark. This mini-golf has served the families of Glen Burnie for almost forty years. And if Angel's flying out here, that means NikolaTV is going to throw a bunch of money at us. We can afford to take on one case, because it's the right thing to do. Did I forget to mention they're applying for a liquor license?"

Rockfish reached across Lynn with his fist, and Jawnie bumped it. Her last bit of information intrigued him.

"Lynn, I'll AirDrop you their contact information," Jawnie said. "Set up an initial client meeting as soon as you can."

Rockfish dismissed Lynn from the rest of the meeting and steered Jawnie back to his office to see if she'd come clean on what was eating her earlier, and by the looks of her, likely still was.

Once in Rockfish's office with the door shut, anxious Jawnie returned. She stood against the wall to Rockfish's right instead of sitting in the chair directly opposite him.

"Spill it, McGee. Just you and me here."

And she did. Jawnie looked no better after finishing up, detailing the high pitch squeals that emanated from the Kia as the mace did its thing. Rockfish loved every minute of her decision making. *It took its toll on her, but goddamn, that made my day.*

"You gonna run that plate past your ex-paramour over at DMV, or are you all out of markers? If so, I can try Decker."

"I've already left Michelle a message. Hopefully, time has made the heart grow fonder, at least for this favor," Jawnie said, and cracked a smile.

"That's my girl!" Rockfish said. "Now, do you think this guy really has it out for you, or did you commit felony assault on some poor citizen?"

"He was terrible or very good at his job. I don't know which. Him, I can handle. I'm pretty sure of that, but it's the emotions all bubbling back to the surface and them fucking with my decision-making ability that scares the ever-loving shit out of me."

Jawnie looked down at her shoes. When she looked up, Rockfish could see what he thought was a tear. She continued to talk and moved from the wall. She ended up slouched in the chair. "I mean, I see how every little thing makes Lynn jump and I'm not sure my nerves are going to last. It's like the first time as a kid you think you saw the boogeyman. You see him everywhere after."

"Seeing that therapist?"

"Once a week, still. Thank God for co-pays."

"Good, keep it up. These things take time. You got this," Rockfish said. "Remember, do as I say and not as I do."

"No more playing WWRD? Because I think it actually helped today."

"In moderation, McGee. Moderation."

Jawnie laughed, and Rockfish felt a little better for her. *A few more baby steps and I can stop worrying.*

"Now sit up in that chair while I go make another drink. Do you want anything?"

"No, I'm going to cut out shortly and go soak in a tub until I'm a prune."

"Excellent call. When I get back in a second, you're going to tell me all about this exotic mini-golf course. Promise me all the drinks won't come with tiny umbrellas in them."

Jawnie smiled at Rockfish as he walked past. He knew two things. She was going to be okay, and they were going to lose money on this mini-golf deal.

****

Friday afternoon found Rockfish and Jawnie headed out to meet her friends, Pilar Dampen and Kara Lipton. Rockfish offered to drive and Jawnie realized he wasn't completely sure she had recovered from yesterday's melt down. His sports car, nicknamed Lana, with Rockfish behind the wheel, would have better odds at running from or chasing down Jawnie's mystery man, depending on what the situation called for.

Lana cruised up I-95 towards downtown Baltimore and Jawnie was giddy with excitement over what she hoped was Rockfish's outlandish reaction to their destination. The wild emotions of yesterday seemed far away to her, except for the times when she found her eyes darting in all directions, looking for a distraction to hopefully put the previous day's events behind her. The good news was that no uniformed police showed up at her condo or the office to question her about the mace incident, and Captain Decker didn't call Rockfish and give him an earful about a complaint filed by John Q. Citizen.

Cut the shit, you're going to screw this whole thing up! Pilar and Kara are counting on you to seal the deal with Rockfish this afternoon. Focus. Can't do a damn thing to help them if your mind is looking for the boogeyman behind every damn corner. We're doing something here for a couple of good people. Opportunities such as this, in this profession, are few and far between. I need to make sure Rockfish buys in and we put the full court press on whoever's doing this.

"Make a right up here and look for a place to park. We can walk the rest of the way," Jawnie said.

With Lana street-parked and the meter fed, Jawnie led Rockfish down the street and through an old alley. The closer they got, the more she scanned his face for any type of reaction, but so far Rockfish was stone faced. She finally got the reaction she wanted when they stopped in front of an old brick building that resembled a speakeasy from the last century. Its current reincarnation was as Maxine's Waterfront Café; a favorite of Jawnie and her friends.

"You stopped," Rockfish said. "Is this—"

And at that moment, she knew his eyes had locked in on the poster in the window.

Maxine's Presents a Tribute to John Waters - The Early Years

"Really, Jawnie? A freakin' drag show at three o'clock in the goddamn afternoon?"

"It's Friday and damn near close to happy hour. Same as one of your business meetings at The Bounce House, out by the airport, if you ask me. Plus, you're the one who said you needed to get out of the office but didn't want to stand around talking shop at a half demolished mini-golf course." Jawnie smiled widely, winked, and reached for the door.

"Not to say I won't go in, but most folks here have had the double jab?" Rockfish said.

"Yes, trust me. Everyone is vaccinated inside. This crowd gets it," Jawnie said.

The inside of the club was dark, despite the time of day. Eighteenth-century brick lined the walls. Jawnie spotted Pilar and Kara at a table far from the stage and silently thanked them. *Being closer to the door for when the EMTs needed to stretcher Rockfish out the door after his heart attack.*

"Steve, I'd like you to meet Pilar..."

Pilar stood up and offered her hand across the table. Rockfish met her outstretched hand with an awkward fist bump. She dressed in jeans and a long sleeve white button-up shirt. Her straight black hair flowed long past her shoulders and down her chest.

"... and this is Kara."

Kara saw the previous exchange and knew to throw rock. She was the polar opposite of her partner, dressed in a green flowery sundress with red hair in a shoulder-length bob and glasses.

The four sat down and a server stopped to take drink orders. Pilar wasted no time in getting straight down to business before Jawnie could help make the smooth transition from social chit-chat.

"Mr. Rockfish, I won't repeat anything Jawnie already told you," Pilar said. "I'm not here to waste your time."

"Good to hear, because the quicker I'm back on my deck, the better," Rockfish said with a smile and a nod.

Pilar then covered the couple's issues in more detail than Jawnie had.

"... not to mention we heard Fulsome Commercial Realty Group also purchased the burned-out Applebee's next door. Whoever previously owned the Applebee's abandoned it and let the building go to hell. Supposedly, Fulsome took ownership of that parcel a year before bidding on Chesapeake Mini-Golf."

"I can have our research specialist pull records from the tax assessor's office to see if Fulsome is on some sort of land grab in the area," Jawnie said. "I'll have her prepare a map of the area with an overlay of properties Fulsome has purchased. It might give us an idea of where they're headed with this."

"Of course, their bid was more about the land than preserving the course," Kara said. "The Applebee's is a total eyesore, and they've done nothing with that plot since buying it. Part of me thinks they'll leave it up, rat infestation and all, to throw a monkey wrench into our grand re-opening."

"Not to mention we've already turned down two large offers from Fulsome to sell," Pilar said. "They followed the last one with a threat left on our windshield after a visit to the property. Although we can't prove it was them."

Jawnie looked over at Rockfish to gauge his interest. He had his poker face on, and she couldn't get a read. *I need him onboard here, not a casual yes that is followed by him always finding himself too busy to help. Time to go for those Rockfish heartstrings. There's a big old softy somewhere in there. I've seen it.*

"Can you fill in Steve on some of the more cowardly bullshit that's been happening since you turned down the second offer? And Anne Arundel County Police's thoughts on the matter."

"Yeah, thoughts," Kara said. "Because talking is all those worthless motherfuckers have done. Defund the lot of 'em."

"Easy, Kara. That ain't going to get us anywhere," Pilar said. "But to a point, she's right. Once we turned down the second offer and began demolishing the course, whoever it is, Fulsome or some other hired goons, increased the heat a few degrees."

Pilar recounted a two-part tale of common vandalism. The first encompassed the destruction and theft of construction supplies and equipment and a second avenue of attack sounded more akin to psyops warfare.

"... tons of gay slurs spray painted on anything with a flat surface. Male gay porn pictures printed off the internet and then strewn about the property, only to have the wind take it down the street where someone's grandma picked it up walking home from the store. You know where they direct that ire at."

Jawnie could hear the inflection in her friend's voice and noticed the napkin Pilar held. Her free hand tore small pieces in time with every syllable enunciated. To the right of her chair, it looked as if a tiny snowstorm had blown through and settled over the table. She shifted her eyes to Kara. Her head was down and her hands rested on the table, clinched tight. *This is more than a business for these ladies. They need us. But what if he's not sold? I can't do this alone, not with the anxiety and the mental gymnastics I perform to get out of bed each morning. I have to. This is bigger than the boogeyman. I promise.*

"... not to mention the flyers left on doorsteps, residences, and businesses alike."

"They are the absolute worst," Kara said, lifting her head and staring Rockfish right in the eyes. "They claim weekends at Little Golf Big Tees will make the old Dinah Shore golf tournament look like an episode of the 700 Club."

"Dinah Shore? That old talk show broad from the 70s?" Rockfish sounded and looked confused.

"I can fill you in on the backstory later," Jawnie interjected. *I need Rockfish to stay on point.* "It's vile the lies being spread and like I mentioned yesterday, this part of community policing doesn't thrill the cops."

"The cops don't give a shit, because I don't have a fucking envelope for them on the weekly," Pilar said with a hefty dash of venom. "They told us we should put up cameras and if we catch someone on tape, then maybe they can do something. But of course, no promises."

"Well, I'm not sure if Jawnie mentioned this or not, but I've got an in with the Baltimore Police Department," Rockfish said, and Jawnie smiled. It actually thrilled her he'd listened. "If we can gather enough evidence and take it to them, perhaps they can lean on Anne Arundel County enough to get them off their ass. Or sell the feds on a civil rights violation."

"That sounds expensive," Pilar said. "Like money we don't have, since we also have a long list of improvements needed before we can even apply for our liquor license."

"Yeah, Jawnie mentioned that. She also mentioned us possibly working this case, gratis."

"It is true. With our books in the shape they are in now," Kara said. "We can't afford your rates, or daily expenses. We're relying on humanity with this one and Jawnie said you might be open to barter?"

"We're not talking chickens, right?"

"No, Mr. Rockfish, no poultry," Pilar added. "I was thinking more like a Little Golf Big Tees lifetime pass with a negotiable discount on adult beverages."

And here we are. Jawnie held her breath.

"You mean I can swing a putter with a beer in my free hand? While my date anxiously looks at her watch? That's some mighty fine evening entertainment there. Hell, I could even swap out the conference table for client meetings underneath the big windmill. This idea might have legs." Rockfish laughed aloud and reached for his glass. "Ladies, you knew before dragging me here I wouldn't go against Jawnie's recommendation. We'll have to change up our normal client agreement paperwork, but I think we're good here. Cheers."

Four glasses met in the air above the center of the table as a Divine impersonator took the stage.

* * * * * * * * *

"See, it wasn't so bad. You survived, right?"

"Gloria Gaynor would be proud, McGee," Rockfish said as they left Maxine's and headed for the car. *For the love of God, some of those performances were brutal. Not as bad as the time she made me watch a Lifetime Christmas movie as an unofficial office Christmas party, but damn close. I'm going to need to go home, dig out Rob Zombie's Past, Present & Future on vinyl and cleanse my palate.*

"And speaking of surviving, why don't you toss me that key fob and let me make sure we both get back to the office in one piece?"

Rockfish complied with his partner's order and crossed himself as he slid into Lana's passenger seat.

"One piece of advice before you start her hemi?"

"Shoot."

"Little miniature Decker's will be out in force until we cross the county line. Second to the last Friday of the month and quotas are coming due."

"The right-hand lane and the speed limit are my jam. Don't you worry."

Old passenger seat habits die hard. Rockfish had Jawnie adjust the side mirror for him and he opened the one on the visor. He made a buzzed, mental snapshot of the cars he could see. He watched as Jawnie repeated the process from her seat and she immediately lowered the volume on the radio to zero.

"He's here. Oh, for fuck's sake."

"Mace Face?"

"I'd bet your half of the next NikolaTV direct deposit on it," Jawnie said. "Silver Toyota across the street, facing the wrong way."

"What the hell?" Rockfish said. *What is with this guy? Street parked and facing against traffic?* Rockfish looked around again. *Probably the best he could do and still monitor us.* "Okay, tell you what. We've done this before in your old Scion when that Jeep forced us off the road in the Pine Barrens."

"How can I forget? It was the day we met." Jawnie couldn't help but smirk.

She thinks she's being funny, trying to laugh it off, but it sure ain't coming off that way. But the tone of her voice, the grip on the steering wheel and the constant revving of the engine paints a different picture. Fuck, I should have stopped drinking during the scene from Hairspray. You knew she wasn't making it up yesterday.

"Exactly like that time, I direct and you execute," Rockfish said. "Better results this time, I promise. Step one, stop pressing on the gas pedal. Don't tease Lana, or she won't be there for you when needed."

Nothing. Not a word. Her eyes glued to that damn side mirror. Fine, let's start the play.

"Step two, wait until someone's coming at us in the other lane. Wait until you think they're too close, then gun the engine and cut the wheel as hard as you can to the left. If you need me to give you a countdown, I'll do it. That clown won't expect us to make a U-turn."

Lana sat on the side of the road as a handful of cars came and went. Each of Rockfish's countdowns went unheeded. He surprised himself with how cool he remained, as Lana never moved an inch every time he landed on GO.

"Okay, Jawnie, you still with me?"

"Yes."

"Good, because you're going to do it this time and then stick to that right lane and speed limit. I don't care if he rams us from behind. Don't deviate from the plan. Unless I tell you, then deviate like a motherfucker." Rockfish reached over and gave her thigh a slight shake. The gesture was the best he could do at the moment.

Three minutes later he said go in a quieter, calmer tone, gave the same leg a squeeze, and the torque threw him against the passenger side door. *Seatbelt asshole. Let's try to make it through this alive.*

The screeches from both Lana's tires as she gained traction and the oncoming car's brakes filled the air. Jawnie steered into the skid like a pro and straightened Lana out before pressing down further on the gas. They both shot a look at a surprised Mace Face as they passed alongside, with Rockfish adding a one-finger salute for good measure.

"Was—"

"It was him. I'm sure of it," Jawnie said.

"Okay. Eyes forward, let me worry about what he's doing. Which is following us at the moment. Remember, right lane, safe speed and listen to me." Rockfish's memory went back to that late afternoon in the Pine Barrens. He hoped the defensive driving lessons he had since paid for would come into play. Add Jawnie's skill to Lana's muscle and he had a better feeling about this time if Mace Face turned it up a notch.

"You holding up, okay?" Rockfish said. His partner was white as a ghost and held the steering wheel as if her life depended on it. *Can't afford for her to break down now. She's gotta hold it together until we're stopped somewhere. In one piece. Maybe I need to give her a refresher course.* His eyes darted from the side mirror to the one on the visor and back. The Toyota had made the turn, but seemed content to hang back and avoid any confrontation.

"You're doing good, kid. He's back there but keeping his distance. I bet he thinks you reloaded with bear spray." The laugh he had expected didn't come. Nor did any kind of acknowledgment, and that ratcheted up the worry meter in Rockfish's gut.

When Jawnie merged onto I-95 South, the pressure on that meter lessened as she stayed in the right-hand lane and kept it under sixty-five. *Okay, despite being unresponsive, she's listening. We're not heading back to her place or the office, that's for damn sure. Think Rockfish. Where do you want this to play out?* He glanced back, and the Toyota continued to follow suit, albeit further than when on the side streets of Baltimore. *He's not on our ass. Perhaps he is really only out to scare us? But from fucking what? Our cases are as goddamn boring as you can get lately. We're going to have to figure out who this clown is and why he's been up her ass for the past two days.*

"Alright, Jawnie. I'm going to assume you're still listening because you're good like that. Do you remember Saburo

Yamamoto? The guy with the grocery store on Deering in Morrell Park? We saved his ass in the slip-and-fall lawsuit?"

Rockfish looked over, and Jawnie nodded but kept quiet. *Better than nothing.*

"I want you to take the next exit. I need to do a little shopping at Yamamoto's Asian Grocery. You need anything?"

She shook her head and put on her blinker, way too early.

He's not on our ass, but no need to telegraph for the next mile we're turning. Fuck, I can't say that. One wrong, negative thing and she falls apart. The tears will flow and then she can't see. Her death grip on the wheel loosens, and I'll be trying to steer this damn thing from the passenger seat. If I can get her parked and safely in the store, I'll deal with the guy.

Rockfish noticed the Toyota had closed the gap somewhat once they left the interstate. He spotted the sign for Yamamoto's up on the right and pointed it out to Jawnie.

"Pull into a spot as close to the front doors as you can and walk with me inside."

Jawnie made the right turn, pulled into the lot and aimed straight for a handicapped space. The spot was a sign to Rockfish that while she looked scared, deep inside, it was worse than he thought. *The kid never breaks the law, ever.* He jumped out of the car, ran around the front of Lana, and opened the driver's side door.

"Let's go, you'll be safe inside," Rockfish said as he held on to her arm and practically pulled her through the front door. The store was the size of an average convenience store. Three well-stocked aisles comprised most space, with a butcher shop running the length of the left wall.

Saburo manned the store's only register at the front of the small grocery and emphatically waved to Rockfish as they entered the store. He was a small elderly man with the beginnings of osteoporosis, which caused him to stand bent over. He dressed in his standard uniform, Rockfish had never seen him deviate from, of a white paper hat with matching t-shirt and apron.

"Hey Saburo, sounds strange but do me a favor, lock that front door and keep an eye on Jawnie for me. I'm dealing with a slight bit of trouble. I'll explain in a sec," Rockfish said as he made a beeline for the rear of the store and cruised through the hanging plastic, separating the back area from the three aisles.

I need something to friggin use other than my fists. I got no idea what this guy is packing and the last thing I want to do is bring a soba noodle to a knife fight. Rockfish hectically looked around the area, a top boxes and work areas. He spotted what looked to be a workbench and grabbed a box cutter and small crowbar from it and threw open the back door. He made his way around to the left side of the store, hugging the wall. The man with a plan had none. He was operating fully on adrenaline and emotion. *Not my finest hour.*

Rockfish stopped and leaned around the front corner of the store. He spotted the Toyota parked directly behind Lana in the next row. Mace Face was staring at the front door, and at this moment, Rockfish chose violence. He looped around the parking lot to come at the car from behind, guessing correctly the man was not checking his rearview. Rockfish approached the left rear tire and released the box cutter. The blade punctured the sidewall close to the tread and the sound of escaping air was music to his ears. Mace Face was still oblivious to what was going on. Rockfish walked up to the driver's side window and tapped the glass with the box cutter.

The man turned his head and jumped at the same time. But he settled back in and gave Rockfish the finger. *Typical mousey little man. Fear turns to bravado real quick when he remembers the thick sheet of glass separating us.*

"Come on, man, I want to talk. I don't have any mace," Rockfish said. He held the box cutter, let it slip from his grasp and fall to the asphalt. The crowbar remained in his right hand, tight against his side and out of sight. Mace Face assumed not rolling down the window meant he was safe. Somewhere in the back of Rockfish's mind, a narrator spoke. *He was, in fact, not safe.*

Rockfish raised the crowbar and brought it down against the glass. It cracked and sagged heavily, but it didn't break. He looked at the spiderweb pattern for a second and tried to figure out what he expected to gain from smashing the window. Those few seconds cost him as the passenger door flew open. By the time his attention moved on from the cracked glass, the man had crawled across the center console and out the passenger door. Mace Face was now ten yards away and sprinting. Rockfish thought better of following. He had more pressing concerns. He walked around and leaned in through the open door and grabbed the keys out of the ignition.

Enterprise Rent-A-Car. Probably the same for yesterday's Kia. Oh, and what's this in the back seat?

A Fulsome Commercial Realty Group lanyard laid on the back seat. *Thank God for company swag.* Attached to the lanyard was a key card, but Rockfish knew someone would deactivate it long before he could ever get the chance to figure out what door it opened.

Rockfish walked back to Yamamoto's front door and tapped on the glass with the crowbar. Saburo ran over and unlocked it. Rockfish patted him on the shoulder and gave his former client a hardy thank you. He then spotted Jawnie squatting against an end-cap display of seaweed. Tears raced down her face. The afternoon had been too much on her. Too soon after the Porbeagle mess.

Rockfish bent down alongside her, ignoring the cracking in his knees, and wrapped his arms around her.

"Never doubt my belief in you. It's just that sometimes I need a little extra convincing."

CHAPTER TWO

The following day, Rockfish forewent his normal coffee and Mack's special breakfast sandwich on the deck to instead head out, pick up some flowers, and check on the second most important person in his life.

He arrived at her condo slightly before noon, or, as Jawnie would say, brunch o'clock. In the elevator to the ninth floor, he contemplated what he would say, how she would look, and if there would ever be a time during the visit for the conversation to focus on work. Rockfish knocked on the door and Lynn answered, looking slightly worn and glad to see someone other than their common patient. She was in matching Ravens' sweats and t-shirt, so Rockfish gave her points for knowing her audience.

"How's the kid doing?"

"Better than yesterday. She had an online session with her therapist this morning. It did wonders for her overall mood. I've got to run out shortly and pick up a prescription for her that the doc called in. I totally get what she's going through. I mean, I can hide behind a keyboard in the office. She's out and about, waiting on a trigger that she won't see coming."

"Oh, she saw this stalker coming a mile away, and do you mind if I step in?"

Lynn muttered an apology regarding leaving her boss out in the hallway and stepped out of the doorway. "Gimme those and I'll put them in some water. She's in the living room, glued to that fancy schmancy massage chair that Costco delivered last month." Lynn yanked the flowers from Rockfish's grasp.

The lady doth protest too much, methinks. It's not like we haven't been here for her in a supportive role. I fucking know she went through ten times as much as Jawnie with that Porbeagle shit. Fuck, does she want a trophy? I'll go back out and pick it up, along with another bouquet. Dancing as fast as I can here.

"Hey, hey, hey, look who's here," Rockfish said as he passed the walkway to the kitchen and stepped into the living room. The large room was more akin to a living and dining room combo. A dining table and chairs were off to his right and typical living room furniture filled the rest of the space. A large sliding door led to a small patio.

Jawnie sat in what looked like the world's most expensive massage chair, with a book and television remote on her lap. She wore a plain sweatshirt, and a crocheted blanket covered her lower half. "I brought flowers. Lynn's taking care of them in the kitchen." He pointed with his thumb over his shoulder toward a wall where he assumed the kitchen was on the other side.

Rockfish pulled a wicker armchair over from under the window and sat down. For a second, he wondered if it would collapse under him like a house of toothpicks. When it didn't, he spoke about anything other than the elephant in the room, dodging any topic that he feared would return her to a quivering pile of lime Jell-O. *Been there a few times now and I'm not eager to return.* After a couple minutes of pleasantries, it was Jawnie that cut through the bullshit and surprised him.

"So, what have I missed? Have you driven past or walked the grounds over at Little Golf Big Tees? Any additional information on Fulsome Commercial Realty Group? What I was thinking, is—"

"Whoa. Full stop. It's been eighteen hours. When I got you back into a semisolid state and here with Lynn, I went home and fully hydrated myself," Rockfish said. "And now I'm here. Baby steps, kid. The case isn't going anywhere without you. Don't assume I plan on working this one alone." He smirked, hoping she would catch it and feel a little better.

Jawnie dropped her chin to her chest and buried her hands under the blanket. She remained in that position for a minute while Rockfish planned an apology in his head.

"Steve, I wanted to say I'm sorry. I fucked things up yesterday and I'm not really sure when this rollercoaster of emotions will hit the upswing. I probably look to you, like Mack did, when he lost that money in the romance scam. Maybe worse. I wonder if my head will ever be screwed on straight since Sommers locked me in that car trunk and you came to my rescue. Turns out, trauma's a bitch."

Rockfish pulled the chair forward a foot and reached out to Jawnie's left arm buried deep under the crochet. "Newsflash, it seems screwed on pretty tight to me and I'm not getting you a dog. You didn't do a damn thing wrong yesterday," he said. "Stop blaming yourself. We got a few positives from yesterday." He pulled the Toyota key chain from his pocket. "It's a rental. That much I know from this nifty key chain. The Kia was probably too."

"That's some mighty fine detective work there, Steve," Lynn said, as she came in from the kitchen carrying a vase and a small charcuterie tray topped with half a dozen types of cheeses and fruit.

"Lynn, can you put that all on the coffee table?" Jawnie said. "Where I can see the flowers but far enough away so I can't nibble myself to death."

Lynn put both items down on the glass surface and looked at Rockfish. "I'll make myself scarce if you two have business to discuss I'm not privy to."

"Steve, I'd like her to stay. In case I forget something that was said."

"All good here. She's an employee. Same as us," Rockfish said with a wink and Lynn took a seat on the couch, within nibbling distance of the food. "What I didn't bring with me is the lanyard.

Based on this solid clue, we have a tie back to the evil corporation. What I don't understand is the fucking with you the day before. Prior to us taking up the case. Doesn't make sense. We had only talked about amending the client agreement forms."

"Maybe they've been watching Pilar and Kara," Jawnie said. "Since I spend a lot of time with them, someone at Fulsome assumed I was involved. Somehow. And if I get scared enough, I'll bring my concern to my friends?"

"Plausible."

"And once they learned who you were, the bad guys made the assumption we were already working the case," Lynn said. "They've had no success with scaring Pilar and Kara into giving in. Why not focus on you? Who might make the professional suggestion that this will only get uglier and they should relent to the next offer?"

"I like the line of thought, Lynn," Rockfish said. "Especially with the lanyard. Mace Face is a Fulsome employee. He's definitely not outside hired muscle. The man rolled down the window for you and ran like a little bitch from me. He's someone on the inside, asked to fill a role he's not accustomed to. That's probably a good thing on our part. Amateurs make mistakes and our job is then much easier." Rockfish held up a pair of crossed fingers for emphasis.

A muffled chirp caught everyone's attention and Jawnie pulled her arms out from under the blanket, holding her phone.

"It's a text from Hasty," Jawnie said. "You remember him? The Chief of the Elk Township Police Department, back in Jersey. Did you tell him about my breakdown?"

"You didn't have a breakdown."

"He says it's important."

"So call him unless you had one. Then I can dial for you," Rockfish said, heavy on the sarcasm.

"I can dial it, smartass."

"Hi Ned, just to warn you, you're on speaker and Rockfish is here."

"Hey Steve. Jawnie, I hope you don't mind me cutting through all the how you're doing bullshit, but have you seen the news?"

"Nope, working and living the American dream here, as Rockfish says. Trying to avoid getting the play-by-play as the country approaches hell in a handbasket. At an unsafe speed, I might add."

"Hold on tight then. A Federal Court Judge overturned Annetta Provolone's conviction on a technicality. He's scheduled the retrial for October 17th."

"Jesus Christ, that psycho is back on the street?" Jawnie said. Rockfish noticed she was now sitting upright in the chair. Her body was at full attention.

"Not yet. Her attorney's arranged a bail hearing set for Monday morning."

"No way they'll let her out," Jawnie said. "Judges don't agree to bail for people like her."

"Never say never. People like her pay good lawyers for exactly that," Rockfish said.

"Agreed," Hasty said.

"Oh my God, I'm going to have to testify again," Jawnie said. She had uncovered the Provolone Crime Family's plan to defraud the Federal Government's Paycheck Protection Program during the height of the pandemic. Without her information, the Feds would have never caught on and the Mafia would have continued to line their pockets with stimulus funds meant for hard working, small businesses.

"Sounds like no one has reached out to you regarding this yet?"

"Not a soul," Rockfish said.

"Well, you're probably on someone's to-do-list here soon," Hasty said.

"You have no idea," Jawnie said.

"Keep your ears out. The FBI should come knocking. I would hope. And Rockfish, keep her safe."

"I can take care of myself, Ned," Jawnie said.

Right, kid. You tell 'em. Rockfish caught the tone in her voice. *Despite how I look and sound, I'm not helpless.*

"I don't give a shit," Hasty said. "You need to stay vigilant, even though odds are there's nothing to fear. No way she gets out on bail. It's not like she's Gotti and hired Bruce Cutler. This is South Jersey, for Christ's sake."

The call ended soon after and a heavy silence hung over the room. Jawnie broke the barrier.

"Mace Face. He's tied to the Provolones. Fuck, that lanyard's nothing more than a red herring."

"No, Jawnie. That idiot was an amateur, and I doubt he's mobbed up. Like you said yesterday, I'd bet your half of the next NikolaTV royalty payment on it."

"I won't run. She can't make me."

"Well then, let's pretend we work in the corporate world. You're working from home until told otherwise. No ifs, and or buts."

* * * * * * * * * *

A beautiful Monday morning found Rockfish in the McDonald's drive-thru for breakfast and his first coffee of the day.

"Bless you too, darling." *A quiet, meeting free day with plenty of time to devote to digging up what I can on Fulsome and write up a handful of late reports. Wasn't I whining the other day about the lack of adventure?* Rockfish had stayed at home on Sunday, choosing not to drive over to the condo again and bother Jawnie. He made a point of checking in with her via text and an actual old-fashioned phone call. Each of which was followed up with a text to Lynn to make sure Jawnie wasn't feeding him a line of bull.

His mood changed one hundred and eighty degrees before the office door closed behind him. The rear tire of Jawnie's bike almost caught him between the legs.

"Cocksucker," Rockfish said. He reached down for his shin. He directed the colorful language at no one in particular within earshot. *Jawnie's first fucking day under my work from home missive and she's already ignoring it. Doing her own damn thing. I will never understand that generation.* Rockfish threw up his hands in disgust and frustration. His eyes immediately went to Lynn at the receptionist's desk.

"What can I say? She's my boss, too. She gave me money to Uber in. I refuse to take sides between mom and dad." Lynn crossed her arms while shrugging at the same time.

"Speak of the devil," Rockfish said as Jawnie walked down the hallway from her office and pulled up a chair at the conference table.

"Steve, don't start," Jawnie said.

"Oh, I'm wondering why I'm even continuing."

"Can I at least show you what I have here, before you rip my name off the sign out front?" Jawnie said and continued without waiting for an answer. "Sit down and eat. I can do all the talking. I've found some interesting stuff regarding Pilar and Kara's case."

"You're focused after Hasty's call? Because I couldn't," Rockfish said. He sat down and pulled the first Egg McMuffin from the grease-stained bag.

Jawnie spread papers and printouts across a third of the table and sat down to Rockfish's right.

"After you left on Saturday, I knew I needed to divert my thoughts in a totally different direction. The emotional ride would have approached the first big drop if I hadn't. Throwing myself at Pilar and Kara's dilemma was what I needed."

"You know there is no way she's getting bail, right?" Rockfish said. He put his anger aside and reached out to place his hand on her forearm.

"I have to testify again. Did it once, can do it again." Jawnie dropped her head into her right hand and rubbed her temples.

"Single-handedly taking down a Mafia family. That ain't no small thing, and this damn prosecutor better get his shit together for the retrial. I'll be in the gallery watching Provolone go down in flames again." In all actuality, he didn't believe a word of this sudden bravado. *Will she do the right thing and kick down all the doors come October? No doubt. But in the here and now, after Porbeagle and Mace Face, she's ain't fooling anyone.* Rockfish laughed aloud at the last thought. *Worst sounding villains since the old Batman's Egghead and The Bookworm.*

"Back to what I was talking about in the first place," Jawnie said and continued on regarding her research.

"Fulsome has been buying up all the property around the mini-golf course the last couple of years. The last purchase, prior to losing the bid, was the burned-out Applebee's plot next door, and that was a year ago. I'm betting they were biding their time till the owners of Chesapeake Mini-Golf were ready to hang it up. Or Fulsome could squeeze them out."

Jawnie stopped, and Rockfish turned and nodded. He was following along and once again said a prayer for having a partner who didn't mind staring at a screen all day. Jawnie grabbed the remote from the table and lowered the screen from the ceiling.

"If you look at this map, the land the course sits on would appear to be the last piece of some puzzle. Not sure what the end goal is, but I bet there are plans for that land, big ones, once they get it all under contract."

"Then your friends swoop in and Mom and Pop give Fulsome the finger."

"Yup."

"And evil corporate America is pissed."

"Double yup," Jawnie said with her own nod.

"With everything I see here, I'm guessing there's a folder in our case management system with all this great information?"

"Somewhat started. I needed to come in today to finish my research."

"Well, you saved me some major computer time today and for that, I'm always grateful. If you're all gung-ho and feeling better, want to swing by Fulsome's headquarters? See what we can see? Walk around and get a feel for the monster?"

"Thought you'd never ask."

Was she ready? Hell no, I know that. But seeing her rollercoaster might be headed back up the track? It would be only a matter of time before she followed up on a hunch and checked out the place. I'd rather tag along for the ride, in case her theory from Saturday proved true. Should the Provolone bail hearing go in the opposite direction, I'll be armed and ready to protect at any cost.

"Lynn, hold down the fort until we get back."

* * * * * * * * * *

The Fulsome Realty Development Group headquarters building resembled a large concrete crypt, on the outskirts of Ellicott City, Maryland, thirty minutes northwest of the office.

"Well, there's no gated entry, so that's a good thing," Rockfish said as Lana turned into the parking lot.

"Doesn't mean there aren't cameras."

"Good point, but this lanyard and keycard should give me the appearance I somewhat belong here. Even brought a sports coat to complete the disguise."

They hustled out of the car and walked to the large glass doors which marked the public entrance.

Rockfish gave the inside visitor's area the once over as he held the door for Jawnie. *This space is bigger than our entire office by a factor of at least two.* The large open room was busy. People entered behind them, others left through another set of doors and even more milled around the center of the room. Rockfish inhaled and tilted his head. *Something really doesn't smell right. The aroma's more like recycled airplane air than an evil corporate setting.*

A visitor's sign-in desk sat against the far wall and further down an old man, glasses on the top of his head, stood behind a podium guarding entry to a hallway. *That's a rent-a-cop uniform and his posture tells me he'd rather be anywhere else.*

"Let's start with seeing what all the fuss is about," Rockfish said and pointed towards the people in the center of the room. They patiently waited for a gap in the crowd to see what drew all the attention of those leaving and entering.

A scale architectural model of a sprawling development sat atop a small stage and was lit better than most television shows. A plaque stood alongside the model and simply read, "Avonlea Crossing".

"It kind of reminds me of the miniature city in Raiders of the Lost Ark," Rockfish said. "The part where Indy shoves the stick in the hole."

"Where do you think this is going to lead us?" Jawnie said as she pulled out her phone and tapped on the keyboard.

"I'd like to try my luck with the half-asleep guard over there. You know, try to continue the tour."

"Hold on a second," Jawnie said, and pulled Rockfish aside. "This article says Avonlea Crossing is Fulsome Project manager Luther Grayson's largest project to date. The plans call for a new retail and residential development to go next door to the re-vamped Glen Burnie Market Square shopping center. This project will include restaurants, shops, a civic center, apartments, townhomes, condos, and residences for seniors."

"Okay, back to the model city over here," Rockfish said. "Where exactly is your friend's investment property located? GPS and Google Maps have spoiled me. Mack would be so ashamed."

They shuffled back to the large architectural display and Jawnie pointed. "There. Pilar and Kara are right in the way of the proposed interstate off-ramp leading into this retail Sodom and Gomorrah."

"Explains why they aren't happy with your friends. They're holding up good old American progress. Let's see if we can continue the tour. You never know what a talkative administrative assistant might say if she's in the mood."

Rockfish led Jawnie over towards the not-so-security guard. The man's glasses remained on top of his head and the latest issue of Bassmaster Fishing magazine seemed to hold roughly eighty-five percent of his attention. Rockfish approached, pointing out parts of the lobby to Jawnie and not saying much of anything. As he drew close to the podium, he grabbed the keycard and held it up as if it were an employee ID. The twosome kept walking and didn't look back.

"Always pretend like you belong," Rockfish said and held open the door to Fulsome's inner sanctum for Jawnie.

The fluorescent lights lit the long hallway, and office doors lined both sides.

"You continue to amaze me, or as the kids say, look at the balls on that guy," Jawnie said. "What's next?"

"Dunno. This is the point where you wing it and hope a little luck shines on you. Let's keep moving and see what we encounter. At the most, someone will order us to leave. Not sure about you, but that won't hurt my feelings."

Rockfish used his keycard and tried the doors down the left-hand side of the hallway, only to be met with flashing red lights. *I was really hoping for a handout here, but it's not looking good. If I have any luck at all, one of these should open.* Something moved at the end of the hallway, and they stopped in their tracks. A door opened and a corporate drone and what was Rockfish's best guess, the man's secretary, stepped into the hallway. She held an open manila folder in front of them and its contents kept their attention from noticing anything else in the hallway.

"Bingo," Rockfish said under his breath. *Here we see the Mace Face observed in his corporate environment. Notice his lack of attention to his surroundings.* Rockfish laughed to himself.

The Fulsome employees took a handful of steps forward and stopped in front of another door. The conversation regarding the folder's contents continued on and appeared to grow more heated. Mace Face began driving his index finger down onto the folder contents while the woman vigorously nodded her head in a subservient manner.

It's exactly the type of connection we came here to find. Now if I can move a little closer without him noticing. Rockfish turned toward Jawnie and waved her forward. Her eyes looked through him and down the hallway. *Fuck. Please don't be a problem, Jawnie.*

He curled his index finger, and she turned her head towards him and nodded. *Good. Thought she froze up there for a second.* They both watched as the secretary closed the folder, spoke a few words, and then used her keycard to go through the door they had held a heated discussion in front of. Alone, Mace Face shook his head in what appeared to be disgust and started walking down the hallway straight at Rockfish and Jawnie.

Without a secretary or folder to keep the man's attention, Rockfish knew he only had a couple of seconds before Mace Face spotted the loiterers. *The closer he gets, the better the odds of his eyes coming off the floor in front of him. If I can corner him, maybe he'll answer a question. Not your greatest plan, but let's go with it.* Rockfish threw caution to the wind, held up his hand for Jawnie to stand still, and strode forward. *I haven't played chicken in a goddamn long time.*

"Excuse me, Sir? Have you accepted Jesus Christ as your..." Rockfish hoped the confusion would give the man pause, and give Rockfish enough time to close the gap before the man slipped away.

Mace Face looked up, and his facial expressions were at full attention. His eyes were enormous, and Rockfish knew the gig was up. Mace Face turned to the door on his right, fumbled with his keycard and threw it open. Rockfish, now in full sprint, hoped to grab the handle before the door fully closed, but arrived a second late and could hear the cylinders lock into place. He tried the handle. No luck. On a whim he tried the keycard attached to the lanyard, but the red blinking light of failure shone back at him. *Worth a try.*

Rockfish pivoted and headed back to where Jawnie stood. Without saying a word, he placed his arm around her shoulder and guided her back the way they came. As they approached the end of the hallway and the doorway that led towards the lobby, he gave instructions.

"We need to get moving before the sleepy security guard's younger, more fit peers come looking for us. Walk fast, but act like you belong."

They made it out the front lobby door and crouched down when they reached the first row of cars in the parking lot. Rockfish led, with Jawnie right on his heels, as the partners zig-zagged across the parking lot and headed towards the thin tree line that separated the Fulsome property and the road.

When they reached the slight cover of oak trees and ornamental grass, he dared to stop and look back. He squinted and leaned into it. Hard. Three rent-a-cops milled around in front of the doors, one speaking into a handheld radio.

"What about the car?" Jawnie said. They were her first words since they faked their way into the long hallway.

"I'll send Raffi back in a couple of hours to get it. No need to give them our faces *and* my license plate on any cameras covering the lot. If they want to watch us sneak across the lot and out onto the main road, so be it. But we need to keep moving. Even those donut munchers luck into an apprehension every once in a while. Not to mention they might think we walked onto the lot and not bother to look at any earlier videotape."

"Gotcha. Learn something new each day." She held out her fist and Rockfish bumped it.

"Let's cross the street and split up. I'll meet you at the dry cleaners. Over on the corner of Clayton and Mullica. Say in a half an hour? Keep your head down."

Rockfish stepped out from in front of Robinson's Dry Cleaning a little after 1pm and approached his partner as she walked up the sidewalk.

"Well, that was close. A little hairier than I wanted or expected."

"Double for me," Jawnie said. "I got too much to worry about already. Can't believe I didn't recognize Mace Face right away. I gotta tell you, the woman drew my attention in."

"Well, that's a given."

"No, asshole. I mean, I know her from somewhere. Not by name, but definitely by face. She and I have crossed paths. And it wasn't too long ago. I just don't know where."

****

Rockfish's phone chirped and his crusted over eyes cracked open early Tuesday morning. *What time is it? How early is it?* His phone was on do-not-disturb, but there were two overrides to those settings, Mack and Jawnie. And usually, Mack walked down the hall and knocked on the door to mention he was having a rough go of it. The notifications, by a process of elimination, were then from his partner.

It's bad. Someone tried to burn down what's left of Little Golf Big Tees last night. You think Fulsome turned it up after Mace Face saw us?

Rockfish closed the texting app and checked the time. 5:51am. *Fuck, I hate that generation. Bad is sometimes clouded with emotion and if you add the verb 'tried', then it's probably not worthy of an emergency text.* He automatically returned the phone to the nightstand and then thought better. *I gotta reply or the notifications won't stop.* He stared at the screen for way too long, knowing there was no way he'd drift back to sleep. Insomnia is a small price to pay in order to have her head screwed on straight.

Hey, glad it was unsuccessful, but does that really surprise anyone after our dealings at Fulsome? I'll be in the office regular time and maybe we'll corral your friends and discuss. If they haven't called the cops yet, now would be a good time.

Rockfish placed the phone back on the charging tray and rolled over. *Surely, she doesn't expect me to jump out of bed and race over to fight the arson investigators for access to the crime scene. It was unsuccessful, so the amateur hour continued. Jawnie probably based her urgency on what's happened the last couple of days, but honestly, who could blame her?*

The Tuesday drive-thru line for McDonald's was no better than the day before. Rockfish ended up rage driving into a parking spot and heading inside to order. The inability of corporate America to pay a living wage caused him to spend more time amongst the un-vaxed than a more civilized time would call for. He jumped back into Lana and headed to the office to see what all the hubbub was from last night. Jawnie met him in the parking lot, coffee in hand, and slid into Lana's passenger seat before the car came to a complete stop.

"They almost burned down the place last night."

"Define almost. I mean technically, if they're demo'ing most of the place, a little fire would have helped them in the long run, capiche?" Rockfish said.

"Don't you start Italian shit with me. I read the news."

"She got bail?"

"Worst judicial system on the planet. But we should all breathe a sigh of relief because Annetta's safe at her beach house in Ocean City under court ordered, monitored house arrest."

"I wonder if she's had that ankle bracelet blinged out yet? But let's not worry over shit we can't control at the moment." Rockfish reached over and squeezed her shoulder. *Need to keep her cool and thinking straight, no matter how this turns out.* "I won't argue with you on our judicial branch. Back to our case. Are we meeting the wonder twins at the course?"

Jawnie stared at Rockfish. *What did I say now?* "You know, that one and the other one," he said. Names were not a strong point with his social skills, especially early on.

"Pilar and Kara. They have names." Jawnie sighed.

"And I've got a shitty memory. Can't all be perfect."

"They are our clients."

"For less than a handful of days now and we've already done a million times more for them than the police have or did last night. I presumed they called 9-1-1."

"They did."

"Well, let's go see what the cops had to say."

Rockfish pulled Lana into Little Golf Big Tees parking lot. *I can't remember what the old place looked like, but goddamn, they've done some serious demo.* He stood in front of the car and took in the landscape. The main building where customers would pick up a putter and ball was a heap of debris, with only the rear cement block wall standing partially intact. There was a small river of water seeping into the parking lot, and Jawnie suggested they follow it as her friends were in the rear.

Construction supplies littered the area. Pallets of boards and bricks lined the far end of the back lot and sat untouched under a tree line. Someone had parked a small backhoe and cement mixer in front of the pallets. *The location might have saved all that from going up.* Rockfish followed Jawnie as she walked towards and then around three large rolls of artificial turf that the machinery had ripped up from the current 18-hole layout. Pilar and Kara waited on the other side of the rolled-up fake grass. The women wore matching white sweatpants and shirts, but black smudges covered the front of Pilar's.

"Love what you've done with the place," Rockfish said.

"We told you it was a total makeover," Pilar said. "Once that last wall comes down and they haul everything away, the pro shop will be the first to go up. We need an office area to work out of. We hope by then we'll have found someone to help design the course."

"Yeah, turn our wacky ideas into something that will be functional, look good, and draw customers," Kara said.

"Don't mind him," Jawnie said. "Is this where it started?"

"Right here. You can make out some of the burn marks on the concrete," Pilar said. Rockfish followed her fingers down to the ground between them. He squinted and bent over. *I still don't see shit.*

Jawnie squatted down, ran her fingers over the faint marks, and raised them to her eyes. Rockfish could see the confusion in her eyes, too.

"Yeah, there's not much evidence left. The fire department hosed the shit out of it, despite it being long out by the time they got here," Kara said. "Then the police and Arson Inspector took away most of the half-burned boards. They threw the rest onto the debris pile over there." She pointed toward where the old clubhouse had stood.

"The cops said it looked more like a fire a couple of homeless would use to keep warm," Pilar said.

"It's July," Rockfish said and shook his head.

"I know. I'm repeating the bullshit they told us," Kara said.

Rockfish looked over at Jawnie and raised his eyebrows. *Kid, I hope you're drawing the same conclusions as me. Homeless, my ass. More like a dumb corporate type following orders or trying to please his boss. Mace Face had also half-assed his surveillance of Jawnie. How about we jack it up and try a felony punishable by up to 30 years in prison? This whole scene screams to me that someone didn't know what they were doing.*

"Have any of your contractors received any threats?" Jawnie said. "Messages not to work with you? Anything like the harassment you told us about yesterday?"

Rockfish nodded along with Jawnie's questions. They were on the same page. *Atta girl.*

"You don't believe the cops' assumptions, either?"

"Not a chance in hell," Rockfish said.

"They are useless every time we call," Pilar said. "One claimed a patrol car might drive by the property at night, but only when resources permit. I can't expect their thoughts and prayers to actually accomplish anything." She held her hands out, palms up. "We hired a guy to install cameras around the property. I know, a day late and a dollar short. By tomorrow, he promises to have most of the area covered in video."

"Good. That might help us," Rockfish said. "Especially if someone returns trying to earn their fire starter merit badge."

"Make sure you have plenty of cloud storage space for that video," Jawnie said. "I don't want you to have an event, only to find out the server overwrote the footage because of limited hard drive space."

"Noted," Kara said. "I'll speak to him about that."

"Excellent. Point him my way if you have questions. I'll make sure you get what you need."

"Now, didn't you say this morning on the phone you found out some additional information on why Fulsome is desperate for this property?" Kara said.

"Yes...," Jawnie recounted her research and what they learned from the brief visit to Fulsome headquarters. "... without your property, it's a windy two-lane road which won't provide the access the development needs to be successful. It is all about ease of entry and exit, directing the flow of potential customers."

"So, we're supposed to sell and watch our dreams become some sort of high-speed entrance ramp?" Pilar said. She kicked at the ground.

"Not if you don't cave to their offers," Jawnie said. "We're going—"

"Jawnie McGee?"

The voice came from the other side of the artificial turf piles, and three of the four jumped.

"Special Agent Thomas," Rockfish said, putting the voice to a face before she came into view. "And to what do we owe this occasion? Isn't the FBI a tad late on providing notice to your potential star witness regarding Annetta Provolone's bail?"

Special Agent Rhonda Thomas, FBI Baltimore, came around the corner, dressed as if she had come straight from the range. Ball cap on her head, ponytail hanging out the back, 511 tactical pants and a polo. Rockfish gleaned from the stern look on her face, she still wasn't a fan of his ball breaking.

"Correct, Mr. Rockfish. The Federal Judge granted Annetta Provolone bail this morning. Jawnie, we need to talk."

* * * * * * * * * *

No one spoke as they walked around to the front parking lot. Agent Thomas asked to speak to Jawnie, but she didn't complain when Rockfish followed along without being asked.

Agent Thomas had parked her Dodge Charger alongside Cousin Lana and stopped in front of the car.

"Do you mind if we chat in the car? I came here straight from a search warrant earlier this morning. If not, we could go back to my office."

"Car's fine," Jawnie and Rockfish said at the same time. She glimpsed his grin as he opened the door and slid into the back seat.

Jawnie reached out for the passenger door and paused. *What could they want with me? They know I know about Annetta. What's the big deal?* Rockfish slammed the rear door shut, and it startled Jawnie. She opened hers and got in.

Agent Thomas started the car and raised the fan on the air conditioner. Jawnie placed the webbing between her fingers in front of the vents. The feeling was cooling, but more to the point, soothing. She stared straight ahead, somewhat fearing what Agent Thomas would say.

"Jawnie, I—"

"Do I have to check my car for some sort of GPS tracker?" Rockfish said.

"I called your office and explained to your receptionist the severity of the matter. She told me where to find you. Understand, this is very important."

Rockfish is back seat driving as usual. Jawnie pulled out her phone and tapped the screen. *Ah, there's all the messages from Lynn. She had to have known I wouldn't have pulled this out during a client meeting.*

"I mean, whatever you have to say can't be that important," Rockfish said. "We learned about the new trial over the weekend and the bail hearing information was all over the press this morning. Seems useless to drive over here and interrupt our client meeting to play online news aggregator."

Agent Thomas whipped her head around and stared. "Mr. Rockfish, I didn't come to trade jabs with you. Nor did I drive over here and interrupt your meeting to speak with you."

"Right, so why are you here bothering us? Unless..." Rockfish shut his mouth and reached around the headrest with both hands. He laid his hand on Jawnie's shoulders. She felt the squeeze and welcomed it. *It's going to be bad, isn't it?*

"My superiors didn't feel the need to come out and get you all riled up over nothing. From our standpoint, that bail hearing was the Hail Mary of all Hail Marys. But this new Federal Judge did not look kindly on the prosecution's error, which forced the original verdict to be thrown out. Regardless of what's happened over the past couple of days, we're going to need you prepared and ready to testify again in October."

A hot flash washed over Jawnie's entire body. Her brain understood the situation and could make a good guess at what Agent Thomas would say next. She was more worried about her sensory organs and nerves. Her right leg twitched and rocked up and down on the balls of her foot. It wouldn't stop, no matter how many times she mentally reached for the off switch.

"Error? Who fucked up?" Rockfish said. "Jawnie's entitled to at least know that."

"The prosecution team. There was a Brady violation—"

"I don't remember anyone named Brady being involved." Jawnie said. Her mouth was dry, and her tongue felt like the size of a bell pepper. *Can they hear the concern in my voice? I sure as hell can.* Her brain added a heaping spoonful of aggravation to Jawnie's current cocktail.

"It's okay, you're not forgetful, Jawnie," Rockfish said. "A Brady violation is a more palatable way to say that the prosecution screwed the pooch and failed to turn over possible exculpatory evidence to the defense. As required by law. Isn't that right, Agent Thomas?"

Agent Thomas nodded.

"We're going to have to live the next three months on pins and needles while Ms. Gabagool lounges on her beach towel and roughs it in her shore house?" Rockfish piled it on.

"Prosecutorial mistakes aside, I came here to discuss a protective custody agreement with the US Marshals. Voluntary, of course, but much like last time we had this conversation, I highly encourage you to accept the offer."

Again, from this same Fed. We know what's best for you. Okay, so maybe they did the last time, but I'm not that same person. I've been through more than she knows. Came out of it a little fucked, but that's being expected. But I'm not running and I'm not hiding. Those days are gone. Show her. You don't need their bullshit protection. She reached over and raised the car's fan before adjusting one vent to blow directly on her neck before speaking.

"That spiel sounds an awful lot like bureaucratic double-talk. A bunch of words to cover your ass. You know, just in case. Your honor, we reached out to her, but she didn't want none of it. We tried. Yes, we did the minimum the law requires of us." Jawnie felt Rockfish's hands give a little squeeze.

"Sounds to me like you've definitely been around this one too long," Agent Thomas said and jerked a thumb over her shoulder. "I'd recommend taking some time alone and giving my words some serious thought. I fully expect you to, especially since you lived through what happened the last time you turned down our help."

"Yeah, that was because of this guy," and Jawnie jerked her own thumb. "Not because of your investigative abilities." Jawnie felt another squeeze. Combined with the cold air, her feet were getting back under her. Not to the point she was no longer scared, but better than five minutes ago.

"But what I'm trying to say here is, I can't afford to leave my friends in a bind. We're working on a case that involves hate crimes and civil rights violations, all going on right under your and the local's noses, but no one's interested," Jawnie said with a tilt of her head. She hoped Agent Thomas felt the barb. "This is my home now and I'm going to stay here and continue to make it a better place. If you want to have a protective detail, follow me around from dawn to dusk, until you get an arrest warrant—"

"It's an order of protective custody. Your safety is that important to the Government's case."

If I'm that important, why didn't she show up this morning, order in hand? If the FBI is on top of the situation, they are watching Annetta's beach house six ways to Sunday. Their technical sources are scooping up every electronic signal that departs the address, re-routes it to Quantico where some serious brain and computing power analyze it. Jawnie turned, looked into the back seat, and shook her head. Rockfish nodded in return.

"Agent Thomas, what I think this pissing match boils down to is, do you have a documented, verified threat targeting Jawnie?" Rockfish said. "Has anyone in Philly overheard something on a wiretap or read any kind of encrypted message, via some Patriot Act man-in-the-middle scheme? Anything that says Provolone has a hard-on for our girl here, despite the mountains of evidence the Government presented at the first trial?"

Agent Thomas's face changed a few shades of red with each Rockfish question, and Jawnie was here for it. She smiled on the inside over Rockfish's correct usage of the man-in-the-middle phrasing and, happier, his questions mirrored her thoughts. *It's like we're in tandem when we feel she's not being forthright.*

"No, we don't. There is some chatter on a wire, but nothing specific. Annetta Provolone holds a grudge longer and more visceral than her father or grandfather. We are trying to be proactive in this matter and not reactive. Surely you understand."

"I do, *we* do," Rockfish said. "It is her decision. I'd hope she'd agree and go with you, for all of our sakes, but again, not my call."

"Tell you what, Agent Thomas. I'll sleep on it and let you know in a day or two. If you don't hear from me, assume I'll be there in October, hand on the bible, ready to fix your screw-up," Jawnie said and took the business card from Agent Thomas' outstretched hand.

CHAPTER THREE

Rockfish didn't agree with Jawnie's decision to turn down protective custody, but he respected it. *I mean, the business isn't going anywhere. She'd have her office when she got back.* Rockfish insisted on a laundry list of precautions, the main one being Jawnie agreeing to work from home as much as possible, leading up to the trial. *Three months, she could do that standing on her head and, like I said, the business ain't going nowhere. I'll handle most of the field work, try to limit our new clients over this timeframe and get her out of the condo every so often so she doesn't go stir crazy.*

Jawnie wasn't hesitant to let him hear her unhappiness with the arrangement, but she eventually relented and gave Rockfish her word. A fist bump sealed it. Her weekly calendar filled with online research, analysis of data from some tools of the trade, and Zoom meetings with potential clients. *I can only hope Lynn and I can throw her enough work to keep her busy and her mind off the fact she's under home confinement, much like Annetta Provolone.*

The following morning, Rockfish had asked Lynn to hold down the fort as he planned on taking the first business meeting of the day on the back deck of his house. Rockfish took the last bite of Mack's greasy homemade breakfast sandwich and gave the small remaining piece to Zippy. The dog had followed him and breakfast out onto the deck, hoping for some scraps. Rockfish couldn't disappoint. He wiped the dog slobber from his hand and looked down at his phone. 8am came and went. Raffi was late. *Expected? Yes. Aggravated? Hell yeah.*

Rockfish would have rather met Raphael "Raffi" Pérez, his high school buddy, and sometimes Rockfish's ears on the street, back at the office, so he could knock out a few other things on his to-do-list, but with Raffi nothing was easy. Rockfish couldn't chance having Raffi and Lynn in the same enclosed area. Lynn continued to harbor resentment against Raffi for talking her into burglarizing Earl Porbeagle's back office with him. She blamed him for the beatings and mental abuse at Earl's hands that followed. *Best to keep them separated and hope that time heals some things eventually. Damn, I'd settle for them being civil to each other and Lynn not spiraling down some PTSD hole every time that afro came through the front door.*

"Stevie, did you save me a Mack muffin?"

Rockfish looked to his left and saw Raffi letting himself in through the side gate. His hair bobbed with each step and, as always, Raffi dressed in a three-piece suit, sans tie. *The man is a true throwback to the hustlers and scam artists that ran Baltimore's streets when we were growing up. Give him credit, Raffi's always one step ahead of the law, creditors and probably a handful of jealous husbands.*

"Hate to tell ya, but the kitchen's closed and I sent the help back inside to watch television. You need to check the hours posted on your way out. Coffee's still on, though."

"Next time I'll call ahead with an order so that it's sitting here waiting, all nice and wrapped in butcher paper," Raffi said. He laughed aloud, poured himself a cup, and pulled up a chair across from Rockfish. "You know, Stevie, I loved your old trailer and the view overlooking the waste-water pond, but this view of actual water is so much better. Which leads to my next question: when are you buying a boat? Isn't your big producer guy headed out here soon with another bucket load of docuseries cash?"

Rockfish mentally shook his head. *This guy. Raffi can smell cash before it even hits your wallet. Ah, you're being too hard on him. Maybe he's looking for some time out on the bay? Right.*

"Correct. Angel plans to travel out for some preliminary discussions regarding a second season of the show. And I'd be lying if I said after moving into this house, a boat wasn't on my list of must haves. The thought of walking out the back door, firing up the engine—"

"Twin engines."

"Maybe, twin engines," Rockfish said. "Taking Mack out for a few hours of croakers, blues, or even run him out at night for some drum fishing. It's an achievable bucket list thing I want to do for him. And obviously myself. Shit, a sweet boat might even help me get a second date."

"I have noticed the bevy of beauties traipsing through your front door has slowed to a crawl. The boat might be a good move. I mean Lana's six years old now, she ain't the draw she once was. But either way, I ain't much for sitting in the sun, but if you buy it, I will come."

"Yeah, that's an image I'll never get out of my head. Ok, enough of the Baltimore episode of Lifestyles of the Rich and Famous. I need a couple of old school Raffi-type favors."

"Shoot." Raffi grinned widely and rubbed his hands together.

"I need you to put that ear to the street for me. A couple of things I'm looking for, or a heads up at a minimum. Has anyone hired a half-assed arsonist and is now trying to spend more, since cheap wasn't the way to go the first time?"

"Got it. If someone accepted a job and then underperformed," Raffi said with a nod.

"Yeah, I'm not sure if this guy watched a couple of arson YouTube videos and tried it himself, or if he drove down the wrong street in a terrible neighborhood and hired the first person he came across. In that case, he might be in the market to purchase an upgrade."

"So, where's the scene of the crime?" Raffi said, leaning in.

I've piqued his interest. A couple of bucks thrown his way should move me towards the top of his priority list.

"The miniature golf place over in Glen Burnie. Can't miss it. An old Applebee's is decomposing next to it. Our clients are putting up some surveillance cameras, so if you come up empty, we'll still have some evidence to work with."

"You know old Raffi won't come up empty for you, Stevie. Hold on a sec, I thought you said someone wanted to burn down the mini golf? Did they hit the wrong place? I'm confused. Más café, por favor." Raffi reached over and refilled his cup and Rockfish let him get in a sip before answering.

"I did and I'm pretty sure the Applebee's got hit by lightning a few years back and is rotting from the inside out. It's a weird coincidence thing."

"I've got a few people I can talk to that offer those types of services," Raffi said.

"Good. Hopefully, they've heard something, or this person approached them. The second thing is if you hear anything, and I mean the slightest hint regarding any out-of-town muscle arriving on the scene. Or, God forbid, a couple of zips from the old country suddenly show up and start asking for directions."

"Stevie, you are everyone's favorite. Bar none. The belle of the ball. Who would want to take you out? Nobody's left breathing from that doomsday cult, or am I talking out my ass?" Raffi's hands moved as if he was juggling invisible oranges.

"This one's all about Jawnie and yeah, it goes back to her time, our time, in Jersey."

"Gotcha. The cheese lady." Raffi said with a slight push of his finger against the tip of his nose. "I'll try to listen in on some contract-type work that Marini's men might sign up for, too."

"Goddamn. Good thinking there. Not sure why I didn't think of those goons," Rockfish said and shook his head. Angelo Marini and the crime family named after him ran the rackets in Baltimore and its suburbs. "I could hit up my old buddy, Gordon Reeseworth. I'm pretty sure he's still in bed with Marini. And not by choice. He might hear something by hanging around those goons. Or at least he can give me a temperature check on the current state of affairs between the two mob families."

"Can do. You think there's any real meat to this Provolone threat?"

"I don't think so. The freakin' prosecution put on an enormous case and Jawnie was less than one day of testimony, but for them to drag their asses out of those cushy Government chairs and come down to talk to us?" Rockfish said and sat up in his chair. He leaned forward, resting his forearms on his thighs. "Maybe there is. That voice in the back of my head keeps spouting on about knowing more, or having heard more than they're letting on. I told you about Hasty, the Chief of Police I dealt with there?"

"Yeah. You saved his and Jawnie's bacon."

"The same," Rockfish said. "He'll let us know if he hears anything. That could be our only warning."

"Holy shit, your government isn't being forthcoming with you. I'm shocked. But above all, how is she holding up?"

"She's good. Not the Jell-O mold I had expected, and that is a pleasant surprise. She's more perturbed because I demanded she work from home until the trial. She needs to keep her head screwed on straight, and it's the only way I can think that she can stay safe. Mentally and physically. She's also been through so much in the past year, more than she deserves, that I can't have her crash and burn on me. Won't allow it." He gave his head a violent shake. "If she's carted off by those guys with the big butterfly nets, I'll never forgive myself." Rockfish's arms pivoted up and cradled his head.

"Alright, boss, I've wasted enough of your time this morning. I'll head out and check with my sources and get back to you when I learn something." Raffi stood up and placed his coffee cup on the small table next to Rockfish. "I'm sure you got plenty of shit to do today. Back to being a one-man band. I'll send you an invoice if I find out anything."

Rockfish picked up his head and looked at his friend. "The sooner the better, you get back to me. I'm not sure how long she'll listen to me and stay on the bench. And I don't know how long I'll be able to keep worrying about all this shit before I lose my mind."

* * * * * * * * * *

"You know Steve's going to flip his lid when he pulls in and sees your car," Lynn said as Jawnie put the Subaru in park, killed the wipers and shut off the engine. The rain was coming down harder since they left the condo. Friday morning's weather wasn't cooperating as they sat and contemplated making the mad dash to the front door. Jawnie played it safe and wore a matching raincoat and hat, but Lynn prepared to carry her backpack over her head for the ten-yard sprint.

"Well, first, he's going to think you drove my car in, as you had the past two days," Jawnie said. "He won't know any better until he sees me in the office. Better he have his tantrum there, out of sight of any potential clients walking by." Jawnie tapped the side of her head with her index finger. "Second, we're partners. One is always going to be pissed over something the other did or didn't do. I'd like to see him last two days working from a coffee table. Not to mention, I'm sure he's not seen the news. The U.S. Attorney's Office is appealing the decision from the bail hearing. She could be back behind bars any minute now."

"But—"

"No buts. I get it. If she's coming after me for some weird vendetta, why now? Why not last year? It is probably as easy to get an order to her minions from her cell as it will be now from her luxurious beach house confinement. Exactly the reason I can't let it get to me on the inside. I'm going to make sure I project the complete opposite. Plus, I promised Angel I'd pick him up from the airport this afternoon. I haven't had a lot of good days lately, so I'm going to enjoy this one. It will be nice to catch up with him in person."

"Is he really going to have you two sign contracts for another season of the show?" Lynn said.

"I don't think so. The way Rockfish explained it was, we're talking about topics lawyers don't have to be present for or have a say in."

"That's clear as mud."

"You're telling me. Another reason to sequester Angel away for a little time this afternoon. I can get a little clarity into tomorrow's meeting without Rockfish butting in and diverting the conversation."

"Good call," Lynn said, reaching down for her backpack. "You ready to countdown?"

"First one under the awning picks the lunch delivery option," Jawnie said and unlocked the car doors.

Once they were safely inside the office, Jawnie headed back to her office and hung up her jacket and hat to dry. Twenty minutes later, the door sensor on her phone alerted and her hands rolled into tight fists. *He's here. Only a few more minutes before he says a few words to Lynn and comes back noticing my light is on. Damn, I left the door open. He's gonna solve this mystery real fast.*

"Jesus Fucking Christ, who do we have to pay off on the Chamber of Commerce to get a couple of dedicated spots right outside the door?" His voice boomed off the walls and down the hall to where Jawnie sat. She stood up and walked towards all the noise.

"The rain soaked my Egg McMuffin. Also, the sausage, egg biscuit is now more like an egg, sausage and gross sponge. You think by 2022, someone would come up with a waterproof to-go bag."

"For your $3.95 breakfast order? I'll call Elon Musk," Lynn said. "You can get a free box of 'em with every NikolaTV subscription."

"Don't laugh. I've got his cell number. Do you want me to call him? Because I will," Jawnie said. She stepped out of the hallway and into the client meeting area, bracing for impact. "He gave it to me at the Pine Barrens premiere."

If looks could kill. Not unexpected. He stood in front of Lynn's desk, dripping from head to toe, soaked McDonald's bag in his outstretched hand. Small droplets of rainwater matted Rockfish's hair to his head and slowly made their way down his cheek. But what stood out to her was the dark crimson color in those same cheeks. *Deep breath. Steer the conversation and don't let him go off the rails and have a tantrum.*

"Steve, you went a little overboard with the H2O Value Meal?" Jawnie said, deflecting right off the bat.

"What the fuck are you doing here?"

"Killing time until I have to head over to BWI and pick up Angel."

"Fuck, that's today. I totally forgot," Rockfish said. Jawnie could see the confusion on his face. "I'm meeting with Raffi this afternoon. He might have a semi-solid lead on the arsonist. Shit. So then, the actual business meeting part is tomorrow afternoon?"

"Noon. He's having lunch catered in. It is only us three, so we'll be in his suite until we tire of each other. How about you get into those dry clothes I know you have in your office, because you taught me to always have a go-bag ready. Then we can finish this and Lynn will DoorDash you a new breakfast."

Rockfish didn't say a word, showed no emotion and dropped his breakfast bag in the garbage as he walked past Jawnie to his office.

That went better than expected. I'm guessing I'm still on airport pickup duty. Jawnie smirked at Lynn, turned, and walked back to her office.

Close to an hour later, the expected knock on Jawnie's door came.

"Steve, it's open. Come on in."

Rockfish walked in, closed the door behind him, and sat down. He put his coffee cup down on her desk and Jawnie slid a coaster underneath. The partners looked at each other. His face was stern and Jawnie could see him trying to set the tone for the conversation. She raised her eyebrows and Rockfish opened his mouth.

"You're going to pick him up, drop him off, and then make a beeline straight back to the condo. I'll worry about getting Lynn home. This is no longer up for discussion. October will be here before you know it and if you feel the need to stretch those legs, call me. I could use a few laps around the block." Rockfish patted his stomach.

Jawnie did not interrupt or try to correct anything he said. She let him vent. He needed it and it would only help them get over this hurdle. She pictured him in his gym shorts or a biking kit and bit the inside of her cheek.

"I see your smirk. Ain't a damn thing funny about this shit. You agreed, we handle this as the worst-case scenario and act accordingly. You coming here is far from appropriate. Lynn can drive to BWI as well as you. This will be the last transgression on the matter. The last time I speak of it. Are you still planning on meeting him at baggage claim?"

Oh my God. At what point will he realize he's not my father? We're partners. Much like him, I'm going to do what I want.

"No, I'll be in the cellphone lot waiting for him to text. Then I'll drive around and he'll jump in. Easy peasy."

"Easy, my ass," Rockfish said, and Jawnie knew what was coming. "He's fucking richer than both of us, times thirty-seven. His newfound wealth and fame came off our backs. Don't you ever forget it. Great guy, but he can afford a damn car service or ride share at the very fucking least."

I get it. He wants me in full on veal mode unless he's within arm's reach. She thought back to his front yard, the shot and the hoodie with the hole in it. *All I can do is put on a brave face and try to live my life. If it's hiding one day under my comforter and being all full of myself the next. My body, my choice, as they say.*

"If you must go, take Lana. You're a big girl and while I can sit here and stomp my feet, you're going to do what you want. This morning and most likely this airport run won't end up being the exception that makes the rule. But bet your ass I'll give you an earful every time." Rockfish reached for his coffee and took a sip. "Like I said, take my car to the airport. That will keep me somewhat relaxed. I'll take your car to my meeting with Raffi. Maybe we'll luck out and someone will try something with me behind the wheel. Put this puppy to bed early and get back to normal."

Jawnie inhaled, took it all in and wondered if he had finished. She knew better.

"Speaking of normal, have you heard from Pilar and Kara? Are those cameras operational yet? Do we have a way to sign in and watch from here, or our phones? Like through an app or website? I'd like to check in from time to time, especially at night. Might get lucky and catch something as it's happening and not wait for the call the next morning.

"Yes, yes, yes, either or and likewise if I see something, I'll call you immediately. And thanks for not referring to them as Frick and Frack."

"I'm learning. I listen. Might want to try it from time to time," Rockfish said with a grin. "Okay, enough lecture and question time. You be super careful, it's a fucking mess out there. Drop him off at the hotel and then go right back to your condo. I'll make sure Lynn gets home and then swap out the cars. I think you're right. It will be nice to see Angel tomorrow."

* * * * * * * * * *

The rain had yet to let up. Jawnie grabbed an umbrella by the door instead of her rain gear. *I can toss a wet umbrella on the passenger side floor and not get the rash of shit I would have if I sat on Lana's seats in a wet rain jacket. Holy crap, he'd never let me live it down.*

Jawnie made the run for Rockfish's baby and slid in behind the wheel. She leaned over to toss the umbrella and noticed an empty Wawa bag on the floor. She placed the small collapsible umbrella inside the convenience store bag and instead dropped it behind her seat. *Let him try to give me shit over that one.*

While it wasn't her first time behind the wheel of Lana's Hemi engine, she still hydroplaned twice before exiting the parking lot. *That's girl power and then some. He's probably watching through the blinds, laughing or cringing. I'm not sure which.*

The ten-minute drive to BWI's cellphone lot ended up taking twenty-five because of conditions and the other drivers confusing the rain for sleet or snow. The small lot was dirt covered with a chain-link fence surrounding it. Jawnie looked around and noticed a majority of cars had parked down by the exit. She pulled to the far end and backed into a parking space against the fence.

Once Lana was in park, Jawnie looked down at her phone. *Half an hour before he lands. Why was I in a rush to leave the office?* She checked Delta.com. Flight 306 out of LaGuardia was still on time. She dropped her phone back into the cup holder. Angel had first flown to New York to meet with NikolaTV executives to clear a few administrative hurdles before meeting with Rockfish and herself.

I've got some time to kill. She thought about the new version of Wordle that had released the previous week. *Never got around to downloading it. Of course you didn't. There were more pressing matters rattling around in your head. Like that middle-aged woman, who dresses and carries herself like she's twenty years younger, who wants you whacked, as they so eloquently put it. But Agent Thomas said there was nothing concrete in what they might or might not have overheard. They don't come out and warn people because they caught a couple of middle-schoolers passing a note in class.* The emotional pendulum had swung hard and fast to the other end of the anxiety spectrum since her talk earlier with Rockfish. The brave front had melted away as she sat alone in the rain. *Leave it for the real you to pop out when you've got no support around.*

Jawnie stepped out of her own head for a minute as Lana's interior filled with the echoes of rain crashing down on the exterior. She reached down and plugged her phone into the cord hanging out of the USB port. She pressed Lana's ignition button once; the dashboard lit up in accessory mode and Cage The Elephant's latest EP filled the car. Jawnie let out a deep sigh and tried to balance out the melodramatic scales. The words effortlessly flowed from her lips, as if someone else was singing, but did nothing to slow her mind as it moved from one negative topic to the next. She could feel the palms of her hands moisten when her phone screen lit up.

Notification - Delta Flight 306 has landed

He's in first class and first off the plane. Maybe another half an hour until his bags come out and he texts me. If I raise the volume, maybe it will drown some of this other shit out.

The intermittent wipers cleared the windshield as Jawnie noticed while lost in her head, two cars had driven into the lot and parked on either side of Lana. On the wiper's next pass, she noticed the increased number of empty spaces closer to the exit. *What the fuck? How did I miss them pulling in and why wouldn't they park closer to the exit like everyone else? I get why I'm all the way back here, but what's up with these cars? Oh, wait McGee, you're the only one allowed to park towards the back of the lot? Not everyone wants to sit up front and fight the mad rush every time a plane lands. Cut the paranoia shit, will you?*

Subconsciously, Jawnie's left hand pried itself off the steering wheel and pressed down on the door lock. She looked through her window and then the passenger side. She couldn't see a damn thing with the rain and the other cars' tint. The voice went straight to where she had tried to deflect it from. *You can't see, but I bet they have Jersey tags. Annetta might not be ready to act, but she's keeping her eye on you.*

"Where had the powerful voice from this morning gone off to?" Jawnie whispered to herself. *How and why had my mood swung so far and fast?* She increased the speed between wiper swipes and tried to focus more on her surroundings. Those forces, not between her ears. She looked in the rearview mirror, but the back window was impenetrable. She searched the dashboard for the rear defrost button.

The phone's screen came to life again and lit up the car's interior.

Angel: Blue Level Door 9

Time to put the brave face back on. He must have his luggage and is standing outside under an awning. Jawnie pressed down on the brake, started the car and dropped her into drive. She kept her foot on the brake and checked all her mirrors. Then a second time before gently releasing and letting Lana roll forward. The exit lay ahead. Another glance in the rearview showed the back window had cleared. Jawnie noticed two things. Both cars had Maryland plates, and neither had moved an inch.

Unbelievable. Get your shit together, McGee. Jawnie pressed the gas. *Lana kicked up a sizable amount of gravel as they left the cell phone lot, heading towards the terminal.*

Jawnie pulled up to the curb in front of Door 9 on the Blue Level and spotted Angel before he noticed the car and waved. He stood huddled under a small overhang with a handful of other travelers trying to stay dry and scouting for their rides. He wore a blue dress shirt and tan slacks. *No jacket? Maybe it's in the bag. Not like him.* Jawnie pulled up and popped the trunk. No way she was getting out in this downpour, no matter who it was. Angel tossed his suitcase and carry-on in the trunk and slammed it. A minute later, he slid into the passenger seat and held out his right hand.

"Holy shit, it's you," Angel said, retracting his hand. Jawnie couldn't miss the shock on his face. He instead leaned over and gave Jawnie a hug and kiss on the cheek. "Sorry about that. I saw the car and just assumed it was Steve behind the wheel. Since when does he let others drive his pride and joy?"

"I guess today's my lucky day," Jawnie said. Her eyes hit all the mirrors before shifting out of park, and then a second look for good measure.

"If I knew the weather was going to be like this, I would have called a car service and met you for a drink later. But I'm damn glad I didn't. It's great to see you again, Jawnie. It has been way too long and you look great."

Forever the bullshitter, but I'll take the compliment. "You too, Angel. It will be fun to catch up." Jawnie took her foot off the gas as Lana pulled up to yet another red light. She did the mirror and window review, her eyes moving clockwise, and settled on a sedan coming up, too fast, on the left. Her eyes darted up to the light. Still red. And then back to the driver's side mirror. Coming in way too hot! The sedan fishtailed as the driver slammed on the brakes.

"Holy crap!" Jawnie closed her eyes and lowered her chin to her chest. After a couple of seconds of not hearing the gnashing of metal, she opened her eyes and looked up. The sedan had come to a stop alongside Lana and then drove off as the light turned green. Jawnie's foot was slow to come off the brake, and she cautiously looked over at Angel. He tilted his head and his concerned look met hers.

"Can you tell me what's going on? You're hitting your mirrors one after another, and the lack of attention you're giving the road scares the shit out of me. Not gonna lie. And I won't mention that scream. I almost peed myself."

"I-I-I thought he was going to slide into us," Jawnie said. "You're staying at The Sagamore Pendry Hotel, right? No changes? I can get you there in half an hour if the idiots stay off the road." Jawnie glanced over at her passenger after the nonsensical rapid fire question segment ended. She didn't like the look on his face. *Can't really blame him.*

"Hmm, yes." There was a long pause before Angel continued. "How about we, instead, swing by your office? Surprise Steve in his natural element. I'd really like to see where you guys make the sausage. Give me a better feel for the atmosphere. It's been so long since I've seen that big lug. Why wait until tomorrow? Let's surprise him!"

There was an awkward moment of silence before Jawnie mustered a reply.

"I really hate driving in this weather. But once I get back to the office, I'll be fine."

* * * * * * * * * *

"You really don't mind coming here? Even after all that cult shit?" Raffi said. Rockfish noticed his friend wasn't dressed in the normal business suit and the sunglasses screamed someone who didn't want to be recognized. *There's a story behind it, but I don't have time for it. I've got my agenda.*

While Jawnie was sitting in the cellphone lot waiting on Angel, Rockfish met up with Raffi at Jamocha Jubblies for coffee and to hear what he had learned about the arson attempt at Little Golf Big Tees. Rockfish looked across the coffee shop. Dad bods filled every table and booth. The mashup of Hooters and Starbucks continued to be standing room only on each visit.

"Nah, not really," Rockfish said. "New ownership. Can't blame them for sticking with a successful theme. Sometimes in a man's day, nothing is more helpful than a cup of Joe with a side of side boob.

I'm no economist, but probably makes damn good business sense."

"Ha! I'm glad you can see past the past, so to speak. Love this place and hold court here often. I think of each dollar I spend here as sticking to old Porbeagle. I know it don't make sense, but fuck that dead guy."

Rockfish laughed. He had been nowhere near this place since the See You Next Tuesday case closed and he thought twice about Raffi's meeting suggestion, but after walking into the place; he knew he was overreacting. "What you got for me?"

"Hey, want to hear something about the new owners of this place? Corporate, I mean," Raffi said, and sat up straight. "I read an article on that dark web about—"

"Raffi, I don't have time for another of your far-out conspiracy theories. We're here to talk shop. My shop. Not what you read on some web page."

"Okay, fine. Some other time." Raffi said. His shoulders slouched back down. "We're not waiting on your partner?"

"She's making an airport run. I can fill her in later."

"I thought she wasn't supposed to be out of your sight?"

"I'm a partner, not a parent. My words only carry so much weight. She'll be alright." *Would she?* Rockfish debated the subject in his head a lot more than he would ever let on.

"You know her better than anyone. Anyway, I was down by the docks, at that filthy fucking place, Slappy Richards, and people were talking."

"I know it well," Rockfish said. "Mack used to take me to a hotdog place right next door when I was a kid, and we'd watch the ships come in."

"Yeah, sounds like a splendid memory. But these days, I wouldn't drag a kid to that part of town unless he was packing more than a hotdog roll."

Rockfish noticed the server headed towards their booth. He tilted his head and Raffi stopped talking.

"I think we're good for right now, darling," Rockfish said and waited for the server to put some distance between them. "Go on now."

Raffi picked up his drink and sipped before continuing.

"My guy said some dude came in and started asking for some help with a particular matter. Problem was, he was trying to contract out but wasn't even offering what's known as a livable wage these days, let alone enough to start this level of felony."

Cheap. That fits the white clueless collar theory.

"From what I hear, everyone passed. He left mumbling something about trying the Mexicans that hung out at the Home Depot. Even Skippy the Torch passed and that guy would burn down his mom's house and pay you for the honor. That should tell you something about the guy you're looking for. He gave everyone he ran into the heebie-jeebies. Weird fucking dude."

Racist too. What a surprise. "He struck out and drove to the mini-golf course. Decided to go the DIY route or found a bunch of degenerate teens. He didn't go the Mexican route. I saw the shitty results."

"What do you mean, teens?" Raffi said. He put his mug back down on the table.

"He might have found degenerates and offered them half up front. They took his cash, put the bare minimum into the job, and never went back for the other half. Easy way to make some fast cash. And that's what scares me. If it is the guy from Fulsome, working to please or on direct orders from his boss, this ain't gonna end until they scare these women into selling. Going to be pennies on the dollar at this rate, but I'm afraid the longer this lasts, the more messy their tactics will get. "

"Gotcha, makes sense. Where do you go from here?"

"Fuck if I know," Rockfish said. "One of those scenarios is dead on, but neither really gets me anywhere. Keep your ears open. Odds are one of two things will happen. He'll raise some more capital to hire a pro, or he'll jump on his home computer and conduct a few problematical Google searches to help his next DIY effort." Rockfish leaned in a little before continuing. "The first one, you hear anything, call me. We'll do a little overnight stakeout in the big windmill that hasn't been demo'd yet. We'll stay out of sight, watching the new surveillance cameras. If someone shows up, we detain them until the cops show up."

"Stevie, you're using the word 'we' an awful lot over there. Much like Skippy, I ain't signed on for anything yet." Raffi folded his arms and leaned back.

"I'll pay you. When have I never paid you?"

"Cut it, Steve. The last time I worked for you, I almost got shot. Thank God, Earl hesitated. Don't forget your old man, with those shaky hands, almost took my head off."

"But he didn't. Mack is an excellent shot, and I compensated you pretty damn generous, if I recall."

"That you did," Raffi said.

"Plus, this is hiding out and calling 9-1-1. At the worst, we run over and tackle some guy. You'll clean up nice."

"And if he tries his luck again on his own?"

"Hope the cameras catch his face and I can confirm it's the same Fulsome employee that's been fucking with us the past week since we first started discussing even taking this damn case. If I get a clear shot, I take the video straight to the local cops or Decker. Jawnie and I give statements about our previous run-ins with the same guy and then wash my hands of it. Once the cops open a case, I'm out. I don't work active cases." Rockfish made a wiping hand motion and picked up his coffee. "Not the ending Jawnie would hope for, but the one I'm happiest with. I got other shit on my plate, especially now that my workforce has been halved."

"Not the first time I've told you this," Raffi said. "But Rockfish, McGee and Pérez sure sounds better now, am I right? Can't give a hundred percent to your clients if you're not staffed at a hundred percent." Raffi adjusted his nonexistent tie and grinned widely.

"Get the fuck out of here with that. You've asked before. Jog your memory back to any of those times and replay my answer. Now what about the other thing? Any paisans fresh off the boat?"

Raffi held up his cup to get the server's attention before answering.

"Imma need another one of these when you get the chance."

"Might as well get me one, too," Rockfish said. The server stepped over and took their empty cups before turning away.

Raffi didn't continue right away, but looked in all directions before opening his mouth.

"Okay, this is a little more dicey, but no clearer than your other issue. I hear the Marini Family has brought in some muscle, outside the family, so to speak, over the past couple of days," Raffi said. His head jumped back on the swivel before lowering his voice. "No specifics. My guy thinks the contract workers have to do with some trouble on the docks. No asks or contracts from up North."

"Goddamn it. I knew I should have reached out to Gordon. So what you're telling me is Jawnie's safe, or some muscle is out to get her under the guise of breaking skulls on the dock. None of this is clear." Rockfish rubbed his temples with both hands. "This is too squirrelly for me. I've got to convince Jawnie, somehow, to go with Agent Thomas. Ain't no shame in sitting out a couple of quarters. That's what the bench players are for. Of course, I don't have anyone sitting on the bench. Don't you even go there, Raffi. If Angel promises to back up the Brink's truck when I talk to him tomorrow, I can easily slow down the new client train until she returns, and the trial is over." Rockfish shook his head, partially in disgust and confusion.

A light to his right caught his attention. He looked down at a text notification from Lynn that had lit up the phone screen. "Hold that thought, I have to take this," Rockfish said, holding up his index finger and opening the messaging app.

Steve - McGillicutty called - he's not a happy camper and on his way down here. Figure you'd want to handle.

Rockfish let out an audible sigh. *The McGillicutty case. The thing that will never die.* Rockfish shoved the phone into his jacket pocket and took one last sip from his coffee mug.

"Sorry about this, Raffi. I gotta run back and deal with an impromptu client meeting. With Jawnie out at BWI, I'm on call."

Rockfish stood up and dug his hand down into his pants pocket when Raffi held up his hand.

"I got this, Stevie. You go handle business."

"Can you see the shocked expression on my face, because I'm pretty sure you could knock me over with a feather right now? Thanks man, appreciate it. Now, don't come at me with that. *You owe me* shit, somewhere down the line."

The old friends laughed, and Rockfish jogged in the rain and across the parking lot to the Subaru. Thirty minutes later, he was pouring himself a drink in anticipation of McGillicutty coming through the door like a herd of elephants. He put the bottle down on the bar when a pair of recognizable headlights came through the glass front door and lit up the office.

"What? I told her to go straight home."

* * * * * * * * *

"Looks like Steve parked my car in the last spot up front," Jawnie said. "I can pull up a little closer for you. You won't get as wet and then I can pull around and park."

"Jawnie, because I'm from Hollywood, you confuse me with someone who'd melt," Angel said. "The question is, are you ready to make a run for it?" He grabbed the door latch and was alongside the front fender before Jawnie realized what was happening. She jumped out and took off. Angel reached the sidewalk first and held the door open. Jawnie walked into the office, dripping rainwater on the carpet as they both stood in front of Lynn's desk, laughing.

"Hey thanks for taking that last spot in the front row," Jawnie said to Rockfish between deep breaths and giggles.

Rockfish shook his head. He looked past Jawnie and Angel to Lynn. She met his gaze and shrugged.

"I couldn't tell ya' the truth and expect you to come back to the office in a reasonable amount of time," Lynn said.

"McGillicutty isn't coming?"

"This guy, all business unless he's the one busting chops," Angel said and walked over to where Rockfish stood. "Steve, great to see you again, buddy." He gave Rockfish a big wet hug, and the laughs continued across three-quarters of the room.

Rockfish stepped back and grabbed a handful of napkins from behind the bar.

"Angel, I figured you'd be about an hour into a two-hour massage back at the ritzy hotel spa by now. What brings you down to the trenches with the little people?"

"What? A rub down? And miss seeing you in your element?" Angel swiped at the wet hair matted to his forehead. "Not on your life. I told Jawnie that tomorrow's the business side of things, but I want to catch up. Like old friends. She's going to order out for us. Now pour me a drink, you miserable bastard." Angel moved in for another damp hug.

Jawnie watched as these two business partners, and now actual friends, went back and forth. It made her smile on the inside. Her most important side at the moment. The anxiety from the drive had diminished.

"Drinks for everyone," Angel added, waving both hands in the air. "I can always Uber to the hotel."

"I drove you here. I'm driving you back. Now, where should I order dinner from?" Jawnie said. She walked towards Lynn to come up with a consensus, while Rockfish remained leaning against the bar with an occasional shake of his head.

"Ah, look at this place. The pictures don't do it justice. I cannot wait to shoot in here." Angel said as he began giving himself a self-guided walking tour. "I love exactly how you laid out the space. I can get the mystery solving vibe from all angles. By the way, Steve, do you have a towel or something I can pat myself semi-dry with? I'll settle for a few of those napkins if you have any left. I mean, can you believe this rain? In LA we'd sell our first born for some like this, flooding be damned." Angel sat down in one chair that circled the conference table, ignoring the couch and recliners he had walked past.

"I thought LA had already sold its first born?" Rockfish said. "You know, when Jeffrey Epstein's guards had to magically pee at the same time?"

"I'll ignore that shot across Hollywood's bow. Save it for the cameras, Steve. America loves you. Jawnie, come sit around the table. You too Lynn, I've heard so much about you."

Jawnie followed Lynn toward the table, but Lynn stopped. She turned and looked at Jawnie before speaking.

"You go. I'll order dinner and be over in a second," Lynn said. "Catch up. I'm in charge of the office admin crap, so let me do my job. I'll grab that cheap champagne that Rockfish keeps for clients and bring a bottle over to the table."

Jawnie reached out and touched Lynn on the left arm. "Thank you. Order something from Manny's Seafood Hideaway. Angel mentioned crabs from the minute he got in the car. He wants to eat like an authentic Charm City resident. Plus, it's Steve's favorite, so that might make him a little more at ease. Drop his name and they'll deliver." Jawnie then walked over to Rockfish and helped herd him towards the conference table and a seat across from Angel. She took the vacant chair next to their guest.

After calling Manny's, Lynn joined the others at the table with a bottle of Freixenet and four glasses.

Jawnie glanced across at Rockfish as Lynn poured the champagne. *He really doesn't want to be here. Damn, it's only a few words. The least he can do.* She watched as he reluctantly stood up and raised a glass.

"Here's to, um... us, um... continuing to um...—"

"Being great friends and all of us making a boat load of more money in the future," Angel said, leaping to his feet. "You two keep working these fucked up cases and I'll keep you in front of millions of American couch potatoes on a weekly episodic basis. Foreign rights, notwithstanding. We have a separate team working on that angle."

Glasses clinked, Lynn poured a second round, and Angel filled the trio in on the latest happenings until there was a knock at the door. Lynn walked back to the front and dealt with the delivery driver.

"Hey, wait. I want to pay for dinner," Angel said.

"We used the corporate card when we placed the order," Jawnie said.

"Yeah, sit down and stop playing the high roller," Rockfish added. "We're semi-successful. We can afford a handful of blue crabs and hushpuppies."

"The least I can do is get the tip," Angel said.

Jawnie reached out but let him go. She pulled her arm back and Angel jumped up from the table, cash in hand, insistent on making the delivery person's night. *Let him do his thing. It makes him happy and the less tension in the room, the less Steve will make me relive it on the way to the hotel in the morning.*

Moments later, Lynn and Angel returned to the conference table. Rockfish had grabbed a stack of old newspapers kept behind the bar for such occasions, and Lynn spilled a dozen and a half blue crabs across the table. Conversation flowed, all dove into the crabs, and jokes were made as the three caught up. Jawnie made a point of keeping Lynn involved in the conversation to avoid leaving her feeling left out. After the second glass of champagne, Jawnie made the switch to bottled water.

She also got a kick out of watching Lynn show Angel how to extract every morsel of meat from the crab's body. Jawnie's occasional glances over at Rockfish and his facial expressions told her he was enjoying the show as well. *He seems to have relaxed, at least on the outside. I really never expected this evening to go as smooth as it has. I, we, deserve it.* She gave herself an imaginary pat on the back for pulling this off, despite her up and down mental health all week.

After dinner, all four moved to the recliners and couch area and refilled their glasses. At one point, Angel called for another bottle of champagne and Lynn stood up from the couch to retrieve it.

"I'm thinking of casting Eladio Woods as Porbeagle," Angel said. "You know, that guy from The Fun House Chronicles. The ladies love him. And it's not like Earl's around to play himself." Angel busted up laughing but stopped when he noticed no one else followed suit.

"Hey, I thought this was friends catching up and not business," Jawnie said, and looked at Rockfish. *Help me steer this thing before we crash into the rocks.*

"Yeah, I think we've got more than enough time to rehash all that shit tomorrow," Rockfish said. "We switched the sign on the door to closed after the food arrived."

Angel threw his hands up with a flourish. "I'm just throwing stuff out there, seeing what you think," Angel said, holding out his arms, palms up. "I didn't know I was crossing some line or Friday night rule. But he's the guy for the role, trust me. And for Lilith..."

Maybe I should have asked how many he had on the plane? Jawnie reached for the bottle, intent on setting it on the table, unopened and out of Angel's reach. *Maybe it's time to call it a night. Steve won't give me any guff if I move in that direction. He might give me a hug.*

"Angel. Cut the shit. There's a lot Jawnie and Lynn haven't processed completely from the end of that case," Rockfish said. "Bringing up shit out of the blue affects people differently. We all have things we are trying to move past. Tomorrow's different. A business meeting, well, that shit's expected to be discussed."

Angel closed his eyes and nodded. "I'm sorry. Maybe I got caught up in the vibe of this place," he said, trying to drink from his empty glass. "Look, if I hurt anyone here, I'm sorry. But whether I say it tonight or tomorrow, you're all going to be a part of this. It is your choice. Actively or passively."

"Is that a threat?" Jawnie said.

"To move forward with this project without us?" Rockfish said.

"No, it is more an insider's view of how the docuseries, the entertainment business, is currently operating. I'm sorry I upset you, Lynn. And you too, Jawnie. I would like to blame the alcohol, but I'm an ass sometimes." Angel sighed and looked down at the ground. "Maybe I should go. I'll call a car." Angel stood up and began walking towards the door, Rockfish right on his tail.

"No, I told you I would take you," Jawnie said, standing up as well. *And give you a piece of my mind on the way.*

Angel stopped short of the door and turned around. "Lynn, please come early tomorrow. Jawnie, you too. Let's do a spa morning on me. With everyone relaxed, we can knock out our discussions and move on from how I fucked up this evening. You too, Steve."

"I'll pass," Rockfish said. He stepped around Angel and reached to open the door.

"Jawnie, do you have an umbrella I could use this time?"

"Ah, no. I'm sorry. I left it behind the seat in Steve's car."

"I can deal with being soaked again," Angel said. "It doesn't look like it's even let up for a second since we got here."

"You know what? I've got a raincoat and a hat in my office. You'll look like Paddington Bear, but you'll be dry."

"I'll take it."

Jawnie walked back to her office and Angel donned the rain jacket and matching yellow hat.

"Alright all, I apologize again for ruining what was a grand night. I'll see you all tomorrow," Angel said.

Rockfish held open the door and Angel stepped outside. Jawnie followed suit but stopped short of the doorway and turned back around.

"Hey Lynn, do you want to come with? This way I can—"

Crack!

Crack!

Crack!

All four let out a scream. Some were louder and in more pain than others.

Angel fell backwards through the open doorway, grasping at Jawnie and bringing her down on top of him. Blood spilt down the front of the yellow rain jacket and onto the floor.

CHAPTER FOUR

"*AAAAAAH!*"

Jawnie awoke mid-scream, her head filled with fog. She blinked half-a-dozen times to focus. *Where the heck am I?* The cold leather against the side of her face and the sunlight streaming in from above brought back a fleeting memory of the U.S. Marshal's arriving on scene before the ambulance had left with Angel.

Angel! Jawnie's stomach folded in on itself and a sourness climbed up the back of her throat. *Where is he? How is he? How could I have abandoned him?* Her eyes slammed shut again. The stress was all too much.

The Marshals had scurried her away to an undisclosed, guarded hotel room for the night before piling back in the SUV this morning. Jawnie lay on her left side, legs pulled in hard against her chest. She moved her left arm, and the pain shot up to her shoulder. *More sore, though. Painful to move and probably touch. Had a bullet hit me? Winged? No bandages, so that was a leap. Had a paramedic on the scene injected me with something? Was I that much of a wailing banshee? Sedated like some wild animal.* She'd look for the tag later.

Jawnie concentrated on her current quandary. At some point, unbeknownst to her at the moment, she had slipped out of the seatbelt and assumed the fetal position. *Wait. Was it a trip? Did anyone tell me where we're headed? Maybe we're headed to the hospital to see Angel.* That would be the best-case scenario, but also the most unlikely. And yet, somewhere deep inside, she

72

understood it. She had laid down to shut off the outside world. The effort failed miserably as she had only succeeded in the short period between closing her eyes and her unconsciousness hitting rewind to replay the atrocious scene again and again.

Angel pulling her to the ground. His arms flailing uncontrollably. Screams. A second shot, shattering the glass of the now closed door. Rockfish cursing and clutching his arm. STEVE! Was that last part real, or just how she imagined it all played out before she shut down? Was any of it real? Are these two really Marshals? Or do they work for Provolone?

Jawnie tried shifting onto her back, but the pain from her left arm, pinned against the backseat, caused her to roll back onto her side. She opened her eyes to fight back and keep the terrible memories at bay. She saw the heads of the men in the front seats. The driver's salt and pepper hair stuck out between the rods of the headrest. Jawnie shifted and her eyes moved to the passenger. The man had twisted around and peered down from between the two seats. His eyes hid behind a pair of sunglasses, the tips of which rested high above his ears, upon his bald head.

Neither man looked like the mob-types she had encountered in the past. Jawnie glanced again at the driver and then back to the passenger. She had no recollection of their heads, faces or names, no matter how hard she searched her short-term memory. If they were from the Marshals Service, surely they would have introduced themselves earlier. *Probably did. It's buried in here somewhere. I need to know where to look.*

The passenger continued to stare and move his lips. She wasn't processing what he was saying and instead stayed deep inside her head. Her new hidey-hole. No more hollowed out space under the stairs, only the space between her ears from now on.

"... Ms. McGee..."

Jawnie couldn't read lips, but those two words stood out. *It's as good a time as any to retry and join the living.* She sat back up and re-buckled her seatbelt. At the same time, the Marshal turned around and pulled down his visor.

He used the mirror to make eye contact, and she preferred this to the way he was, all twisted around and staring down at her. Jawnie returned to the world mid-conversation.

"... glad to see you're back with us. Doc said that shot should have worn off a couple of hours ago, but either way, here we are. Welcome to the program."

"Here? Where? Who?"

"Okay, looks like we're going to have to start from the beginning here. I'll take it slow. You tell me if any of these affect you. My name is Agent Kevin Sorbelli, and this is my partner, Agent Walt Winters. We're with the U.S. Marshals."

Jawnie looked at the driver, who tipped the ball cap he was wearing while keeping one hand on the wheel. The rest of his hair matched the salt and pepper she noticed previously.

"There was a shooting—"

"Angel! Steve! I didn't imagine it," Jawnie said. "Are they okay? Are we going to see them?"

Agent Sorbelli pushed up his visor and spun once more in his seat. Jawnie leaned in towards the space between the front seats as to not miss a word. Sorbelli flipped his Oakleys atop his head before answering. "I'm going to have to ask you to take it easy. You have been through a lot in the past eighteen hours. Please sit back and I'll try to fill in the holes and answer what questions you have."

Jawnie locked eyes with Sorbelli. She didn't budge; her face almost resting atop the center console.

"Alright then. I don't have a recent update, but I can tell you what I learned before we got on the road this morning. Mr. Davenport is in the ICU. I haven't had an update on him in a few hours. Your partner, Steve, got, as we say, winged. A through and through on the fleshy part of his bicep. He's going to be fine. Might even have been discharged by now, with a sling and some fresh bandages—"

"He's still in the hospital. He would never leave Angel."

"He could be, but I'm not privy to that type of information. What I know is that Mr. Davenport's father chartered a plane and flew out as soon as he heard. The family's plan is to take him back to Los Angeles on that same charter. Apparently, the East Coast doctors leave a little to be desired, at least according to his dad. The two of them are most likely headed back cross-country this weekend, if the doctor provides the proper medical clearances. Once we get to our destination and check in, I'll get an update for you."

Jawnie felt her cheeks go flush. *Embarrassment, anger or good-sized portions of both?*

"Can't you get on that radio and call someone now?"

"No reason to worry about things that aren't in your control," Sorbelli said. "Our job is to get you to the safe house in one piece. That includes mentally. So sit back, close your eyes, and I'll let you know when we're close."

"The bullets were meant for me. Weren't they?"

The pause was all she needed. Jawnie reached across and unhooked her seatbelt. She assumed the position once again, pulling her knees tight against her chest. She closed her eyes and tried her best to turn off her ears and fight away the tears.

* * * * * * * * * *

Sunday afternoon, less than forty-eight hours after the shooting, Rockfish was home and not well rested. His pain came from two distinct areas. His left arm, where the bullet entered and exited through some fatty tissue a few inches above the elbow, and FBI Agent Thomas, who now sat across at the kitchen table.

The hospital hadn't kept him overnight for observation, as someone in pink scrubs classified his injury as not-life-threatening. The on-call doctor discharged him around 2am Saturday morning after an ER doctor picked glass shards from the door out of his wound, cleaned it up, let him know he'd be sore for a long while, and stuck two sheets torn from his prescription pad in his hand. One for pain and the other to prevent infection. The same doctor claimed the sling would also help with healing and pain relief. His parting words to Rockfish were to wear it for most waking hours.

Despite the early hour and his pain, Rockfish hadn't gone straight home. He sent Mack out to wait in the old man's pickup, while he worked his conversational skill set to see if he could get in to see Angel.

"Just because you both were injured at the same crime scene, don't make you kin," the lead ER nurse said. She had crossed her arms when she spoke and shuffled in front of the big button on the wall that would have opened the door Rockfish needed.

She used the same line of excuses when he downshifted and only wanted to hear how his friend and business partner was doing. A few Anne Arundel County police officers still milled around the ER, but they didn't know him from Adam and remained tight-lipped. *Maybe Decker could make a call over to the PD's chief and get an update for me?* He remembered Mack sitting outside. Not to mention Zippy sitting by the front door, back home, his Labrador legs crossed for all they were worth. *Ah, I'll bug Decker when the sun comes up.*

Rockfish still hadn't heard from Decker, nor had he begun tackling the Sunday crossword puzzle, when the video doorbell announced he had company. It took him three tries to open the app with his right hand, all the while the house's two Alexas continued to announce motion detected at the front door. *Fuck, I hate this goddamn thing.* He equally shared that feeling with most smart devices and his temporary assignment on Team Right-Handed.

When the live video feed filled his screen, Agent Thomas stood on the top step. She dressed more professionally this morning than the search warrant getup Rockfish last saw her in. He glanced down at his shirtless belly and boxers. He tapped the microphone icon.

"Hola. No hablo ingles."

When Agent Thomas didn't bite, Rockfish stood up from the table. "Dad, get the door. Put her in the kitchen. Least comfortable chair we have. I'll run Zippy upstairs, put him in your room, and throw on some clothes."

The Kitchen Summit had started with niceties and honest inquiries about how Rockfish was getting along, both physically and mentally. His salvo of one-word answers did not appear to dent Agent Thomas' bureaucratic armor.

She's clearly working from a script of questions written by a government shrink to avoid any kind of liability issues. Feel me out, if I plan to sue. Rockfish put his one working elbow on the table and dropped his chin into his palm. He stared across the table. He waited until she took a breath and then dove in. Feet first.

"Let's cut the shit, Agent Thomas. I'm fine, life couldn't be better," Rockfish said. "You know who it's not so great for? Angel and Jawnie. How about you tell me how they're doing? Matter fact, I'll do you one better." Rockfish slammed his right palm on the table. "You scratch mine and I'll scratch yours. I'll tell you about my new receptionist who's probably suffered her second mental breakdown in the last six months, but she's loyal to a fault. Still will drag herself in each day. Big Pharma'd up six ways to Sunday, and I wonder if she'd even be capable of doing her job. She goes home each day to a condo filled with Jawnie's stuff the Marshals didn't pack, and that's her fucking cue to medicate again." Rockfish shook his head in disgust. "Your turn Agent Thomas."

Agent Thomas stared back and didn't say a word. She took a deep breath, exhaled, and kept her lips pursed before speaking. "Steve—"

"*Mr. Rockfish.* Let's keep this on a professional level. Because it's nothing else."

"Mr. Rockfish, I am very sorry to hear about the troubles Ms. Hurricane-Tesla is having. We have an entire division of the FBI dedicated to victim/witness matters. I can have someone get in touch—"

"Don't need it. Don't want it. I'll get her whatever she needs."

"As for your first question. Regarding Mr. Davenport's medical status, you are not family and thus not privy to that information," Agent Thomas said with a stern face. "Off the record, I can tell you his long-term prognosis is good. But it will be a long road. His father is already making plans to take him back to LA for further treatment, then rehabilitation."

"I'll call the studio. They'll tell me."

"You do that. As for your partner—"

Rockfish dropped his head into his hands and vigorously rubbed his eyes. "Jawnie. Her name is Jawnie McGee. You spoke to her not a week ago. Face to face."

They stared at each other and if Rockfish could read her face, and he was damn sure he could, Agent Thomas' patience was wearing thin. *Check.*

"Her situation is completely out of my hands and with the U.S. Marshals Service. From what I know of their procedures, no one, not even the immediate family, will be told of her location. Eventually, at some point, the Marshals will set up secure comms, but again, those in charge will restrict them."

"But technically, I'm the only family she has—"

"Here." Agent Thomas said between pursed lips. "She has plenty in New Jersey. They are aware of her situation."

"Alright then," Rockfish said, putting his one good palm on the table. He pushed away, and the chair slid back. "If you're going to be absolutely useless in providing information or keeping me safe." He pointed to the sling and bandages sticking out from under his short-sleeve shirt. "Then I think we're done here." *Checkmate.*

Rockfish stood up, walked around to where Agent Thomas sat, and headed for the front door. He didn't wait to see if she followed. He unlocked the deadbolt and threw open the door to see her out. Agent Thomas was right behind him, as expected, but stopped short of stepping outside and instead turned to face him. Her face looked void of emotion to him, but Rockfish thought he spotted a slight slouch in her shoulders. *I'm getting to her.*

"Mr. Rockfish, you're a smart guy. Don't take this into your own hands. There is an investigation ongoing, and if I recall from your past rants, you don't work pending cases. Let's not reverse course with this shooting."

"Yeah, that won't cut it. But you told me, so no liability to you now. You're safe."

"I mean it, no Death Wish, Charles Bronson shit, Rockfish," Agent Thomas said, turning away and not waiting for an answer.

Rockfish watched as she walked down the steps. A car pulling into the driveway caught his attention.

Raffi. This is going to be the cheering up I need, or the aggravation I don't. He's always a flip of the coin. He waved goodbye to her and welcome to him.

Raffi bounded up the steps and Rockfish felt the morning's tension dissipate into thin air.

"Damn, Stevie, you look like the Crypt Keeper with a bad wing. You sleeping much?"

"Get in here, you dumb sonofabitch. I'll have Mack put some more coffee on."

The Kitchen Summit II convened under much better circumstances than its predecessor.

"... yea, it only nicked me. Nothing major. It's only been a day, but I'm fucking tired of doing shit right-handed. Have you ever tried to wipe with your non-dominant hand? It ain't easy. Fingers slip and suddenly I'm on the back deck writing poetry and cheering on the Cowboys. The damnedest thing."

"That sounds pretty major to me," Raffi said with a hearty guffaw. "The Cowboys? Where do you keep the hand sanitizer? You know, get a bidet. You'll never go back to the sandpaper."

The laugh was exactly what the doctor ordered after dealing with his first unexpected guest of the morning.

"I gotta tell you they didn't keep me overnight. Kind of shocked me. That Omega variant doesn't fuck around. Not an empty bed in the place. Nurse told me, with a gunshot wound, it was standard to admit, but times are a changin'. Goddamn, COVID is going to be the death of us yet." Rockfish rapped his knuckles on the table.

Mack walked over from the far side of the kitchen and put two mugs down on the table before refilling his own. He stepped into the doorway and leaned against the jamb.

"We're good here, Dad," Rockfish said. No need for you to stick around unless you want to be bored to death."

Mack took one step back into the kitchen and locked eyes with his son. He then turned and gave Raffi the once over, except his gaze didn't move on from their guest. "Sonny, you sure? I might not be around the next time this fella loses a fist fight to a meth head."

Rockfish bit his tongue as to not laugh out loud at his father's crack. But with a slight nod, he acknowledged game and Mack walked out of the kitchen with a wide grin.

Raffi shook his head and turned to Rockfish across the table. "You dad will never let me live that down."

"Not in a million years. He enjoys busting your balls too much." Rockfish now let out his laugh and stood up. "Hey, these coffees need a little something, especially after my first visitor," Rockfish said. He walked into the other room and emerged with a bottle of Jameson. Irish coffees in hand, they got down to business.

"Other than being a sweet friend and checking up on me, whatcha got?"

"Not much of anything on your deal there," Raffi said, pointing to the sling. "But word has it your arson guy was back looking for potential applicants. Claims to be working on a real short deadline but with a larger bankroll. Last night he was asking for someone that would provide a customer satisfaction guarantee if you get my drift." Raffi raised his eyebrows and nodded. "I'm betting he's heard you and Jawnie are most likely out of commission, if not the picture, and looking to move forward to squeeze your girls out of that prime real estate."

"What's his deadline?"

"The guy tossed around an end of the week bonus."

"Hmm," Rockfish said. He tapped his fingernail against the side of the coffee cup. *I can call Jawnie's friends and make damn sure the cameras are up and operational. Do a little surveillance. Catch this piece of shit in the act and call the police. Wash my hands of this. As Agent Thomas so eloquently put it, I don't work on active cases. But there is a difference between being active and the cops not doing shit. This is the one I need to make time in my schedule for.* "You up for some night work? Paid, of course."

"You know me, Stevie. You're down a man. I'll pick up that flag," Raffi said.

"Glad to hear it. Pack some snacks and a thermos of coffee. You'll be in the big windmill. I'll set up behind the construction supplies along the tree lines at the back of the lot. This way, we've got him in the old pincer maneuver. You come busting out of the Windmill and I'll come from the rear. He'll have nowhere to run, except smack into one of us." Rockfish's finger moved across the table and drew out exactly how the plan would go down.

"You sure you don't want to be in the Windmill? Safer in there, I bet. Less wear and tear on your wound." Raffi's head nodded with each word he spoke.

"And way more cramped, too. You're a long way from having your name on the marquee, pal. But I'll chip in a little hazard pay for you. If it comes to it."

* * * * * * * * * *

Winters turned the SUV up the long dirt driveway. By this time, Jawnie was back upright and looked at the old, white farmhouse as they drew closer. The SUV stopped alongside the right side of the house, and Jawnie could make out a barn but not much else in the backyard. The tree-line driveway reminded her of *Forrest Gump*, or maybe *Gone With The Wind*, but this house was much smaller and, according to her captives, she was outside Lancaster, Pennsylvania. A far cry from a plantation in the South.

Both Marshals threw open their doors. Jawnie released her seatbelt and did the same. She stepped outside onto the gravel and looked around. The house was set far back from the road and corn field stretched in all directions. *Will the Children of the Corn be the death of me?*

Winters pulled her bike down off the rack and wheeled it into the barn's open doorway. Once he removed the rack, Sorbelli pulled all of Jawnie's bags from the back and grabbed what he could on the first trip.

"Let's get inside, it looks like rain," Sorbelli said and walked towards the front steps.

Jawnie grabbed her backpack. It was lighter than when she packed it, but chalked that feeling up to memory misfires and followed Sorbelli.

As she drew closer, the house was older and in more disrepair than she noticed when they pulled up. The board and batten siding appeared to have been painted a century before. Jawnie thought the top coat would fall off with the brush of a finger. The steps leading to the large wraparound porch didn't look to be in any better condition. Her eyes went from Sorbelli, struggling with her larger suitcases, up the steps to the front porch. Annetta Provolone held the door open and beckoned Jawnie to come inside.

"*AAAAAAH!*"

Her scream brought her upright, her eyes so wide, she momentarily wondered if they would ever shut again. She was in bed. Her new bed. *The temporary bed.* The sunlight streamed in through the white lace curtains to let her know it was the start of day three in paradise. Ninety-seven to go, unless Provolone's attorney would successfully lobby for a continuance, and then all bets were off on when the trial would actually kick-off.

Knock

"Are you okay, Ms. McGee?"

"Just my Amish Mafia Haunted House alarm clock, all good here in the Matrix, Agent Sorbelli."

"Huh? Are you alright?"

"Ah, don't worry about it. I'll stop having nightmares at some point."

The Marshals had bedrooms on either side of her, and like clockwork, when something seemed amiss, one or the other would knock. Their reactions were the first of the ground rules she had learned on Sunday. Jawnie had expected some sort of indoctrination lecture on Saturday after unpacking, or at least after dinner. Instead, the men instructed her to unwind, decompress and try to get acclimated to her surroundings. All she was told was the name of the small town. New Chilltown. A small Amish city, close enough to Lancaster, Pennsylvania, should any emergencies arise. But both Sorbelli and Winters were quick to downplay any talk of those.

"Take it easy the rest of the day, but don't go outside. Unless one of us is with you," Winters said. "I need you rested and full of attention tomorrow. It's going to be a huge learning curve. Consider it almost like a classroom environment. Protective Custody 101, if you will."

Bodyguarding for Dummies. Knock it off. You're not dumb. These men are here to protect you because you have a pretty poor track record of doing it on your own. Take a deep breath. The sooner you understand they are here to help, the quicker and less eventful the stay will be. Jawnie nodded to herself and took a relaxing deep breath.

Dinner that first night was courtesy of the Old Chilltown Diner. The eatery was a long-established family restaurant a few miles down the road. The owners had a long history of working with the Marshals and could cater to whatever strange dietary restrictions Jawnie had. Her first thought had been to Google the restaurant on her phone and check out the main menu before she began making wholesale substitutions, but in this crazy action movie, because to her that was the only comparison she could make with her anxiety filled brain, the Marshals had confiscated it. She remembered the incident the following morning and learned why Winters had pulled it from her hand.

Sunday morning brought coffee and the three of them seated around the dining room table. The theme of the morning session was communications. To emphasize the point, a large desktop computer sat at the opposite end of the table.

As the lesson droned on, Jawnie couldn't help but think that Winters and Sorbelli could have condensed all the key points into a single PowerPoint slide. No one was to know where she was. Any wanderings or walkabouts outside the house were to be accompanied. And last, all electronic communications were to go through the desktop computer while on location. *It's like when I was growing up and the computer couldn't leave the first floor of the house. Only these two Marshals have replaced Mom and Dad. Would they be as easy to fool? Probably not, but I'll figure out some way to get word to Lynn or Rockfish.*

After a brief break for lunch, Winters had walked over and showed Jawnie exactly what she needed to do, with either Marshal's help, in order to log in and begin communicating with the outside world. The portal appeared pretty easy to grasp and understand. *Must be for all the knuckle-draggers and turncoat mobsters they've hosted here in the past. No way those types can do complicated technology.*

There were tabs across the top of the portal's browser window for Read and Send. Winters explained a Tech Agent set up the portal to accept both Jawnie's personal and business email accounts. With a simple click, she could bounce back and forth between them. As explained prior to the hands-on workshop, the firewall's rules, a proprietary AI program, and then human eyes monitored the incoming messages prior to being posted in the portal. Outgoing messages received the same treatment, but in reverse order.

"Oh, well, that's strange," Winters said after clicking on the Read tab. "Our system has already flagged a bunch of messages." The program had already quarantined thirteen messages sent within the past thirty hours because of malicious attachments and links. The anonymous sender had targeted all thirteen messages to Jawnie's work address, while her personal account was cc'd with every message.

Her mind, not firing on all cylinders, still came to a quick conclusion. *Chenzo. That little computer dweeb phishing piece of shit. He's related to one of Provolone's goons and did some work on the side for the Family. They're aware I'm gone. Apparently, the hunt is on.*

"Someone's trying to get you to click and give up your location or monitor your every keystroke. Pick one, but this is a prime example of why we handle comms like this."

"I think we all know who's trying."

"Your partner," Winters said with a grin. "He was pretty riled up that we gave him the silent treatment before leaving."

"Yeah, right? I'm sure he's jonesing to figure out where I am, but he sure ain't the one sending malicious payloads via email. USPS? Sure, but not the information superhighway."

"I know. It was a poor attempt at levity," Winters said. "If I hover my mouse over the quarantine folder, I can click and it will ask me for an administrator pass phrase. Then myself, or Agent Sorbelli, can read a short preliminary analysis on that flagged item. Then we can ask you any follow-up questions in order to determine who might have sent it."

"Again, I already know, hence, so should you. Unless I'm overestimating your investigative skills."

Winters cleared his throat and moved his head from side to side as if he was stretching his neck muscles. "No, I don't mean the

Provolone family. We would want to drill down further than that and learn exactly who is sending these."

"Ok, you read your reports and come find me. I'll tell you it's some kid named Chenzo. He's her go-to for shit like this."

Sunday ended with the gnawing feeling that Provolone wouldn't call it a day after her minion's failed attempt to determine her location. *She won't stop. The emails won't quit. Chenzo was only her first avenue to try. How long before they figured everything out and knocked on the door, guns blazing? This time, making sure they don't miss and I'm the one in the line of fire?*

The constant attention her brain gave to those thoughts led to increased tossing and turning. In between rolls, she stared at the ceiling and tried to make out shapes from the stains from previous water damage. Without her phone on the nightstand, Jawnie didn't have a clue at what time she finally drifted off, but she went straight into a nightmare that bled into the following morning.

After she had awoken screaming, Jawnie went back to the water stain game for a little while until her breathing returned to normal and she felt comfortable dressing and heading downstairs.

"You okay?" Sorbelli asked as Jawnie walked through the living room.

"Can I at least sit on the porch swing?"

"Sure. Let me open up the curtains and move to this other seat. Are you sure you're doing okay? I can make a call and get a doctor out here before the end of the day."

"I'm good thanks, Agent Sorbelli." Jawnie opened the front door and walked over to the hanging porch swing and collapsed. She wasn't close to okay, but there was no way she was ever going to admit that to her babysitters.

I'm a grown adult. A growing private detective. A partner in one of the best firms in Baltimore. I can do this. Country mouse living for a couple of months? Should be a cakewalk. But while I'm supposedly safe in this bubble, what about Angel? Steve? Lynn? I need to know they're okay. That despite this being my fault, it, they, me, will be alright. Physically and mentally. Why can't we fast-forward to the end?

Voices from the road drew Jawnie's attention from the woe is me record playing in her head. Three young boys rode bikes down the road. They rode three abreast, the very occasional car not a worry. *Not a care in the world. What I wouldn't do to go back to times like those.* They spoke and laughed, but Jawnie couldn't make out the words from this distance.

That's what I need to clear my head. It's worth a try. Even if it's for only the duration of the ride.

She jumped back off the swing before her seat grew warm and threw open the front door.

"I want to go for a bike ride. Mental health and such."

Sorbelli looked up from the tablet in his hand. "We went over this yesterday. No leaving the property alone—"

"Did I say I wanted to go all rogue and sneak out? Why do you think I'm announcing my intentions?"

"I get it. But give me a second to explain. You asked us on Saturday to pack your bike, I put in a requisition for one. It will be here in the next day or two and then we can go. Although how far, only my legs can tell you. It's been a while since either of us rode. Accept what I tell you, and your time here will be more tolerable."

Jawnie got it, but it didn't mean she had to accept it without a fight. She had a Plan B, and that was something she learned from Rockfish.

"Anyway, this is going to happen. Which one of you is going to grab the keys and follow behind me at the rip-roaring speed of seven miles an hour? Don't make me give you a bad rating on my customer satisfaction survey in our first week together."

* * * * * * * * * *

Three hours to the east, Annetta Provolone opened the French doors to her ocean view deck and stepped outside. She said a silent thank you to her lawyer, Oscar Rosenthal. The man had gone above and beyond, but she had paid him to do exactly that. And she expected it. He was the one who had lost at trial.

The warm summer breeze from the water bounced off her hair. The Aqua Net Extra Super Hold did its job. Annetta looked out over the water, dressed like every other guidette beach-goer down below. Her shorts, too short. T-shirt, too tight. Hoop earrings, too large and platform flip-flops. Yet she was light years, literally, and figuratively, from being one of them. *Age is only a number.* Ankle monitor, or not, *I'm the goddamn John Gotti of this family. No charge is gonna stick to me. Fongool that prosecutor and the Feds.*

It had been one week since Annetta left federal custody, flashing an extra wide shit-eating grin at every member of the prosecutorial team and then the press on the steps of the courthouse. Her car, a new G-Class Mercedes SUV, waited at the bottom for her and, being the strong independent mob boss she portrayed, Annetta slid behind the wheel and drove herself away. She headed across the Ben Franklin Bridge and down the Black Horse Pike to her shore house in Ocean City, New Jersey. There were worse places the Government could have confined her to. The U.S. Attorney's Office knew exactly how luxurious her home was. Hence, the forty-page brief submitted only hours prior to her release. Rosenthal argued the restrictions were Draconian, but the judge that morning felt differently.

"Counselor, your client should be damn glad she's getting out. Period. Next Case on the docket."

Besides the ankle bracelet and home confinement, Annetta was to have no contact with any of her previous associates. Rosenthal was the only permitted guest allowed through the front door. His office, her only allowed trip, other than various physicians. The FBI monitored all calls to and from the residence and disconnected the internet prior to her arrival. Or so they thought. *It wasn't very hard to stay one step ahead of a team of bumbling bureaucrats if you knew where they were headed. Let them think I'm sitting here reading*

Agatha Christie novels, one after another. That report could have been a hundred and forty pages. They ain't gonna win. Fucking frocios.

Three days had passed since the failed attempt to remove one obstacle to Annetta permanently remaining a free woman and regaining access to her AOL account. *I want answers. People need to be held accountable. I refuse to be seen as weak. What of the fucking chooch that failed? A case of the goddamn yips, or what? The next steps better be already underway or so help me God. I am not going back. Fuck metal toilets and one hour of sunlight a day. I want to soak it up every time I throw open these doors.*

She walked away from the railing towards the French doors and stepped back inside. *Air conditioning. One more thing to be thankful for.* She leaned against the back of a leather couch and stared, lost in thought, at the large flat-screen television mounted on the far wall. In a few minutes, Annetta planned to violate two conditions of her bail without thinking twice. Specifically, the 'no contact with those involved in any type of organized criminal activity' and the one underlined in the ruling, that she have no access to the internet. *Tell me we didn't see that one coming a million miles away and planned accordingly.*

Annetta fixed herself a tall glass of iced tea before walking across the family room, past its floor to ceiling windows and into her office. The small room kept with the house's nautical theme and painted a calming light blue. Two portraits graced the wall above her desk. Her father, Angelo and grandfather, Julius. The two heads of the family prior to her ascension. Their paintings reminded her of the power she inherited and wielded. The men were always there for her to listen, to weigh in on the tough decisions. Her desk was an old walnut roll-top desk that also served those men in the past.

Annetta pulled the curtains before taking a seat. She placed her glass down on a coaster and made sure she had everything needed for the surreptitious meeting.

Russian-made Tablet? Check. Some janky Ukrainian software and the finest VPN from the dark web that cryptocurrency could buy? Check and check. The last piece was a financial arrangement made a long time ago for such an occasion. The pass phrase to the neighbor's secured Wi-Fi. Check.

She logged onto the call and wasn't surprised at all to see she was the first one. Her consigliere, Giovanni Bianchi, was next, a few seconds later. Capo Anthony Bologna would have been the last attendee, but he was still serving time at The Federal Correctional Institution in Hazelton, West Virginia, a medium-security federal prison. Annetta felt bad, but Rosenthal and the additional laundered funds thrown his way were to concentrate on getting her conviction overturned. Everyone else in the RICO case was second. Someone had to be on the losing end. And to that effect, she welcomed her acting capo over the Bologna crew, Salvatore Bertoni, aka Sally B, to the call.

"Okay, so let's keep this short and sweet," Annetta said. "The longer we're on, the better the odds someone realizes what the fuck is going on. Now, where is the puttana?"

She stared at the three blank faces before Giovanni visibly swallowed hard and replied. "Not a clue. No one is talking. The Feds wrapped her up tight and spirited her off after the misfire. Our consolation prize is he tagged Rockfish, although it ain't gonna keep him out of the game for very long. Matter of fact, we've gotten word he's back in the office this morning." Giovanni ran his hand through his hair and shrugged his shoulders.

"I don't have time to yell, but if I did, you know I'd come down on this amateur hour you hired, with both feet," Annetta said. She hoped her anger came across in 4K. "Please tell me that yip-having, fucking moulinyan is in worse shape than Rockfish?"

"I can vouch for that, boss," Sally B said. "He's hand crabbing at the bottom of the bay. One of my guys was there with our friends when he went overboard."

"Five minutes in and I finally get some good news, madone!" Annetta noticed her consigliere glancing down at his watch. "Here's what you're gonna do. Dig up the sweetest of honey traps and find some U.S. Marshal with a vice. It shouldn't be hard. Gambling, hookers, blow, little boys. Find it! Doesn't matter where, they'll all have access to the same databases. Get 'em over a barrel and find out where this cunt is. Someone in one of these families has an in with that agency. We need to find it. Exploit it. No fuck-ups, capisce?"

The two heads on the tablet nodded in unison.

"Alright. Let's wrap this shit up. How is our in-house attempt to locate McGee coming along?"

"I spoke with the kid yesterday," Sally B said. "He's not had a bite on any of the emails."

"Any contact between Rockfish and McGee?"

"Our guy at the cell company said her cell's gone silent since she bolted," Bianchi said.

"Obviously. The Feds don't want her bouncing off God knows what cell towers, in some godforsaken podunk town. Are we doing anything with the dick? He's gotta know something."

"A few of my men are on their way down to chat with him," Sally B said.

"Good. No more outside contracting. You see where that got us. Let Angelo's men know you'll be doing business in their town. Don't want any mistaken identities causing an incident between the two families. The blood is bad enough with that one already."

And with that, Annetta cut off the call. Nothing anyone had said left her with a positive outlook, except the image of Rockfish being worked over. Now that gave her a warm and fuzzy feeling, she embraced. *Maybe they'll bring him back here and I can watch. Vaffanculo, Rockfish. And your puttana, too.*

CHAPTER FIVE

Tuesday morning was the first morning Jawnie hadn't awoken in the farmhouse to her own screams or soaked in a cold sweat. *Baby steps.* It could also have been the two glasses of wine. *You know you don't want to make that a habit each night.* She glanced over at the corked, half empty bottle on the nightstand. *Let's get out of bed and start the day.* She threw the dry sheet off her body and got dressed. Before going downstairs, she poured the rest of the wine down the sink in her bathroom. *No one's gonna call me Rockfish junior.* Not that the other two are aware of his proclivities. *Or are they? What do they know of my, or our, past?*

Jawnie came down the stairs and turned right. She walked through the family room and then around to the dining room. She took a seat at the end of the table, turned on the monitor and logged into the Marshal's portal.

"Hey, don't forget I need to look over your message before you hit send," a voice said from the kitchen.

While the Marshals were opposites in looks and age, Jawnie had yet to differentiate their voices. She stood up from the table and walked through the doorway into the kitchen. Sorbelli was at the kitchen table, alone, with a cup of coffee in one hand and a tablet device in the other. *It's always in his hand like it's freakin' attached. You'd think he's a teenage girl with her first smartphone.*

"Yeah, I remember from Remedial Comms 101 on Sunday. You look at it, then someone at Marshal's headquarters reviews it. If you both agree I'm not passing any state secrets, then it gets scrubbed by an AI program before finally heading through the firewall and to its intended recipient." Jawnie looked at Sorbelli and gave him a forced smile as she took down a mug from the cabinet and poured her own cup.

"You paid attention, at least. It's been a while since we've had one of those here."

Jawnie nodded and stepped back into the dining room. She noticed Winters wasn't sitting in his normal spot in the living room.

She leaned towards the kitchen doorway and asked Sorbelli, "Where's your buddy? It's a workday. He can't be sleeping in."

"He's out. Handling a few things," Sorbelli said. "Should be back any minute now."

From what she could see, Sorbelli never lifted his eyes from whatever kept his attention on the tablet. Jawnie sat back up and looked at her primary link to the outside world. The first thing that caught her attention was the increase in quarantined messages. *Atta boy, Chenzo. Never give up. You do you, boo.*

Jawnie looked at the folders for her business and personal email. She grew frustrated that someone else had read these prior to her. Each message, her only tie back to normalcy and a life she was desperate to return to. Her mouse hovered between the two. She couldn't decide where to start. *Would the business messages mean anything to me? Wouldn't Lynn and Rockfish have already reviewed and responded? Perfect. Yet another set of eyes reading my messages before me. The Marshals or Rockfish can't expect me to somehow work from here.*

Get used to it, kid, at least for the short term. Rockfish's voice filled her head. Suddenly, she wasn't so interested in catching up with what was happening on the other side of the wall and razor wire. The sound of tires on gravel gave Jawnie pause, and she locked the screen. *Plenty of time in the day to play catch-up and get depressed.*

"He's back," Sorbelli said. "Go give him a hand. He's got something you're probably interested in."

"Aye aye, Sir," Jawnie said with a mock salute. The words had left her mouth before she could stop them. *Okay, Rockfish, get out of my head.* She laughed to herself and stood up from the dining room table.

Jawnie stepped back into the kitchen and walked past Sorbelli. He hadn't moved, his eyes still glued to the tablet. Must be some kind of trick to get me to carry in the groceries. *Jokes on him. I'm a guest here, not hired help.* She walked to the rear of the kitchen and opened the door to the backyard. The SUV had parked facing the house. She could see the back hatch of the SUV was up and it looked as if Winters was fiddling with something inside.

Jawnie closed the door behind her and headed down the steps. She made her way around the side of the vehicle. Winters stood, a bike leaning against his waist as he reached up and pulled down the hatch.

"Wow, that's some fine piece of machinery you got there."

"Yeah, I know, a Dick's Sporting Goods special," Winters said. "It will not win any awards sitting pretty next to your Cannondale, but it will keep up. Or die trying."

"No, I'm thrilled I don't have to pedal down the road with two tons of steel inches from my rear wheel. But I have to ask. I thought the federal government always overspent? What's another thousand dollars to the already ballooning deficit?"

"It's August. The fiscal year is drawing to a close and money is tight," Winters said. "I'm lucky I know someone in procurement who could approve even this piddling amount. You want to test her out?"

Jawnie couldn't say yes fast enough and ran back inside the house. She logged off the portal, changed, and grabbed a water bottle from the fridge. She noticed Sorbelli hadn't moved from the kitchen and his fascination with whatever was on the screen had not diminished. *To each their own.*

Winters was faster and waited for her in the driveway. She wheeled her bike out of the barn and off they went. The ride was straight and flat. Nothing exciting about it at all, but Jawnie couldn't be more at ease. *The breeze, the sun, I love all of it. So much better than being cooped up in that house where my imagination can run wild.*

Hey kid, it runs just as wild out here, but you're oblivious to it.

Go away Rockfish. This is the only place I can relax.

Jawnie pressed on, changing her speed. She combined sprints with casual rides and glided to the bottom of what little downhill areas they came across. All the while taking in every sight and smell the countryside offered. The fields were planted with waist-high soybeans, tomatoes and other green crops she couldn't identify. Others were barren, and by smell alone, Jawnie guessed they were used for livestock. The shift in wind told her a cattle or pig farm was around the next bend.

Her bike straddled the white line separating the road from a small dirt shoulder, and she casually glanced back. Winters was a couple of bike lengths behind, but after seeing him in shorts this morning, there was no doubt he could catch up and leave her in the dust if he wanted. He was physically the complete opposite of Sorbelli.

They continued down the road, cutting through the heart of the farmland. Jawnie turned her head and admired a brightly painted Amish hex sign overtop a barn's enormous front doors. She squeezed her brakes and slowed down to keep the sign in view for a few seconds longer.

"Beautiful, aren't they?" Winters shouted as he drew closer. "They're a form of Pennsylvania Dutch folk art. Two schools of thought. One being a talismanic nature to the signs; the other sees them as purely decorative. Funny thing is, the Amish don't use them, so if you see one—"

At that moment a pickup truck passed by both riders on the left, close enough to shake Jawnie's confidence, and her front wheel wobbled. She struggled to straighten out the handlebars and not end up going over them. The truck had given little margin for error. But Rockfish found his way into her mind, no matter how narrow.

Too close for comfort? Didn't that truck pass you in the opposite direction like five minutes ago?

Go away Rockfish.

Like I said, just as wild out here, but you don't notice it.

Most likely running an errand and on the way back home, or to a job site. Get off my case.

"Goddamn, that was close!" Winters said. "Maybe next time we can stick to some back roads. Or closer to where the Amish actually do their farming. It has to be easier to deal with horses and buggies."

Jawnie didn't answer. She kept her head down and contemplated turning around until she spotted a sign for a custard stand ahead. *One more mile, some nice soft serve, and then we'll head back.* She pointed at the sign and Winters nodded. *I deserve some custard for all I've been through.*

"This cone is on Uncle Sam," he said, returning from the window, a black and white swirl in each hand.

Jawnie mouthed a thank you.

Dippy's Custard Stand was a white painted wooden building off the road. It sat between a small parking lot and a strip of grass lined with three picnic tables. The building resembled a large detached garage, more than a small road-side custard stand. Two open windows, with large sills, faced the road from opposite ends of the structure.

Winters had come from the first window. The small menu for custard orders hung to the left of the sill. Jawnie could make it out from where she sat. Vanilla, chocolate, or swirl. Chocolate jimmies were the only topping. *No rainbow?* The second window had a different sign, hung on its right side, but it was too far and the print too small to make out. Curiosity got the better of her. Jawnie held up a finger to Winters.

"Be right back. I want to check out what the other window is for." Jawnie passed a mother and young daughter, who had ordered before Winters, and had sat at the far end of the picnic tables. The daughter leaned in, whispered, and pointed as Jawnie walked by. *Your mother should teach you some better manners. Mind your business.*

The sign next to the window simply said, rounds $2.50. Jawnie leaned over and looked around the building's corner and understood. Behind the custard stand was a nine-hole mini-golf course that had seen better days.

Pilar. Kara. Her mind turned to her friends for the first time since her arrival and the trouble they were most likely in. *Is Rockfish taking their case seriously? Has he already gotten Mace Face in a headlock and forced the piece of shit to spill the beans on Fulsome's plan? Just a few more things for your little old mind to worry about.* She shook her head as if half of her problems would fly out one ear and make life that much easier. A loud sigh escaped her lips before she turned back around and concentrated on her cone. She skirted around the mother and daughter this time and didn't look over as she passed.

"Okay, Winters, here is the point in our adventure that you tell me I'm imagining or overreacting to things," Jawnie said. The child was pointing again, this time less obvious, but aggravating to Jawnie the same. "I think that mother and daughter at the other table recognized me. They've done nothing but whisper and point since you went up to get our order. And not to sound totally paranoid, but that truck that almost hit us had passed by a few minutes earlier going in the opposite direction." Jawnie hoped Winters could see how much both incidents had affected her. She could hear herself speaking faster than normal, and the sweat in the small of her back wasn't from the ride.

"Totally expected from someone in your situation, only a few days in," Winters said. He bit into the side of his cone and swallowed before continuing. "Dark colored pickup trucks are quite common out here. As much so as a horse and buggy. Just how it is. Nothing nefarious in it passing a little too close. And as for those two, you're out in the sticks. Closed community. It's only natural that a child would be curious about an African American."

"I'm the first black woman that kid's ever run across?" Jawnie closed her eyes and shook her head.

"I'd bet my paycheck. It's not because you're The Jawnie McGee from Television. Especially after only one season."

Wow, the arrogance with this one is real. I'm definitely not parading around this place or the damn farmhouse like Paris Hilton. My shit does, in fact, stink.

"We've been using this location for years with no issues, and there isn't one now. This is my third assignment here. Trust me, I know what I'm talking about. The sooner you do, the sooner the days will start flying by and you'll be back home. Now excuse me, I need to use the can before we head back. Please do nothing stupid like leave without me."

Jawnie stared hard enough to almost see through Winter's sunglasses as he stood up, adjusted his fanny pack and walked around the backside of the custard stand. She glared at the back corner of the building, long after Winters turned the corner. *How dare he treat me like I'm making all this shit up out of the blue? I'm not some clueless child or housewife he's dealt with before. How can he—*

The tug at her right sleeve caused Jawnie to jump, her right knee slamming up into the picnic table.

"Excuse me. Are you Jawnie McGee? Can I get your autograph?"

* * * * * * * * * *

Neither one spoke a word during the ride back to the farmhouse. Winters fell farther back than on the way out, but the distance was nothing where he couldn't close the gap with a few hard pedals. Jawnie appreciated the extra space, as her mind paid less attention to the white painted line and more to the conversation she had with Sherry Shall, New Chilltown's biggest *The Pine Barrens Stratagem* fan.

It had taken Jawnie a minute to shake her own thoughts, fears, to turn and listen to what the little girl had said. Her eyes darted back and forth, from the girl's enormous eyes to the corner where Winters would emerge at any moment.

"What makes you think that?" Jawnie had said. The question was the only one she could come up with. By this time, the girl's mother had walked up and immediately apologized for her daughter's interruption.

"Oh, she's alright. I'm not her. Believe it or not, this isn't the first time it's happened."

"My name is Sherry Shall," the girl said over her shoulder, and her mother led her by the arm to their car in the parking lot. "I'm a huge fan."

All Jawnie could do was wave. She was afraid to say anything more that might put her in danger. Not to mention Winters would be back from the can any second. She couldn't be more right.

"What the hell was that all about?" Winters said and sat back down. "Did they approach you?"

"Winters, you were dead on. Little girl had never seen a black woman before. She walked over when her mother looked the other way. Asked if I lived around here. Barely got that sentence out before the mother came over and apologized as you were shaking or zipping up."

Jawnie shook her head and pedaled faster. It had surprised her that Winters had let it drop so quickly and after such a lame cover story. *It's like living with mom and dad as a teenager. I'll be stealing the SUV and coming back home as the sun rises, at this rate. Should I stick to pedaling and not stopping for a cone, rest stop or anything? If Sherry could spot me out of nowhere on my first real interactions with locals, how long before her school newspaper came knocking for an exclusive? I know Winters was trying to be calming, but I actually have things to worry about here.*

Back at the farmhouse, Jawnie put her bike away in the barn and went straight to her room. She feared Winters interrogating her with a sudden barrage of questions regarding her first dealings with citizens of New Chilltown and then retelling it all to Sorbelli.

Jawnie wasn't stupid. Hiding wouldn't wipe Winter's memory; it would only postpone the inevitable. Plus, she wasn't sure how she was reacting to being recognized and didn't want to crack under pressure and admit to Winters what happened. *If I tell him what happened, they'll pack me up and ship me somewhere off the coast of Nova Scotia in a matter of days. There, they'd lock me in a small room and feed me through a slit in the door.*

Happy to have someone recognize me. Who wouldn't be? Especially by a young girl who probably looked up to me. Somewhat. Maybe. Either way, it beats having it be a creepy old man. I've had enough Sugar Daddy offers to last a lifetime. Reading fan mail wasn't always an uplifting experience. *Had Sherry sent something? Had I read it and replied?* At the moment, Jawnie wished she'd had a few more minutes with the young girl and had been more open and honest. She tried to push the fear of being recognized to the back of her mind and replaced it, for a change, with thoughts of Angel.

He was the one. Swore to her she'd be a role model to young girls of all ages and socioeconomic backgrounds. "You're going to be someone these girls look up to," Angel had said. "Down the road, they'll come up to you and thank you. You're the reason they ended up at the police academy, an FBI agent, or choose a career in STEM. You might not have been the big push, but you were definitely the inspiration. The kick starter, so-to-speak."

It had been less than a week since Angel stepped in front of a bullet that was meant for her. And despite all that filled her head each day, there was always the nagging feeling that she let him down by being whisked away to the so-called safety of New Chilltown. *I don't even know how he's doing. Alive? Dead? They would have told me if the shot was fatal. Would they? Was he still on the east coast, or had he flown west without seeing her or allowing her to speak to him?* Jawnie stayed upstairs in bed and let loose with a good cry. The one that had been building for a couple of days now.

There was a knock and some muffled words from behind the door, but she ignored both.

Later, after a short post-cry nap, Jawnie was at the terminal typing a message to Lynn. She spotted Winters in the living room and pretended not to notice as he stood up and approached. After a minute, she sensed him towering over her, but didn't look until she was ready to click send along with a silent prayer. *I hope she understands this and doesn't think I've totally lost my marbles here. Stop thinking about yourself. Imagine what she's been through? Did she break? Will she ever get this? Is she in one piece and doing better than me?*

"I'll look at that message in a minute and get it to the next stage of review, for you."

Jawnie finally looked up and acknowledged Winters. "Okay," she said and stood up. She held the chair out for him, with plans of watching him and holding him to his word. "Might as well do it now, before there's a line."

"Hey, speaking of chairs, earlier I dragged those Adirondacks and the small fire pit out of the barn," Winters said. "Here's a lighter. The fire's ready to go. I'll be out in a jiffy. Figured you could use a little venting time. Want me to bring you out a beer?"

"Is that allowed? Aren't you technically on duty until the trial?" *I can imagine him, three sheets to the wind, shooting at anything that moved in the night.*

"Technically, yes. But a couple days a week, the local PD sends a couple of men over to give us a break. It's usually young cops, thinking about a future career as a Marshal," Winters said. He fidgeted, shifting his weight from one heel to the other and back again. "You know the mutual back scratching thing. They'll be patrolling the area until 8am. Trust me, it's a standard operating procedure. Our management doesn't want men burning out, running full tilt all day every day."

Not a word of that made Jawnie feel safer. She had to assume they knew what they were doing.

"Okay, then. I'll grab a coozie so it's not warm in ten minutes. I could use some mindless relaxation." Jawnie took the torch lighter from Winters and guessed the stench of a cigar would join them. "Sorbelli coming out?"

"Nope, he's got a ballgame he's more interested in."

Jawnie wanted to mention the tablet isn't tethered to anything. It is portable, after all. But it was better not to ruffle feathers when the man was sitting in the kitchen, within earshot.

Jawnie watched as Winters sat down at the dining room table. She then slipped out the back door. He had put the chairs and small fire pit between the barn and the house, where the straight driveway curled around the back of the house. She walked over and lit the kindling before plopping down in a chair. The only other outside light came from the small bulb by the back door. Her body slid forward, but she was too comfortable to care. The fire wasn't too much for the sultry August night and her eyes watched the flames dance. They were hypnotic. Calming.

How have I not thought about doing this earlier? I need to go and really explore what's in that barn that could make time here feel like this. Thoughts of the barn turned to her bike, which led her down the road to the custard stand and Sherry. *Was this post-sunset fire a way for Winters to finally question me about what happened? Does he not believe a word I told him? Had he actually heard what Sherry said as he walked out of the bathroom? The man's a U.S. Marshal. I bet he read me like a book.* Jawnie could have come up with a few more questions to dwell on, but the backdoor slammed shut and she looked up.

"Nice job on the fire, oh, and I approved the message," Winters said. He handed Jawnie a beer from the small cooler he carried. He placed it on the ground between the two chairs and took a long drink from his. "Not sure what you were trying to get across to this Lynn person, but I don't think it's threatening national security or your safety."

Either he thinks I tried to sneak a secret message to Lynn, which I did, or I'm totally off my rocker. I guess that's a win?

"You mentioned Davenport, like half a dozen times. I don't think it would hurt to let you know we got an update this afternoon. His father got the all-clear and they're flying him back home. Cedars-Sinai, Hollywood's hospital to the stars. The docs say he's got a long road back, a ton of physical therapy, but he's expected to make a full recovery. He might need a cane to get around, but all things considered."

"Good to know," Jawnie said. She made a mental note to plan a trip immediately following the retrial. The PTO was hers and Rockfish had no say in when she used it. *It shouldn't matter that I've been away for three or four months by that point.*

Each stared into their respective beers after that exchange, and it was only when he reached for a new one that Winters went where she expected.

"So that kid, today. Just excited to see a person of color? That was it?"

"Totally. Trust me, it did not thrill me being considered an exhibit. Or her mom's half-assed apology. You should have been there to hear that beaut." Jawnie paused, half expecting him to say he was, but Winters didn't reply. It was dark. The fire didn't provide that much light, but Jawnie still wished she had a pair of sunglasses. Anything to hide behind at the moment. Time to change the subject and drive the boat for a while.

"I'm guessing your supervisor had you read a complete dossier on me before dragging me out of my condo. But I don't know a damn thing about either of you, other than your names." Jawnie tossed her empty on the ground next to the cooler and pulled another out. "You know, something like that goes a long way to making me feel a little more comfortable in this shitty circumstance." She cracked open the beer and took a healthy swig. "Let me ask you, what's the deal with Sorbelli? He's always got his nose buried in that tablet. Is that where you keep your marching orders? He doesn't look like the type that likes to read." *Or even knows how.*

Winters let out a slight laugh and picked up his beer before replying. Jawnie wondered how much they could share and how much farther the alcohol would push that conversational boundary as the night progressed.

"Homesick, maybe? I'm not really sure. He's out here from our Vegas office. Not sure if it was by choice or not." Winters tossed his empty on the pile and stood up. He walked over to the small pile of wood to his left, grabbed a few hefty pieces, and placed them on the fire.

"Yeah, I didn't think he was here for the apple butter. How about you? Raise your hand or volun-told?" Jawnie fired off both questions before Winter's ass had touched back down in the chair.

"Volunteered. I believe in the mission, but it's also one of many bureaucratic hoops I need to jump through to qualify for promotion."

The conversation continued to scratch the social surfaces and professional boundaries as the beers flowed and Winters added more logs to the flames.

Jawnie asked about Winters' wife and kids. How do they deal with the separation? What's his new gig after this? Promoted or goes back to his home office. Where is that? Was that home, or did he grow up elsewhere?

Winters countered with the perils of dealing with new-found fame and Jawnie soon realized the man had done his homework. He peppered her with what he considered possible liberties taken with the storyline in The Pine Barrens Stratagem episodes, from a law enforcement perspective. Jawnie swore that the story he watched was one hundred percent how it happened. Winters shook his head, and they agreed to disagree on that point. He asked how it was working with an older, more grizzled partner. He was still learning.

"You know, with Sorbelli working this gig with me, we're more alike in that situation," Winters said with a laugh. "Here's to our bonding moment." He leaned over and tapped the side of her beer with his.

They shared a good chuckle over their one commonality. Jawnie's was deep and hearty. Enough so, her bladder knocked on the front door. She needed to go. If not, a small Dutch boy would need to plug the leak.

"Hold that thought. I need to head inside. No walking around the corner of the barn for me," Jawnie said. She stood up and headed for the back door.

She climbed the steps, opened the door, and stepped inside. She turned to close the door quietly, in case Sorbelli was asleep, but heard his voice coming from the direction of the living room. *At least he had changed chairs.*

"... listen, I'll have it for you. No, I don't want to hear your proposition... The Yankees should have covered."

Rockfish whispered in her ear before she even stepped into the bathroom and put the seat down.

* * * * * * * * * *

Rockfish drove back to the office on Wednesday afternoon after a contentious meeting with Jawnie's friends, still his clients, Pilar and Kara. What started out as a normal catch the client up on the status of the investigation quickly turned adversarial. The women were quick to question Rockfish's game plan, especially without Jawnie present to ease their concerns. Their main point of contention was the fact that Rockfish was working solo and seemed to them no closer to any resolution, even in the smallest matter.

If I had a dollar for every time I rolled my eyes behind these sunglasses, I wouldn't need the aggravation of this damn case. Not like I'm doing it for the money.

He left the meeting, still not sure if they understood what he had laid out. One, he was close to identifying the Fulsome employee behind all the vandalism, slander, and attempted arson. Two, how the police should be brought in to see some real consequences, as the real estate management group would be under the law enforcement microscope instead of being watched by a local PI with his handheld magnifying glass and his rogue temp employee.

Rockfish shut Lana's door and walked towards the office when his phone buzzed in his front pocket. He pulled it out and looked at the screen. *Raffi.* He contemplated sending it straight to voicemail, but that would only result in him blowing up his office number.

"Hey Raffi, go. I'm walking into the office. If I lose you, call me back at my desk."

Raffi was out of breath, but Rockfish could follow his friend's story.

"Hey that's great news," Rockfish said. "If I only had it two hours ago, I could have saved myself a ton of grief, not to mention slander about my work ethic and historical case closure rate."

He reached for the door, admiring the work done in a very short time frame to replace the glass. The same glass that the ER doc had pulled out of his arm. He smiled at Lynn, the phone still pressed to his ear. *What is she doing here?* Despite his smile, Rockfish was pissed. He had ordered Lynn to stay home, with pay, until further notice. *Christ, the last thing I need is for her to fall apart on me after all she's been through. Angel's shooting is icing on her PTSD cake.*

"Yeah, so we're on for tomorrow night. I hope your guy knows what he's talking about this time... uh huh... uh huh... I'll touch base tomorrow to make sure we're all good on the stakeout... uh huh... uh huh... not a problem... yup wrap this guy up and the case, too."

Rockfish hung up, dropped the phone back in his front pocket, and turned to address the elephant in the room.

"All quiet today, boss, for a change," Lynn said. "Except, Angel's publicist reached out. The flight back to LA leaves tomorrow. I asked him to let us know as soon as he's settled at Cedars-Sinai and can accept video calls."

The grin on her face reminded him of the joker. It was big enough to make him question what type of meds she was on. *Okay, dipshit, we're going with kid gloves here. I can't have her cry and run out the door. You can do this.*

"Lynn, I'm surprised to see you in today. Are you sure you should be here? I've felt like I'd be a shitty boss if I didn't reiterate that you don't have to come in. We've all got a shit ton to process. If it's better for you somewhere else, then by all means."

"It's okay, Steve. I'm part of the team and we're down a member right now. I really feel I should be here to support you."

Rockfish looked down at Lynn's hands. They rested in her lap, unmoving. Despite his intuition, she seemed calm, cool, and collected. *That's a load off my mind.*

"You don't have to be brave for me. I've seen you in action. Everyone can use some time to step back and recharge those batteries. Goddamn, I hate that phrase, but you know what I mean?"

"I got a message from Jawnie last night."

"You got what?" Rockfish shook his head and for a second thought he was hearing things.

"An email. From Jawnie. It's kinda cryptic, and I wasn't sure what she wrote at first. But just hearing from her, a little voice in my head said I needed to be here. Suck it up."

"Really?" Rockfish said. He stepped closer to her desk.

"Yeah. Cryptic is a good way to describe it. I read it last night, but I didn't crack it, so-to-speak, until this morning."

"You're a code breaker now?" Rockfish said. "I thought you wanted out of the field work?" They both smiled, and he felt another step better about her.

"Still do. Might at some point again. But I did this sitting at my desk with coffee and a piece of lemon cake. I think she's somewhere close to Lancaster, Pennsylvania."

"Pennsylvania Dutch country. Great."

"Don't seem so thrilled."

"I'm not. One, the bad guys could trick anyone of us with that knowledge into giving it up and putting her in danger. Two, it's not like we can jump in a car this weekend and drive up to say hi."

"But she wanted us to know. The clues were all there. I had to research a few of the words across old cases she mentioned. I mean, Google helped some." Lynn shrugged her shoulders.

"Okay, she wanted us to know. Mission accomplished. I guess we could hang a banner. What I'm trying to tell you is as smart as she is, she doesn't always know what she's doing. You know the town. I know the general area. There are people out there that would kill for that information, do you understand? We are now liabilities."

Rockfish stopped and looked at Lynn. Her head was down, the smile long gone. He had slipped off the kid gloves without noticing. *The last thing I want here is a shame spiral. She needs to think in situations like this. I can't berate her and expect her to learn from it. Ratchet it down, idiot.*

Rockfish stepped behind Lynn and laid his good arm across her shoulder. He didn't say a word until she turned her head and looked up.

"I'm sorry, I went about that all wrong. I can blame half a dozen things, but I fucked up. You should be thrilled. You figured out the message she was trying to get across. That is great work. I mean it." He squeezed her shoulder for emphasis. "But you know, in this industry, there are always half-a-dozen buts. Keep what you think you've figured out to yourself. Better yet, forget you got that message and delete it. The last thing you want to do is cause the Marshals to move her again." *Good choice. Better than saying the reason the bad guys found her and Jawnie suffered. Or worse.*

Lynn bit her lip and nodded. Rockfish hoped she understood and wasn't placating him. He turned and walked back to his office, where he found a small package on the desk. The container was half the size of a shoebox, and when he picked it up for further inspection; he saw the return address label. He knew he hadn't ordered it.

"Lynn," Rockfish shouted. "Who ordered something from Apple?" *Was this some new goddamn gadget I'm going to have to learn how to use?*

A second later, she was in his doorway. "Yeah, more Apple Airtags. Jawnie ordered them a while ago. She read a news article on how high-end car thieves use them to track the expensive cars they want to steal. She's been putting them on all the equipment valued over five hundred dollars for tracking. You know, in case they're stolen or lost in the line of work. This way, we give the cops a leg up on getting the particular thing back to us. Or us, if we need to track an asset down ourselves. "

"That's what I love about her and what she brings to this office. Okay, here ya go," Rockfish said, and he handed the box back to Lynn. "Go tag some shit or put the box on a shelf. It really doesn't matter to me which."

"Sorry about that. I thought you'd want to see stuff like this as it comes in. You know, since she's not here."

"Good call, but I'm gonna audible. I don't need to see everything. You're the office manager, so manage."

"You got it, Steve," Lynn said. She turned with the box and walked out of his office.

I did not know about these apple tag things. How much other shit goes on behind the scenes here that I'm clueless about? Not enough. Not goddamn enough. Rockfish grinned. He pulled out the bottom right desk drawer that he used as a footrest and leaned back in his chair. It took a minute for his left arm, sling and all, to find a comfortable resting spot on his chest before he closed his eyes. Rockfish contemplated calling it a day when the phone in his front pocket came to life. After Raffi's call earlier, he had forgotten to put the ringer back on. His right hand reached across his body for it, but he thought better of it and let the call go to voice mail. Whoever it was would leave a message or call back. He needed a little me time. At least until Lynn came and woke him up before she left for the day.

"Steve," Lynn called out from the front. A second later, his desk phone rang, the intercom light flashing.

He sat back up and picked up the receiver. "Yeah, Lynn?"

"I've got a Gordon Reeseworth on the phone. He said he tried your phone earlier, but it went to voicemail. He said it's very important and his voice sounds the part."

"Transfer him back."

A second later, the desk phone chirped again.

"Gordon, I was about to call you. Good timing."

Gordon wasted no time with greetings or any kind of small talk. The men had a history, going back as far as high school, much like he and Raffi.

"Your back deck. 8pm and I'll come in the back way. Get your ass home and wait."

Click

Rockfish held the receiver against his ear long after Gordon hung up. He shook his head and then placed it down.

The back way is the inlet. Why wouldn't he park in the driveway? Because someone's watching it, dumbass. What other reason could there be? To him, Gordon's urgency and abruptness meant only one thing. Provolone ain't done. She's coming for me. Probably thinks I know where Jawnie is. Fuck! Now I kinda do. Goddamnit, Lynn. Think. What now?

He picked up the phone again and dialed his friend and Baltimore PD Captain Dan Decker. Local law enforcement swore to be there if Rockfish felt sketchy or saw something out of the ordinary after they shot Angel. *You promised. You better be there.*

Decker picked up on the second ring, and Rockfish filled him in. The best Decker could do on such short notice was to have a uniform patrol to drive by the house a handful of times on second and third shift. He'd work on stationing a permanent detail outside the house first thing in the morning.

Rockfish hung up the call, feeling better about the situation. *Time to fill Lynn in on my plan.* He walked from his office to her desk and glanced at the front door. For a second, he pictured a circle with cross-hairs inlaid on the door's fresh glass. *Gotta keep a tighter grip on that imagination, buddy. Don't want the doc to give you one of those big fake medicated Lynn smiles.*

Lynn's head was buried in her monitor. She didn't glance up until Rockfish stood in front of her.

"Can I bug you for a second?"

"Sure. I'm entering those new tags into the inventory spreadsheet alongside the others," Lynn said. "In doing so, I came across something exciting."

Rockfish raised his eyebrows.

"In order to check out the first batch we ordered, Jawnie put one underneath the seat of her bike. You know, as a test case. I know what you said a few minutes ago, but with this information I could—"

"If you know what I said, then you'll drop it. Don't pull it up, don't see where the fuck it is."

Lynn's head dropped and Rockfish lost eye contact. *Fuck me. Back to good cop.*

"I really, really appreciate the work you've done here since the incident with Angel. But grab a laptop. You're working from my house for the next couple of days. Transfer the phones."

"Um, what?" Lynn's eyebrows arched across her forehead.

Rockfish expected the confusion and continued. "I've heard some stuff. Better to be safe. I'll drive you to the condo. Pick up a few things."

"What is all this about? Jawnie? The shooter is still around?"

"Trust me, you'll be safer there," Rockfish said, ignoring her questions. There would be plenty of time back at the house to explain. They needed to get moving. "I spoke to Decker. A uniform car will keep an eye out for us there."

He looked at Lynn to make sure she understood. She replied with a blank stare.

"Hey, anyone home?" He said, waving his palm in front of her face.

"Come with me if you want to live," Lynn muttered.

"What?"

"Nothing, only a line I heard you used once."

"Start shutting this place down. I'll be back in a sec."

Rockfish walked back into his office and pulled his handgun from the desk drawer.

* * * * * * * * * *

As the clock ticked closer to 8pm, Rockfish had gotten Lynn settled in and calmed down an anxious Mack over the situation. He had waited until he had seen the cruiser Decker had promised make its second run past the house before he grabbed the bottle of Jameson, two glasses, ice and walked out onto the back deck. He poured himself a drink and tried telling himself he was being hospitable. After all, he was entertaining here shortly, but Rockfish really knew it was for his nerves. *The older I get, the worse they get.*

Rockfish left his drink on the table and walked to the back of the deck overlooking the inlet. He placed his gun on the railing and stared out over the water. He waited on some sort of signal, something out of the ordinary, to show Gordon's arrival. *Are two lanterns in the old church tower too much to ask for?*

Rockfish had seen little of Gordon since the night they rescued Jawnie and Ned Hasty from a couple of Provolone's goons and one dirty cop a little over two years ago. *Silly of me to think this would have all gone away after the trial. History is repeating itself. Not in a good way. They would not have shot Angel had I not taken on Gordon as a client originally. It was a long string of dominos. Gordon's visit to ask for help to locate his wife, before the mob did, who she stole a quarter- quarter-million from, was the first to fall. What, almost two years ago? Damn. Pre-pandemic.*

Rockfish watched as a small skiff entered the inlet. He reached for his gun, in case it wasn't Gordon and ended up being whoever Gordon was coming to warn him about. The sling prevented his left hand from extending far enough to grab it. *I ain't gonna be able to hit the broad side of a barn doing this right-handed, but it might scare whoever away.*

The skiff came directly toward the house and then took a hard right. It docked at the neighbor's pier. A shadow made its way along the waterline and then across into Rockfish's backyard. He took a few steps backwards and raised his gun as the figure approached the deck's back steps.

"Whoa, Steve, you can put that away. It's me, Gordon."

Rockfish took a step closer but didn't lower his gun. The man pulled down his hood and Rockfish quickly recognized Gordon. "Could you dress in any darker clothes? And what's with the hoodie? It's fucking August, for Christ's sake."

"Trying not to have anyone see or recognize me." Gordon pulled off the sweatshirt. He followed Rockfish back to the small table and chairs. He draped his sweatshirt over the back of one and sat down.

In the deck's soft light, Rockfish didn't like how his friend looked. Gordon seemed to have aged twenty years in the last two. His baggy clothes sagged. *I guess working off a never-ending debt to the mob isn't the afternoon at the spa he pretends it to be.*

Rockfish sat down and placed the gun down on the table next to the bottle of Jameson.

"You know, Steve, it kills me that a television star bought a house on the water but still hasn't put in a dock yet."

"Mack's still trying to figure out what boat we should get. Once he makes a damn decision, then the dock issue will fix itself. Make yourself a drink. I have a feeling your story is going to be a bumpy one."

Rockfish watched as his old friend poured his neat, took a gulp and put his glass down. *He's trying to figure out the best way to say whatever drove him to come out tonight.*

"Well, I'll start this one off. You're here to tell me Annetta's dipshits are back to finish the job they fucked up in the first place," Rockfish said and gave his left arm a wiggle.

"As you probably guessed, I'm still tied pretty close to Marini. Working off my dead wife's debts will be the death of me yet. Steve, being close to Angelo, I hear things." Gordon reached for his glass again. "Most of the shit they say in front of me makes little sense or rings any bells. But this morning the old man took a call from Provolone's consigliere. I thought it strange as the families ain't as close as they once were."

"Today, Gordon."

"That broad up north is sending a couple of goons down to *talk* to you. You know the drill, rough you up enough that you'll spill what they want. I'm guessing you know what that is?"

"Yeah." *Damn you, Lynn.*

"He made a point to Angelo that it won't go further than that. Doesn't want to bring any heat down on him or his men, should something more nefarious happen to you."

"How nice of her to be so concerned about Marini's current love/hate relationship with law enforcement and concern for bad press."

"She claimed speaking to you was one of a few options she was trying out. No idea what the others are. But these idiots are probably here already. Waiting for the right moment to approach. Be careful. More than you usually are."

"They want to know where my partner is. Where the Marshals have her stashed. Maybe your guy can play telephone again and let Provolone know I do not know. Tell these meatheads to work smarter, not harder. Jesus Christ, why would they tell me where she's stashed when I'd be the number one target of those wanting to know?" *Well, buckeroo, at least it's only a beat down they expect you to walk away from. Unless it gets out of control. Never can tell with these bozos. Remember that meathead Sommers?*

"The boss don't take too kindly to indentured servants making suggestions," Gordon said and shrugged his shoulders. "I don't know what else I can do, other than what I am now. I mean, if someone spotted me here, I'd end up like my wife." Gordon ran his hand through his hair while simultaneously taking a shot.

Nice party trick. But I can tell the guy is concerned and worried. Maybe he forgot our past and how I handled myself in that situation? Time to reassure him and me with some positive affirmations.

"Gordon, it's been great to see you. What's it been? Two years? And I appreciate the heads up, I really do, but don't worry about me. I can take care of myself. You might recall the fun we had with you riding shotgun the last time we dealt with Provolone. I hope you've learned to shoot better."

"Shhh. My current employer doesn't have a clue about that. Christ, if anyone's in the bushes, I'm fucked."

"Lighten up, Francis, ain't no one in the bushes," Rockfish said and shook his head. "I do this for a living, remember? Listen. I got a business to run. I can't shut down my paying clients because of the fear of taking a few blows to the gut or the side of the head. Hell, one set of those clients ties directly back to my partner, I will not leave them in the lurch. I sincerely hope to have that fucker tied up in a nice bow by this time tomorrow night. Less than twenty-four hours."

"I'm only saying, watch your back," Gordon said. "You need someone riding shotgun again?"

"Thanks, but I got a guy. We should be good."

"Yeah, Raffi. That's why I asked. He's a well-known commodity. And not highly rated among my associates."

"I'm good. You'd be surprised about him. Not the same jerk from high school. Okay, maybe sometimes. But you gotta understand. Since the shooting, I've been more careful than ever. No one's been following me or staking out the office or house. I've kept a pretty good eye out."

"Her men probably got here this afternoon or could pull into town any minute. Give them a day and they'll be on you like white on rice. Odds say, at some point they'll send competent types to get the job done."

"I'll believe it when I see it. I need twenty-four hours," Rockfish said. He picked up the bottle of Jameson and shook it. "One for the road?"

* * * * * * * * * *

The sun had long set by the time Rockfish pulled Lana over to the side of the road. He and Raffi would walk the quarter mile to the mini-golf course to avoid anyone watching. Especially if the arsonist had beaten them there and was in the middle of doing his thing. Headlights pulling into the parking lot would only continue to prolong this case.

"Here, take this," Rockfish said, and handed Raffi a couple of zip ties. "We don't want this guy making a run for it after we call the police."

Raffi stuffed the ties in his back pocket and held out his phone. "Hold on. All I have to do is open this app and I'll be able to switch between the cameras set up around the place?"

"That's all. There are four now. They added one on the pole out front that covers the parking lot. I even tested the signal the other day inside the big windmill. AT&T has a good signal there."

"He won't pull up and park all nice and neat," Raffi said, ignoring half of what Rockfish said.

"Don't overestimate the dumb mind of a half-assed criminal for hire."

"And I don't care about your strength of signal test. I'm the one going to be stuffed inside that thing, for who knows how long.

There's gotta be a better place for me to hide and jump out of. Come on, Stevie."

Rockfish had expected the push back but thought his partner would have started the bitch-moaning when they were closer to the actual windmill, not a hundred yards down the street.

"Look, you're smaller than me and once inside, you'll be surprised how roomy it actually is. It's the best spot. I had my clients dump a gigantic pile of construction debris behind the building. He won't be able to pass it up. This way, we're on either side of him. I'll start off in the tree line at the end of the back lot, but when he approaches, I'll sneak around and wave my gun, so he thinks twice before running. When you see me walk into the lighted part of the lot, that's your cue to come out and be ready to take him down."

Raffi didn't reply. His smirk told Rockfish his new partner questioned every part of this plan.

Once Raffi was situated inside the windmill, halfway down number 8's fairway and had finally shut up, Rockfish moved into position. He positioned himself at the far corner of the back lot, where pallets of boards and bricks sat in front of a tree line. The small backhoe and cement mixer remained untouched from his and Jawnie's first visit and would provide perfect cover. He settled in for a long night; the tablet showing the cameras in his right hand.

Well done, girls. The four cameras covered most of the property, and with the lighting, the visuals were perfect.

A breeze had picked up from when they first arrived and the hairs on the back of his neck stood up.

"Not a move, Rockfish. Step out onto the asphalt."

Fuck, not a breeze, but some cold steel on the back of my neck. His eyes closed and his head dipped. *How the fuck did they find me? Gordon told you, but you thought you were smarter. Knock this one job out before concentrating on them. Smooth move.*

The gun moved from his neck and pushed into his back, propelling him forward.

Once out from behind the equipment and into the parking lot, Rockfish got a better look at his captors. Two men. One stood behind and the other in front. The man standing before him was dressed all in black, with a baseball cap and pistol pointed at Rockfish's chest. He took a leap and assumed the man behind looked the same.

"Drop the iPad." The direction came from behind him. He did as instructed. The tablet fell to the ground, the screen facing up, and the man behind him stepped aside and placed a boot heel through it.

"Search him."

The man in front separated Rockfish from his phone and gun and handed both to the man behind him.

"Okay, where's your partner?"

"I'm alone. I swear. Doing a little surveillance, hoping to catch an arsonist in the act."

"Bad luck. You'll be long gone by the time the firefly gets here. Junior, go find the other one. He's out there somewhere pissing in his pants." The man in front turned and disappeared around the demolished building's last standing corner.

Rockfish stood at attention. His mind raced on how he could get out of this jam and what would happen to Raffi if he came up empty. *A solid beating, that's what Gordon had said.*

"Don't you worry, we ain't gonna bust you up, too bad," said the man from behind.

It's like he's reading my mind.

He walked around Rockfish's left side and gave him a punch in the arm for good measure. Rockfish bit his lip from the pain but tried not to show how much it hurt.

"We've got a few questions the boss needs answered before we let you drive yourself to the hospital. But we ain't gonna do it here. Somewhere a little more secluded. Where we can take our time. Get out of you what we need. And maybe a pint or two of blood."

The man had stopped at Rockfish's left, and he expected another punch. Rockfish turned his head to get a better look. The man didn't have a hat on, but from the looks of the mook, there was no second guessing. The welcome wagon Gordon had warned him about had indeed arrived.

The men stared at each other, sizing the other up, but neither spoke. Seconds and then minutes passed.

"Hey!"

The sound from the direction of the mini-golf course was loud, and Rockfish knew instantly it wasn't Raffi's voice. *Fuck. They found him. So much for him riding in to save my ass for once.*

"Looks like your buddy came out of hiding. Good, I didn't want to spend all night looking for him."

"I don't know what you want," Rockfish said. "I'm a dumb PI."

"Oh, you know what we want. You're going to tell us where your partner is."

"Um, sounds like your buddy found him."

"That's the attitude we were told to expect. Stupid shit like that will also get you taken to pound-town unless you tell us her location."

"Yeah, I definitely don't want to go there."

"Wait. Nobody's fucking—"

The man dropped to the ground face first. His gun skittered across the asphalt and under a pallet of bricks.

Damn. Could have used that. Rockfish glanced from the pallet back to where the man had stood a minute ago. Raffi stood there grinning, a hefty-sized chunk of two-by-four in his right hand. Raffi reached behind him and pulled out the other goon's gun from the small of his back before shoving it back into his pants.

"Took you long enough," Rockfish said with a shit-eating grin. "Where's the other one?"

"He's taking a dirt nap between the windmill and the giant gorilla. I spotted them with you on the camera and circled around on him. Never heard me coming. Just like his partner."

Rockfish bent over and searched through the unconscious man's pockets. He took back his gun and phone. "Here, drop the Jim Duggan act and secure this guy's arms and legs," Rockfish said, tossing his zip ties onto the man's back. Raffi dropped the board to the ground and kneeled. A second later and the mobster wasn't going anywhere.

"Neither one looks like the pyros I've worked with, err, heard about in the past," Raffi said, still kneeling and looking back up at Rockfish.

"Yea, these are out-of-town muscle. I had some advanced warning, but they still caught me by surprise. They probably scared away our arsonist. A couple of Provolone mooks wanting to know where Jawnie is. We need to get the other one over here before he does the worm and is halfway down the street before either of us notices," Rockfish said. He looked around and saw what they needed next to the cement mixer. "Grab that wheelbarrow and bring him back here. I'd help, but I can't lift shit with this arm."

"Better than dragging his sorry ass, I guess." Raffi said. "Do you want me to slap them around, see if they'll answer questions now that the shoe is on the other foot?"

"Wheel him back here. I'm going to get the cops rolling here."

Raffi headed back towards the mini-golf course, pushing the wheelbarrow while Rockfish took a few steps back from the goon on the ground and made the call. When Rockfish hung up, he turned around. Raffi had parked the wheelbarrow next to the unconscious man on the ground.

While they stood around waiting for the police, Rockfish noticed Raffi reach for his phone and gaze at the screen.

"Sudden urge to swipe right at a time like this?"

Raffi didn't reply and instead held up his phone. Rockfish saw the surveillance cam app was open and two men approached the short driveway that led to the parking lot. One was carrying something that could very well pass as a gas can. Not even trying to hide it.

"We should have had all these guys take a number," Raffi finally said. "At least my guy was right on with the information."

"Scoot that wheelbarrow behind the supplies. I'll start dragging the other one. Gimme a hand when you're done because I've only got one that works."

The two men crouched and waited in the darkness. Rockfish was happy to have the upper hand this time. He tapped Raffi on the shoulder and pointed for him to circle around and come up behind where the two men were likely to come to a stop. Raffi nodded, pulled his gun, and took off. Rockfish gave Raffi a minute to get into place before stepping out from behind the front loader. He knew the enormous pile of debris would be too tempting.

"Put that down. The police are already on the way."

Rockfish aimed his gun at the man with the gas can. It slipped from his fingers and landed on the asphalt. Liquid splashed the insides, and Rockfish knew he had his man. He glanced at the other and waved his gun.

"Stand closer to your buddy. And don't even think about it."

The man stepped closer to his partner and partially into the light.

Mace Face!

"You!" Rockfish shouted. "You son of a bitch! Don't move!"

Mace Face spun around and ran straight into Raffi. The gun flew out of Raffi's hand and both men fell. As they struggled on the ground, Rockfish stepped over to the discarded gun, never taking his barrel off the other man. He reached down with his bad hand and plucked it off the asphalt.

"Don't move. Tell your buddy, fun time is over."

"Cut the shit, asshole!" the man said. The words did nothing to stop Mace Face from struggling. Rockfish thought about firing a warning shot, but with the cops ready to arrive at any minute, he didn't feel like taking the chance of friendly fire. He watched as Mace Face and Raffi wrestled on the ground. Neither man had thrown a real punch at this point.

"Ahhh!" Raffi said as Mace Face broke free and scampered off into the night. Raffi remained on the ground, nursing what had been a clear nut shot.

"What are you doing, Raffi? Go! Get up and get that sumbitch," Rockfish said, totally forgetting about the guns he held.

"No need, boss," Raffi said, rolling onto his back. He held up the man's wallet. "I know where to find him. Or should I say, where to send the cops."

Sirens soon filled the night air and Rockfish could see the rolling lights off in the distance.

CHAPTER SIX

Annetta walked over to the plush couch against the large window. She drew the curtain as a precaution and sat down. The wall across from her was one long bookcase. Awards, framed newspaper articles and family pictures outnumbered actual law books ten to one. She'd have to turn to her left to see Oscar from where he'd sit behind his desk. His choice was a minor inconvenience she'd deal with. The couch was more comfortable than the two prissy French Louis XV-Style Armchairs that sat in front of the lawyer's desk.

She had not planned the late Friday afternoon meeting. The call jarred Annetta awake from a catnap and Rosenthal's secretary on the other end was equally surprising. It wasn't what the woman said, but how she had said it. She dropped a few keywords into the conversation, and whether the former exotic dancer knew what they meant or not was of no concern to Annetta. She informed the rotating set of babysitters outside, watching her house, she had simply forgotten a long-scheduled meeting with her lawyer. Yes, she knew they would have to follow her there and back. *Fucking minchioni. No idea how you're being played.*

When the office door finally opened, Annetta stood, expecting to greet an already late Rosenthal. Instead, his secretary walked in, a glass in hand. The woman teased her hair high. Her white dress, while form-fitting, was more conservative than Annetta would have expected.

"Large mint iced tea with extra ice. Exactly how you like it, Ms. Provolone."

She remembers. Maybe she ain't all tits and ass.

"I apologize, but Mr. Rosenthal is on his way up. Traffic on the way back from another meeting delayed him."

"Not your fault, my dear," Annetta said and took the glass.

Five minutes later, Rosenthal entered the office and filled the air with apologies. He was a small man with a receding hairline. What gray he had was combed straight back. Small wire glasses sat on the bridge of his nose. His apologies didn't fly with Annetta as the man stood before her in khaki shorts and a pink polo.

Did this meeting pull him off the back nine? It must be important then.

Rosenthal approached the couch and greeted Annetta with a kiss on her cheek. He took her hands in his before speaking.

"I'm so glad you could make it on such short notice. I felt the issue required the privacy this office provides."

Annetta watched with intent as he stepped back. In the past, if he were bringing good news, he'd drag one armchair over to the couch. If he were the bearer of bad news, Rosenthal would retreat to relative safety behind his desk. Annetta didn't have the arm strength or aim she once had, but shoes had taken flight in this office from time to time.

"Oscar, will Giovanni be joining us in some capacity?" She glanced over at the phone on the desk. "Surely, if we're talking business, my consigliere should be on the line." With their previous meetings, Giovanni Bianchi always sat on the party line.

"I spoke with him earlier. He and I agreed this meeting would be best served if I only updated you on some events that transpired last evening." Annetta watched as Rosenthal ran the back of his hand across his forehead.

"Jesus Fucking Christ," Annetta said.

And like clockwork, Rosenthal walked over and slid behind his desk.

"Understand, fewer cooks in the kitchen today, the better."

Annetta nodded. *Yeah, too much of Our Thing is never a good thing. Someone sprinkled extra yips in the goddamn gravy. Golfers, second basemen unable to find first and now her men. Shaky hands led to misses, time and time again.* She realized it more and more with each day as the head of this family and she reached over for her tea.

"To get it out there, the local police picked a couple of Sally B's men up last night down in Maryland. They were on site to get some answers, as you know."

"Wait. Sally B's men? He wasn't one of them?"

"No, he sent two down for the chat with Rockfish. He remained local."

Annetta bit down hard on her bottom lip, a tad shy of drawing blood. Without thinking, but knowing it would happen at some point, she launched the glass of iced tea towards the bookshelf next to the door. It fell short by a few feet. The carpet prevented the glass from shattering.

Rosenthal reached for his phone and pushed the intercom button. "Gloria, can you—"

"Clean it up later. You're on my fucking dime!"

Rosenthal slowly replaced the receiver. Annetta noticed he now sat at attention. She stared him down for a couple of seconds before continuing.

"Motherfucker. The balls on that guy to disobey my order and send underlings. Are these two morons still in jail?"

"It's going to be harder to get them out with this incident. Felons in possession of firearms are not getting released on their own recognizance. They'll be in the local lock-up for a while. But my team will resolve the issue and get them out."

"No. Don't lift a hand to help them. Now get that fakakta consigliere of mine on the line."

"Annetta, I don't think—"

"Now!" She instantly regretted throwing the glass. *Fuck, I'm all out of bullets. What's with these types I surround myself with? They all lose their hearing and balls when promoted?*

Rosenthal picked up the receiver and dialed. He shook his head, hung up, and pushed redial.

"He's not picking up. Probably a good thing for us. My guy at the courthouse does not know what devices they're up on since your release."

"So help me God, when you win this retrial, I'm going to make a shitload of changes."

"Before you rearrange the deck furniture on the Titanic—"

"What did you say?" Annetta pursed her lips. *Was Bruce Cutler still practicing? If not, what would it cost to dust him off?*

"Apology, a piss poor attempt to lighten the mood," Rosenthal said, and lowered his chin. "Bad jokes aside, it gets a little worse if you can believe it. When the cops picked up Sally B's men, they also picked up an associate of Angelo's in the same sweep."

"What? That fucking old man wouldn't lift a decrepit finger to help us, but had a guy keeping tabs?" Annetta dug her nails into the arm of the couch. She felt one puncture through the fabric.

"Not a made guy. A hanger-on. Jack of all trades, so-to-speak. From what Giovanni could find out, one of Angelo's guys made introductions to a paying client and this other guy to burn some shit to the ground. Rockfish was waiting for them when your guys chose the same time to approach."

"And Angelo's pissed. Right?" Annetta said.

"That, my dear, is an understatement. Word is he assumes the guy will roll over and implicate one of his crews to save their own ass. You know that would only lead the authorities upward, looking at additional parts of the Marini Family. What little love was left between the families is fading fast."

Christ, now I have to worry about hurt feelings. Annetta tilted her head down and rubbed the bridge of her nose, anticipating the pain before her sinuses did.

"Okay, I'll back burner that mess for a minute. What about the other avenue?"

"Your friends in Vegas might pay the best dividends," Rosenthal said and stood up. He walked around to the front of his desk and leaned on an armchair. "Seems they've got a U.S. Marshal over the barrel because of a shitty run at the ponies and baseball. Turns out, he's away on a temporary duty. Guarding a witness." Rosenthal raised his eyebrows with the last word.

"Get the fuck out of here," Annetta said, and stood up.

"Yeah, we lucked into this one."

"I'll take this over someone checking a computer for us and then two of my men fucking it up even further."

"Vegas says the guy is turning into a liability," Rosenthal said. "They're willing to do, you know, two birds, one stone type of deal."

It's a good deal, but do I want to involve yet a third family? Shit's stretching my span of control pretty goddamn thin. Think girl, think. Not to mention the heat a dead Federal agent would bring. Shit, as long as it keeps my ass out of jail, it's worth it in the long run. To me.

"You know, Oscar, if you think about it, we're as bad as the goddamn Feds. The Baltimore family is pissed at the one in New Jersey for overstepping. Vegas has a problem and thinks they can take care of it by also taking care of yours. Then you owe them. We're turning into a damn bureaucracy. Sometimes, too much of Our Thing is bad."

"For business?"

"For everything," Annetta said as she walked towards the door. "Tell Vegas they have a green light. As for Rockfish, get word to Giovanni to handle it. Personally. Do not delegate down." In her mind, the meeting was over. She stopped short of the door and kicked the empty glass the rest of the way across the room, where it shattered against the wall.

Cheap piece of shit. Like so much around me at the moment.

* * * * * * * * * *

"Well done, buddy. You stayed as quiet as a church mouse," Rockfish said. "What did you think of your first client meeting? Everything you thought it would be and more?" He turned to Raffi and smirked. The two men had met with Pilar, Kara, and their attorney as Saturday morning rolled into the early afternoon.

The private eye and his temporary partner walked down the steps and across the sidewalk in front of the large sign for Ross, Giacchino & Day - Attorneys at Law. The meeting had gone off with little fanfare. It did not thrill their audience that the case was now in the hands of the police. Based on their previous interactions, the lack of actual police work undertaken from the women's filed reports was of concern. Rockfish did the best he could to reassure them. When he covered the events from the previous night, he promised the police would handle the case differently this time.

Once Raffi had turned over the wallet to the responding police at the mini-golf course, it didn't matter that the man with the gas can had clammed up. The driver's license and credit cards in the wallet identified the man who fled as Brett Brick. The Fulsome Commercial Realty Group Recreation Association card also helped solidify the identification. With an address, the police sat on the residence until the wanted man thought it was safe to return in the early hours of Friday.

Once in custody, Brick couldn't wait for officers on scene to activate their body cameras before he spilled his guts. He implicated Fulsome's Project Manager for Avonlea Crossing, Luther Grayson, as the brains behind the plan to terrorize Pilar and Kara and ultimately force them to sell before a cop could even push Brick into the back of the patrol car.

By the time Brick went through central booking, the detective assigned to the case had called Rockfish and asked if he and Raffi could come down to the station to make a visual identification. The detective filled Rockfish in on Brick's rantings.

"The man continued to rant about his superiors at Fulsome being in bed with the Marini Crime Family and that there was proof. Tons of it," the Detective had said. "Kept repeating that she's got it all."

"Any idea who she is?" Rockfish said.

"Not a clue. Then he shut up. We'll sweat it out of him, don't worry. Maybe even call in the Feds to sit in on it."

The last part caught Kara, Pilar, and their lawyer's attention. Federal intervention gave them a glimmer of hope that all their problems would go away.

As the meeting had wrapped up, Rockfish warned the women that if the police weren't taking things as seriously as expected, or stop returning calls, they should immediately reach back out to him. But to keep in mind one thing:

"Property development companies like these are always in bed with the Mafia. Once the police investigate Brick's claims that a Marini Family capo put him in touch with the arsonist, it may seem to you that the case has slowed down. Add in the gas can guy clamming up. I bet it will be a while before the cops catch a break. These types of cases go on for a while before you see any justice served. Remember that. Think big picture if something else happens and you're not seeing immediate results."

Deep inside, Rockfish was happy to wash his hands of this case, but tried not to let it show until the meeting concluded. He could now give that much more attention to Provolone's next attempt to pick his brain. *Damn you Lynn for sticking that nugget in my head.* And he knew with two of Annetta's soldiers sitting in the county jail, it would only be a matter of time before she ramped up her quest to figure out where Jawnie was being held and bring in the big guns.

Back in the car, Rockfish let Raffi know he was going to swing by the bank before it closed. Pilar had handed him a check as they left. While Rockfish had agreed to work the matter gratis, Pilar felt the need to cover some of their day-to-day expenses. If there was one thing Rockfish understood, it was ego.

"... then back to the house to kill some time before a meeting with Gordon."

"Reeseworth? I hate that fucking guy. Have since high school. Mr. Big Shot knows it all. How come you didn't mention it before?"

"Yeah, him. And last time I checked, you're serving in an acting capacity. Not a full-fledged partner. I don't have the time or the patience to run all my shit by you. You coming along for the ride, or picking your spots?"

Raffi nodded. Rockfish knew his current running partner would be by his side.

They killed Saturday afternoon at Rockfish's house. Steve pulled a laptop out of Lana's trunk and set up his work from home office on the dining room table. He documented the meeting with Pilar, Kara, and their lawyer, officially closing the case. Raffi hung within eyesight, in the living room with Mack, watching Joe Kenda's latest adventure on The Murder Channel. Zippy lay at their feet, content.

As suppertime rolled around, Mack asked if he should set a plate for Lynn.

"I wouldn't, Dad, unless you want to take it upstairs to her," Rockfish said. "She won't come down here with Raffi roaming the first floor. Still a ton of bad blood there from her view."

Dinner ended up being takeout on the back deck. At one point, Mack wandered out and brought out homemade brownies for dessert, a bottle of Jameson and an extra glass for Gordon. He scooped up the Styrofoam empties and carried them back inside. Rockfish and Raffi waited somewhat patiently for Gordon's skiff to tie up at the neighbors. Raffi's right leg was bouncing a couple hundred miles an hour.

"Hey bud, let's give it a rest," Rockfish said, placing a hand on Raffi's knee. He wasn't sure why Raffi was so nervous, but he also didn't want to put his friend on the spot with Gordon due any minute.

Right on time, as the sun dropped below the horizon, the sound of an outboard motor filled the August night. Gordon didn't waste any time as he poured himself a drink and pulled up a chair.

"One of Marini's capos asked me to set up a meeting between you two. I don't know the guy that well and it was unexpected. Claims he wants to make you an offer, one that is mutually beneficial."

"What's his deal?" Rockfish's eyes shot over to Raffi, who shrugged his shoulders.

"I don't know," Gordon said. "I'm following orders here." He took another sip of his whiskey. Rockfish noticed the whitecaps in his friend's glass.

"Well, it can't be about that Fulsome idiot, Brick. I get that he's tied to the arsonist-for-hire, and that guy's a Marini associate. But I really don't care at this point. I don't have a case anymore. The cops have my statement. I'm done with it." Rockfish lifted his own glass and smiled at the calm seas.

"I don't know about you, Stevie, but the hair on the back of my neck is standing straight up," Raffi said. "Something ain't right here. My two cents."

Gordon let out a long sigh and stood up. He stood in front of Rockfish and pled his case.

"It's not a setup. Don't turn this into a movie of the week, Raffi. The man wants to run a business proposition past Stevie. No funny business. I'll be there and will guarantee safety. I'm basically one of them."

"Sit back down, Tessio," Rockfish said, throwing out the name of the turncoat who promised the same thing in *The Godfather. I mean, if we're talking movies of the week, he should have gotten that fucking point.*

Gordon did as told, but it didn't stop him from pressing for the meeting.

"We go way back. You and I. Them and me. I know these guys. I've worked alongside them most of my life."

"You said that last time. But you're not one of them. If we're spitting truths here, you're nothing more than an indentured servant working off a never-ending debt," Rockfish said. It was his turn to stand up. He walked over to the back of the deck and stared out over the inlet before continuing. "Because they let you eat at the kids' table, doesn't mean they're reserving the empty spot at the grownups' for you."

Gordon followed suit and leaned on the railing next to Rockfish. The men stood silent for a minute, the only sound being the ice violently crashing against the side of the Gordon's rocks glass. Rockfish tilted his head slightly. *Last time he drank neat. Why the sudden interest in rocks? Was it anything or am I looking for something that ain't there?*

"When I said I can guarantee your safety, I meant every word," Gordon said. "I would never put you in any kind of danger. It's a friendly, you scratch my back, I'll scratch yours type of conversation. Don't let Raffi convince you this is something it isn't. I have Marini's trust, his men's and that's what matters."

"Forgive either of us for being overly cautious. But there are two goons in the county lockup right now after a failed attempt to talk with me. And now another capo wants to chitchat."

"But those were from up North."

"North, South, East, West. I don't give a fuck. Too much gabagool, if you ask me. Fucking hate that shit. Tell me, Gordon, what's all this scratching really about? And why come to me?"

"It's got something to do with your case—"

"Again, I deposited the client's check a few hours ago. I don't have a case."

"They don't know that. Sometimes, I listen closer than I should. The Capo and some bigwig over at Fulsome have a long-standing thing."

"Big surprise," Rockfish said. He wanted to drop his head into his hands and give his temples a good rub, but that would mean putting his glass down. *That ain't happening.* Rockfish took a gulp before continuing. "What realty management companies don't have mob ties? You need builders to build and who controls the unions? Not to mention most every other aspect of construction."

"That's all I got. I'm assuming it ties back to something you were working. I think he's going to make an offer to get Provolone off your back. That's what you want, isn't it?"

"I do, more than you know. But not at the price he's going to dictate. I lost a partner to all this wop-shit. That means I'm handling half the caseload I should. They shot my producer." Rockfish leaned in and exhaled. "I can't afford any more damage." Even Rockfish could hear the anger as that last sentence trailed off.

"Hey, I'm not one to call in a marker, but I will if needed. You called me and I showed up. Rode shotgun to rescue your partner. Didn't hesitate one iota. Trust me on this one, Steve. I got you. I got this."

Steve let out his own long sigh and stared out over the water. *I owe him. Fuck me. If all this is, is a sit-down, what do I have to lose listening? If it's a setup, it isn't like Annetta's soldiers will ever stop coming. It's going to happen sometime. I'd rather lead from the front than the rear.*

"Gordon, I'm in. After this meeting, we're even. Hell, you might even owe me a little. When and where?"

"I'll be in touch, Steve. They won't plan shit until you agreed."

Gordon left his glass on the railing, and the two men embraced. Gordon then bounded down the steps and across the yard to where his ride waited.

Raffi got up out of his chair and walked over to the steps where Rockfish stood.

"Hey, I didn't want to ruin the love connection you two were having over there. Not to mention, I could hear perfectly from my seat. Stevie, I kept my mouth shut, but I don't trust that guy as far as I could throw him, and he's put on a ton of weight since Mr. Oberg's gym class. I'm tagging along. I'll be the one guaranteeing your safety. Make sure everything stays kosher." Raffi slammed his own glass down on the railing, but Rockfish wasn't buying it.

"Dude, I can't put you in danger if this all goes to shit. It's my deal. I got it."

"Stevie, consider it my last test before you add my name to the sign over the front door."

Rockfish rolled his eyes. "I'll tell you what. Stay out of sight, but follow me. Watch for any signs of fuckery. Call Decker if you feel so inclined. Make sure I don't go the way of one James Riddle Hoffa."

* * * * * * * * *

The rooster crowed. Jawnie's eyes snapped to attention. She rubbed the gunk from out of the corners and rolled over to check the time. *Shit. No phone. No clock. You think you'd learn by now.*

Day eight at the safe house and she had yet to lay eyes on the damn bird. Was it some sort of U.S. Government illusion to make it appear the farm was fully functional? *I'll have to check the barn eves for some sort of speaker. Or I'm still in the Matrix. One or the other. Get your head screwed on right, girl.*

Virtual reality or feathers and comb, the persistent crowing had pulled her out of yet another nightmare. Bad dreams, puss-faced Sorbelli, and the rooster were some of the reoccurring wonders of the farm.

This morning's cinematic masterpiece had Winters and Sorbelli chasing Jawnie through the woods. The setting seemed awfully familiar and could have passed for the Pine Barrens. In that case, she would have been the infamous Russian, but that was another lifetime ago. If the man behind the curtain really wanted her to be scared shitless, the setting should have been a cornfield.

The back door slammed. Jawnie sat up and leaned over to see out the open window. Winters walked over to the SUV and opened the rear hatch. He lingered there for a second before closing it. Then he got in the driver's side and pulled away.

Ah Shit. That means another morning of trying to avoid Sorbelli. The man's creepiness was off the radar. Not to mention, in the five days since overhearing his phone call, Jawnie was pretty sure they each looked at one another differently. For sure, she did. On the tails of listening to Sorbelli's call with his bookie, there was another instance that caused Rockfish to shout *DANGER* from the back of her mind.

Two days earlier, lunch had not turned out the way she planned, and she was sure both men heard her cursing fit. No smoke alarms were injured during this home economics class, but the meal was destined for the trash can. Winters had picked up a handful of no-name frozen vegan meals on his last trip out to civilization. Not one she had tried so far was worthy of a second bite. *He tried, and that's what counts. Except these things tasted exactly how everyone else perceives vegan food.*

Jawnie had held the foul-smelling dinner at arm's length as she walked across the kitchen. One klutzy stumble later, the trash can was on its side, trash spilling out, but somehow the microwave meal landed in one piece atop of the previous day's garbage. She sat there for a second, head in her hands, cursing to herself. She waited for one of her keepers to rush in, making sure she was okay, but help never came. Jawnie lifted her head and wiped away a tear with the back of her hand. *This won't clean itself up.*

She noticed a crumpled-up piece of paper had ended up under one of the kitchen chairs. She paused, scooping up the empty food containers and coffee grounds, and leaned forward to retrieve it. Three handwritten digits caught her eye. *856. South Jersey's area code.* The paper fell from her hand. Her heart jumped into her throat where no amount of hard swallows could dislodge it.

When she gathered the courage to pick it up, she flattened the paper out and saw it had a second phone number written below the first in the same shaky old man's handwriting. *702. Has to be*

Sorbelli. Vegas? Her throat pulsed harder. *It's probably his home or office number. Didn't Winters say Sorbelli was from their Vegas office? The 856 number is probably for the US Attorney's Office. Of course, they need to stay in touch regarding the trial. Lighten up, Jawnie, not everyone's out to get you.* But she could only eighty-seven percent sell herself on the suggestion.

Now, thinking back on that day, she wondered. *Should I have brought it up to Winters? Maybe he'd listen?* They'd gotten closer since the bonfire.

Oh, really now?

Shut up Rockfish. You know better. Bike rides, binging some television shows. I'll have you know I served as the unofficial DVD commentary with each episode of The Pine Barrens Stratagem. Can you believe he's never seen it? But it didn't stop him from talking shit on it earlier.

With the mention of the show, Jawnie's thoughts turned from her trash-fueled anxiety to her early morning revisit to the Pine Barrens. Both Marshals chased her. Or was one chasing her and the other chasing his partner? *He'll probably blow it off. Chalk it up to my overacting imagination. Again.*

Then it's up to you, kid. Figure it out.

Jawnie said goodbye to her imaginary partner and got dressed. She headed downstairs, no less conflicted than when she went to bed. She hoped some oatmeal would help settle her stomach and that feeling would spread throughout the rest of her.

Sorbelli was waiting for her in the kitchen.

"Hey your biking partner is going to be AWOL until later in the afternoon. Care to give it a shot with me?"

His request surprised Jawnie and her agreement left her lips before she could actually comprehend the situation.

"Good, I've got a pleasant ride plotted out, more scenic than you've done with Winters. There are some impressive sights to see out here, if you know where to find them. What do you say, round ten?"

Jawnie finished eating and was ready by 8:45am. The ride would do her good. Clear her mind, at least until they turned back into the gravel driveway.

She harped on Sorbelli. They needed to leave early, before the scorching August sun rose too high. *If he says 10am, he'll finally be ready by 11am and out of water or breath by 11:45am.*

"Ah, I need to make a call," Sorbelli said, glancing down at his watch.

"I can go without you," Jawnie said. "Figure out my route. You know there's no car here and you couldn't keep up if you pedaled your heart out."

"Okay, fine. I guess we can go now."

Shit, he probably agreed to shut me up.

****

As Jawnie expected, Sorbelli, an older, out of shape man, lagged from the start. She continuously had to slow down for him. A few minutes later, he would then drift further back. Rinse and repeat. And without a clue as to the route, Jawnie was reliant on his shouts from behind on the direction as they approached each intersection.

"Next left... Hawthorne... can we stop?... Bottom of the hill... coming up..."

Jawnie waited to see if anything came after the last gasp for air, but Sorbelli was silent.

Probably waiting for an answer. Jawnie raised her left arm and gave a thumbs up.

Hawthorne Lane was beautiful. The scenery was everything she wanted on a stretch of road. Open space gave way to fields filled with chrysanthemums of all colors, which led to trees that grew denser with each tire rotation. Fresh air filled her lungs. The air was the same as she breathed back at the farmhouse, but the flowers gave it a little something extra. The ride was the relaxing, de-stressing thing she needed that day.

Sorbelli. Who would have thought? How come Winters never took me this way? I can only picture what this ride is like in the fall with the change of colors. Well, you won't have to imagine for long, you'll still be here in October. She hated when the voice was right. *So much for the distressing part.*

Jawnie squeezed her hand brakes as she approached the bottom of the large ravine. She came to a stop on the thin dirt shoulder and hopped off her bike. *Hopefully, he won't need more than a minute or two to catch his wind and start walking his bike up the other side. There's no way he's peddling up that hill, especially from a full stop.*

Sorbelli coasted to a stop directly behind Jawnie's bike and his heavy breathing filled the otherwise quiet morning forest air. He struggled to get off his bike before putting down the kickstand. He mumbled something under his breath and turned to look out and over the right side of the ravine.

Too goddamn early? Is he really complaining about how I pushed him out the door before he wanted to leave? We get out from under these trees, and he'll be damn happy the ride is on the downslope. That pasty white skin won't take kindly to the midday sun.

"You going to be okay, Agent Sorbelli?" Jawnie said, and she walked over to where Sorbelli stood.

"Yeah... I need a minute," Sorbelli said. "Lesson learned. Next time I'll look at the elevations before I plan."

He took up a seat on the dirt incline where the shoulder met the edge of the ravine and rested his forearms on his knees.

Well, this looks like it will not be a short pit stop. Let's see if I can get him up and moving again. It worked this morning.

After a couple of minutes, Jawnie walked over and stood next to where Sorbelli hadn't moved from. She offered her arm to help get the party back on track.

"Here, you need a hand getting back on your feet?"

"I gotta pee," Sorbelli said, ignoring her offer. He ran a forearm across his sweaty forehead before rocking side to side and eventually getting up under his own power.

"Alright then. When you get done, we can get back on the road," Jawnie said. "I don't know how much longer you planned for us to be out, but the sun is high in the sky."

She watched as Sorbelli lifted his wrist to his eyes again and then turned. His neck strained to look back at her.

Was that a sneer? What's his problem?

He stepped towards the edge of the ravine and steadied himself before inching down the steep incline at what appeared to Jawnie like a large maple tree. The large base was twenty feet down and would give him the privacy they both needed. He reached out, grabbing small branches from other trees to keep his balance with each step.

Jawnie had second thoughts about standing on the side of the road while the man peed. It didn't matter how far down the gigantic tree was; she decided she wanted, no needed, to be out of earshot of the stream as it soaked the dry leaves on the forest floor.

"I'm going to get to the top of the hill. My legs are tightening back up. I'll wait for you there. Don't you try to pedal. Walk your bike up. I'll be waiting."

"Don't you... go anywhere."

He didn't lean out from behind the tree to speak, but his voice was loud. Booming. Authoritarian. Jawnie heard the leaves crackle and assumed he was starting his ascent.

"Stay away... from the bike... McGee."

Jawnie walked over to the edge for a better view. Sorbelli was using the same branches to pull, to will himself back up to the road.

"You... we're not going anywhere. We've got time."

"Relax, I won't make you lose your job. I'll do a little back and forth here to stay loose," Jawnie said.

"I can't... let you... do that," Sorbelli said. His hand slid around his belly and reached for his waist.

Jawnie's eyes grew wide and multiple WTF scenarios postured for the entrance lane to her mind. *His constant glances at his watch. Are we waiting for company? The company?*

As her mind raced, Jawnie's eyes followed Sorbelli's hand. It moved from a branch to the roll of belly fat that had tried to free itself from the t-shirt on either the climb up or down. His eyes were as wide in surprise as Jawnie's and both their heads swiveled from the exposed belly, up to Sorbelli's bike, where the fanny pack was jury-rigged to the handlebars.

Jawnie stepped over to his bike and Sorbelli tried to increase his speed, his arms flailing at any branch within reach to propel himself forward. His feet continued to slip on the dead foliage that littered the forest's floor. It wasn't a contest. If Jawnie wanted the fanny pack, it was hers.

Jawnie stood in front of the handlebars and unsnapped the plastic latch.

"Don't... you fucking cunt."

"But I did."

"They're... coming... for... you!"

Jawnie froze in place. She felt her legs shake and then give out. In desperation, she reached out for Sorbelli's bike to stop from collapsing on the ground. Up to this moment, she knew something was way wrong. But she hadn't put together any of the clues. Or had she and didn't want to face the outcome? Now, with the last hint, it was apparent. Provolone. Someone had gotten to him. *That was why he didn't want to leave earlier than planned. Kept looking at his watch. This is a meeting place, not a freaking rest stop.*

At that point, her mind reestablishing the connection with her eyes, Jawnie realized Sorbelli had moved closer. *Too goddamn close for comfort.* His face was dark red. Sweat soaked hair was plastered against his forehead and steam poured from all visible orifices. *Fuck, stop daydreaming!*

Before Jawnie could comprehend exactly how close, Sorbelli leaned forward and reached out. His footing gave way, and he dropped to his knees to prevent sliding back down the ravine.

Do you want to live the rest of your life like this? Jumping at shadows? No... Trust yourself and the progress you've worked so hard for. You won't let yourself down. Jawnie swung the only weapon she had. The fanny pack shot out like a lasso from her right hand and Sorbelli twisted to his left in desperation. He reached for it with both hands, eyes wide in anticipation.

With his arms and eyes occupied, Jawnie twisted, lifted her right leg and connected the bottom of her sneaker with the side of his shoulder. Sorbelli teetered and in that second his face changed. Gone was the red blustery anger and instead, it took on the surprised look of Hans Gruber falling from Nakatomi Plaza. He tipped over backwards and rolled ass over elbows down the ravine. Sorbelli shouted or screamed. Jawnie couldn't really tell which, but the noise stopped as abruptly as it began.

Jawnie didn't wait around to see how far or hard he fell, but on the inside, she patted herself on the back until it hurt. She grabbed his bike and wheeled it to the other side of the road, and gave it a solid push. She then twirled the fanny pack again and let it fly.

Fuck, what if there was a phone inside? She contemplated going down after it. *At least for the gun.*

How would you unlock the cellphone, Einstein?

Thanks, Rockfish. Always sunshine and full of help.

You're welcome, and you need to get moving.

Jawnie ran over to her bike and glanced back over to the spot where Sorbelli fell. Disturbed dirt and leaves were all she saw. Her left foot pushed down hard on the pedal, and she was back on the asphalt.

She headed up the hill, still following Sorbelli's directions for the day's ride. Her muscles screamed out at the steep incline, but fear kept them pumping until she could reach the top. There, she paused. Part morbid curiosity about whether someone was hot on her tracks and part needing her own rest.

The trees thinned out at the top and unused farmland blanketed the two-lane road on both sides. With her feet on the ground, Jawnie turned and looked back down. She half expected to see a car stopped at the bottom with a couple of goons helping Sorbelli back to his feet. Nothing. No Sorbelli, or anyone else.

Turn around and head back to the house? Winters would be there to help. What if he was the person Sorbelli was waiting on? You can't trust either of them, plus if you turn around, what if he's waiting down there? A stick in the spokes as you pass and over the handlebars you'd go. My kingdom for a car to drive by. What if it's who Sorbelli was waiting for? You threw the gun away, dumbass. Keep riding, you'll figure it out. Put some serious miles between you and the ravine.

Pedal she did with head down and eyes glued to the white line separating the road from the now nonexistent shoulder. Her mind raced. *What to do? Where to go? Who to trust? The local police? Surely if Provolone could get to a U.S. Marshal, she would already have the locals deep in her pocket.*

A glance in her peripheral vision caused Jawnie to lock up her hand brakes and come to a skidding stop. Hawthorne dead ended. Valley View Road ran north and south. Or was it east and west? She didn't know, and was even less sure about which way to turn.

Where the fuck am I? Remember when schools paid me to delete porn off middle school Chromebooks? Tears mixed with frustration and fear. A car approached from the left with its blinker on. *Turning on to Hawthorne? Do I wave them down or keep my head down and turn away?*

You can only trust yourself. Rockfish was back.

Tell me something I don't know. That's a huge issue. I'm a fucking wreck. But WWRD? The voice didn't reply.

The car passed without incident, and Jawnie lifted her head. With no phone or GPS, she flipped an imaginary coin and went left.

A gas station, maybe? Could I buy a map? Do they even sell those anymore? I need to get out of sight. I can't ride till my legs fall off, hoping that some amazing idea will come to me.

A few miles down the road, Jawnie spotted an old, abandoned farmhouse coming up on her right. It reminded her of her temporary home the past week, but this one had seen better days. Dilapidated would be a compliment for this structure. *The perfect hideout, or the first place they would come look for me?*

The giggling and shouting of young schoolgirls filled her head as she stared at the approaching house. At first, Jawnie thought the sounds were trauma based. She didn't know why, but thought it was the only answer. *If you can't explain something, blame the hallucinations on the shit you went through this past week.* When the noise continued, it drew her attention from the house to the large oak tree halfway between it and the road.

"Jawnie?!"

The sound of her name shouted aloud, laser-focused her attention.

Sherry? The ice cream girl? Couldn't be? Could it?

Jawnie took a chance her guess was right. She steered the bike over the shoulder and back across the front yard to the large tree where the girls' bikes lay. *What's one more to the pile? Maybe behind the tree?*

Sherry ran up as Jawnie stepped off the bike with rubbery legs. Sherry wore high pig tails and a too large t-shirt, but Jawnie knew it was the same girl from the other day. Jawnie walked the bike behind the large tree before laying it down in the grass.

"Are you okay? You look like my mom when she cries about my dad. Wanna check out our tree house? We've got soda and cheesy poofs up there."

Jawnie couldn't speak but she could think, despite all of it being way too much to process at the moment. She simply nodded and followed Sherry up the slats of wood nailed to the tree. Her arms and legs ached with each rung, but she needed to get out of sight before a vehicle slowed its approach and took in the scene. It would only be a matter of time.

The inside of the clubhouse was small. Someone had dotted the walls with pictures of teen hunks, ripped from the modern-day version of Tiger Beat Magazine. Small backpacks sat piled the far corner. Jawnie moved from her knees and collapsed into her new hidey hole.

Dreams of the cavalry, any cavalry to come save the day, soon flooded her unconsciousness.

CHAPTER SEVEN

Six hours later and ninety-four miles from where Jawnie remained safely passed out, hidden eight feet above the ground, Rockfish paced the office floor as his dinner performed a mini-gymnastic show in his stomach. Gordon was late, which meant the meeting wouldn't start on time. Rockfish had a feeling their hosts would not appreciate the tardiness.

Another ten minutes passed before a car horn sounded and Rockfish looked up from counting the floor tiles. He walked out of the office and locked the door behind him. Gordon's Chrysler 300 was double parked.

"Nothing to worry about, right Gordon?" Rockfish said. He slid into the passenger seat and shut the door.

"I got you. We're all good, buddy. Where's Raffi? I figured he would have tried to tag along."

"I dunno. Not my day to watch him." Rockfish said.

Gordon laughed, and Rockfish allowed himself to relax a little in the seat. Gordon sped up and pulled out of the parking lot. Rockfish smirked to himself. He didn't lie. He couldn't pinpoint exactly where Raffi was at the moment. Now if he had to take a guess, the man should be a few car lengths back, following at a safe distance. *My ace in the hole. Well, more like a ten of clubs.*

Gordon stopped at a traffic light, and Rockfish leaned a little to his right. He tried to spot Raffi out of the side mirror. It would make him feel better if he could lay eyes on the man and not continue to hope his backup was in place.

"You doing okay, pal?" Gordon said.

"Yeah, I'm not very comfortable in the passenger seat. I'm a behind the wheel and in control kinda guy."

"Relax. If you go into this thing all fired up, neither one of us is going to get out of it what we want." Gordon said and turned his eyes back to the windshield.

What WE want? Other than guaranteeing my safety, what is Gordon attempting to get out of this? So much for this doing the right thing for an old friend. Rockfish knew to listen more closely to each word that came out of Gordon's mouth from this point forward. *Does he have an alternative outcome in mind? Fuck, what am I walking into?*

Rockfish craned his neck for the rest of the trip. He tried to catch a glimpse of Raffi, but never did.

Soon after, Gordon pulled off the main drag and zig-zagged through the middle of an industrial area that had seen better days. Trash littered the roadway. A homeless person who thought better of setting up camp in the area had abandoned a shopping cart on the sidewalk. Gordon signaled, turned off the street and pulled alongside a row of pumps of an abandoned Mobil station.

Rockfish gave the building the once over. *Is this where we're meeting? Or is it where I'm pushed into another car?* His previous crack to Raffi about Jimmy Hoffa flashed across his memory. The front door, roll-up bay doors, and the windows were covered in plywood. Taggers had covered every inch of the building with graffiti.

Rockfish saw an arm stick out from the right side of the building and wave them around. *This must be the place.* Gordon shifted back into drive and pulled around the side of the building. Two men stood there waiting. One held up his hand as the car rolled to a stop.

Rockfish gave each man the once over as he reached for the door handle. Nothing would scream gangster to a directionally challenged tourist, but to Rockfish the signs, albeit hidden, were there. Both men were of average height and had matching sunglasses. One had them set high on his head and the second had them hanging from the collar of his shirt. The telltale sign was the outer garments. Each wore lightweight, zip-up jackets that stood out to the disconcerting eye, considering it was early evening in August. *Obviously concealing today's weapon or persuasion option of choice.* Rockfish had left his own piece back at the office, as he knew the minute he walked into the meeting, someone would ask him to bend over and cough.

They exited the car and Rockfish walked around the front, holding up his hands the entire time. He wanted no misinterpretation of any sudden movement. Each was patted down, and cell phones confiscated.

"Ouch, watch the arm."

"You hurt it jerking off, old man?"

"No. Supporting your mom in reverse cowgirl. She leaned too far back. That bitch put on the pandemic thirty. Maybe forty. At least," Rockfish said. He expected more pain, and the mobster didn't disappoint. The punch landed squarely on the stitches. Steve ground his teeth but knew the verbal shot was worth it.

Once both men were separated from their cell phones, the man with the sunglasses atop his head flipped them down and slid behind the wheel of Gordon's car. He drove the car around the back of the building and reemerged a minute later.

The other man opened the heavy metal door and ushered Rockfish and Gordon inside. Rockfish's eyes slowly adjusted to the lack of light. The door slammed shut and two overhead lights came on. One high above their heads lit the way forward. The second lit a small card table and three chairs in the open area of the garage where grease monkeys lifted and fixed cars.

One man, Rockfish could no longer tell them apart with what little light he had to work with, pointed at two chairs on the side of the table closest to them. They did as instructed, and Rockfish gave a stern look to Gordon. Alarms were going off in his head, but his friend shrugged his shoulders in return. Gordon walked over and sat to Rockfish's left. They sat in silence for a couple of minutes before one man walked back into the darkness and disappeared. The other stood at attention directly behind them, barring any type of rush for the door and run to freedom.

The second man reappeared, leading an older gentleman through the shop and to the vacant chair on the other side of the table. The goon then took up position a few feet behind the old man.

Rockfish immediately recognized Ignazio Conti, despite the shitty hanging sixty-watt bulb above. Their paths had never crossed, but the Marini Capo had a tendency to headline the evening news and morning paper with accusations of every criminal violation the locals or Feds could throw at him. His presence at this meeting told Rockfish a couple of things. The discussion about to happen was more important to the other side than he could have imagined. Second, he exhaled and felt better about walking out in one piece. Gordon's promise rung truer. This wasn't some trigger-happy crew trying to make a name for themselves. This was an old school sit-down.

Conti dressed immaculately, despite the summer heat and sweltering cinderblock they found themselves in. He proudly wore the Paulie Walnut wings and had appeared to have left his suit coat wherever he had come from. Rockfish imagined the old man had to be sweating through his vest and white dress shirt.

"Mr. Rockfish, Gordon tells me you are a reasonable man. One who listens and understands the cost of doing business," Conti said. "I'd like for that to be true. For us to work through the matters at hand, in an efficient time frame."

"It is hotter than balls in here," Rockfish said and leaned back in his chair, the front legs lifting slightly off the cement floor. "I don't know what you want or if I can even deliver, but I'm here because Gordon asked that I hear you out. Here I am."

"Yes, he also said you had a way with words. And I won't mince mine." Conti's lips curled into a sly smile.

Rockfish nodded and slowly raised his hand to his forehead. He wiped the sweat from his forehead. It would be a losing battle in this building.

"I understand, Mr. Rockfish, that your little dance with Annetta Provolone won't be at the amateur level anymore. She's sending down a seasoned professional to be your new partner. It's no longer only the location of your partner they're after."

Rockfish squinted and tilted his head ever so slightly. He wanted Conti to see the confusion on his face.

"Her two men, the ones currently sitting in county lock-up. Someone's gotta pay for that." Conti shrugged and tilted his head slightly to the side.

"For their stupidity?" Rockfish said. "I did not know their affiliation when I called the cops."

"No one's calling anyone—"

"Shut up, Gordon," Conti said. "You played your part by getting Mr. Rockfish here. Obligation fulfilled. Now sit there and shut up. I don't have Angelo's patience." He turned and spit on the concrete floor with the last word. "Now I've been around the block and then some in this game. While I play with them, I don't make the rules. But here's where I can help bend them to help you, Mr. Rockfish."

"And then I owe you what? Neither one of us deals with the other out of the goodness of our hearts."

"In due time, Mr. Rockfish," Conti said. He pulled a handkerchief from his pocket and dabbed his forehead. "I'm sure Gordon has told you that these two families aren't exactly on the best of terms right now. But like families do, when someone is in need, we're here for the other."

"Your family? My family? Gordon's? Governor Hogan's? Look, you need me to do something for you. Can we get to the point before my insides poach in this heat?"

"Gordon, let me know you are a brass tacks type of dick. So, before I get down to them, let's hydrate. I apologize for the location, but it was a last-minute decision." Conti snapped his fingers and the man that stood behind him walked into the darkness. He emerged a minute later with three water bottles.

The three seated men turned their attention to the bottles and Rockfish drained half of his before putting it down on the table. He gave his forehead another swipe, this time with his upper arm, hoping the fabric of his shirt would absorb the sweat.

"Okay, now that I can talk a little easier," Conti said. "Here's where the scratches comes in. They're coming for you. I can keep them at bay. Perhaps make them think you zigged when you actually zagged. Don't ask, just know I can."

"That would be helpful from my standpoint," Rockfish said. "But I fear you will ask for more than I could deliver today, tomorrow, or next year."

Conti stopped and padded his head and neck with what was now a fully soaked handkerchief. The man reached down and took a sip from his bottle. He pursed his lips and gave Rockfish a slight nod.

"All I ask is you do whatever it takes to get those two dykes to sell that piece of shit property. There are a lot of powerful people that have money tied up in the Avonlea project. It needs to move forward."

Rockfish tried his best to look surprised. He figured it was coming, but didn't want Conti to know. He pretended to compose himself before answering and glanced at Gordon, then to Conti and back down to the water bottle on the table.

"I can't do that."

"Listen, Ignazio, perhaps there is something I can do. I've got Angelo's ear. The boss listens to me. Like I said, Stevie—"

The gunshot echoed off the walls and Rockfish fell in slow motion backwards off his chair and onto the concrete. All he could hear was the ringing in his ears. His cheek landed in some godawful mixture of oil and grease. His left arm landed beneath the weight of his body. Rockfish let loose a whimper. There was no holding this one back. But those superficial wounds and grime were all he felt.

The goon behind Conti still held his gun, and Rockfish followed the barrel down at an angle to where Gordon lay. The force had flipped his chair backwards and while Rockfish couldn't see his friend's face, there was no mistaking the liquid pooling quickly beneath his head. It puddled, then flowed towards the trench where a tech once stood to change oil. Memories flooded Rockfish's mind. They kept him glued to the floor and his body didn't listen to any commands his brain gave. He only watched the mental picture show as it moved from Gordon to his wife, Ginny, that Rockfish was hired to locate, the car chase, with Gordon riding shotgun to save Jawnie from the crooked cop, to the warning from the other day. *I'm not walking out of this place under my own power. Raffi, if ever there was a time...*

"Gordon served his purpose in getting you here. He thought he was a friend of ours. He thought about a lot of things. Fuck him. He didn't have the boss's ear. And if he did, I'd have to question Angelo's judgment. Too many have come to me and told me of his tattling to Angelo. People like Gordon really should know their role. I hope you understand exactly how important it is we come to an agreement today. Yo, Christopher, help get Mr. Rockfish back on his feet so that we may wrap this meeting up on good terms."

Conti's tone and words didn't affect Rockfish, and he remained on the floor, not moving a muscle. A large part of him was failing to comprehend exactly what happened. Christopher stepped over Gordon and hooked his arms under Rockfish's and lifted. Despite Rockfish's best attempt to remain limp, the goon easily placed him in the now upright chair.

"Finish your water, Mr. Rockfish."

Rockfish shook his head. He looked over at Gordon's lifeless body. He focused his ears, wanting to hear even the slightest moan, but the only sound rattling around in his ear canal was the echo of the gunshot. *If you ain't walking out, it's defiance time. Going out on my terms. Fuck this guy and his like.*

"Your choice. Let's move on from this nastiness and get back to the subject at hand," Conti said. "I'm going to need you to force those women to come to the table and sign."

Rockfish paused. This would only be his one chance to walk out of here.

"They are my partner's associates. I don't believe I have any influence over them. What are you going to do, shoot me, too? How's that going to solve anything?"

"No changing your mind? Not a second to rethink this horrible position you're taking up? Tick Tock." Conti drummed the fingers of his right hand on the table.

"No."

"Then it won't be pretty for them. They will wish they'd had accepted any of the previous offers from Grayson. Now I'm the one across the table making offers. It ain't gonna be pretty. And you won't be around here to read the story or watch the news. It may be months before they're found. If they don't do the right thing."

Rockfish braced himself for what was coming. He closed his eyes and gripped the seat of the chair with both hands. The blood pulsed through his veins, and he took a deep breath.

"Relax, Mr. Rockfish. I'm not giving you the Gordon treatment. My men would have two bodies to dispose of. Truth be told, we're stretched thin at the moment, more so without your cooperation. You're being out-sourced. I gotta tell you, Annetta knows her shit. Not worthy of the wrap the boss is laying on her."

Rockfish opened his left eye and squinted across the table.

"Call Bianchi. This schifoso is all his. The transfer will happen as arranged." Conti stood up and grabbed his water. He turned and walked into the darkness.

* * * * * * * * *

Raffi had followed Gordon's car to the industrial area and finally to the boarded-up gas station. He was proud of himself. Hoped Stevie would be too. He doubted Gordon noticed the tail. He parked in the parking lot of a flooring wholesaler, which was across the street and elevated. The location gave him the perfect view down to the side door where Rockfish and Gordon had entered through. *Another step closer to partner.*

An hour after Rockfish walked into the building, Raffi pushed in the clutch and started the car again to get the air conditioning flowing. The windows were down, and he was eating through gas, but Stevie could reimburse him at some point. Or once he joined the team, the petty cash drawer would be accessible. The sun had sunk below the horizon and the heat radiated through his windshield. *Shit, if I'm bitch moaning about the heat, I'm betting you could wring old Stevie out by the time he walks out of that cinderblock building.*

Raffi picked the binoculars off his lap and gave the target location the old once over. He could see as well with the diminishing daylight as he could when he first arrived. *These probably cost a pretty penny. Especially after the lecture, Stevie made me sit through before finally handing them over. Maybe these are standard issue to partners. After tonight, I might not have to hand them back in.*

He scoped out the exterior of the building. Moving left to right, Raffi gazed across the front and stopped at the narrow driveway on the right. Based on the same thin lane on the left, the path around the gas station was u-shaped.

Same as the last time. Nothing to see here. What the fuck are they still doing inside? He should have brought me along. I could have moved this shit along, brokered some type of agreement, and we'd already be back on Stevie's deck. The man needs to see what I can bring to the business table.

He moved the binoculars across the front of the building and came to a sudden stop. Movement to his right caught his attention, and Raffi swung the binoculars back. *Whoa.* He gripped the binoculars tighter, feeling the sweat forming on his hands. The side door had swung open. Raffi sat up at attention, never taking his eyes off the right side of the building. *Go Time!*

A goon from earlier emerged and walked around the corner to the back of the garage. Gordon's car circled out from behind the building and returned to the side door.

The door opened and Raffi helplessly watched as one man pushed Rockfish at gunpoint. They climbed into the backseat. The other man slid behind the steering wheel. *Where are they taking him and where is Gordon? I knew Stevie shouldn't have ever trusted him.* Raffi noticed a second figure emerged from the doorway. *Fucking Gordon. Pulled some shit on Stevie.* His hands brought the binoculars back up, and he instantly realized he was wrong. This man was older and dressed more for a night at the opera than a sit-down in an abandoned gas station. *Okay Gordon, where the fuck are you?*

The older man leaned over; his forearms firmly planted in the open window. The conversation was brief, and the man straightened up before walking behind the building. *To grab his own wheels, I bet.* A few seconds later, Raffi patted himself on the back as a small sports car emerged on the left side, headed towards the street.

Porsche 718 Cayman, if I know my shit and I do. The outfit wasn't for the occasion, it's part of the persona. Good to know. Raffi kept one eye on the Porsche and the other on Gordon's car, which continued to idle along the right side of the building. It wasn't until the old man worked his way through the gearbox and was long out of sight that the other car followed around the building. Raffi dropped the binoculars into his lap for easy access and shifted into reverse.

Raffi's mind turned back to the missing puzzle piece as he followed behind the car at a safe distance. With the binoculars, he felt he could let Gordon's car get further ahead and not worry about losing them. *It was Gordon's car, but where was he?* Still inside that gas station, if Raffi read the situation right. *That right there ain't a good sign for Stevie's friend. Something must have happened. I missed it. Was that not a truck backfiring? Maybe whatever went down happened when I had the air blowing full blast?*

Gordon's car had left the industrial area and made a beeline for I-95. It took the northbound ramp. Raffi followed suit. *Careful. These guys are a level above following old Gordo. Here's your actual test. Rely on technology and not your old eyes if you still want that promotion.*

Raffi read the signs above for the Fort McHenry Tunnel. *Fuck, I don't have an E-ZPass. WWRD? If they go that way, I'll follow suit. What's the worse they can do? Send me a bill in the mail? What if a cop is sitting there, drinking coffee?* Raffi knew if he rolled the dice and got pulled over, the game was over. He thrust his right hand into his pants pocket, grasping for any bills he could find. It would be the cash lane for him and a prayer that Our Lady of Blessed Acceleration would come when needed. Raffi silently crossed himself. He took one more look through the binoculars and cursed the setting sun. As the evening continued to roll through, the darkness would cancel out his slight advantage. The spyglasses were expensive, but not night-vision-expensive.

The car ahead slid into a cash only lane and Raffi let out a loud, long sigh. *Of course, you chucklehead. If they're the bad guys, why would they want a digital footprint by rolling through this E-ZPass lane, when the cops could look into it?*

Raffi paid his toll and hurried through his gears. He needed to make up a ton of valuable distance. All the while, his mind continued to race. *How far will this go? How far should I go? Do I need to cut them off before I'm in unfamiliar territory? Do I attempt a rescue or call for help?* The driver of Gordon's car put on the right turn signal and moved into the exit lane for the Dwight Schultz Rest Stop. The car's movement answered Raffi's question.

Raffi slowed and followed suit. The car turned into a parking space, past the actual rest stop facilities and away from other travelers. He slowed even further and crept into the spot immediately to the car's right. He glanced over to his left and made eye contact with all three passengers. Raffi thought he glimpsed confirmation on Rockfish's face and picked up his empty travel mug. He pretended to take a drink when he noticed the passenger side window of the car open. He looked over. The driver made a circular motion with his finger, and Raffi rolled down his window and prepared to play the traveling rube.

"Get lost. Plenty of places to park here. Gimme some space." The driver waved his piece at Raffi and did not wait for an answer. The window went back up.

WWRD? The answer came to Raffi in a flash. He didn't question the plan. He executed it.

Raffi reversed out of the parking spot and cut his wheel to the right. He shifted into first gear, popped the clutch, and the engine stalled. The car was perpendicular to Gordon's car, directly behind it. Raffi jumped out of his car and popped the trunk. He hoped to have caught the men in Gordon's car by surprise. By the sound of the driver cursing as his door swung open, he had.

"I told you to move that pile of shit!"

"Look man, she died. I'm trying here," Raffi said, noticing the flash of silver that now stuck out of the front of the man's pants. Raffi leaned forward over the engine and pretended to know what he was doing. He ignored the man's shouts and continued to fiddle until he sensed the man standing behind him. Raffi waited another five seconds.

"FUCK!"

The mule kick landed square in the family jewels and the man dropped to one knee. Raffi heard commotion coming from the car, but his man still had a piece. Raffi's next kick, a roundhouse, caught the man on the side of the head and he went down. The gun skittered across the parking lot and Raffi was on it. When he turned, Rockfish emerged from the far passenger side, brandishing a handgun of his own.

Rockfish jumped into Raffi's passenger seat as the hood slammed back down. Raffi threw open the driver's side door and fumbled around in the console before pulling out a folding knife. He made eye contact with Rockfish before stepping out and slashing both left tires of the other car. He then slid back behind the wheel and laid rubber. They were miles down I-95 South before either spoke.

"Holy shit, did you see that?" Raffi said.

"I did. I was there."

"That couldn't have gone off any better if I had tried."

"You did well, my friend. Enough of a disturbance to cause the knucklehead in the back seat to look over and I took it from there. A glass jaw is a liability you shouldn't have in that line of work," Rockfish said.

"Where's Gordon?"

"Back at the garage. Or maybe in the bay by now. Not the best time for my pea brain to process it." Rockfish's answer was short, and Raffi could feel the emotion in what little he said.

In return, Raffi said nothing. He wasn't good at consoling people. Deep down, he wanted to replay the last ten minutes repeatedly and let the adulations from Stevie keep flowing. But even his egoistical mind knew there was a time and a place. This was neither.

Raffi hoped his buddy realized his savior deserved some words of encouragement.

"Did you watch a fucking Bruce Lee marathon on your phone while waiting? I mean, back there, you resembled a solid fuchsia belt."

"Not to brag, but I've listened to a few Joe Rogan podcasts."

"Well, next time, try not to when on the job and you won't miss the gunshot. Mind if I borrow this?" Rockfish said and picked Raffi's phone up out of the cup holder without waiting for an answer.

"Unlock is 814591."

A second later Rockfish switched to speaker phone and Raffi could hear it ringing somewhere off in the distance.

"Decker, it's me Steve..."

* * * * * * * * *

A loud noise filled the night and Jawnie's eyes snapped open. *The condo? The old farmhouse? Sherry's tree fort?* It took her a moment to gather thoughts about where she was and why. The why was important and because of it, Jawnie chose not to sit up.

A blanket covered most of her body and despite it being August, she was thankful for the warmth. She pulled it up under her chin. Darkness filled her immediate vision, despite small streaks of moonlight making their way between the boards. *Would it provide enough protection if I pulled it up over my head? Can I blend into the darkness if someone climbs the rungs?*

Rays of yellow light filled the gaps between the pieces of wood that comprised the club house's walls. Jawnie turned on her side to get a better glance through the cracks. *Headlights? If the noise was a car door that woke me, those were high beams. Someone's here and since the house is abandoned, they aren't here for a late-night booty call.* She shut her eyes and listened. The crackle of dry brush under feet filled the night. *Someone's searching for me.* Jawnie cringed as the steps grew closer and a second beam of light joined the headlights. *Flashlight. But whose?*

Jawnie rolled to her other side and watched through the floorboards. The beam of light stopped at the base of the tree. Jawnie held her breath. An invisible arm then moved it up the wooden two-by-four rungs nailed into the tree. The light moved up through the hole in the floor. She shuffled her body and tried to become one with the wall against her back. It would only be a matter of seconds before the person began the climb. The flashlight moved in a circular pattern through the opening in the floor. Jawnie tried to move even further back. After a few revolutions, the light dropped, and the footsteps began again.

It can't be Sorbelli. No way it's him or any other guy he was meeting up with to hand me over. If they were searching this area, it would have been long before the sun went down. WWRD? He'd be damn proud of what I accomplished today, or at least until this person shines that light in my face and I piss my pants. What if Sherry or one of her friends said something? Hey mom, remember that famous TV star we met the other day at the custard stand? Well, I'm hiding her out in my clubhouse. The tree fort on the old Lannister property? Yeah, that's it. She's there now, hiding out from some big evil men who are after her. I'm going to be part of her next big case. You watch!

The crunching stopped, and the flashlight searched behind the tree. Jawnie leaned over towards the hole in the floor and tried to glimpse who was out there. All she could see was the back of an individual. The person had lifted Jawnie's bike off the ground and pushed the kickstand out. The flashlight moved across the bike from wheel to wheel. Inspection. *Making sure it's mine and then determining their next move. Up, I'm guessing.*

The light moved on from the bike and back near the tree. The person below had seen what they wanted or was moving on to another phase of their search. They stood again in front of the small wooden rungs and climbed. Jawnie rolled back, pressing against the wall, and pulled the blanket up over her head in pure desperation. She had run out of creative escape plans earlier that day. Despondency was all that remained.

Jawnie watched through the thin blanket as the light reached through the hole and now made sweeping arcs across the inside. It stopped square on her face, and she shut her eyes tighter. She held her breath and almost reached for her chest to see if her heart was still beating.

"Jawnie? Are you okay?"

Winters. Jawnie sighed and pulled the blanket down. She stopped. *Wait, what if he's involved and here to finish what Sorbelli screwed up?* She could play twenty questions all night, but her only option was to make herself known.

"I'm not hurt, if that's what you're asking."

"Let's go then."

Jawnie threw the rest of the blanket off and crawled over to the opening in the floor. She peered down. By this time, Winters was back on the ground and shined his light on her face and then on the rungs. *Would he catch me if I fall?* She swung her legs over and moved methodically down.

Winters shone his light on the idling SUV. Jawnie took the hint. She walked across the yard to the road and climbed into the passenger seat. She watched as Winters wheeled her bike over and slid it into the back of the vehicle. He closed the hatch and opened the driver's side door. Winters clicked his seatbelt and looked over, but Jawnie beat him to the punch.

"How did you find me?"

"Don't underestimate the power of big brother."

"NSA?"

"You've got an Apple AirTag on your bike. It took an expedited subpoena, but we have our ways."

"Who told you? Was it Lynn?"

"No, we've not been in contact with anyone in your office. Remember, I loaded your bike into the truck after you had a conniption about us leaving it behind? My fingers wrapped around the seat. I lifted and felt it. I put the knowledge away in case something ever happened and we needed to use that resource. And by the looks of things today, something happened. Want to tell me about it?"

Jawnie dropped her head into her hands and rubbed her eyes with all the energy she had left. She kept her head down, buried in her palms until she felt a hand on her shoulder. The short but supportive squeeze caused her to sit back up straight and recount her day from Sorbelli's offer to ride to Winter's arrival and subsequent ascension up to the tree fort. When she finished, her eyes didn't move from his. Instead, she asked him a question.

"How about you?"

"How about what?"

"How did you end up here? Winters, make me believe, even for a second, that you're not part of this. That you won't drive me back to some desolate area where that rogue partner of yours is sitting on a log, sharpening a knife. Fuck, maybe even Provolone tunneled out, all Andy Dufresne-like, from her beach-house and is sitting alongside him, twirling her weapon of choice. Both waiting. For me."

"No one is waiting anywhere. I've got a team coming up here to primarily locate Kevin and to search the farmhouse for any clues. I've found you, but we still have a missing US Marshal out there somewhere and we won't stop until we bring him home."

"If by home, you mean jail, I'm supportive every step of the way," Jawnie said. She saw the doubt in his face from the overhead light. "You weren't there. You don't know how it went down."

"Look, we'll figure out what happened and why it happened soon. I want you to know that the farmhouse was empty when I got back. It was late in the afternoon and I assumed with the bikes gone, the two of you had gone out for a ride. At some point I got concerned. Called Sorbelli, he didn't answer. Pinged his phone and drove out to its location ASAP. Found it and the bike in a ravine. Tried to find him or any sign of which way he went. I came up empty, and the clock was ticking. You were my next option to search for after I called in the situation."

Jawnie couldn't get a good read based on Winters' facial expressions. *Good, bad or something else, I'm in this vehicle with no other options. Can't go back and fucked going forward.*

"Listen, I can't risk taking you back to the farmhouse. I think it's safe to say everything here is compromised. I've got a team on the way to secure it, but they're an hour out, at least. We've got an office in Harrisburg which is closest—"

"Take me home."

"I can't do that. You're in the program."

"Yes, you can. I've seen *My Blue Heaven* at least half a dozen times. When I want out, you have to let me. If Annetta can get to me here, through a Federal Agent, then she can get to me anywhere. And if that's the kind of shit that's going to happen, I want to be home surrounded by friends. I'll sign whatever stack of waivers you want."

"Go," Winters said. "The U.S. Attorney's Office will put out a warrant for you. They'll send a team of Marshals to take you back in as a Material Witness. We can hold you for your own safety and to ensure your testimony."

"Yada, yada, yada. Tell me something I don't know."

Jawnie reached out and tried the door. The handle gave, and the door cracked. He hadn't locked it. *That's a good thing, right?* She went with her gut and stood her ground.

"Home. You can have me there in less than two hours."

* * * * * * * * * *

Rockfish turned and watched Dan Decker walk out the office door. He stood up and stretched. It had been a long night, and he pretty sure it would not end soon. Rockfish moved from the conference table over to the bullpen area and collapsed into his recliner. He waved Raffi over to follow suit. The conversation had gone on a lot longer with Decker and his officers than Rockfish expected. *His rapid response time once I got through to him was unexpected by all and appreciated. I wish more could have been done. At least for Gordon's sake.*

Decker ended up calling in two separate teams. One set of officers raced to the rest-stop and found Gordon's car abandoned. No sign of the two goons that had taken Rockfish at gunpoint. *They had beat feet into the night and I hope for their sake, they're still walking. Straight into a dangerous neighborhood.*

As luck would have it, as officers searched the immediate area, a Cadillac CT-4 with New Jersey plates was stopped by members of the team as it pulled into the rest stop. The driver wasn't really important, but the other passenger? Giovanni Bianchi, Annetta Provolone's consigliere. At that point, with all that he had witnessed and gone through that previous evening, Rockfish realized he was at the rest stop to be handed over and most likely driven back to some torture chamber in the Garden State. *Would they even have waited to beat on me? Or would the drive be one long, continuous battle with consciousness?*

The cops targeted the consigliere's car solely because of the license plate. Rockfish had given them his version of what might have happened if not for Raffi. Turns out Bianchi was late for the exchange thanks to a wreck on I-95 South, which caused the Cadillac to arrive on scene much later than scheduled.

I haven't been this messed up in a while. Arm's throbbing. Head too. Watching what happened to Gordon and then being saved at the last minute by the guy who hasn't stopped reminding me of it. Gordon. Is he alive? Is this the second time in my life that me and the cops assumed the Marini Family has done him in? Will there be a second surprise resurrection? Doubt it. And what was Conti's problem with the man? There were too many questions for his brain, running on fumes, to even contemplate.

What little relief Rockfish felt with the news was short-lived. Decker had let him know that with nothing to hold him on, the officers let Bianchi go. The consigliere claimed to have been on the way to Florida. Not thrilled with the current state of the airlines, he opted to be driven. People gotta pee and they pulled into the rest stop. Even if they could work up some charge, Bianchi's lawyer would be on the phone and they'd be lucky to have him through central booking before the release order came down.

He's halfway back to Philly by now anyway, probably doing double the speed limit and thanking his lucky stars. Might have been for the best, Steve. If he had pulled in on time, maybe Raffi never gets to play hero.

The second team had taken longer to get dispatched and when they arrived on scene at the vacant garage, it was clear someone had recently completed a professional power washing job on the whole inside. The scene commander radioed in that they would maintain the scene until the morning when the forensic team could arrive, but no one was hopeful of any real evidence recovery.

"They need to go all Gil Grissom on that place. Tonight! Find the smallest thing and follow the goddamn evidence," Rockfish had begged. But procedures needed to be followed, and Decker was by the book. By the end of the conversation, the authorities had both their statements, but didn't sound too reassuring.

"I get it, Steve, I really do. But we ain't got much to go on other than an abandoned car and a freshly cleaned gas station. I know your statement should hold weight and it will. I've got a ton of circumstantial evidence to sort through. Circumstantial, not exactly rock solid, but leads nonetheless. If I had something less soupy. I don't know, something I could grab and hold on to without it spilling out between my fingers. That's what I'm looking for. What I need."

Rockfish had seen the dance before. He knew the next few steps without really having to watch or listen.

"I'll reach out to the FBI and see if they know of any reason Bianchi would be in this area. I know, to pick you up, but let me do my job. We'll double the teams monitoring those ladies, Dampen and Lipton. Based on what you said, Conti might look to tighten the vice on them."

Rockfish didn't listen too much more after that. Decker continued with his BPD Captain two-step. He knew his friend would be there if called or texted, but Rockfish also knew he'd have to add some solid proteins to that soup before reaching out again. Decker saved the worst news for last, basically on his way out the door.

"I was going to stop by in the morning and tell you this, but I'm here. So, Brett Brick, the guy we picked up for the arson—"

"I know who he is."

"He's recanted every bit of the story he spilled when picked up," Decker said.

"Get the fuck out of town," Rockfish said. It wasn't surprising, but still came as a blow to the gut.

"I wish I was fucking with you, Stevie. He's totally reversed course with the story. The way Special Agent Thomas told it, they had every Three Letter Agency in the room and he clammed up. Claimed he was not in his right mind when he made those allegations. There is no hoard of evidence tying his employer to the Marini Crime Family and thus, no mystery woman securing it. The latest line is that he'd been off his meds for a while. You know the story. The guy's lying through his teeth."

"Sounds like someone got a new lawyer and is following the playbook given to him."

"My guess is someone got to him," Decker said.

"No shit. Conti most likely. Or fuck, after tonight, maybe Provolone? I do not know what the fuck's going on with these goombas anymore. They all blend. Wait. He's taking the wrap for the whole thing?"

"Yeah. Our case went south. Fast. From Fulsome management and the Baltimore mob to a lone wolf probably acting on behest of the voices in his head. Worse, the incredible shrinking case pulled some of mine and Anne Arundel County's resources with it."

Rockfish felt a hand on his shoulder, and he jerked back to the present. A shake of his head cleared the cobwebs, and he looked up. Raffi stood alongside him; his head tilted like a dog that didn't understand.

"Hey Stevie, you still with us? Making sure you hadn't gone all catatonic on me," Raffi said.

"Yeah, I'm here. Just rehashing this mess. Saying a prayer I didn't end up like Gordon and that I escaped Provolone again."

"I know, I saved you."

"Cut the shit, man. What do you want me to do? Knight you? Write a fucking check? I said thanks. Now's not the time to ask me to break out the gold fucking star for your forehead. Gimme a day to put my head back on straight. Grab a seat on that couch or head home. Either way, I need you to gimme some goddamn quiet right now. I got a ton of shit to process."

"Okay, Okay. I'll leave you to your thoughts," Raffi said. "Know that I'm a text away and can be here even faster. I worry about you, dude."

"I know, but don't."

"And I want to help. Shit, you saw Gordon popped right in front of you."

"And I keep seeing it. That's a big part of the problem. But again, my problem, not yours."

Raffi shook his head, shrugged his shoulders, and held out his hands. Rockfish wasn't buying the routine and tilted his head towards the door.

"I can take a hint," Raffi said, and walked out the front door. Rockfish leaned back in the recliner and considered a drink, but quickly realized it would put him to sleep and there was plenty still to ponder.

Now, some peace to do exactly what? Morn for Gordon? That guy's got some lives left. I have to believe that. The cops will have spoken to Pilar and Kara by the morning. How can I protect them any better? Fucking Conti. He'll go way over the line, further than

Grayson or anyone at Fulsome to get the girls to sign on the dotted line. No line too dark to cross. The result is too valuable. Shit, I watched the Sopranos. These idiots will do anything to earn. The no-show jobs, kickback from a dozen or more union reps and we shouldn't forget all those valuable materials (on the black market) that will mysteriously fall off the backs of delivery trucks.

The chime notification that someone walked into the office went off on his phone.

"GODDAMN IT RAFFI. For the love of God, what is it now?"

Rockfish looked up from his chair and immediately began forming an apology.

"I'm sorry, Lynn. I thought you were the nudnik coming back. But what the hell are you doing here at this hour?"

Lynn stood in the open doorway and smiled. She didn't move out of the doorframe but stood there, grin widening.

I really don't have the time or the patience to play twenty questions. "And? I mean, my night's been a pile of shit. I can't rehash for your benefit. Just spill it, Hurricane-Tesla. My attention span, along with what's left of my patience, is dwindling fast."

"Look what I found," Lynn said, and she took a long sidestep to the left. She continued to hold the door open with the tips of her fingers as she stopped alongside her desk. Rockfish's eyes followed her outstretched arm all the way to her fingertips. His stomach dropped for the first time since that kiss from Rosanne Slendig back in the eighth grade.

"Hey boss," Jawnie said, stepping out of the darkness.

Rockfish leapt from his chair, shaking his head and praying that the hallucinations from exhaustion hadn't started. The partners met halfway, embraced, but each too spent to say a word. Jawnie eventually pulled back and spoke.

"I've been through some shit."

"You and me both. Wanna catch up?"

"I got nothing but time."

* * * * * * * * * *

Jawnie took up her assigned spot on the couch and, with an active dance partner, Rockfish poured them both a drink without asking. He turned from the bar, glasses in hand, and looked over at his partner.

Somewhere in the world Peaches & Herb are jealous as fuck. But they were right. It feels so good.

He stepped back over to his chair and waved Lynn over. Rockfish figured the odds she could go back to the condo and fall asleep were minuscule. He also didn't offer Lynn a drink, and she didn't ask. They both silently knew someone had to get Jawnie home, safe and sound. And so be it if the conversation took them long into the early morning amid normal business hours. He had no problem sending them home, making sure the last one out flipped the sign to closed, and then catching roughly three days of needed sleep on the couch.

When he was back settled in his recliner, Rockfish took her all in. From head to toes and arm to arm. He assumed he equally looked like shit and she was drawing the same conclusions. The concern on her face matched his.

If I didn't know better, I would think she aged ten years in a little more than a week since she'd been gone. The girl's been through hell and I'm betting the same fucking guidette bitch is behind it.

"Provolone got to the Marshals," Jawnie said, letting out a larger-than-life sigh. "Can you believe that shit?"

"Of course. I'm pretty sure she's pulling the strings down here, too. This greaseball Conti seems more enamored with her than his own freakin' boss."

"All of this when she's out on bail and supposedly on house arrest. Who's fooling who? How can she do this? Are the Feds and the US Attorney looking the other way?"

Rockfish shrugged. The gesture was all he had left in him. But each needed to fully understand what the other had gone through the last twenty-four hours before the team could move forward.

They took turns keeping the other's attention, recounting each's adventures. It amazed both at what the other went through and that each wasn't slowly sinking into piles of liquid emotions on their respective couch and recliner.

"You gave up your protection," Rockfish said. He wasn't sure if she was bold or plain not thinking correctly. "They could have moved you far away. Assigned a small army to watch over you."

"And she would have found me again. I'm tired of running. Winters hoped they had enough evidence to take to the US Attorney and have her put back in jail until the trial. News flash. He doesn't. They won't." Her shoulders slouched and then straightened as quickly. "I choose to make a stand for myself. By myself. I signed every piece of paper and liability waiver they wanted. If she can get to me there, she can get to me here, but at least I'll be happy." Jawnie dropped her eyes into her palms and gave each eye a solid rubbing.

"I'm going to go out on a limb here," Rockfish said. "Did you have anyone, like a lawyer, look at the papers you signed?" He knew the answer, but the question slipped out before his tired mouth could stop it.

"Surprisingly, no. My guy over at Ross, Giacchino & Day, didn't pick up his office phone at 11pm. And before you ask, no, I don't have an evening number for the guy."

"We're fucked. I bet one of those highfalutin government lawyers snuck in some language in the middle of a four-page clause that garnishes any royalties we'd make if Angel turned this bowl of slop into a Season Three."

They both let loose with a solid belly laugh that hurt, but for that one particular moment, all was right in the offices of Rockfish & McGee.

"Okay, in all seriousness. How is Angel?"

Rockfish stopped and inhaled. He really wanted to keep her laughing and upbeat as they both seemed headed for an emotional and physical crash. *Three days of sleep doesn't sound too bad. The kid deserves an update, though. She'll always carry the burden of that night, heavy on her shoulders. Her voice sounded like those two nudniks hadn't updated her with any info on Angel's condition. What? Did they just let her stew in her own shame spiral? Fucking bureaucrats.*

"He's doing better than expected. You probably didn't hear, but his father had him flown back to LA. Something about better care at Cedars-Sinai than he could get here in Baltimore."

"That's where I left off."

"Really? I'm surprised they filled you in that far. You know as well as I do, money talks and Angel's getting the best aftercare and physical therapy there is. His shoulder shouldn't give him any problems in the future, but he's always going to have a hitch in his giddy-up. He's still wheeling around, but with the physical therapy, I hear the most he'll need is a cane to get around in six or so months." Rockfish stopped and gauged Jawnie's face. He spotted the tears welling and watched as the first one let loose from her eye.

"I'm glad he's going to be close to his old self. I want to go out there and see him. As soon as I can." Jawnie wiped her eyes with her sleeve and then grabbed a tissue from the coffee table to help staunch the flow.

"I agree. A visit might be the best thing for right now," Rockfish said. *I really mean it. She needs to disappear. I know she'll fight me the entire way, but maybe, just maybe, LA is enticing enough to get her on a plane or anonymously slow driving cross-country. That Subaru can't have that many miles on it. Do it and her both a world of good.*

"Nice try, Steve," Jawnie said. "I'm not going anywhere. We got the team back together. We do our best shit when we're side-by-side and not when separated by a couple thousand miles. Need I remind you how the last goddamn week went for both of us? I'm here until either that damn construction project is officially cancelled, or those clowns are in jail. When I say clowns, I'm including that old bitch from Jersey."

"You're a partner, so I will not argue, but respect your decision."

"There's a first time for everything."

"All I ask is you complete the training, both classroom and field work, to get that concealed carry permit. You ain't gonna be able to pull yourself out of the quicksand with that T-Square and USB drive you carry around."

She laughed aloud again, and he felt the tiniest bit better about the mess they were in.

Rockfish looked at the other end of the couch and realized Lynn hadn't moved a muscle or said a word the entire time. Her face was expressionless. Rockfish hoped she wasn't having flashbacks of her own. He made eye contact with her and gave his head a slight tilt.

"You doing okay over there? Anything to add?"

"Not really," Lynn said. "I'm still new here, so I'm taking it all in. Also, glad to know I'm not the only one here with reoccurring bouts of PTSD. The deal with Porbeagle was one thing, but here I'm sitting in the office, trying to get my head back on straight and BAM. Angel falls right next to my desk."

"Never a dull moment. I'm pretty sure he put that in your employment contract," Jawnie said. "Better go back and look at the fine print." She held up her fist and Lynn bumped it. Both women chuckled at their boss' expense.

"Okay, kids. Back to the matter at hand," Rockfish said. He pursed his lips and nodded. Once the giggles stopped, he continued.

"I can't help but think Provolone is behind all of it," Rockfish said. "It's not only what Conti was spouting off about, but based on our history, I can't put any of this past her. She pulled the strings in Lancaster with you and I'm sure I saw her paw prints all over

Conti's suit. Does she have her hand in the Fulsome's Avonlea Crossing pie, without Marini knowing?"

"If she's the problem, let's cut the head off the dragon," Lynn said. "Go up there. Guns blazing. I saw how you took out Porbeagle and that fuckin' cult. Let's end this once and for all."

"Easy does it, Lynn. Not every case goes down in a hail of bullets. With any luck, especially with Jawnie back in the fold, we're gonna outsmart these fucks. I never want to have a case end like that, ever again. We need to work smarter. Get the better of them and not extend our current round of therapy sessions. Lord knows I'd like to cut down on the Blue Cross Blue Shield co-pays. We keep Jawnie safe. Provolone heads back to prison. Then get Fulsome's project cancelled and hopefully Grayson and some of his underlings thrown in the cells alongside Brick."

"Don't forget Conti," Jawnie said.

"Oh, I never do," Rockfish said with a shit-eating grin. "His kind are the most slippery. I'd love to see him make prison lipstick and play Adebisi's cellmate, but we all need to come to terms that there's a chance he could live to scam on."

"Adebisi is a character from one of Rockfish's favorite TV shows," Jawnie said. She had spotted the confusion in Lynn's face and answered. She then used the floor to ask a ton of her own instead.

"Do you think she's working some sort of power play? Eventually elevate Conti to a boss she knows she can control? A boss that maybe owes her everything? Or is he a pawn she'll eventually toss aside and designate her own puppet?"

"Like her damn consigliere. I get where you're coming from and to tell the truth, I've thought along those same lines. Everything Decker has told me is that the working relationship between these two families ain't the best and is continuing to slide downhill. Maybe we're on the right track. Like I said, when he had my attention, he sure talked better about her than his own boss."

With a nod of his head, Rockfish retreated into his own thoughts. His mind kept repeating Conti's threat. He needed the girls to do the right thing. To sign on the dotted line. And poof, it would all be over. He reran those couple of minutes in the garage through his mind. He rewound it and hit play again. And a third time. That was the key. He was sure of it.

"You know what? This Fulsome retail plan is too big to fail," Rockfish said, his mind back in the office and alert.

"Like the banks in '08?" Jawnie said.

"Sure. I'll take your word for it and look it up later. But we need a plan. Fulsome, Grayson. Marini, Conti and likely Provolone. They all have way too much invested in this fucking Avonlea Crossing project to allow Pilar and Kara to not give up the land. By check or violence, they're gonna get that property. The amount of stuff they plan on stealing and reselling off an enormous job site, kickbacks galore from each contractor and union representative. Not to mention all the no-show jobs Conti's crew will get, ensuring the flow of cash. And you gotta remember, the mob doesn't pay health insurance. No-show jobs do. They won't stop with the pressure on your friends. Our clients."

"It's up to us," Lynn said. To Rockfish, it sounded more like a question, and he answered.

"It is. And then the police, but in the meantime, I've got a plan to take the attention away from the ladies. I think I've got the beginnings of a way forward. Let me sleep on it and I'll run it past you if it passes the smell test once I'm not emotionally spent and physically exhausted."

"Deal," Jawnie said. She leaned over and returned Rockfish's fist bump.

CHAPTER EIGHT

Annetta followed Oscar into his office. She turned and made sure she shut the door behind her. Annetta took a slight detour and walked over to the couch under the large floor to ceiling windows. She drew the curtains, as was her normal routine. Oscar sat down behind his desk and waved her over. Annetta walked over to one of the guest chairs in front of the desk instead of her normal spot on the couch. *If he wants to think he's leading this for a change, who am I to rain on his parade?*

"So, Annetta, what do I owe this last-minute meeting to? By the way, you look amazing this morning. Headed anywhere afterwards?" Oscar laughed at his little joke and looked across the desk to see Annetta didn't find it so funny.

"You're my lawyer. You know I'm only allowed to come here. Don't joke about shit that you're obviously failing me on. I've still got this thing," Annetta said. She lifted her leg and pulled up on the pants fabric to show the ankle monitor and its ever-present red dot. Despite the accessory, Annetta dressed to impress this morning in a Salvatore Ferragamo light blue pants suit and heels. *I see you, Oscar. Giving me the once over twice with those beady eyes, but I didn't get dolled up and put all this together for you.*

"I apologize. How did your babysitters take the last-minute request?"

"They weren't happy, but they never are. Miserable bastards drew the short straw and have to sit outside my house and do nothing when they could be out saving this country from real criminals. Speaking of which, Giovanni should be here shortly with a couple of guests. I hope you don't mind that I'm going to throw you out of your own office and hold court. Go have lunch or bang your secretary. I don't care as long as you're not around."

"Of course not. Mi casa es su casa," Oscar said.

"Goddamn right. I probably paid for three quarters of this place."

"And the firm appreciates your generosity. But while we wait on your guests, is there anything you'd like me to cover regarding your upcoming re-trial? The bond revocation hearing the Government is pressing for? They really hate the press you're getting, holed up in that beach front house."

"Fuck 'em. Oscar, I could bitch and moan about your efforts from now until next week," Annetta said. "And trust me, if I hadn't made plans for the rest of the morning, I would." She shifted in the chair and recrossed her legs. "But I've got bigger problems. My plans for McGee went right down the shitter at the beginning of the week. The contract shooter, Sorbelli, and now Conti's men. All a severe case of the goddamn yips."

"I see. She's still available to testify in October?"

"Yes, she's still scheduled. Why the fuck wouldn't she be? I don't know where the fuck she's at. I've got a man in Vegas at this very moment trying to figure out what the hell went wrong. The Marshals probably have her wrapped super tight now. Anchorage for all I know. Maybe Guantanamo Bay."

Despite the deadpan facial expression and killer posture, Annetta was at her wit's end. The L's were stacking up, and it wasn't something she was used to, despite the previous encounter with Rockfish and McGee that ended with her in federal prison. *An anomaly, nothing more. Yet here I sit, stuck, putting my future in this horndog's hands. I can't throw any more cash at him and expect anything less than a hung jury at the minimum. I will not go back. But for future business, I'd like to fuck that girl sideways. If I can't get to her, then her partner will pay and that's where the second meeting today comes in. There is one thing both families need to understand. Grudges and egos are hurting the joint-earning dollars we all used to enjoy. If Angelo won't see past this petty animosity, maybe Conti would. I can use him as a conduit. Words or violence, it didn't matter.* But deep down, Annetta knew she wanted to go the second route. She smiled widely and chuckled inside.

"... and even with Ms. McGee's testimony, I feel with lessons learned from the first trial, I can undoubtedly inject reasonable doubt into the minds of the jury. Solely on the horrible testimony of the bankers and executives at Farmer's National Bank that flipped. Barring one of your men getting to a juror. That is our best plan of action. But I look forward to cross-examining that moulinyan. Make her squirm this time."

Annetta watched Oscar as he spun his tail. *The man was sure of himself. I'll give him that. Even despite losing the first trial. Yet based on that and this goddamn US Attorney, I've got doubts about Oscar's ability and this working out in my best interest. One of my crews needs to come through in the clutch and get to a juror as soon as they're in the box. Between now and then? I need that cunt's head on a platter. Or her partner's.* Annetta didn't care which one ate it first. If she ended up in that prison cell, the thought of one or both idiots in an urn on someone's mantel brought warmth to her icy heart.

"That's fine, Oscar. But here's the deal." Annetta then launched into the intricacies of her half of the *Keep Annetta from shitting on a steel toilet* plan.

"If you do your job and I'm back living the American dream, I can tell you circumstances are going to get very heated, quick. A consolidation of South Jersey and Baltimore will most likely be in the cards. I'm going to work with Conti. Perhaps feed his ego and such. You know, make him believe he's the leader he really isn't. Fill his nudnik head with nonsense and sit back while he makes his move. Then I make mine. And if things work out, I'll install Giovanni down there as the boss. Make sure Conti takes the rap for the power play and is no longer in the picture. Get these families back over the fucking grudge hump and to making money. Everyone will be happy. Excluding Angelo's wife and kids, but fuck 'em."

"Ambitious."

"I am nothing less. But during all of this, I'll need you to—"

The sound of a ship's sonar cut Annetta off, and she watched as Oscar's cellphone skittered across his desk. It vibrated to his right a good six inches before he reached out, picked it up, and stared at the notification.

"I don't recognize the number, but I'm betting it's Giovanni. Yes, they're down in the parking garage."

"Excellent. I'm going to need your conference room. Now," Annetta said.

Conti and crew had yet to impress her with actions, but in her current predicament, Annetta didn't have many other options. *Time to pump up some egos and lay on the charm.*

* * * * * * * * * *

Annetta made sure everyone sat at the conference table before she made her entrance. She let them stew for five minutes while she touched up her makeup in Oscar's private bathroom.

"Welcome, gentlemen, I'm glad you could make the long drive on such short notice," Annetta said as she walked into the conference room.

A long oval table took up most of the room, with four chairs on each side. The left wall contained what she could only think were law books, running the length of the room from floor to ceiling. Framed pictures and newspaper articles lined the right side. A small credenza sat against the far wall.

The three men, all seated, rose and walked over to kiss the ring, so to speak.

Luther Grayson was first in line and last in dress. He was a short and round man. His stature and the way he tucked his polo shirt into his Dockers reminded Annetta of former Governor Chris Christie.

"Ms. Provolone, so nice to meet you," Grayson said. He reached for her right hand and cupped it between both of his. Annetta nodded.

"Likewise, Luther. I hear good things about your business savvy and commitment to the Marini Family coffers."

"Thank you. On the drive in, I see a lot of potential with some of those dilapidated boardwalk piers. Perhaps we could talk some business after we talk business," Grayson said with a wink.

"I look forward to it. I can always find time for money making conversations."

Grayson peeled off and returned to his seat. Next in the procession was Ignazio Conti. He dressed impeccably in a three-piece charcoal suit and matching pinky ring. Annetta warmly smiled and reached out her arms. Conti took the cue and moved in for a hug before kissing Annetta on both cheeks. He stepped back, but Annetta held on to both of his hands.

"Ignazio, it's been how long? Ten years?"

"Longer than that, I'm afraid. Back in '08, as the Great Recession was in full swing. We were earning, hand over fist, with that consolidate your bills, improve your credit scheme. Rung every last cent out of it before burning it to the ground."

"Of course. How could I forget such a productive, boiler room? Forgive me, sometimes with promotions comes the loss of cherished memories. Only so much room in there," Annetta said, and she tapped the side of her head. "But it is so great to see you. Please stick around afterwards and we can, no, we should catch up. Also, thank you for the reminder that our families can and have worked well in the past. Unlike our current predicament."

"I fully understand and agree," Conti said. "There is a long and mutually beneficial past that neither of us can ignore. That is why I didn't hesitate to come when called."

"Does Angelo know?"

"He does not. I felt the need to not worry him about trivial matters, if you understand where I'm coming from," Conti said with raised eyebrows and a curt nod. Annett smiled and released his hands. "He'll understand later, at some point. It's strictly business."

Holy shit, did I hear that right? Is he already thinking along the lines of what I want?

Last was Giovanni Bianchi. He greeted his boss and took the chair to Annetta's right after she sat down. The two factions sat across from each other, Annetta deliberately not sitting at the head of the table, as to not ruffle any egos. Keep the illusion that all parties were equally represented. Obviously, she and Giovanni knew differently.

"Ah, before you get started," Oscar Rosenthal said from the doorway. "Gloria put some water and snacks over on the credenza. Please help yourself."

"Jack and a splash of coke," Conti said. The others quickly followed with their own cocktail orders, while Annetta recommended Oscar have someone call down to Caccamo Osteria and have lunch catered in.

"Order a little of everything. We'll pick out what we want. You can disburse the rest to your staff after we leave."

Oscar nodded subserviently. He waited for Gloria before backing out of the doorway, closing the door behind him.

"Madone, I can see why he hired her," Conti said as he watched Gloria walk out of the room.

"Some things never change with you, Ignazio," Annetta said. "We've got limited time and a shitload of things to discuss. I'd like to start with moving past any recent issues the families have had. No one is earning jack shit if we can't move forward."

"I couldn't agree more," Conti said, with Grayson's head nodding in agreement.

For the next twenty minutes, Annetta deliberately observed more than she spoke, lulling Conti into the false sense that he was leading the meeting, resolving problems, and setting the group's objectives. She was content, for the moment, to play the wide-eyed country mouse.

Giovanni and Conti brought up areas where lack of communication and jealousy between crews and families have cost each side millions over the past year. The conversation even determined a line of demarcation for the state of Delaware. Provolone crews would work the state north of Dover and Marini's could run rampant south of the city. Annetta enjoyed this part, as any decision in a matter as lucrative as this would require Angelo at the table, but Conti signed off on it as if he had Angelo's proxy.

The man is already planning for his reign. That's nice. Let him keep thinking that way.

Grayson eventually asked permission to talk and brought up the subject of Avonlea.

"Yes, Luther, I was about to bring it up myself," Annetta said.

"For every day those women remain in control of that property, we are losing hundreds of thousands of dollars," Grayson said. "The county needs proof of ingress and egress rights before they will issue the proper permits for us to begin construction."

"This affects all of us. The girls are your problem and they've hired Steve Rockfish to help fight off your less than legitimate attempts to gain ownership. Am I right?"

"Yes, Annetta. Dead on as usual," Conti said.

"Okay, then I'm here to ask a favor. Avonlea is a Marini golden goose."

"My goose, actually," Conti said. His tone was stern and gave Annetta pause.

"Understandable, but you kick up to Angelo, correct?" She didn't wait for his answer. "Rockfish, and those women, to a lesser extent, are preventing business. He's a thorn in both of our sides. We've both dropped the ball, individually, regarding him, and I would like to propose we work together. As a force multiplier, as they say nowadays. With him out of the picture, I don't need to say you'll be able to squeeze those bitches out of that property in a matter of minutes and I, well, I'll have sent a message to my own little bitch."

Annetta surveyed the table as the last words left her mouth. She wanted to get a good read on the room before continuing. *Grayson's leaning forward like he depends on my next word. Conti's probably wondering where I'm headed with this. After all, I've got the smallest dog in this fight.*

"I couldn't agree more, Don Provolone," Conti said, and the respect surprised her a little. "Before I continue down this road, I would like what we say to go no further than this room. I'm not speaking for Angelo or any other Marini capos, but if words were to filter back, taken out of context, well, that wouldn't be good business for any of us. I, for one, do not want to leave this meeting constantly looking over my shoulder. Again, business will suffer." Conti finished speaking and folded his hands on the table in front of him.

"I understand, Ignazio," Annetta said, and stood up. She leaned forward, her hands on the table. *Here's where I guide these simpletons and plant the seed.* "When I hear of what's going on with Avonlea and the piles of money, Angelo is leaving on the table by not wanting to use the force necessary to have those finocchi sell. Well, it boggles my mind. Giovanni's too. We are earners if nothing else." Annetta could see she had their attention, and she leaned slightly further in. "In the old days, he would have given the order and we would have moved past this problem, before the thought of even hiring a two-bit private-eye ever crossed their minds. Ignazio, you know him better than anyone here. Is it age? I mean, healthcare isn't cheap and I saw the news footage a couple months ago of him. He isn't looking so good. Is it the early onslaught of dementia, the thought of eating grilled cheese off the radiator until you keel over from cancer, or a combination of both?"

"Grilled Cheese. Nothing more, nothing less. He measures decisions these days on the heat index. How much will come down on us and how will it affect him? Not how much we could make on a particular deal, but what attention will it bring on him. Will it be local, state or federal heat? He has made it crystal clear with the current cultural climate. If someone whacked either of those two, well, it would make the BLM protests of last year look like a freakin' Girl Scout parade. He don't want no part of that, especially if you throw in the woke media."

"Fucking cancel culture," Bianchi said, and threw his hands in the air. "Back in my father's day, you could knock off a few dumb lezbos and no one would care. Someone might even give you a citation and a key to the city, depending on where you were and who the mayor was."

Annetta let the boys get out their anger over the country's current state of social affairs. She nodded in agreement, but let them drive the complaint session. She waited until there was a break and then dove back in.

"I mean, I've got my own girl problem. McGee is among the missing, and the only way I see to draw her out is to have Rockfish taken out yesterday. Isn't there something you can do to help me out, Ignazio? For old times' sake?" Annetta said, with a tilt of her head and puppy dog eyes. "If Angelo continues to be a stumbling block, perhaps I could figure out a way to get Rockfish on my home turf? It wouldn't take much to associate the deed with me, and Angelo could keep his panties un-bunched."

"You don't have to lift a finger, Annetta. I'll take care of it personally. You have my word. Top priority as soon as I get back to Charm City, and I'll deal with Angelo if he raises any stink. Then onto the lesbians."

Giovanni reached over the table, and the two men shook on it. Conti stood and walked around the table to Annetta. They embraced. "I'll support any action you might take," she whispered in his ear, and then felt his grip tighten on her hands.

Once Conti returned to his seat, Grayson turned to Annetta. Assuming the official business part of the meeting was over, he floated the idea of Fulsome's potential interest in buying some of the rundown portions of the boardwalk. His pitch included restoration and the development of luxury condominiums and retail spaces.

"I'm sure you have some contacts with the city council you, me, we, can exploit? I'd like—"

A knock on the door interrupted Grayson, and Oscar stuck his head into the conference room.

"Luther, we've got a call from your office on hold. Gloria will transfer it to that phone on the credenza against the wall. Pick up the receiver and you should be good to go."

"Thanks, Oscar, that's what I get for putting my phone on silent," Grayson said. He stood up and walked over to the credenza. "My apologies," he said before picking the receiver and turning his back to the group.

Annetta looked at Conti and then at Grayson's back. He shifted his weight from foot to foot, but she could not hear his end of the conversation until his voice rose.

"Goddamn it!" Grayson slammed the receiver, and it slid off the phone and hung off the credenza, twisting in the wind. Grayson grabbed the base, pulled it from the wall, and threw it on the carpeted floor.

Annetta threw a puzzled look over to Conti. *Ok, he's paying for that. What got up his ass? Only I get away with throwing shit up here.*

Another second passed before Grayson then turned and faced the group.

"My apologies for the outburst. The lawyer, representing those bitches, called our general counsel's office a couple of minutes ago. The conversation was brief. They claim to have a new party interested in purchasing the property and have gone in that direction. We are to cease with all negotiations."

"WHO?" Annetta and Conti said at the same time.

"They claim confidentiality, but all will be a matter of public record soon."

"Ignazio, may I suggest—"

"Annetta, I'm on it. Don't you worry. Let's go, Luther, leave your credit card info with that broad at the front desk."

* * * * * * * * * *

Rockfish left the offices of Ross, Giacchino & Day - Attorneys at Law, early Monday afternoon, after meeting with Pilar, Kara and their attorney Susan Giacchino. The August sun was overhead, and the humidity was as high as it could be without rain falling from the sky. It shocked him that Susan could have the appropriate legal documents drafted in such a short period, but here he was, the proud owner of a half demolished miniature golf course. His current out-of-pocket expenses, to date, was a dollar. Susan mentioned additional fees for filing the documents with the county and state, but she had his credit card on file.

Pilar and Kara were no longer part of the equation, and Rockfish felt good about that. *Innocent people shouldn't have to endure the shit those two have endured. Not to fucking mention the violence certainly headed their way. Now me? Bring it on, fuckwads!*

Rockfish picked up his pace and walked around the corner to the back parking lot. When Lana was within eyesight, he double-tapped the key fob and imagined the air conditioning filling the insides at full blast. Her doors unlocked as he drew closer. Rockfish slid into the driver's seat, leaned forward, and patted the dashboard as cold air shot at him from all angles. He instinctively reached for the seatbelt before removing the phone from his pocket and dialed the number Lynn had texted. He held the phone to his ear, ignoring Lana's Bluetooth option, and listened to the ringing as he waited for Jawnie to pick up.

"Hey Mack, what's going on?" Jawnie said.

"Jawnie, it's Steve."

"I'm going out on a limb here. You haven't received your replacement phone yet?"

"No, no, no. Well, kind of. The new iPhone is back at the house," Rockfish said. "I dumped it right in the garbage. I like Mack's Cricket Wireless piece of shit here better. It's got the gigantic number buttons for old fucks like me."

"Okay, I get it. Your phone is still somewhere in the shipping process. The supply chain is really taking a hit these days."

"Trust me, I know. I had to call Lynn just to get your number. I'm leaving Giacchino's office and am now the proud father of a jacked-up piece of property with a more fucked up recent history."

"Congratulations. I mean, I understand what you're doing and wish I could have been there."

"You are doing fine, lying low and keeping people guessing," Rockfish said.

"I know. You should also know that Pilar and Kara are so thankful for this. Except they really don't understand why you're taking this chance on their behalf. To be honest, we're all worried about how this is going to turn out. Not that I don't have faith."

"You know as well as I do, it's the least we can do," Rockfish said. "Especially with the locals in Anne Arundel dragging their feet. Only so far the Baltimore PD can push. There's a line in the sand and the locals could always pull the jurisdiction card. Look, they were kinda still are our clients. I feel a duty to protect them. The firm feels the same duty. Not to mention those ladies are like family to you, which means family to me."

There was a long pause on the other end of the phone. Rockfish could hear a faint sniffle and then a second. *She's trying to compose herself. Either very emotional about what we're doing or pissed off. She can't actively be a part of it.*

"It's okay, Jawnie. This is what we do."

"Gimme a sec, will ya? I'll call you right back. I remembered something last night and want to run it by you. Unless you plan on stopping by the condo later?"

"I don't think I have time today to swing by. I wanted to drive over and inspect my new purchase. Show my face around in case anyone's scoping the place out. Raffi's meeting me there and we were going to game plan a little for what might come down the pike. It is violence or another sit-down. There really is no other with these people. Plus, it's not exactly my first rodeo."

"That's a favorite line of yours," Jawnie said with a quiet laugh.

Nice one, kid. Your recovery time is getting better and better. I'm going to need you at one hundred percent long before this thing is over.

"I'll deal with these people and when I've got their nuts in a vice or behind bars, I'll sell it back to Pilar and Kara for seventy-five cents. Call me back when you can. I'll be in the car for another twenty minutes. No rush."

Rockfish dropped Mack's phone into the cupholder. He reached for the touchscreen and paired the phone to the car's Bluetooth for when it rang next.

After catching three calls about Mack's expiring car warranty, Rockfish contemplated turning off the ringer. He knew how to silence unknown callers on his iPhone, but after pulling over and looking at this Cricket monstrosity, he couldn't even locate the settings menu. He worried how Jawnie's mind might take being sent straight to voicemail. Rockfish kept the ringer on.

The meeting with Raffi was uneventful, as both men had expected. After half an hour of standing around and coming up with some cockamamy ideas, Rockfish called it. They agreed to continue the conversation the next afternoon back at the office. Rockfish was cutting it close with meeting a potential new client on the other side of town. After the meeting, he expected a call later that night from Angel's dad with an update on the recovery of their favorite Hollywood producer.

Mack's phone rang the minute he dropped Lana into reverse and began pulling out of the property's small lot. He glanced at the display, but at first, he didn't recognize the number.

Car warranty? Maybe my computer has a virus on it? Or my favorite, I've won an all expenses paid vacation to Timeshare Land.

"Hello."

"Hi, Steve."

"All good in condo land?"

"I'm good. I got distracted by my research and lost track of time," Jawnie said. "It happens now that I've got my laptop back and have unfiltered and, more importantly, unmonitored internet. That being said, I wanted to apologize."

"No need. Ever."

"Steve, this condo is like being trapped in Lancaster but without the dread and fear of the unknown hanging over me. I know I'm not all there during some of our conversations. But I'm good right now."

"Glad to hear it. Now what has my favorite web sleuth uncovered?"

"Do you remember our brief trip inside Fulsome's headquarters? Afterwards I said the woman with Brick looked familiar."

"Yeah, you and her had run across each other. Somewhere."

"I remember."

"Stop. Call Lynn. Reschedule the meeting with Owen Vass. I don't care what excuse she uses. Fill me in on which she uses, so I don't make an ass out of myself when I sit down across from him. I'll be there as soon as I can."

* * * * * * * * * *

Jawnie had cleared the coffee table in anticipation of Rockfish's arrival. She pulled the bottle of Jameson, untouched since his last visit, from the bottom of the pantry and a rocks glass from a cabinet. She made a plate for herself, knowing full well Rockfish wouldn't come within an arm's reach of anything in her refrigerator. Jawnie then sat back on the couch and waited. All she could do was shake her head when the aroma of his McDonald's takeout reached her nose as he walked through the doorway.

"You're carrying that bag in your right hand," Jawnie said. "The arm giving you trouble still?"

"Nah, it's close to normal," Rockfish replied as he walked past her to the couch. "I keep forgetting to use my dominant arm after switching things up for the past couple of weeks."

Jawnie grabbed her plate off the kitchen island and joined Rockfish on the couch.

"It's been a while since we've had a working dinner," Rockfish said as he shoved three fries into his mouth.

"I wonder why?"

"Okay, okay. I'll save the McNuggets for after," Rockfish said and placed his grease-stained bag down on the floor. "What did you remember about the woman in the hallway with Brick, 'cause I totally blanked on her after that day?"

"Yeah, me too. With Provolone, Angel and all the shit afterwards, I hadn't given her a single thought since then either."

"She looked like his assistant or secretary that day. You know, based on Brick's actions and tone of voice."

"Can we go back to calling him Mace Face?"

"We could compromise and shorten it to MF," Rockfish said with a sly smile.

"Deal," Jawnie said and held out her fist. Rockfish bumped it and she continued. "Her name is Rosa Mangold, but it's more about what I remembered. Lynn was out for the evening, and I was sitting here, feeling the downward spiral starting. Asked myself WWRD."

"Looking at the empty wine bottle and glass on that dinette over there..."

"Exactly."

Jawnie recounted her previous evening's decision to crawl into a wine bottle and get all sentimental. To her, a trip down memory lane was long overdue and a self-prescribed cure for what ailed her. A few glasses in, Jawnie opened her phone's photo app and tapped on *For You*.

"One memory that Apple was nice enough to curate a slideshow for was this past Labor Day. From what I remember, it was a good time, and I thought I'd relive it. I topped off my glass and hit play."

Jawnie had sat on the couch, her mind traveling back a little over two months earlier, when a drunken night at an old haunt flooded her consciousness.

"Rosa was in almost every picture with me. We flirted pretty heavy through a margarita haze, but the following morning, sober heads prevailed and neither of us followed up on it. I know it's her! And then I went and found her on Facebook. The account is pretty locked down but I think I should send her a friend invite. Maybe I can get her to chat? Open up?" Jawnie knew she had to downplay her over-the-top enthusiasm. It had been a long time since she had done anything positive to move the firm's case forward. *Slow down, kid. That's what he's going to say if you keep trying to break some sort of speed talking record. Just the facts, ma'am. It will all come out.* Jawnie opened her laptop. The change from the phone to the larger screen gave Rockfish's old eyes a break and larger images for his brain to process.

"Is that Jamocha Jubblies?"

"Yes, they had a big inflatable pool in the parking lot and crazy drink specials," Jawnie said. "It was not one of my prouder nights."

"Mediocre expensive coffee with a side of side boob. Sometimes the unofficial slogans are the best."

"That place closed up fast. I mean, I liked the original theme. Who wouldn't love a mashup of Hooters and Starbucks? I think the liquor license was the beginning of the downfall."

"No fucking way? Raffi and I were there not too long ago," Rockfish said. "Hmmm."

She had seen that look before on his face. *He's got his thinking hat on. WWRD? Do I smell smoke?* Jawnie couldn't contain the giggle and Rockfish looked over.

"What's so funny?"

"Nothing. Looks like you're onto something."

"Partial idea, if there is such a thing. The Jubblies mention gave me an idea. Stay with me on this. But maybe it's time, with you lying low here, to do your best *Sunshine West* imitation."

Sunshine was an online scammer from the Porbeagle case. She used her womanly wiles to win over men online in order to separate them from their money. Jawnie did not have that skill set. But there was one she had.

"Wait, I think I see where this is going. Especially since I'm not planning on selling Rosa on some whacked out investment con. Also, need I remind you Sunshine is no longer with the living? You want me to friend her and then send a virus to hack into her computer? It's clear as day on your face."

"Get cyber chummy and get her to click a link. It's an idea. I mean, she seemed pretty damn close to Brick, professionally speaking, of course. And we have no other choice but online reconnaissance. I can't have you out socializing, pumping her for information and get recognized by someone in the next booth. *Hey Jawnie, you working a big case?*"

"I see where you're coming from and respect your faith in my computer skills. I'm not thrilled with the delivery mechanism." Jawnie folded her arms across her chest. She knew he'd blow past her verbal and non-verbal opposition to his plan until he made his point. *Then he should be ready to listen, if history's told me anything.*

"They discussed that damn folder. He shoved his finger in it. She looked back at him. What if? What if she has taken over some of his duties? The man is sitting in jail taking one for his superiors. Is it really that much of a stretch that she's keeping the seat warm?"

Rockfish smiled and reached down alongside his McNugget bag. He took a long draw from the straw in his Diet Coke and placed the cup back on the floor before continuing.

"And hack is such a dirty word," he said, imitating Jawnie's crossed arms. "All I'm asking for is a quick look around. Let's call it online investigating for anything of interest. I'm not asking you to download her nudes or anything. A little meander through cyberspace to see if you can find anything that can help us."

"Define help," Jawnie said, uncrossing her arms. *Maybe if I appear less defiant, that look on his face will change. And then he might be open to suggestions.*

"I can't. It's like what that one old crotchety Supreme Court justice said years ago about porn. I know it when I see it. Also, maybe run across other things she's got access to?"

"I have to bring you a ton of files or other digital evidence to review and then you'll know how this will help us?"

"That's a Texas-sized 10-4."

"I'll sleep on it. But I'll definitely send the friend request. That can't hurt anything. Fuck, let's do it right now and get the ball rolling, at least. You never know what could come of a simple move like that. Let's hope she's an outright Gabby Hayes and will online chat my ear off."

Jawnie reopened her laptop and closed Photos. She navigated the browser window to the Rosa Mangold profile page.

"You were correct about it being properly locked down," Rockfish said. "Not much more than her name and a slightly blurred profile picture." Rockfish shook his head. "Cyber security conscious. You might need to send a spicy picture in order to get her to click on it."

"Relax. One step at a time, horny old man. You went from sending her a malicious link to me learning steganography to hide some sort of executable code within an image. I appreciate game acknowledging game, but I'd have to study up on that. If it came to that."

"Keep me advised, and I agree. Fire off that request."

Jawnie moved the cursor and clicked the track pad. "Done. I'll be honest, the steganography bit makes me want to research it a tad more. Not promising anything, but thinking it would be a suitable tool to add to the arsenal at some point. Speaking of, I need to swing by the office and pick up some stuff. Perhaps you'd like to escort me tomorrow at some point? Or I can have Lynn drop me off if someone will be there after sundown? Cover of darkness and all."

"I can fit you into my post-dinner plans. Sundown's a little after eight. It could be like old times. And we have our normal Thursday meetings, but on a Tuesday. Cover a lot of those admin issues I've been ignoring for the past couple of weeks."

"Good thing we hired Lynn."

* * * * * * * * * *

The next evening, Rockfish was running late. Or going to be. He glanced down at the clock on Lana's dash. *6:30pm. I'll never get there by eight. What the fuck else is new? Gotta text Jawnie when I can.*

"Hey, how we doing back there? Throw up on the blanket buddy, not my leather seats," Rockfish said over his shoulder. Zippy lay stretched out across the back seat, alternating between the dry heaves and actual vomit spilling from his mouth.

Rockfish diagnosed the foamy, yellow slime mixed with grass as soon as it began spilling across his wood floors. It had been an issue in the past with Zippy's unsupervised playtime outside. Yet this time sounded the alarm bells as it seemed more violent. The dog's body shook with each heave.

"Are you letting him eat grass again? Or not watching him when he's outside," Rockfish had said to Mack as the first blades of regurgitated grass hit the floor.

"Grass ain't never killed nobody," Mack had said.

"Right, but the pesticides that the fucking lawn company sprays all over it do."

That's the simple answer. The one I need Mack to accept. The only other option is someone did it on purpose. Weak ass intimidation, if you ask me. Man up, come at me, you piece of shit. Not my old man's dog. Rockfish shrugged off the idea, but stowed it away in the back of his mind for future consideration.

The unexpected trip to the after-hours Animal Hospital after they had cleaned up the dinner dishes meant he was on a path to not arrive at Jawnie's on time. *Unless they decide quickly to admit your ass and keep you overnight. Not that I'm hoping for that boy, but it would be best for business.*

The vomit had slowed to a trickle as soon as they crossed the hospital's reception area. *Never fails.* And the two of them ended up leaving for home ninety minutes later with two prescriptions and orders to keep a better eye on Zippy if Mack continued to insist on having the best lawn in the neighborhood.

Rockfish opened the passenger door to pull the seat up, but Zippy stood there and looked right through him. *Okay boy, front seat it is.* Rockfish reached down, picked the dog up, and softly placed him on the front seat before gently closing the door. On the way home, Zippy remained somewhat sedated and inattentive. Rockfish didn't care. He was a friendly ear, and he sounded off about Raffi's no show in the office that afternoon.

"I can't believe fucking Raffi. First, he no-shows our meeting and then he won't answer his phone. Three messages I've left. Him? No, I doubt anything nefarious happened to him. I mean, it's always a consideration in this line of work. But I'm betting a better money-making opportunity has come up. He made a business decision to move old Steve to the back burner. Not the first time."

By 8:50pm, Rockfish had handed Zippy back to Mack and raced across town to Jawnie's condo. The warm body in the passenger seat might have changed, but it didn't stop Rockfish from continuing his rant, even as they arrived at the office and settled into their seats in the bullpen area.

"Yeah, I don't know what to make of that guy sometimes," Rockfish said as he sat in the recliner and instantly regretted not pouring a drink.

"Are you worried about him?" Jawnie said, sitting on the couch, laptop open in front of her.

"Does it sound like I am? Not my first rodeo with this guy."

"There it is again."

"What?"

"Never—"

BZZT BZZT BZZT

Both heads swiveled towards the locked front door. Someone was pushing the buzzer on the other side of the drawn shade.

Jawnie opened a separate browser window and brought up the feed from the outside security camera.

"Hey, it's Raffi."

"I knew there wasn't anything wrong with that piece of shit."

"He doesn't look good, and he brought company," Jawnie said and spun the laptop so Rockfish could see the scene on the other side of the door.

Conti! Motherfucker. And by the grin on his face, the two of these guys just didn't run into each other in a vacant strip mall parking lot. The condition of Raffi's face gave Rockfish reason to pause. *I was wrong and should have known something was up.*

Raffi had taken a beating. His face was swollen, not to mention his left eye looked to have the makings of a nice shiner. Dried blood caked under his nose and bottom lip. They had put him through the wringer, but he was alive. Rockfish gave a quick thank you to the Man above for that. He had lost one friend to this fucking low-life a little over a week ago. He wasn't about to run headfirst into a dangerous situation and signal Raffi's death knell.

"Jawnie, get in your office! Lock the door and don't come out for any reason. Matter of fact, get under the damn desk if you hear footsteps. This ain't good."

Rockfish jumped out of the recliner but didn't make another move until he heard Jawnie's door shut. Once he felt she was as safe as she could be under the circumstances, he headed for the front door.

"I'm fucking coming," He shouted over the buzzer. "Knock it the fuck off. I said I'm coming!"

Rockfish pulled the string, and the shade shot up to the top of the door frame. Conti's smile grew wider, if possible. The man was impeccably dressed for the late hour. He waved a French cuff covered hand with a giant diamond cufflink, signaling Rockfish to open the door. As Rockfish reached for the deadbolt, he could see two of Conti's men positioned behind Raffi. Each towered over their boss and dressed similarly. *I had a feeling it wouldn't be as easy as whooping this old man's ass.* He opened the door and Raffi fell into his arms.

Rockfish half carried, half dragged Raffi over to the couch and set him down against the right arm. Raffi hung there for a minute, leaned left, and then fell the rest of the way down to the couch cushions.

Conti and only one of his men walked through the door and past Lynn's desk. The other remained outside. The gangster stopped at the recliner across from Rockfish's and looked around the office.

"Harold, go check the place out," Conti ordered and Rockfish held his breath. "Make sure we're alone."

Harold headed straight down the hallway leading to the partners' offices. Rockfish recognized Harold from the garage with Gordon. This meathead wasn't the shooter, but odds were he was packing more than the fists he used on Raffi.

"Hey boss, we've got a locked door."

Conti said nothing. He looked at Rockfish and raised his eyebrows.

"That's McGee's office. She locked the door as the authorities spirted her away after the shooting. I have a key if Harold wants to go in and dust."

"That's okay, Harold. Come sit with us next to the punching bag."

An awkward silence hung over the bullpen as Harold pulled up the only couch cushion left.

Conti reached into his suit jacket, and Rockfish winced. He pulled out a single dollar bill and placed it on the coffee table. "Now we're going to make that same sweetheart deal, if you know what's good for you." Conti smiled, leaned back in his chair, and nodded at Rockfish.

Rockfish might have had an idea for the late-night visit, but the crisp bill three feet in front of him told him all he needed to know.

"How did you know it was me? No one has even filed the paperwork yet."

"Mr. Rockfish, I've been in this game longer than you've played pretend-cop. Do you think Giacchino pays her damn secretary a livable wage? Of course not. That bitch has three kids and a seven-hundred-dollar car payment. You wave some cash in front of a desperate person. Doors open, they spill information. It is the world we've always lived in."

"I have half a mind to—"

"What? Tell that stupid broad her assistant has loose lips? You gonna feed those three kids and buy them school clothes when she loses her job?"

Rockfish ground his teeth and searched for the right thing to say. He came up empty.

"That's what I thought. Now Harold and I have places to be. Our business meetings are never-ending these days and nights." Conti reached down and picked up the bill. He folded it, lengthwise, and placed it between the middle and index fingers on his right hand.

He then began tapping the bill on the table as he spoke. "I'm going to give you one more chance to take this dollar and do the safe thing for all parties involved."

"And if I don't?" Rockfish said. *I gotta weigh all my options, no matter how dark it looks.* Memories of Gordon lying in the grease and blood filled his mind while he stared at Raffi, curled up in the fetal position on the couch.

"That old broad up north wanted you whacked yesterday, but I'm a reasonable man. Plus, you got cameras inside and outside this joint. I've done my homework and want to give you one more chance. Despite what she wants, I'd rather not have Harold work late running you out to where we dumped Gordon. Take your time and think about it, Mr. Rockfish."

"I see," Rockfish said and gave his ten o'clock stubble a good rub. He wanted to give the appearance he was thinking. Give Conti's offer the thought the old man thought it deserved. *Fuck that dude if he's dumb enough to leave me, at a minimum, in better shape than Raffi.*

"Yeah, that's gonna be a hard pass from me."

"We all make our own decisions and live with the consequences, Mr. Rockfish," Conti said as he stood up and pocketed the dollar bill. "Harold and I are going to walk out that door and the next time you see him, you might wish you had turned it over for free. Look at this guy over here." Conti tilted his head at Raffi. "You keep this shit up and no one will want to be friends with you."

Harold joined Conti, standing behind the couch. The men turned and walked over to the door. Rockfish shook his head and regretted the words before they had finished spilling from his mouth.

"Hey stronzo, vaffanculo!" Rockfish cocked his right arm and grabbed the bicep with his left. The old Italian salute. *That they should understand.*

Harold continued to hold the door open, but Rockfish's comment stopped Conti dead in his tracks. He turned around toward Rockfish, pursed his lips and shook his head. The old man didn't say a word, but gave Rockfish a solitary finger gun and then melted away into the dark parking lot.

Rockfish stood in silence. He stepped over to the couch and crouched down.

"When the fuck did you learn Italian?" Raffi muttered.

"The Italian profanity wiki is a wonderful thing. I knew a thirty-second internet search would pay off with these idiots. You hang tight. I'll get you some ice."

"Jawnie! All clear!" Rockfish called out as he hunted behind the small bar for the ice pack he knew was there.

He attached the ice pack to the side of Raffi's face, thanks to an old-fashioned ace bandage he kept around for such occurrences and hangovers. But mostly hangovers.

"Hey buddy, I'm going to get you to an urgent care or Saint Luke's if you think an x-ray is necessary."

"Home" It was all that Raffi could muster with his new mummy look.

With Raffi as comfortable as he could be with the supplies on hand, Rockfish turned his attention to Jawnie.

"Not sure how much of that you heard."

"The only thing I heard was that doorknob jiggling. My heart now has a permanent spot in my throat. I dove under the desk. I would have put money on Conti ordering you to hand over the key." Jawnie said, wrapping her arms around herself and giving a tight squeeze. "Glad he didn't. Hiding under the desk wasn't as easy as George Costanza made it look."

"Finally, a reference we both understand."

"Yippee for that," Jawnie said, and kneeled down alongside the couch and put her hand on Raffi's shoulder. *She'd be a thousand times better a better nursemaid than I would make. I need to think quickly on my feet. That's my skill set. Come up with something quick to get that asshole back on his heels. And drive.*

"I gotta get you home and you need to speed up that honey trap game. I can't help but feel this entire mess is barreling towards an end," Rockfish said, running both hands through his hair. "We need something to give us an advantage. But for right now, we need to get the fuck out of here. Grab my key fob off the bar and start her up. The cold air will do Raffi a world of good until we can get him home and in bed. I'll get him into the car. You'll have to ride backseat."

"He doesn't want to see a doctor?" Jawnie stood up and walked past Rockfish's recliner to the bar.

"He's like me. Can't get diagnosed with something bad if you don't—"

BOOM

The glass from the windows and doors blew out before the sound reached anyone's ears. Those left standing fell to the floor while Raffi rolled off the couch. Pieces of the wood blinds, shards of glass and chunks of ceiling tiles rained down on all three.

CHAPTER NINE

Dan Decker, now acting in an unofficial capacity, pulled into Rockfish's driveway long after midnight and killed the engine. Mack and Lynn met Rockfish, Jawnie and Decker at the door, woken by Zippy's barking and the headlights lighting up the inside of the house. No one was up for an early breakfast, so Mack headed back up to bed after the third time Rockfish told him the story would be the same in the morning. Lynn followed suit because the small group needed time alone and unfortunately, the office wasn't available at the moment.

Decker and Jawnie followed Rockfish to the opposite end of the house. The kitchen was far enough away to not wake anyone if someone raised their voice or if the conversation went on long past sunrise. *I hope. Can't promise anything after this night.* They squeezed around the green Formica table, littered with small boomerang designs. The table was an heirloom from the seventies, if Rockfish remembered correctly. His mother had picked it out and Mack had sworn to never throw it away. It had been repaired and refinished more times than Rockfish remembered.

Rockfish looked around at Decker and Jawnie as they all pulled out the metal, vinyl covered kitchen chairs.

For the first time in a long while, Jawnie looked angry. As if she wanted to be back on the street at that moment, tracking down whoever had done this. It was the opposite of the retracting turtle that Rockfish had seen since the beginning of this case. *If she's pissed, she's ready to ride shotgun again. It's been a long climb up this hill, but, girl, we're going to enjoy the ride down the other side.* Rockfish also surprised himself. Despite all that had happened, the man had a positive outlook. There had been no yelling as the cops arrived on scene. No screaming for vengeance on the ride back to the house. For the first time since he met Kara and Pilar, he felt whatever move he was going to make would be the right one.

Decker had arrived on scene without Rockfish making a call. He showed up in his minivan dressed for a late night trip to the gym. That's when Rockfish knew the man was present not on business, but as his friend. Any issues the two men had in the past were just that, in the past.

The EMTs were the next on scene and despite his vocal opposition, Raffi submitted to the once over before loading up for the quick ride over to Saint Luke's for x-rays. *Could an x-ray even see CTE? I bet they said a bunch of other things that, in the heat of the moment, I missed. Angel, Gordon and now Raffi. I can't sit on my ass and hope the police or now the ATF plan on bringing any kind of justice for them.*

Last, his mind wandered to the one remaining back at the strip mall parking lot. There would be no salvaging Lana. One of the ATF men in white coveralls had Rockfish sign a couple of forms after they completed processing the scene. The same technicians gathered all the pieces and placed them on the back of a flatbed truck. From there, she'd go to a local lab for further analysis. They would release the body to the family, but it would be a couple of months at the earliest before they could plan the funeral. *I'm fucked trying to replace her. It's not like I can go on some Russian dating website, find another and buy a plane ticket for next week. The news was full of supply chain issues and microchip shortages.* It would be months before he could slip behind the wheel of her replacement, if Rockfish could ever replace a gal like Lana. *Maybe that guy over at Fair Oaks Dodge could move me to the top of the waiting list?*

"Hey, I know you all turned down Mack, opening up the kitchen and getting out eggs and hash browns, but what about water?"

"You got something stronger, Steve?"

"Read my mind, Dan."

Rockfish returned to the table with three water bottles, two glasses, and a bottle of Tullamore Dew. Each sipped their own until Decker broke the ice and returned from the freezer with some of his own.

"Those heavy blinds you had installed saved you from the shards of flying glass. Count your lucky stars there. To me, and this isn't official, it doesn't look like it was meant to emulate the Oklahoma City bombing and wipe out a good portion of this strip mall." He stopped, sipped his whiskey, and rubbed his hands together before continuing. "Whoever did this wanted you inside that car when the ignition turned over. Pray to the idol of your choice, Steve. You were very lucky to afford a remote start, what almost six years ago? Anyway, I would have preferred one of you or, better yet, both had gone with Raffi to get checked out."

"I know. Better safe than sorry," Rockfish said. "Thanks for the concern, old buddy, but I'm raring to go and this one over here..."

"I've cut, run and hid under way too many desks. I'm a signature away from my concealed carry permit. Big girl pants have been acquired."

What the fuck?

"I'm ready, Steve. Don't look at me that way," Jawnie said and reached for her water. "I'll be there in October to hang that witch. Put her back on that concrete cell. Let her die alone behind the walls of a Supermax. Ready to stand by your side and do whatever it takes to bring that same justice down on Conti and his crew."

"Easy does it, kid," Rockfish said. The growling in his stomach made him think for a second about waking Mack. *Time to eat later, man. Finish keeping her head on straight. Can't be great for her going from one extreme to the other in the snap of a finger.* "I need a partner with a clear head. Not one clouded with vengeance and vigilantism. Not that either of those are bad, but you know, moderation."

Jawnie cupped her hands and rested her chin on them, elbows firmly on the table. He could tell she was rip roaring to go. *But we've got to go about it smartly. Hey, exactly when did we change places?*

"I have to agree with Steve. Let the Feds handle this," Decker said, his eyes clearly focused across the table at Jawnie. "They've got all the tools. RICO, maybe a domestic terrorism charge depending on how they look at the explosion. And who knows, maybe this fits like a glove into a current large scale Marini investigation. You would hope the Feds already have one in the works. Both of you need to take a step back and see all you have to lose. And speaking of the Feds, what was on the flash drive you handed over to the site supervisor?"

"He asked me if we had any archived footage from the security cameras," Rockfish said. "Talking cloud shit, so I pointed him over to our resident expert."

"I had landed on my laptop when Lana went, but it was still working and had a decent charge," Jawnie said. "The ATF guy gave me the USB drive, and I looked to see what video we had prior to our guests showing up. I auto-save it to four different clouds, so I sat down on the asphalt and looked to see if it captured anything. The feed caught someone a little over ten minutes prior to when Conti and Raffi showed up, walking past the front door and then back the other way. On the second pass, he reached under Lana before hurrying away. Dressed all in black, including shoes. Hoody up, ski masked-up for an August night. Not much to go on."

"Enough time for Conti to claim pure coincidence." *Hey, I was here to talk about buying some property. We found his friend all fucked up in the parking lot. Maybe the mad bomber beat the shit out of him.*" Rockfish shrugged his shoulders and held up his palms for added effect.

"Jawnie, is there any chance I can get that footage?" Decker said. "I know I'm here as a friend, but I've got friends in our lab that owe me favors."

"No offense, Dan, but what can your guys do that the AFT and their billion-dollar budget can't?" Jawnie tilted her head to add emphasis to her question.

"Not a damn thing, but I can bring speed," Decker said. "Something actionable and timely. I won't be dealing with red tape or evidentiary chains. I'll have my guy look at it and see what he can pull from the video."

The partners' eyes met across the table and each nodded. They were thinking along the same lines. Rockfish could imagine Dan standing behind the lab tech's back, looking over his shoulder, yelling 'Enhance' at various intervals. *Was Jawnie clearly stifling a laugh? He's here to help. Offering us pretty much any marker he has or can work under the table. Be fucking grateful, you bum.*

"Sure thing, Dan, we'll get you it before you leave."

"I also want to stress what they told you before we left the scene," Decker said. He took a second and rubbed the back of his neck. Rockfish leaned forward, expecting the parent-son talk. *Is he trying to frame what he's going to say to make it more palatable? Christ, I know what's coming. Out with it.*

"Lie low. Let the investigators do their job. If Conti thinks you're dead, the better the chance he'll not be so cautious. Make that mistake. The one the Feds need to bust the case wide open. Not to mention if you go sticking your head up out of the sand, Conti will come at you twice as hard. This is a delightful house. Remember, your father lives here." Decker pointed up at the second floor and then over to a picture of father and son from a recent fishing trip that hung on the wall over the kitchenette. He then turned to Rockfish and raised his eyebrows.

"I've seen this episode on television, not that I watch much. Steve is supposed to roll over and play dead," Jawnie said. She saw Decker's ask coming a mile away. "You want Mack to hold a fake funeral for Steve and then see who shows up? Hide microphones throughout the church and cemetery to catch the murderer's incriminating confession."

"Yeah, Dan, that's some Hollywood bullshit," Rockfish said. "The only funeral around here will be Lana's. I'm going to call The Wolf and have her crushed down to one of those giant metal blocks. Put her in the office, after the new construction finishes. Great topic of conversation for attracting new clients. Or maybe over there in the living room as a coffee table."

Two of the three laughed out loud. The third chose his words wisely.

"I get it. Everyone deals with shit differently, but having Moe and Curly on either side of me is fucking with my last nerve. I'm here to help. Not play the straight man. You want it or not?" Decker shook his head and held out his hands, palms up.

"We're sorry, Dan."

"What she said," Rockfish said. "But truth be told, wasn't the stand aside shit the same line you gave me when the state and locals looked into the happenings at the mini golf course? Same when Gordon disappeared. A soup sandwich with not much consistency, if I remember your words, right?"

"Okay. You're the big man on campus. What's your plan then?"

Rockfish blinked and swallowed the saliva that had pooled in his mouth. He had the floor and all the attention. He looked at Jawnie and then at Decker. *One's trying to guess what I'm about to say, and I scare the other to death with what's about to tumble out of my mouth.* Those thoughts could describe either set of eyes on him.

"I ain't going anywhere. I ain't hiding my head in the sand. It's time the media and the people of Anne Arundel County learn of the change in ownership of Little Golf Big Tees. What the new proprietor has in store for the land and the community."

* * * * * * * * * *

Investigative Specialist and an FBI Newark surveillance team lead by Keith Black was the first to spot the unidentified car. He checked the time, 8:15am, and marked it in his log. The car crept down Annetta Provolone's street, at roughly fifteen miles an hour, as if the driver was searching for something. He reached for his telephoto lens on the passenger seat, picked it up, and scoped out the car.

Wednesday the 17th was halfway through FBI Newark's week of watching Annetta as she flaunted the justice system and toughed it out her house arrest at her luxurious beach house. Black led the team responsible for reporting, observing, and surveilling comings and goings from the house for the week.

While the RICO case and upcoming retrial were the investigative responsibility of FBI Philadelphia, the Ocean City, New Jersey beach house in question, sat smack dab in Cape May County. And according to the FBI's area of responsibility map, FBI Newark covered the county. It never made much sense to Black, and he hated these early mornings when he had to leave his home north of Trenton and make the trek down to the small town south of Atlantic City by the crack of dawn. But to his superiors, it was less of a long drive before sunrise and more of an example of how two offices could work in coordination without either puffing their chest and enduring an unproductive power struggle. The offices were working well, and Black hoped it would set the tone for future joint operations along the shore.

He had sat on the street catty-corner to Annetta's house since 6am. He cracked the van's windows, but the heat was coming.

Humidity spilled in and filled the surveillance van. He'd kill for a sweet ocean breeze at some point soon, but wasn't counting on it.

He zoomed in and made out the driver of the Chevrolet Spark. A young woman, maybe late twenties, was behind the wheel. She wore a baseball cap that didn't contain her long blonde hair. He had called in the plate as soon as he could make it out, but the radio had squawked in response it was a rental. The next thing that came to mind when he saw the small white car was delivery. He picked up the radio again and checked in with the rest of the team and FBI Philadelphia's Radio Room back over the bridge at 600 Arch Street.

"Are we aware of any food or merchandise orders scheduled?"

Negative responses came back over the radio, one after another.

"Okay, the car's stopped directly in front of Provolone's walkway. Everyone on their toes. Rollins, I need you on a beeline for that car in case she needs to be stopped and questioned."

"Copy that."

Black leaned forward and squinted to see what the woman carried in her hand. The breeze finally came, and a piece of paper fluttered in the woman's grip. He watched the woman traipse up the walkway where the paper flapped in the wind. In a matter of seconds, the woman jogged back to the car.

"Rollins, stand down. Looks to be a flyer on the door."

"Maybe it's an eviction notice."

"Always with the jokes, Rollins. Run up there and check it out. Grab a picture before the old goat realizes her Ring alarm's gone off."

* * * * * * * * * *

Rollins quickened his pace and watched over his shoulder as the Chevrolet Spark shifted into drive and headed down the street at roughly three times the speed of its approach. He hit the walkway and took the porch steps two at a time. *In and out, don't loiter and have to deal with the witch.*

When he reached the landing, the flyer hung at eye level. Rollin's brain read it as his hands fumbled with his cellphone. It wasn't an eviction notice or even a Jehovah's Witness pamphlet. *Only a promotional flyer. What's the purpose of ignoring every other house on either side of the street and only papering this one?*

LITTLE GOLF BIG TEES - PROMOTIONAL EVENT - FREE VIRTUAL REALITY MINI GOLF GAMES FOR CHILDREN 15 AND UNDER

His eyes moved to the second line as he looked through the phone to frame the photo. His thumb pressed the screen at the exact time the heavy steel door flew open. *God, I hope I fucking got it.*

Annetta Provolone stood in the doorway, fresh from the shower in a hot pink bathrobe and curlers. Rollins watched as she ripped the flyer from the door and stared him straight in the eyes. His eyes couldn't move past her large gold hoop earrings.

"What the fuck are you looking at?" Annetta said and slammed the door in his face.

****

At the same time Rollins realized his photo opportunity had shit the bed, one hundred and sixty-one miles to the west, as the Chevrolet Spark flies, Steve Rockfish readied for his camera time. Seven days prior, Decker had given the partners stellar advice regarding lying low. Rockfish had ignored each word.

Two hours after Decker had pulled away from Rockfish's house, the plan was hatched. Another six hours passed before the phone rang alongside Angel's rehabilitation bed. And now, a week later, Rockfish's giant fuck you to Provolone, Conti, Grayson and any other steaming pile of turds tuning in was about to kickoff.

Rockfish had hired a clean-up crew to clear the mini golf course's parking lot and hang large backdrops in order to keep the eyesores of what the clubhouse and course had become out of camera range. Hired help had rolled artificial grass, measuring one hundred feet on all sides, across the large swath of asphalt. Small tables placed ten feet apart across the AstroTurf. Atop each table? An N95 mask and the latest metaverse VR headset. YouTube would stream the promotional event for Little Golf Big Tees live, thanks to Angel calling in half-a-dozen favors owed him on the east coast. *Today, I settle all family business. Or at least piss many people off.* Rockfish could picture Angel saying those words.

Angel was more excited than Rockfish about the revenge plan. His assistant arranged for a camera crew to be on site, with the capability to cast individual kids' rounds of VR mini golf over the live stream. Angel took care of all things modern day technology and Rockfish handled the old school end of moving rocks.

A call to WPVI's Ann Arundel's news desk and a little sweet talk secured a five-minute taped remote from the parking lot that would run on the noon broadcast and then again on the 5pm show. No one could promise the piece would run on the prime news show at 6pm, but Rockfish didn't care. By that time, the intended audience would have either watched the stream live or caught wind of the news story. When Annetta Provolone picked her jaw up off the floor, heads would roll. Rockfish was sure of it. He counted on it.

Invitations went out via bulk email the previous evening to guarantee a large online audience. Jawnie tapped into the local YMCA day camps to make sure enough kids would be on hand to play. Their counselors and even a handful of parents would make up the on-scene viewing audience. Rockfish wanted enough kids to flood the property to make the event everything they expected. He had no problem staying until the early or even late afternoon to make sure each kid got a VR experience of what was coming to the property. A few invitations with the link to the stream had been hand delivered through the night and early morning to those expected to view online and perhaps throw various heavy objects at their smart TVs or hand-held devices.

Thirty minutes prior to the day camp bus's arrival, Rockfish checked his watch and then looked up and down the street to see if Lynn had arrived. Her text from earlier let the partners know the delivery had gone off without a hitch and she was well on her way back down I-95, with an estimated arrival time of before the camera rolled and the children set loose upon the field of play. He would need her to help Jawnie herd cats once the festivities kicked off. He, as the face and spokesman of the event, would not have time. Not to mention he wasn't a huge fan of kids under thirty.

Rockfish remained off to the side, admiring his well-oiled machine. *That we're actually pulling this off without Mr. Murphy showing up says something about our team. There will be fallout from this, and I'm going to step up and take it. Take it all. Give me all the fallout. I'm here, you dumb broad. Come get some. Fuck your minions and Conti, too.*

"Hey Steve, whatcha got going on here, buddy?"

Decker's voice startled him, but not as much as the hand on the shoulder which had Rockfish swinging around in some sort of defensive stance, ready to throw hands.

"Relax, it's only me. Nice moves through. You're going to need them after this fucking stunt."

"Dan, you can't plan a business and not give potential customers a peek into what they can expect. Good press never hurt no one."

"You couldn't tell me? My wife found this damn email invitation in our spam folder," Decker said. "I'm not sure if I would have liked it better had she not found it, or if I'd come across it last night when it came in." Rockfish could hear and feel the anger and hurt in his friend's voice.

"I'm sorry, Dan, but you know better than anyone. Sometimes it's best not to be completely forthcoming. I'm trying to get a little payback here and perhaps throw some doubt in the bad guys' minds. Plant that seed that all isn't exactly as they thought in their friendly little alliance."

"God forbid you let the authorities do their job. How can you be sure they'll be watching?"

"I had personal invites hand delivered to all of them. If they choose to not watch, well, not my problem. Someone they know or are criminally associated with will tell them about it. Either she'll call Conti screaming, or they both will shove the video down Grayson's throat. You watch what I do here today." Rockfish smiled and fully felt he was in the zone. His friend could watch, help, or both. Rockfish didn't care.

"At the very minimum, the Baltimore-based turds will sit down to watch the news over rigatoni at lunch or dinner and see the story on the local news," Rockfish said.

"I'm glad to see you have this all worked out," Decker said with a grin. "Hey, how's Raffi doing?"

"He's laid up, healing the best he can. Most likely contemplating our friendship or how he can hold this mess over my head in the near future."

"Glad I'm not the only one," Decker said. He winked and Rockfish hoped theirs was still salvageable.

"Did you spot my new wheels when you got here? Check her out," Rockfish said and pointed over to an orange Toyota Yaris parked up behind where the tarps hung.

"I would not have expected you to pick that off a car lot. What made you pick that?"

"It's a rental. Fucking Geico, man. It's the best my policy will allow. I can't even toss in some of my money for an upgrade. Dumb broad on the phone told me I would need to upgrade my entire policy instead."

"You got the money to go out and rent whatever the fuck you want."

"Principle, Dan. I have a policy that I pay for. They want me to drive that clown car. I will. But I'll make sure I whine about it to everyone I know and each customer rep I can get a hold of at that damn company."

"Never change, Steve. I'm going to hang back and watch this morning. You good with that?"

"Of course."

"I'm worried about you, bud."

"Don't be."

The friends said their goodbyes and Rockfish walked over to the news van to kick the shindig off.

Claire Spires was a one-woman remote crew, and she was setting up the camera as Rockfish approached.

"Morning, Claire. I can't thank you enough for coming out to cover this. Gonna be a hot one here shortly." Rockfish gave Claire the head-to-toe treatment, if only for her outfit of the day. She was business from the waist up and cut-off sweatpants and flip-flops from the waist down. *Hmmm, the interview will be a close-up shot. I should have really worn a better shirt.* He looked down at his Kohl's white polo. It had been free with the amount of Kolh's cash Mack had accumulated. *I really need a girlfriend before I totally give up on dressing myself like an adult. At least it was breakfast stain-free.*

Claire was the Anne Arundel community reporter for WPVI, and Rockfish had caught a handful of her stories while the news played in the background. But their history went further back, as Rockfish had secured the evidence that put her ex-husband over a barrel in their divorce case. He was an abusive bastard and Rockfish was happy to be the first domino that eventually caused the man's life to spiral out of control.

Claire had always told Steve that aside from the firm's fee, she'd be eternally grateful and, if he ever needed a favor, call. It had been eighteen months, but he finally picked up the phone a couple of days ago.

"Steve, it is so great to see you. When you called and told me what you were planning, I marched right into my supervisor's office and told him we had to cover this amazing community event."

"Thanks for coming on such short notice."

"No, thank you. I'll always owe you one."

Rockfish let Claire return to setting up the shot. He turned back towards the field of fake grass and noticed Lynn had finally arrived. *Thank God she's back and nothing happened, especially after all she's been through. Kinda surprised it took little to talk her into playing messenger. The only other option was Craigslist.* Lynn walked over to where Jawnie helped direct the kids off of the small day camp buses and onto the playing field.

"How about we give them a couple of minutes to get started over there and then we'll go," Claire said. "The kids in motion will make a great backdrop. Remember, look at the red light and follow my lead. This won't be streamed lived. We can always take a mulligan if you get flustered."

"Let's do this," Rockfish said. He was ready, willing and five minutes later he stared at the red light and took the fight directly to Annetta and her group of sad lackeys.

"... a great thing you're doing for the children today. What can you tell the viewers about your plans?"

"I want to get the word out there that we're going to reopen, despite any rumors to the contrary. Claire, I'm here to respect the wishes of the previous owners of Chesapeake Mini-Golf. We'll be open and ready for mini golfers of all ages by the Spring. I cannot wait to see parents and children back out on the course, enjoying wholesome family fun. But until then, this virtual reality shit, whoops, sorry, you can bleep that, right? This VR stuff is really cool. We'll be working with a Hollywood artist and game developer to incorporate the actual holes we will construct here into the VR game. Come down and practice up before the big opening. We'll be here today until mom rings the supper bell."

"That sounds like a lot of fun. Do you mind if I head over as soon as we're done and give it the old college try?"

"Nice one, Claire, but if you look over my shoulder, that is one heck of a line of kids waiting to take their shot. But you know the owner, so I'm sure we can fit you in before you have to head back to the studio." Rockfish said with a grin and a nod at the camera.

"That would be great! One last question, Steve and I'll let you get back to the fun and games. What about the big retail plaza plans for Avonlea Crossing and the attempted acquisition by Fulsome Commercial Realty Group of this property? Previous reports showed they tried to purchase the land for use as a proposed interstate off-ramp leading to and from the proposed retail behemoth."

"Claire, you sneaky devil. Today is for the kids. How dare you ask me a business question!" Rockfish said with a huge grin. "But I'll fill you in on something few people know. The good folks over at Fulsome promised me they were no longer interested in purchasing this property or gaining access to it by hook or by crook. Little Golf Big Tees appears not to be part of their grandiose plan after all. Matter of fact, they now see it as a great addition to their proposals. The perfect lure for families. Parents can drop off children. The kids can play a round of eighteen, enjoy a slice of pizza, and a fountain soda while their parents empty those same kids' respective college funds to buy whatever overpriced retail shit would be sold at Avonlea Crossing. Whoops, you got another edit."

Rockfish winked at the camera, but it was really intended for a much smaller audience.

* * * * * * * * *

"... *The good folks over at Fulsome promised they are no longer interested.... appear not to be part of their grandiose plan.*"

Annetta's eyes and ears were glued to the eighty-five-inch 8K television mounted over the gas fireplace. She had contemplated taking the call in her office, but the family room was larger. She expected pacing back and forth with the possibility of throwing items. The family room was cleaner, less of a chance for an errantly thrown item to do much damage. Except for the television. *If you lose it, aim downward. Ain't shit gonna bounce up off of this carpet.*

Her hands held the janky Russian-made tablet. Ignazio Conti's profile stared up. Annetta had stopped listening a couple of minutes ago to what he was saying. She focused on the stream from the television and Rockfish's stupid fucking face. *He's a dead man as soon as he signs over the property. Conti too, for all intents and purposes. He's Angelo's Barney fucking Fife. I know what I saw in him all those years ago, but how the fuck have I stuck with his incompetence this time? I won't have it on this level, fucking with my money and plans. When I resolve this in my favor, I'll talk to Angelo and tell him what I know. What Conti confided in me regarding the need for regime change. Yeah, so what? I may have put the thought in his head, but I ain't letting anyone else come out on top here."*

"Annetta, are you still there?"

"Where the fuck else would I be?" She regretted the day she agreed to his proposal for a nice cut from the Avonlea project. *I'm surrounded by idiots. How did I ever think I could drive this thing from the backseat and it would turn out successfully? Not every good earner or soldier from the past can transition to a management role. That family needs leadership and Conti ain't it. Angelo neither.*

"Are you absolutely sure the Feds haven't tapped into this?"

"They can't, because I said so," Annetta said. "How the fuck are you not watching this?" She looked down and all she could see was the man's nose hairs and eye gunk. *Christ. Is he licking the damn screen? Is it even worth the effort to tell him to pull it away from his face? Good gangsters of yore. They could still clip a guy over a perceived slight, scam a grandmother out of her last bit of retirement savings, but add a few rings to that tree and try to get them to use technology? Good luck with that.*

Annetta firmly believed she was the exception to the rule. *I will be Boss of Bosses; Capo di tutti capi even if because of these bumbling assholes, I'm giving orders from a goddamn Supermax and eating grilled cheese off the fucking radiator. RIP Phil. South Jersey, with a Baltimore merger, will put Philly back on their heels.*

"I'm on my iPad talking to you," Conti said. "Is there another way to watch YouTube?"

"Don't you have a smart TV? Jesus Christ, you can't tell me one hasn't fallen off the back of a truck in front of your guys and they didn't bring it over for you? It's 2022, for fuck's sake."

"Smart TV? I've got boxes of shit in the basement. Might be a decent TV down there, I don't know. I don't watch the idiot box. It turns your brain to mush. Not to mention I had to get my nephew over here to help me with the encyclopedia of instructions you sent so that we could do this video chat. Do you want to talk business or do you want me to open the YouTube app? Pick one. I can't do both."

Annetta took a deep breath and tapped the mute button. The stream of expletives that flew from her mouth would have had her mother blushing and her father taking her out for a congratulatory ice cream cone. *I'm backing the wrong horse in this race. The man isn't what I once thought he was. Clearly. I need to lead. No more faking it.* She unmuted Conti.

"I'd be happy if you fucking listened to me or even did a tenth of what I've asked in return for my support." She looked down at the tablet, frowned, and shook her head. Annetta wasn't sure if he could see the disappointment in her face, so she made sure Conti heard every last bit of it. "Should I hang up here and talk to Angelo? It's been a while, but I've still got his number around here."

"Annetta, don't you threaten me. Do not forget who I am. Do not misunderstand or underestimate me when I tell you this is salvageable."

"Salvage this," Annetta said, grasping her non-existent testicles over her slacks. "I thought you said you were going to take care of him? From my viewpoint, all you did is give a couple of general contractors serious hardons over how much scratch they'll make from the remodel. I throw my support behind you for the big move and this is how you repay me? Seems like amateur fucking hour down there. Time and time, again."

"Don't give me any of that crap. I'm paying you outta my cut from Avonlea. And the plan, *MY* plan, was solid. I put the fear of God into him and the ATF should have been picking up pieces of him and his fakakta partner from that parking lot for the next month. You remember her? The one you failed to get. But we're not pointing fingers here, are we?"

"Not at all," Annetta said. "Ignazio, you didn't even know she was there until you read about the three survivors in the paper the next day. Don't you dare throw this back on me." She was done. And if he even tried again after that smart remark, she'd reach through the screen and bend it so far back it would snap the fuck off. *Brittle old fuck, probably osteoporosis out the ass.* The shine was clearly off this new partnership.

"... Rockfish has no family to speak of, just his old man. If that ass didn't remote start his car, his old man would have had the screws put to him and caved the next day. We wouldn't be having this conversation."

"But we are, you fucking coglione. Rockfish is spitting in my face, live. He's fucking us royally with the biggest smile."

"If what you're telling me is true—"

"Why wouldn't it be? You continue to question every goddamn word I say. You need to stop with that shit."

Annetta stared down at the screen. Conti wrinkled his brow, and she assumed he was trying to think of what to say next. She prepared for some off the wall scheme or excuse but his line of thinking pleasantly surprised her.

"Then it has to be Grayson. Without that property, there is no offramp. No offramp, no Avonlea on the grand scale we expect. Fulsome may have caved. Downsized the scale of the project and no longer need a highway exit to accommodate the flow of traffic previously estimated? What if, for a second, what Rockfish said is true?"

Good point, not that I'll ever let him know I think that. It's easy to corroborate. Maybe an in-person visit was necessary? Yet again, but this time, my men won't trip over their own dicks.

"I'll give you that one, Ignazio. Reach out to the rat bastard. But I'm telling you, Rockfish is throwing all this shit right back in our face. He's literally saying it straight to the news camera. I don't care if Grayson called Rockfish and worked out some sort of side deal in both their interests. Can we trust this culattone? I don't think so. He's fucking us, Ignazio. Don't you feel that in your gut? If Grayson needs to go, so be it. We'll bend the next project manager over a bigger barrel and fuck him twice as hard. But I will not have my bottom line impacted any further."

"Our bottom line," Conti said.

Annetta laughed aloud. The man was nowhere near his camera. It currently pointed down at the carpet and she took that as a win. If he was scared to look her in the face, then he'd be too frightened to stand up to her next move.

"Well, my friend, my piece of that got a little bigger. I'm clearly driving this boat now. I'm sure you'll agree to a sixty-forty split in my favor. And don't even think about it. Because I'll counter with a sit-down with Angelo, and he won't like what I have to say."

Silence greeted Annetta this time.

Click click click.

She could hear a gas burner being lit in the background. *The bastard is frying up some sausages. What a pretentious cunt. The amount of disrespect.*

"Ignazio, I'm going to need that face of yours back on the tablet. What I'm going to say is very important and I need to know you understand, even if you don't agree with a damn word of it." Annetta dialed down the tone in her voice with the last sentence. She still needed him on the team and capable of taking her orders. *For the time being.*

"If you still want my help and support getting you into Angelo's chair, you're gonna have to pull over and let me drive. I can't expect you to do the right thing anymore. No offense, but your recent track record speaks for itself. Yips out the ass." *That's right. You bring up McGee, and I'll jump down your throat so fast it will make your head spin.* Annetta paused and Conti remained silent. *Good boy. Know your role.*

"Rockfish thinks he pulled one over on me today? No fucking way. I'm more determined and focused. He can have his brief minute on the news and pretend to be fucking Peter Pan to all those latchkey kids. I'm going to send Giovanni down there to work with you. Finish this once and for all."

"If Angelo gets wind of that—"

"Did I ask for your fucking opinion? What Angelo doesn't know ain't gonna hurt that old fuck. Are you implying your crew's gotta leak?"

"No."

"Good. Now this is what I want you to do..."

She told him exactly what she needed in the short term. No more, no less.

Annetta hung up the call and dropped the tablet onto the couch. She looked up at the big screen. The stream showed kids spinning around with large VR headsets on and the other half of the screen showed their avatars playing mini golf in the Metaverse. She had to admit: they looked like they were having the time of their lives.

CHAPTER TEN

Two days post Rockfish's first ever internet live stream, he continued to soak in the positive press. Lynn printed off tens of emails coming in from community activists saluting his stance against Big Retail and promised to lend what support they could. When Jawnie showed him the morning's paper and the op-ed in support of his efforts, she realized she hadn't seen him smile that widely since she'd met the man. With one hare-brained idea, he had brought sunshine and calm back to the office.

She and Lynn moved around with smiles that rivaled Rockfish's. Jawnie didn't know how long it would last but embraced it like a lost love. *The mood around this place has been through the roof since he rallied us to fight fire with fire.*

After reading the op-ed, Rockfish had walked around the office, purposely ignoring the large sheets of plywood where the tall glass windows had previously stood. He talked aloud about staying on after the shitstorm blew over to help Kara and Pilar. He mentioned leaning towards not completely walking away after selling Little Golf Big Tees back to them and getting his dollar back.

Jawnie was as happy as he was. The success of the event far exceeded her expectations, and she let him know at every opportunity. It had been a cause dear to her from the start. *I dragged him to a drag show to meet Kara and Pilar and hear their plea for help. He had answered the call in spades. Anyone of the three would continue to remind me. It was really more than a revenge thing for him. I hope.*

"If you're willing to throw your dollar or more into the ring, it's only right that I match it," Jawnie said. "Whether it be a silent partner or investor, I'm there beside you. Watching those kids play yesterday, I know this is going to turn out in our favor."

"Only a matter of catching that break," Rockfish said. "A little positive energy to fuel the fire."

Each walked back toward their office. With the doors open, they didn't have direct lines of sight, but the acoustics made their voices carry. *It's not as personal as sitting out in the bullpen area.* However, she knew that each needed time to get research done and reports filed. There were other clients, and many of them were probably not as sympathetic to their current predicament.

"I'll tell you what, I feel good mentally," Rockfish said through the open doorways. "Even my arm isn't bothering me anymore. Last couple of days it's felt as good as new."

"Good karma will do that to you."

"Speaking of which..."

Jawnie looked up from her laptop to find Rockfish standing in her doorway.

"... how's things with Rosa?" Rockfish didn't wait for an invitation and instead stepped in to re-settle himself in her guest chair.

She closed her laptop and prepared for the barrage of questions that were about to come her way. They weren't unexpected and Jawnie had a measured response for her partner's eagerness to cross the Federal Government's Computer Fraud and Abuse Act, Title 18 U.S.C. § 1030. The US Attorney she had met during the Provolone trial didn't differentiate between hacking good and bad guys. Jawnie was slow walking Rosa, hoping to not have to resort to breaking the law to find any tidbit of information that would help. *Her computer is the nuclear option for me. She's talkative and*

I should be able to get her to open up about her job. I'm sure of it. Now if I could only convince this lummox.

"Gonna need you to speed it up, McGee. Only a matter of time before my good deed from the other day causes a reaction from the other side. My bet is that it won't be a repeat of Lana's murder. I think it will actually be something legitimate, but with enough pressure to convert a Zippy turd to cubic zirconia. It may not be today or tomorrow, but it's coming. It would be fabulous if we had even the slightest advanced warning."

"I'm working on it. You don't rush these things. I push too hard, she ghosts me. I need to dance a little. Make her think she's leading." Jawnie reached down and grabbed a couple of folders off the floor. She put them on the desk and piled her backpack atop them. *Packing up, I gotta run. Let's wrap this up. Take a hint, Steve.*

"You do your thing. You know better than I. I ain't been on a date in God knows how long. But find us something. At the very least, come across the official and unofficial Fulsome party line regarding this stunt."

Jawnie nodded and kept shuffling the items on her desk before standing up. *Hint, hint.*

"Not too much longer," Rockfish added.

"I know, but I really have to get going. I've got the final reports completed for the Bauers and Cooney cases. The plan is to drop them off, pick up the checks and hit Sterling Optical for a checkup. The eyes are bothering me. Lynn says it's stress, but it's been a while since my last exam. I'll be back here later in the afternoon. I'll be on my phone if you need me."

Jawnie picked up the items on her desk and didn't wait for an answer. She hustled past Rockfish, waved to Lynn, and was out the front door before Rockfish had stepped back to his office.

The walk to her car took Jawnie past Rockfish's rental, and she laughed. *That ride really is the complete opposite of his personality. Hey, remember Lana? Can I get the opposite end of the spectrum?* She knew he was still in the beginning stages of the grieving process. He'd soon have his new girl, depending on when the microchip shortage ended. Bigger. Better. Faster. But in the meantime, he seemed content to spend part of his day on Dodge.com building new versions.

Jawnie climbed into her Subaru and placed the stack of manila folders down on the passenger seat. She punched in the address for Jim Bauers' office and hit *go*.

Four hours, two meetings that could have been emails, and one eye exam later, Jawnie stumbled out of Sterling Optical's front door. She instantly regretted not listening to the doctor. He had dilated her eyes for the exam, an experience Jawnie had somehow forgotten about. At the conclusion, he had recommended killing some time in the waiting room before heading outside. Especially if she didn't have someone picking her up.

The sun's rays defeated her heavily discounted designer sunglasses the moment the door opened and her foot hit the sidewalk. *You'd think these were a pair of cheap Chinese knockoffs. Damn, did I get ripped off?* Jawnie spun around, felt for the door handle and retreated to the safety of the waiting room and soft lighting. The room was small and she bounced off the magazine rack in her hurry. The receptionist from behind a glass window stared.

"Can I help you, ma'am? Did you forget something?" The receptionist said. "Do you need us to call someone for you?"

Holy crap, how pathetic do I look right now?

"No, I'm cursing my stupidity, but thanks for the concern. I think if I squint real hard, I might make it to my car. At least there I can wait out the eye drops and maybe get something accomplished."

The woman nodded and returned to her computer screen. Jawnie gave it ten minutes before the anger of being completely helpless lessened. She stood up and approached the door. "Okay, wish me luck."

Jawnie didn't wait for any words of encouragement from the receptionist. She pushed open the door and stepped outside. The pain and lack of visibility were everything she remembered. She squinted and attempted to navigate the sidewalk, using the world's smallest crack between her eyelids. Jawnie had parked the car two blocks over on the third level of the parking garage. She reached into her pocket to double check for the parking ticket the receptionist had validated. *Now let's hope I can see well enough to give the attendant the right credit card.*

Her pace was slow and methodical. Sidewalk square by sidewalk square. By the time she reached the parking garage, Jawnie felt proud of what she had accomplished. She chose the stairwell on the outside corner of the garage instead of walking inside and attempting to locate the elevator. The stairs were closer to her car, and if she remembered right, there was only the one set. She moved faster up the stairs, using the handrail as a guide and lucked out that no one else came down in the opposite direction.

Once out of the stairwell and onto the third level, Jawnie looked for the red painted markers along the columns. Those in front of her were orange. *I think they're orange.* She squinted harder and the dimness inside the garage made her almost think she could see again. *You need red to make orange, so I must be close.*

"Excuse me, ma'am."

The words hit her ears at the same time a hand landed on her shoulder. Jawnie spun around and assumed a defensive stance. A shadowy figure stood before her, their arm still outstretched.

"Who are you!" Jawnie's lack of vision, a dark parking garage and the stranger before her had every one of her senses tingling and not in a good way.

"Look lady, I was told to give—"

Jawnie caught the flash of a shadow rising from her left. She acted out before the expected blow could land. The kick landed square between the man's legs and he crumpled to the cement floor with a long moan. Jawnie stepped back and held her hands up in case the man leapt up, but he remained on the ground, both hands grasping between his legs.

"Holy hell, lady, I have a delivery for you. What the fuck is your problem? Aggggggh."

Jawnie looked around on the concrete and spotted the white envelope. It stood out against the dirty floor. She shuffled over and picked it up, keeping one eye on the man on the ground. *Was he telling the truth or was he some sexual predator with a daylight and parking garage delivery kink?* With the envelope in hand, she stepped back and began her own line of questioning.

"Are you a process server?"

"No. Some guy outside pointed you out and gave me thirty bucks if I followed you to your car and handed you this envelope." The man struggled back to his feet and, for his own protection, stepped away from where Jawnie now stood. *He's not over twenty. I've had better facial hair than this kid.* His clothes spoke volumes. They were dirty and torn. *I'm sure he could use thirty dollars for a couple of decent meals or one solid fix.*

Jawnie took a step forward, no longer in fear, fully intending to apologize for her actions. She hadn't gotten the offer to drop him off at an Urgent Care out of her mouth, before he shot her the finger and took a wide path around her towards the stairwell. Despite her vision slowly returning, there was nothing wrong with her hearing. It sounded as if the messenger boy was taking the stairs two at a time. He would be out and down the street before she could make it to her car. *He moved pretty good there for taking a Sergio Rossi leather boot to the junk. Was he really alone? Get your ass to the car. Don't think. Do.*

Jawnie found the Subaru and fell into the driver's seat. She locked the doors and exhaled. Despite being shaken, she was never in any real danger, but that didn't mean she couldn't be happy with her performance. Rockfish had pressed for her to take self-defense classes since she joined him in Maryland. She had put it off, much like getting her concealed carry permit. Now that the permit was days away, she'd give serious thought to signing up for some Jiu-Jitsu or Krav Maga. She owed it to herself.

When her breathing slowed, Jawnie hoped her pupils were close to returning to their normal state. She wouldn't be able to tell sitting in the dark garage. Her options were to hang out in the car a little longer or roll the dice and head out. Jawnie checked her mirrors and when looking right, she spotted the envelope. She had thrown it down as she collapsed into the seat and, despite it being the center of all that had happened, she had completely forgotten about it.

She reached for it and held it close to her face. The return address and logo in the upper left corner slowly came into focus. Fulsome Commercial Realty Group.

****

"... to meet with Fulsome Commercial Realty Group's Avonlea Crossing Manager Luther Grayson, members of the General Counsel's office and other managers tied to this vital community revitalization project."

The partners sat in Rockfish's office. The lights dimmed for Jawnie, despite her still wearing sunglasses. She had driven straight back to the office, without causing an accident, nor playing Roshambo with anyone else. When she handed Rockfish the envelope, his eyes grew large, and he hustled her back to his office.

"I mean, it kind of makes sense," Rockfish said, still holding the letter in front of his face.

"The meeting?"

"Sort of. Not long after you left for Bauers, the phone lines started blowing up. The caller ID showed Fulsome Commercial Realty Group and Lynn said the person on the line was an administrative assistant wanting to speak with you or me."

"What did they say?" Jawnie said.

"Beats the hell out of me. I let them all go to voicemail. If it's important, they'll call back. And they did. Again and again."

"You haven't listened to them?" Jawnie said. Rockfish could hear the agitation in her voice.

"Not yet, which also explains why they sent someone to physically reach out. It makes me wonder if you were being followed the minute you left this parking lot. And why?" The confrontation was one more thing for him to worry about. Slowly chipping away at all the good feelings from the past couple of days.

"I didn't catch anyone on my tail. I've been more cautious and observant than ever."

"I'm sure you were kid. Sometimes the unavoidable happens and we have to be ready. Based on what you said, one of those boots did the heavy lifting for us today." Rockfish let out a laugh and shook his head. "I have to ask, when you kicked him, did you go all Bobby Hill and scream, *That's my purse, I don't know you?*" The laughs came from Rockfish again, and despite the look on Jawnie's face, he rolled with them. He laughed harder and felt a tear emerge from the corner of his eye. "You don't know what I'm talking about yet again."

"Another pop culture reference from last century. Whoosh, right over my head," Jawnie said. She rolled her eyes and took a step away from him.

Rockfish kept laughing.

"I am scheduled to pick up my concealed carry permit soon. Next time, I'll wave it around, scare him, and save future generations." Jawnie pursed her lips and Rockfish could read the room.

It's time to get back to the matter at hand.

"Okay, last thing on this. I'm glad you finally finished with the gun safety instruction. Well, after today, hell after the past year, I might suggest you finally take me up on the firm paying for some self-defense classes. Someone else in this office needs to throw a punch. I'm getting too old for this shit."

"I'd be happy to sign up with you, Jawnie," Lynn said, her voice traveling from her desk up front.

"Are we that loud?" Rockfish asked, lowering his voice substantially.

"You were getting quite full of your jokes there the last five minutes," Lynn said.

Rockfish took a deep breath. "Let's get back to the letter. I could do nut-shot-jokes all day long."

"I figured as much," Jawnie said. She reached across the desk and picked up the piece of paper.

"Okay, then gimme your thoughts on it," Rockfish said. He leaned back in his chair and crossed his arms.

"It reads like a simple mediation request," Jawnie said. "The last step before they consider some sort of legal action on their part. What legal leg do they have to stand on?"

"You're asking me? I don't know. I'm more of a 1-877 CASH NOW kinda guy. It all might be a shitty legal scare tactic, since everything else up to this point has failed. They probably don't have any kind of legal standing. We might need to bring in Giacchino to weigh our options at that point. She might be in a better position to advise than the lawyer we currently retain."

"I think we need to slow down here. I'm trying to process all this," Jawnie said. Her eyes were back on him, staring across the desk. She had stopped reading. "Do you seriously think with all that's gone on, they'll lay down their arms and try to beat us in court?"

"I absolutely think it is odd, but we can't look past it," Rockfish said. "Stranger shit has happened. Like I said, their intimidation tactics have failed. Both by Brick and then Conti's men. Violence, heinous violence at that, has gotten them nowhere. Should it surprise us if they switch it up and go all hardcore business negotiations? This is a huge win on our part. At the very least, I think the initial offers made to Kara and Pilar will be back on the table. Let's consider someone at Fulsome realizes that kind of shit ain't working and some of that stench is sticking to them. Grayson and Brick's actions aside, they've got shareholders to think of. If any of this got out... Remember, since we learned about this project, it's—"

"Too big to fail. I know."

"Trust me, kid, too many important people have way too much invested in this project for it to go tits up. We might as well listen to what they have to say. Can't hurt and it might give us options to play with."

"Listen, but not even remotely consider, right?"

"Not in a million years. So what does that piece of paper say about a date and time? I never got that far. Not to mention I can't believe you didn't rip it open in the parking garage or at a red light."

"Sorry I saved my squinting for the road. I wanted to get back here in one piece." She glanced down. "Next week. Tuesday, late afternoon. 3:30pm. We've got some time to work with."

With their initial strategizing session coming to a close, Jawnie got up and walked back to her office. Rockfish turned off his computer monitor and dropped his head into his hands. He contemplated support options for the meeting, besides a legal mind. *Support as in muscle. They probably won't let me walk in with a small army, but at least one other person who looked like they mean business might be of some help. I doubt anyone around that table intends to bring the pain. After all, that was Conti's job, and he had failed time and time again. Albeit, Gordon would beg to differ. Better to be safe than sorry.*

Rockfish reached over for the remote on the desk and turned off the television. He hoped that with the screen off, it wouldn't distract him. He could think more clearly and, of course, faster. *Because that's what I need right now. I wonder if Decker, in an official or unofficial capacity, would want to attend? He showed up to VR day. Couldn't hurt to ask. Shit. What if the bad guys are there?*

I bet someone there would recognize him. Can't chance it. Bad guys know cops. It's part of their job.

Rockfish stood up and walked across the hall and stood in Jawnie's doorway. A moment passed before she noticed him and lifted her eyes from the laptop on her desk.

"Jawnie, I've been thinking about this meeting. We need to let someone important know where we'll be and that we'll give any offer they make lip service. That way neither of us will be worried or feel in any danger. That I can see."

"So, us alone?"

"Do we really need anyone else?"

"Absolutely not." Jawnie stood up and leaned across the desk. The partners' fists met, and they each nodded in agreement.

"We're good, kid. This ain't no abandoned gas station. There will be a tape of us walking into the building, and I'll let Decker know where we'll be. And if shit goes sideways, you aim for the first set of nuts you see."

Jawnie laughed aloud. Rockfish saw his in.

"The real reason I made the long trek across the hallway is I want to speak about this whole Rosa Mangold deal." He stepped into her space and sat in the guest chair. He reached behind him and pushed the door shut. *No need for Lynn to hear any of this, but I'd bet my bottom dollar these two talked back at the condo like schoolgirls.* Mentally, he shrugged his shoulders and moved forward with the topic at hand.

"We need some kind of inside baseball before we walk through those sliding glass doors. I feel we're at a severe disadvantage, not knowing what their game plan is. I don't work well with surprise. If there's going to be an 'A-HA!' moment, it needs to come from our side. "

"We're back to this, huh?"

"Yes."

"Exactly what federal law are you looking for me to cross? I can repeat Title 18 U.S.C. § 1030 verbatim because I've read it that many times since you've wanted me to go down this road."

"With everything that's happened, they aren't running to the police. Plus, I got faith in your skills. Ain't no one going to catch you creeping on their network. Look at all these computer brainiac books you got along the wall."

"I've seen how eager you are when you've got an idea you won't let go of," Jawnie said. "I dealt with it back in Scrumsville when you wanted the GPS-tracking data on Porbeagle analyzed every hour. But you listened to me and my skills then. Worked out for us, didn't it? I told you I would exhaust every other option before I entertained that one."

"Well, we're kind of under a short deadline now. It's why I brought it up. You know me. I'll push and push, but if the end call is yours to make, I'll agree with your decision every time."

"I know. And that's why we make such a good team."

"But if I can continue?" Rockfish said.

"I also knew that was coming."

"What if it's a work laptop she's using?"

"And using company property for non-official stuff? Like flirting with me over?"

"Not everyone has the high ethics of our team here," Rockfish said. "*If* it is, then there really are no concerns about running roughshod over her privacy concerns."

"I see where you're coming from. But here's mine. What if I start this by sending a document, picture, or a malicious link to fool her? What if it sits untouched prior to the meeting and we walk into that conference room on Tuesday and she's sitting right there?"

"Maybe nothing?"

"Nothing? How long has it been since you actually flirted with a woman? And don't include any on the job experiences." The look on Jawnie's face told Rockfish she knew exactly how long it had been.

"I plead the Fifth," Rockfish said.

"Exactly. Her hackles would go up so fast and she'd be on the defensive from the get-go the next time I reached out. If she even responds. I'm betting in this scenario she'd block me before we got back to the car."

"All the more reason to move now." Rockfish raised his eyebrows for emphasis.

"Stop me if you've heard this one before," Jawnie said. "This is the case of last resort, and I'm not there yet. You'll be the first to know should I swap my white hat for a black one. Trust me."

"Okay. I'm officially laying off."

"Speaking of the meeting, for the four-hundredth time in the last hour, are you going to return those voicemails and RSVP?"

"Let's make them sweat a little more than they already are. I'll have Lynn reach back out on Monday and confirm."

"Agreed. Now I'm going to get back to my research here before heading home," Jawnie said. "This has been a fucked up day. There's a nice bottle of red wine with my name on it."

"One last thing, if you don't mind."

"What do you need?"

"That's my purse! I don't know you!" His belly laugh echoed through the space and Rockfish could see Lynn covering her face at her desk.

****

Saturday night found Jawnie and Lynn sitting in different parts of the condo, dateless, and each contemplating different ways to kill time until their eyelids refused to stay open. Lynn had piled various cheeses and crackers on a plate and dropped half off for Jawnie on the coffee table next to the couch. She then retreated to her bedroom with the rest, a book tucked under her arm along with a full glass of wine. It wasn't long before Jawnie spotted the flashes of light coming from under Lynn's door and assumed she had moved on to a movie or the latest action-adventure streaming series. Roommates practicing common courtesies were never easy to find. Lynn loved her superhero universe and had no second thoughts about streaming through her ear buds.

Jawnie got up off the couch and grabbed a piece of cheese. She dimmed the lights in the small living room and flopped back on the couch. She piled some pillows behind her back and sat up, longwise, with her knees drawn up and the iPad leaning back against her thighs.

Rockfish's words had bounced around in her head as she checked for any messages from Rosa throughout the day. Anytime the notification bell rang, Jawnie was on the device hoping to accomplish whatever she was supposed to and praying those actions would ratchet her anxiety down a few notches. *Because sitting in this condo, on pins and needles all day, ain't doing a damn thing to help lower it.*

Her thoughts turned from the annoyance of anticipation of actually having to mislead someone. A person who might be totally innocent when it came to Fulsome's tom-fuckery.

What if Rosa started a more serious line of conversation about what I did for a living or the company I work for? We've been able to keep the subject pretty generic in our first couple of chats. Rehashing and playing coulda woulda shoulda regarding the Labor Day flirt-a-thon has been the go-to topic and easy to maintain. I could go with the flow and lie. Tell her I'm the Executive Vice President over Acquisitions at Mergers at Wilhelm, Gicobe and Stottlemyer? With my luck, I'd walk into that meeting on Tuesday and she'd be in the seat at the right hand of Grayson. Then I've killed Steve's dreams of any chance at inside information and set myself up to look like the bad guy. Jawnie kicked at the pillows by her feet in frustration. *Damned if I do, damned if I don't.* She kicked again and a large yellow pillow fell to the floor. She stretched her legs out and pressed the bottom of her feet hard against the couch's far arm.

Damned if she invaded an innocent person's digital privacy. Damned if she didn't make sure her team walked into that meeting armed to the teeth, in every respect expecting the other side's home run swing. *Not to mention Pilar and Kara's dreams, plans for a business and all they've gone through.* That line of thought filled her head and played devil's advocate, pushing for Steve's way of progressing forward.

What exactly Rosa's employment was, at Fulsome, was next up on the anxiety hit parade. If Rosa does work for Grayson in some higher up capacity, other than making copies, and is involved in the Avonlea Crossing project, she sure would know about the meeting and the names Steve Rockfish and Jawnie McGee. *Maybe I'm flying under the radar as Steve is the focus now because of his dollar investment? But if she knows more about me than I think, then why is she doing this online dance with me?*

Rockfish's voice filled a small sound void in the back of her brain. Jawnie had a feeling he had been listening all along. *You better get to her first before she spins you into revealing something you shouldn't.*

Jawnie put the iPad down on the table next to the small plate of cheese and let out a long sigh. The mental gymnastics left her exhausted. She stood up and stretched, arms far above her head. Jawnie picked up her wineglass and headed to the kitchen for a refill. *And maybe a handful of Triscuits.* She ended up settling for the box over her small hands when the notification bell went off.

Jawnie walked back to the couch, put down the crackers and picked up the iPad. She swiped down and hoped the notification was for Mack posting yet another picture of Zippy and tagging her. He didn't really understand that if they were friends, his posts would automatically show up on her wall and she was too tired or frustrated to play help desk. But the minute the sound burrowed deep in her ear canal; she knew who it was. *Just thinking it was for a cute dog picture won't make this any easier.*

The Notification Center listed only one, and it wasn't a surprise or something as cute as Zippy balancing a treat on his muzzle. Facebook's Messenger Icon was prominent, as was the name Rosa

Mangold. The message under those was short: *U up?* Jawnie swallowed hard and opened the app.

There was little flirtatious chit-chat and Jawnie soon realized something wasn't right and Rosa was looking for an ear to bend. Someone who would read her bitch moaning and make her feel better than at the start of the chat.

Rosa Mangold had done the right thing. She felt sick and stayed home from work on Friday. Not long after calling in, she received one herself. Her step-father relayed her mother had fallen at their house in the Outer Banks. The old woman was more sore than anything but was under doctor's orders to remain off her feet for the next week. Rosa didn't listen or remember the rest of the call. She packed a small bag and then spent Friday night making the drive while running through an entire box of tissues. She awoke to the smell of salt water and feeling worse.

"You're positive?" Jawnie typed.

"Yes. Now I can't even help my mom. I'm stuck for the next two weeks in their guest bedroom. My step-dad is going to have to take care of two now."

"I thought the CDC had knocked it down to a week. You're all vaxxed and boosted, right?" Jawnie typed. A weight was lifted off her chest as the news sunk in as she hit send. There would be no Rosa sitting around Tuesday's conference table. And without direct knowledge of Fulsome's HR manual, Jawnie assumed the chances Grayson would have her video conference into the meeting were slim and none.

"Fulsome policy is still two weeks. I'm glad my boss is understanding and not one of those hoax believers. I offered to VPN in with my personal laptop and he shut that down right quick. Said to rest and come back to us when you can. He's a great guy."

And there's the direct knowledge. Maybe Tuesday will only be a nine on the fuckery scale now, instead of the ten or more I assumed it would be a few minutes ago.

Jawnie wrapped up the conversation soon after, lecturing Rosa to get as much rest as possible. She wished her a quick recovery and left the door open to reach out anytime during quarantine.

Mission somewhat accomplished. Jawnie had learned of Rosa's ability to Remote Desktop into her office computer and gain access to the Fulsome network. The information wasn't much, but she hoped it would satisfy Steve for the time being. Jawnie still couldn't get over the ethical hump of what Rockfish wanted done.

She remained on the couch and finished the glass of wine. She lay there, hoping Mack would post a late-night Zippy picture as a palate cleanser. It didn't come and her eyes grew heavy. She'd text one more person before she could collapse into bed.

"You awake? Rosa reached out. Got a little something, not much. Will fill you in tomorrow."

"Hey Jawnie, it's Mack. Steve got his new phone up and running today. You can reach him at his old number. Want to see a picture of what Zippy did?"

"Of course!" While Jawnie waited for the picture, she copied and pasted the first message and waited for Rockfish's response. It came before the picture of Zippy.

"We're running out of time and you're spinning your front wheels. I'm headed over to see how Raffi's doing around lunchtime tomorrow. More than welcome to come."

Jawnie could read the disappointment and potential anger in Rockfish's reply. She tried to keep hers upbeat. "I know and I will. Text me when you leave the house."

She walked to the bedroom and was half undressed when Mack's upload finally arrived. The silver Labrador looking as innocent as ever atop the kitchen island gave Jawnie the smile she needed.

CHAPTER ELEVEN

Late Sunday morning, Rockfish battled traffic as churches along his route had set their parishioners loose on the roadways. Each car or SUV exiting its righteous parking lot would find its way into the tight space between Rockfish and the car in front of him. He had no choice but to let them in as yet another claim to Geico was not on his to-do list for the day. Although the thought crossed his mind. *Maybe I could get an upgraded rental if I somehow total this damn Yaris?*

The offending vehicles, loaded with annoying, pro-life families, or giant boats from the late 80s with a couple of blue hairs in the front seats, would immediately start tapping the brakes. *Damn rubberneckers.* They slowed, looking for the least crowded Bob Evans or Cracker Barrel to continue soaking in the Holy Spirit through sweet tea and a biscuit with gravy.

Each set of brake lights reminded Rockfish of how late he was running. His eyes searched the strange dashboard for a clock to no luck. He reached down and felt for his phone. The quick glance almost cost him as the Yaris' front collision aversion system, the only real accessory in the elongated rolling orange, locked up the brakes and brought the car to a stop inches from the rear bumper of a Cadillac Fleetwood Brougham from the previous century. Rockfish let loose with a flurry of curses. He stared down at the driver, but the large blue beehive never once looked back in the rearview. A drink at Raffi's settling his nerves couldn't come soon enough. *Maybe four. Jawnie could drive me home if needed.*

He pulled up to Jawnie's building almost half an hour late. She was waiting outside and slid into the passenger seat.

"Here, I know how much you like the coffee from the lobby," Jawnie said. She handed Rockfish a Styrofoam coffee cup.

"Thanks, I didn't get you anything," Rockfish said. He followed her eyes as they stayed on the cup and his shaky hands.

"Please don't tell me those shakes are from the DTs. Is there something you're not telling me? I have nothing on me to help stop them."

"It's more from a shitload of horrible drivers circling the city looking for the cheapest shit on a shingle they can find."

"Shit on a shingle?"

"A Navy classic. Mack force-fed it to me while growing up. I'll make sure he whips you up a vegan version, if there is such a thing." Rockfish took a sip of the coffee and placed it in a cup holder before pulling out onto the street.

"I know you're bullshitting me, but I look forward to anything that Mack whips up when I'm over. So, about the rental. I see you haven't won your battle with Geico yet?"

"I hate that freakin' lizard."

"More than you hate Apple? I'm glad your new phone is finally operational."

"Yup, and I still haven't figured out how to transfer over half my shit. It's supposedly floating around in the cloud somewhere, but I'll be damned if I can lasso it. Mack's Cricket thing ain't looking too bad right about now."

The drive from Jawnie's condo to Raffi's apartment was short. The Yaris took a slight detour so the partners wouldn't arrive empty-handed. Rockfish hit the strip mall's liquor store and remembering it was Sunday, waited in line the last ten minutes until the clock struck noon with the other degenerates. When the line finally moved, he grabbed two twelve-year-old aged bottles of

Bushmills Single Malt. *What's good for the goose, and shit at that price, why not grab one for home?* He met Jawnie back at the car and saw the enormous bouquets of flowers now taking up the entire backseat.

"He didn't die."

"I know, but it's the thought that counts."

They parked the Yaris as close as they could, and it still took two trips to carry all the flowers. Jawnie knocked and Raffi opened the door in a long sleeve t-shirt and basketball shorts. Rockfish gave his friend the once over and nodded to himself. *The guy didn't look half bad after many days of rest and ice compresses. At the least, he could tell people he used to be a boxer.*

"Wassup mis amigos? If I had known you were stopping by, I wouldn't have taken that extra pain pill. You'll forgive me if I doze off. It's not a direct reflection on the company, you understand."

"Oh, we do. Now can we come in?" Rockfish said, his arms straining from the weight of two of the arrangements.

"Sure, sure. Put the flowers down on the dinette. I'll grab a couple of glasses."

"You sure that's a good idea with the meds?" Jawnie said, while throwing a sideways glance at her partner.

"It's a great idea," Raffi said, stepping into the kitchen. "Ask Steve."

"Can confirm, good buddy."

For the next hour, Rockfish sipped Irish Whiskey, and they both listened as Raffi talked about revenge, his newfound love for big pharma, and how the unique shape of his nose would hurt his dating prospects. He wasn't a happy camper about lowering his standards. But he mostly raged about revenge.

When Rockfish slipped up and mentioned the meeting at Fulsome the day after next and Conti may or may not be in attendance with Harold, Raffi insisted on attending.

"There is strength in numbers. If they've got hangers-on there, I need to be, too. Plus, I want them to see me. See that I'm behind you and not backing down after that half-assed beating." Raffi leaned back in his chair and crossed his arms.

"I get it, but I need you on the sidelines. Not where one of these clowns can come across you. Out of sight, out of mind. It's all about convincing them you've taken your beating and retreated. Pulled yourself out of the game, so to speak. Then we spring your ass on them when they least expect it. You get where I'm coming from?"

Raffi sat back up and Rockfish thought for a second his friend was going to keep on insisting.

"Stevie, I ain't in any kind of shape to go against your wishes like I could before. Now this could be all the meds talking, but whatever you need, you got it. If listening and doing exactly what you say for a change will get me a shot at kicking Conti's head in, so be it."

"Good. I need a secret weapon," Rockfish said. He was thankful for the booze and pills helping calm the man who otherwise was way too energetic and erred on the side of going off half-cocked. "My, or should I say our, other attempts at working up some sort of surprise for these fuckers of late have fallen flat." Rockfish regretted saying it as soon as he did. He gritted his teeth and kept his head straight, but his eye swung hard right to glimpse Jawnie. She had a pissed off look and stared back at him. *Well, I guess I set the talking points for the ride back.*

It wasn't long after his faux pas that Rockfish and Jawnie stood up and quietly crept out of the apartment and left Raffi in his chair, head tilted back and snoring away, in his chair.

Rockfish started the Yaris and tested the waters. "Do you think he'd be okay doing a little work for us? Down the road at some point? When he's in less pain, of course."

Silence and crossed arms met and answered his question.

Okay, asshole, how are you going to fix this before you pull up to her building? You can't ignore it and hope everything is puppies and roses Tuesday when you show up at Fulsome. Think dumbass.

"Jawnie, I'm sorry for that perceived slight back there. I know you're doing what you can with what you have," Rockfish said after an additional couple of minutes of silence. He owned up to it, hoping Jawnie would get whatever she's holding back out in the open and get them past it. "Not to mention how you feel about it."

"I was going to tell you, I had a conversation last night with her," Jawnie said. She slouched in the seat, arms firmly crossed. "She's vaxxed but currently quarantining at her mother's house in the Outer Banks after testing positive for Omicron 3.0."

"No chance of being at the meeting, then?"

"Obviously."

Rockfish smiled to himself. She was talking again, and he needed to listen. He threw on his blinker and merged into the right lane. The blinker remained on and he swung the Yaris into a parking lot. He pulled into a space off to the side, away from where others had parked.

"What are you doing?" Jawnie said.

"I need to concentrate on what you're saying," Rockfish said and slid the car into park. "Not the other cars. Not trying to figure out where the damn air conditioning knob is on this piece of shit. This strange car needs a lot of attention when I'm driving. Attention I can't give you."

Jawnie smiled, and Rockfish patted himself on the back for learning. A year ago, they would have ridden back to her building in silence with nothing settled.

"Thanks, Steve. I learned a little nugget last night," Jawnie said, and recounted Rosa's request to her supervisor to work from home. "She can work remotely, but her boss told her not to worry about it. It sounded to me like she uses a Remote Desktop program. That software is notoriously riddled with vulnerabilities that are never patched."

"Then you can do that voodoo that you do," Rockfish said, trying not to rub his hands together over their good fortune. *I can't afford to piss her off again.*

"I can and I won't. Based on everything she's told me; she's not involved in this at all. And before you ask, yes, I believe her," Jawnie said. She turned in the seat so she faced her partner instead of staring straight out the windshield. "If she had any part in this deal, or whatever the hell tomorrow is, she'd teleconference in from the Outer Banks. But her boss explicitly told her to take the two weeks off and concentrate on her health. She's a small administrative cog in the Fulsome wheel, no more, no less. We won't get a damn thing from her if we execute your plan. Well, other than a guilty conscious and maybe, if we're lucky, a knock on the door from the FBI or Secret Service." She re-crossed her arms and shifted slightly in the seat.

"No one's threatening Biden."

"They also handle computer crimes," Jawnie said with a grimace.

Rockfish shook his head. He wanted to throw a couple of hard punches at the steering wheel. *Damn Yaris. Fucking Geico.* Instead, he gave it a tight squeeze with both hands. *All I can do now is bottle it up and wait for Jawnie to get out of earshot before I shake it up and pull the tab.* The old Rockfish was a pro at stuffing his emotions down, deep inside. It wouldn't be hard to channel his former self. He asked one last question.

"You said this a minute ago, but honestly she didn't move up the food chain with Brick getting three hots and a cot?"

"It doesn't sound it. If she was an admin assistant to Brick, she's still in that role to some other schlub. I don't see any reason to keep hoping this avenue will offer us up something of importance."

"Unless you're making a love connection."

Rockfish never saw the punch to his shoulder coming.

* * * * * * * * * *

Tuesday afternoon found the partners dressed in business suits and looking more professional than they had in a while. Jawnie had mentioned searching her memory for the last time they were both dressed to the nines. She settled on the day the office opened and the Chamber of Commerce was on site for the ribbon cutting. A lot had changed since that day, ninety-nine percent of it for the good. *As for today, I'm not sure which side of the ledger it's going to fall on: the good, the bad or the ugly.*

Jawnie had offered to drive to Fulsome headquarters building, but Rockfish insisted on taking the Yaris. He mumbled something about putting as much wear and tear on the shitty rental as he could before Geico asked for it back. Plus, he needed to make a stop on the way. Jawnie didn't ask where, but he could see the curiosity in her face when he wasn't forthcoming.

Rockfish put on his blinker and pulled into the Giant shopping center.

"Hang out here, I'll be back in a jiffy," he said. He returned ten minutes later with a box of supermarket donuts and a carafe of coffee.

"You will not win them over with that," Jawnie said. "Oh, look a Boston creme. I love those. Of course, we'll re-route the off ramp around your property. Thanks for coming."

"Who said it's for them? But seriously, office jockeys love this shit. Don't they?"

"Maybe twenty years ago, or if the attendees are as old as you and need that sugar high to stay awake this afternoon."

"See, that's why I have you," Rockfish said. "I did not know. I've never worked in an actual office until I met you." He smiled and tapped the steering wheel with his hand.

For the rest of the ride, Jawnie peppered Rockfish with questions regarding the outcome he was hoping for, expected, or would settle for. His answers didn't disappoint or surprise.

"Nothing. Zero. Zilch. We ain't selling or dealing. I expect extreme frustration to where we're escorted back out, not long after sitting down."

"Make sure you grab the snacks on our way out. Giant won't give you the deposit back without the carafe."

"Funny, McGee. This is a fishing expedition. Too big to fail, remember? Both sides of the table will do a little dance. The other side will think they are leading and hopefully spill something about their plan. That's all I can hope for with this boondoggle. Because we need something. Anything."

Jawnie nodded, her facial expression hoped Rockfish would continue. He saw the interest in her eyes and did.

"I need a piece of their plan. Every option to date has failed and now I'm holding the deed. Not Kara and Pilar. In the end, maybe they'll build around us. We'll, uh, I mean the girls, will need to invest in some of those noise barriers you see on the interstates."

"I knew it. Power of the donut." The partners fist bumped over the center console and shared a laugh.

Rockfish pulled into one of the guest parking spaces up front. Jawnie glanced toward the front of the building and spotted two security guards, dressed in the greyest of uniforms, standing on either side of the visitor's entrance.

"Looks like they rolled out the welcoming committee for us. This time," she said.

One guard exchanged guest stickers for the donuts and coffee. The partners peeled the stickers and placed them on the front of their suit coats. The other guard held the door open. They were led inside, past the main security desk and down a long, familiar hallway.

"Déjà vu," Jawnie whispered as they entered the hallway where, on their previous visit, they'd glimpsed Brick and Rosa. This time, the hallway was empty. The guards led them to an elevator, which they took to the fourth floor. Then led to the right, down a hallway, around a left corner and to a conference room door.

The hands-free guard held open the door. Jawnie stepped towards it but stopped when she heard Rockfish arguing with the second guard over his party favors.

"Right through that door. They're waiting on you," the taller guard said as his partner waited.

"What about my donuts and coffee? I paid for those. Need them in the meeting. I have a medical condition." Rockfish said.

The guard ignored Rockfish's pleas and instead handed them to a petite woman, who turned and carried them further down the hall and eventually out of sight.

Jawnie heard Rockfish grumbling under his breath as he followed her through the doorway and into the conference room.

The room was smaller than Rockfish expected. A large oval table ran perpendicular to the door. Three older, distinguished men sat on the far side of the table. He only recognized the one to the far left, Luther Grayson. A retractable video screen, like they had back at the office, was in the down position directly behind the men. Pictures of what he assumed were previous real estate development projects hung on the walls. Rockfish gave Jawnie an elbow to the ribs to get her attention. She followed his eyes to the right wall, where another trio sat below the pictures.

"Conti, Bianchi and Harold. He's Conti's personal bodyguard and driver," Rockfish said under his breath. "They're the intimidation factor. Probably to make sure we take the deal. You know, because they've done such a bang-up job until this point."

Jawnie nodded and pulled out a chair facing directly across from the three men at the table.

"Hey guys," Rockfish said with a wave to the men along the wall. The men stared back with stern faces and angry body language hidden by pinstripe suits. "Youse waiting for the kid's table to be brought in? By the way, Raphael Pérez, sends his sincerest Fuck You." Rockfish placed his fingertips under the chin, pointing toward his neck and then swiftly flicked them outward at the mobsters. *Italian salutes. I got a few up my sleeve.*

Harold stood up, but an arm across his chest stopped him. Rockfish looked at Conti. The man smiled widely and nodded. His facial expression screamed confidence and intimidation. *He finds this whole thing funny. I got news for—*

Rockfish felt Jawnie pull at his suit coat. She had already sat down and wanted him to do likewise. *I gotcha. You want to get this started and be on the road before rush hour. Not to mention keep Harold's back planted firmly against that wall.*

"Mr. Rockfish, the sooner you take your seat, we can get this meeting started and the sooner you can carry on your conversation with the others, if you so choose," the man seated at the middle of the table said.

"Hey Luther. How's it hanging?" Rockfish said as he slid into his chair.

"Mr. Rockfish, Ms. McGee, I'm Winston Warrington, Chief General Counsel for Fulsome Commercial Realty Group. To my left is Chadly Slanderson, Associate Chief, and you already know Mr. Grayson, Avonlea's Project Manager."

"Good afternoon," Jawnie said. She looked over at Rockfish. He had pursed his lips and stared straight through Warrington. The look was his normal game face. He once told her, don't let the sarcasm fool you. It's a distraction for the other guy.

"Let's cut to the chase here," Grayson said. His injection into the conversation didn't appear to go over well with the other lawyers at the table. "You need to come to your goddamn senses and take this offer."

"Ah, let me speak to the compensation package, Luther," Warrington said. "I understand you are the new owner, Mr. Rockfish. I haven't had the pleasure of dealing with you on this matter, but from what I understand, both sides made mistakes early in these negotiations." Warrington leaned forward and folded his hands on the table. "You need to understand for the betterment of the community, this project needs to move forward. Fast tracked, as the younger associates say. No one has seen the growth and income it will bring to the area in that part of town since the 1950s."

Slanderson reached down and placed a large maroon folder on the table. He slid it across the table in Jawnie's direction, but Rockfish's hand shot out and stopped the folder directly in front of him.

"This is our latest proposal for the property. It is more than any sum offered to Ms. Dampen and Ms. Lipton," Warrington said. "You are welcome to take it with you and have proper representation throughly review the contents."

"If you know what's best for you," Conti said from the side. He confidently rubbed his hands together.

"Not interested," Rockfish said and sent the folder sliding back toward Slanderson at a high rate of speed. The man fumbled for it before the folder ricocheted off his vest and onto the floor.

"Mr. Rockfish, you didn't look at the compensation number, nor any of the other stipulations that weigh heavily in your favor," Warrington said. He lowered his head and shook it from side to side. When Warrington looked back up, he furrowed his eyebrows. "Please take the folder. See for yourself what we're offering you."

"That's going to be a no from me," Rockfish said. "You lost any good faith you might have had with me, thanks to those jack-offs." Rockfish pointed at the delegation from Italy, sitting along the side wall. "Winston. Can I call you Winston? It doesn't really matter. Check with those against the wall. They should be able to tell you, one, I ain't too bright. Second, it ain't about the money. It's about doing what's right for Kara, Pilar, and the rest of the people in that neighborhood. Trickle down this, economic windfall that. I never voted for Reagan." Rockfish said.

"I see. Mr. Rockfish, is this your ultimate position?" Warrington said.

"Yes," Jawnie said. Her forthcoming and courage behind that single word warmed Rockfish.

"Bet your sweet ass, it is," Rockfish said.

Warrington turned to Conti. His look was met with a shoulder shrug and a tilt of the head. Warrington took his cue, looked over at Slanderson and tapped the table. Slanderson put the file he had retrieved from the floor back on the table and the two men stood up.

"We'll see you in court, Mr. Rockfish. This company has the ability and resources to drag this litigation out for much longer than you can afford." Warrington shook his head at Grayson, and Slanderson followed suit. Warrington pointed at the door. Grayson reluctantly stood up. The three men picked up their belongings and marched in a single file. The procession headed around the end of the table to Jawnie's left.

Grayson caught Rockfish's attention and mouthed, *dumb ass* as he moved past the table and continued towards the door.

Rockfish didn't have time to respond in kind. Jawnie tugged at his suit jacket for the second time that afternoon. He turned and her facial expression was pure disbelief. *I feel the same way, kid, but I hope my poker face is a lot better. What the fuck is going on here?*

Jawnie said what they both were thinking. She leaned in and lowered her voice.

"I thought you said there would be back-and-forth negotiations. Something we could use to maybe get them to slip up on. Steve. What just happened? You said there would be dancing. Quick footsteps to gain the upper hand. There was no dancing. No one led. I felt no hand in the small of my back."

"I thought so. I didn't expect the take it or leave it stance. But if we go the legal route—"

Each partner had more to say, but movement along the right side of the room drew their attention away from the shared mood of befuddlement with a slight hint of danger.

The mobsters stood up. *Christ. The Fulsome General Counsel bolting out the door made me forget about the goon squad. Here we go.* Rockfish curled the fingers on both hands into fists and waited for someone to ring the bell. *Harold, it's payback time, you piece of shit.*

Rockfish rose while Jawnie remained seated. But their adversaries walked to the opposite side of the table and sat without saying a word. They took the seats previously occupied by Grayson and Slanderson. Harold remained along the wall, choosing this time to stand and stare a hole through the partners.

"Mr. Rockfish, please sit back down. The intermission is almost over," Conti said, folding his hands on the table before him. "It is time you seriously listened and considered the consequences. They won't be good for you and I'm talking more than just Harold over there."

Rockfish sat back down and swallowed hard. But couldn't resist another jab. "I brought donuts. Now would be a good time to bring them out. The coffee, too."

"Fuck you and your donuts," Bianchi said with an evil smirk. And as if right on cue, the room's overhead lights dimmed slightly.

The partners again turned to the other, each not even attempting to hide their *WTF* expressions.

The screen flickered black and Jawnie screamed.

"Nice to see you too, Jawnie," Annetta Provolone said.

* * * * * * * * * *

Jawnie stared at the face on the screen, perfectly placed in-between Conti and Bianchi. The muscles in her thighs twitched and her legs rocked on the balls of her feet. She interlaced her fingers and pressed them down hard into her thighs. It didn't matter how strong she thought she was this morning or as she stepped off the elevator half an hour ago. The giant head floating over the men's shoulders shook her to her core. She could feel her knees buckle and her stomach imitated the elevator. In this instance, it dropped fast with no bottom in sight.

She looks more ready for the sun and surf than whatever this is turning into. The mafia chief wore a simple yellow t-shirt with the telltale strings of a bikini underneath tied around her neck. Her long hair was up in what Jawnie thought was an old school banana clip. Blue sky filled the background. *She's nonchalantly grabbing some sun on her deck. No matter what I said earlier, I'm not ready for this. No fucking way.*

With each word Annetta spoke, and no one to bar the door, memories flooded her subconscious. Rosenthal's cross-examination during the original trial. Angel crying out and falling backwards as the sound of gunshots filled the night. Sorbelli's surprised look before she sent him careening down the ravine. *The woman had proven time and time again she could get to you. Any time, any place. Why is this so surprising to you?*

Jawnie sniffled and her legs shifted into a higher gear. *How many times does it have to happen before you realize it? Are we going to leave this room? Of course, you're going to leave this room. How many people watched you come in? Yeah, but how many actually care? They're all Fulsome employees, not neutral observers.*

A sudden rush of warmth flowed through her hands, and Jawnie looked down into her lap. Rockfish's large left hand covered hers. The verbal back and forth in her head slowed. She looked up at him and he winked.

"It's all good, kid."

"... some terrible things will happen to you if you do not get on board this train, but you see what I'm working with. My sharp shooters have been anything but. Offense intended, gentlemen. But let's not kid anyone. It is why I've had to step to the forefront."

Bianchi tilted his head down an inch, but Jawnie caught it. She also noticed Conti's subtle shake of his, implying the opposite. There was a divide there, to be sure. *It's a nice nugget, but not the prime piece of intelligence we're hoping to come out with.* But she filed it away, as she was sure Rockfish had too.

"Ah, excuse me," Rockfish said, raising a hand with the index finger outstretched. "I brought donuts. There was coffee, as well. A carafe. I'll need that to get my deposit back. Some woman took them when we arrived and promised to put the spread out on the table. I've asked these all-stars about the snacks, but they're ignoring me. Perhaps if you ask them to check? I would hope they're capable of a simple task like that."

Yes! He had caught on.

"Ever the wise ass, Rockfish," Annetta said. Her nose wrinkled. The disgust was clear to all in the room. "Does the act ever get old? Don't answer. It doesn't matter. I'm here for her." She turned to the side and addressed her consigliere. "Giovanni, did they accept Fulsome's offer?"

"No, boss."

"Well, that seals the fate of your little company. This group of shysters will bury you so far in litigation you'll need seventeen freaking reality shows to stave off bankruptcy. Speaking of which, how's your producer fairing?" Annetta's wide grin made Jawnie want to leap over the table, but Rockfish's hand still covered hers, letting Jawnie know it wasn't the best of ideas. She could feel him squeeze a little harder.

"To be honest with you two, I couldn't have given a shit less whether you did or didn't. But I guess in a perfect world, I'd like to see your life totally fucked. Tied up in litigation for years while they build the exit ramp around that piece of shit property of yours. And if I know Ignazio, he'll pay the local truckers union a little extra to run eighteen-wheelers up and down that ramp every day until they drive whatever customers you had left to the new state-of-the-art Avonlea Crossing Mini Golf. It's not in the plans, but I'd suggest it as the perfect *FUCK YOU*. You can thank me later, Luther."

Rockfish lifted his hand from Jawnie's leg. He raised a middle finger and smiled widely before returning his hand to support his partner. *He's not taking a damn thing from her. Rolling off his back like water off a duck.*

"You'll be so poor, you'd wish you still could afford that shit box trailer you used to live in. That fucking dollar was the worst fucking investment you ever made, you dumb son of a bitch." Annetta said. Her words were coming faster, and she had increased the level of venom in her personal attacks. She didn't seem to care who she shit on.

Small things seemed to pepper the screen and drew Jawnie's attention away from the verbal abuse. *Spittle. She's really losing it up there.*

"... My recent run with levels of incompetence not experienced during my time in this life has made me rethink my stance to support this project. I'll miss the money, but Luther has assured me there will be other opportunities, some close to home, which will be of greater benefit to me and my family."

Silence hung in the air as the woman on the screen paused and inhaled deeply. *She's trying to catch her breath. Acting a raving lunatic has taken a lot out of the old broad. I'm sure she didn't sign on with that intent, but here we are.* Annetta's head turned slightly when she began again, and Jawnie knew Annetta had reloaded for her. *Okay. Bring it on. I think I'm ready. Maybe. Probably.* She pulled her hands off her lap, placed her elbows on the table, and leaned forward.

"I'm only interested in this one. You, my pretty, need to come down with a sudden case of amnesia and make the conscious decision not to testify." Annetta moved closer to her camera and on the other end, her head took up most of the screen.

Macy's Thanksgiving Day Parade. She gave Rockfish a quick kick to the shins under the table, knowing if she had thought of it, he was about to say it. He turned, cocked his head at her and shook it side to side. *Good.*

"... and if that dyke brain of yours does the right thing and I'm sitting in this same chair minus the government's ankle bracelet, life will be good. You can go back to chasing adulterers or cats in a fucking tree. I could care less."

Jawnie took a deep breath and stood up for herself. *You can do this!*

"You can't scare me into not taking the stand." Jawnie said. She sat up straighter in her chair. Annetta's slur meant nothing. *She thinks that penetrated?* It wasn't the first time Jawnie heard it and it would be far from the last. *Piss poor effort, granny.*

"Giovanni," Annetta said. She leaned back in her lounge chair.

Bianchi dug into the bag on the floor to his right. He pulled out a black folder of his own and Jawnie noticed this one didn't have the giant Fulsome logo across the front. With a flick of the wrist, he slid the folder across the table. Jawnie turned and looked at Rockfish. He nodded, and she flipped it open.

Her audible gasp drew concern from her partner and shitty grins from those on the other side of the table.

"That's your boy, right?" Annetta said. "The only person you really keep in contact with back in Jersey. I got a bone to pick with him, too!"

The folder contained pictures of Hasty. Both on the job and off. She stopped flipping through the first couple. *Message received.* A tear formed in the corner of her right eye. *This isn't right! He has no part in this!*

Rockfish reached over and took the folder from Jawnie's hands. "Provolone, you piece of shit. You wouldn't. The amount of heat this would bring down on you would be monumental. You'd have the Feds so far up your ass you'd have to ask your cellmate to disimpact you."

"You, Mr. Rockfish, confuse me for Ignazio's boss. Angelo is the one who decides on how difficult the result will make his life in the short term. I decide on how the outcome will eventually affect me in the long run. I run this family and make all decisions. Don't worry, I can handle the heat. My plans do not include leaving the kitchen soon. Not to mention the damn US Attorney could choose to call that local yokel to the stand this time. He's as guilty as the two of you in fucking up my Paycheck Protection Program scam."

The slur didn't get to Jawnie but the threat to her friend, peer and sometimes unofficial partner, was as close to a kill shot as she could take. She lowered her head, stared at the table, and said nothing.

"Bitch, eyes up here!" Annetta said. "Don't you fucking crawl away from me in that head of yours. Hasty is not innocent. I owe him a little something. But of course, you can stop that thought dead in its tracks before I even give the order. You clam the fuck up and Rosenthal does his Jew lawyer dance. There ain't no way this retrial is successful. We. All. Win."

Annetta winked at the camera. Rockfish couldn't miss the woman's tense jawline and the tendons stretched, looking to escape the confines of her neck.

Jawnie's head sunk another inch and she tried desperately to wish it all away.

"Look at me, now! I'm offering you the chance to keep living that miserable, unholy, shit life of yours. You should be thanking me."

Jawnie's chair violently rocked to the side as Rockfish leapt to his feet. He stood, his hands gripping the side of the table, and let loose with his own barrage of expletives. His left arm shot out, snatched the folder, and side armed it at the screen.

Silence came from those in the room, but the shrill of Annetta's rantings continued to come through the speakers. Her words ran together and neither of the partners wanted to spend the energy to figure out what she was railing about, but both assumed the subject at hand was them.

Rockfish reached down and grasped Jawnie's jacket by the bicep. She felt as if he practically lifted her up out of the chair. She wobbled for a second, but his hand helped steady her.

"Meetings fucking adjourned, Fuckos," Rockfish said and turned to Harold. "Don't move a muscle if you know what's good." He flicked his fingers under his chin at each of the men at the table and then the screen for good measure. He spun Jawnie and navigated the path towards the door. Initial laughter followed by a string of what Jawnie assumed were Italian curses lingered behind them.

When Rockfish opened the door, Jawnie finally found her footing. She bit the inside of her lip, hard, and followed Rockfish out into the hallway.

* * * * * * * * * *

When the conference door swung open, Jawnie saw the expression on Grayson and Warrington's faces. Their exit had caught the men off guard. They had stood outside the door, but close enough to keep track of what was going on and being said. The two men took a couple of quick steps backwards, but to Jawnie, each looked guilty. Grayson moved quickly to step forward, back to his previous position, and shut the door in order to stop Annetta's diatribe from echoing down the hallway.

"Over s—s—so soon?" Warrington said, still surprised by their exit. "I can have Pentworth escort you back down." He pointed at a young man standing behind him. "And, Mr. Rockfish, you still have some time to consider the offer. I'll have my secretary send over the folder and documents via courier to your office. Please have an attorney review them and advise you accordingly."

"Can't wait," Rockfish said and looked back at Jawnie. She watched over his shoulder as Warrington and Grayson walked around the corner and out of sight.

"Neither can I, Steve," Jawnie said. "Mr. Pentworth, is there a bathroom close by I can use?" *More to compose myself. I probably look godawful.*

"Right over that way," Pentworth said and pointed in the direction Warrington and Grayson had disappeared. "We'll wait for you by the elevator." Pentworth pointed down the hallway as if either partner couldn't remember where they had walked a short while ago.

"You okay, kid? I could walk with you." Rockfish said, leaning in close. "Say the word."

"I'll be fine. Gimme a sec to compose myself."

"Take your time. Me and Pentworth got a lotta catching up to do." Rockfish winked, and it brought a smile to Jawnie's face. "Plus, find out where my carafe went."

She walked in the hallway's direction where Pentworth pointed. Jawnie approached the turn in the carpet cautiously. Her head took the turn first, hoping to not run smack dab into Warrington or Grayson. Yet there they were. The two men stood a few paces past the small alcove where the sign above showed the bathrooms. Jawnie went up on tiptoes as she drew closer and then slid into the opening.

The doors for both the men's and ladies' room were directly in front of her, separated by the mandatory water fountain. She pushed open the woman's door and slipped inside.

Jawnie placed her purse on the side of the sink and walked back to check the occupancies of the three stalls. With no one home, she then headed back to the door and checked for a lock. *Damn, not from this side. Come on, girl, do your shit and get out of this damn building.*

Jawnie stood in front of the mirror and ran the cold water from the tap. She rinsed her hands and face, not caring what it did to the morning's make-up routine. The cold felt good against her skin and the paper towels from the dispenser were softer than she imagined. *Big companies got money to spend. I bet the toilet paper is ten ply, too.*

Only when her face was dry did Jawnie allow herself to look into the mirror. *Damn, girl, you look rode hard and put away wet.* She glanced at her pocketbook. *Not enough time to reapply a lot of this. Gonna have to go all natural.* Jawnie joked with herself, to fight off the concern that built in the back of her mind. The concern for her own safety and Rockfish was ever present. But now, her actions directly affected another. Hasty. She'd have to call him ASAP.

How long will it take? I can't stay in here forever. Hasty. Buddy, please forgive me for dragging you into this. She knew he would. *I need to get up the courage to get out of this bathroom and let you know how badly I fucked up. This time, it isn't Steve coming to save you. IF something happens. My kingdom to get my hands around that old bitch's neck!* Jawnie gripped the sink with both hands and stared long and hard into the mirror. She found it hard to believe the eyes staring back were hers. A peek at her watch let her know she'd been in the bathroom for close to five minutes. *Steve is probably getting antsy. Will he bust down the door to make sure some Fulsome goon didn't come through the ductwork to get me? Get your shit together, McGee, and get out there.* Jawnie slowly released her killer grip on the sink, picked up her pocketbook and headed for the door.

She stepped out and noticed that Warrington and Grayson were still standing a few feet away, their backs turned. She bent down to wet her lips on the water fountain when her ears perked up.

"... the McGee broad..."

Jawnie recognized Grayson's voice, and, with the mention of her name, she slipped over to the alcove's corner by the men's room. The position allowed her to eavesdrop without being seen. The men's conversation continued, both clearly expecting Pentworth to have walked the twosome out the front door by this time. Their voices were louder than a normal hallway discussion, as if neither didn't have a care who in the company walked by or overheard.

"... I don't care if she's got Ebola. Certain things take precedent if she wants to get out of the secretarial pool." The anger in Warrington's voice contradicted his reasonable demeanor in the conference room.

"Rosa will step up, Sir. You have my word," Grayson said. "I'll get her in touch with Freddie down in IT. I've spoken to him. He knows to expect her call."

Rosa! Was I wrong about this, her, the entire time? She's not a simple pawn?

"... She's flown right under that dumb broad's radar. Freddie will work with her to find the best way into that shitty business network of theirs. I'll make sure you have every bit of information regarding those two and their operation before we file the first legal document in this battle."

"Agreed. I don't want any surprises when we're in that courthouse. Get me everything. I'll have my clerks go through every document for an advantage or some leverage we could use to crush them," Warrington said. "Do whatever it takes."

Jawnie realized what the men's words implied and her knees buckled. She spun around and latched onto the water fountain to avoid collapsing onto the alcove's tile floor. After a minute, she straightened back up. *Trying to beat us at our own game? Well, Rockfish's at the least? Malicious payload in bound. It's intended for me, but we all need to be ready for it.*

"... One last thing, Luther. Our insurance policy. Is it safe?"

"Absolutely. I gave her my personal card to purchase a small safe," Grayson said. "She promised me it's well hidden in her house. No one would think of her involvement in this. Safe and sound, until we need it."

"Let's hope it's not too well hidden if Annetta comes after us. We could always sacrifice Rosa for the good of the order. You heard how crazy she was in there. It didn't matter that we stepped out, that shrill came straight through the walls. Make sure Rosa keeps it secured and you know exactly where it is. With this one, you never know when we'll need to use the nuclear option and blow this whole thing up to save our asses."

"Trust me, Sir, she's more responsible and trustworthy than her old boss. Brick was a moron."

Jawnie remained out of sight until the men's voices faded and she realized they had moved away. She approached the alcove's doorway and looked at where the two men had stood. The hallway was empty, and she willed her legs in the opposite direction, towards Steve and the safety she hoped the elevator would bring.

Rockfish and Pentworth were right where they said they'd be. Rockfish was very animated, his mouth moving almost as fast as his arms. As she approached, the conversation became clearer.

"... that lady took the box, and no one ever put them out. Are you going to pay me the five dollars because I sure won't be getting back my deposit on the carafe?"

"I'll look into the situation. I'm sure someone has your number and I can reach out to you."

"Here," Rockfish said, thrusting a business card in the man's hand.

Pentworth had pushed the call button when he spotted Jawnie coming around the corner. The door opened almost as if on cue as she approached. Jawnie didn't slow down her stride until she was in the elevator and the doors closed. Only then did she turn around and face the front of the car.

"How you holding up?" Rockfish said. He put his hand on her shoulder, but Jawnie didn't answer. She tilted her head and grimaced.

They rode in silence, and Pentworth escorted them to the front door. He wished the partners a safe trip wherever they were headed and hoped they enjoyed their time at Fulsome.

"I had a blast, Junior," Rockfish said over his shoulder before the glass door shut behind him. "Five out of five, would recommend. Dipshit." The last part was under his breath.

"Any thoughts?" Rockfish said as the two stepped off the curb and into the parking lot.

"Can we wait till we get in the car? I wouldn't put it past these scumbags to have mics placed out here to catch what a competitor or potential takeover candidate might say."

"If you feel that way, let's hold off until we pass Robinson's Dry Cleaning. That parking lot has served us well in the past."

The orange Yaris pulled into the dry cleaner's parking lot faster than their previous walk from Fulsome. Rockfish picked a parking spot with a few empty spaces on either side and shut off the engine.

"Okay, what's in that bonnet of yours?"

"They're trying to beat us at our own game. Well, your game," Jawnie said. She recounted the conversation she overheard between Warrington and Grayson. By the end of her short story, she could see the color change in Rockfish's face. The crimson red wasn't his best look, but it was exactly what she had hoped for.

"... I'll text Lynn and give her the plan for tonight. It won't take me long to compile and insert the code. Despite my words to the contrary, I've been practicing."

"You were right. My idea must be evil if the bad guys go that route."

"Or smart enough for them to copy it."

"True, but thinking about it makes my head hurt," Rockfish said with a laugh. "We need to strike while surprise is still on our side. They don't know that we know. She doesn't know that you know. Send the picture. Even if this Freddie has reached out to her, she won't expect you getting the jump on them. They're in offensive mode, not thinking defense."

"It should be an adventure," Jawnie said. "Lynn is about as thrilled to be playing photographer as I am a Rockfish's Secret model. It's a good thing I've got skills with Photoshop."

"Make it a good one. Tantalizing enough for her to not think straight and click immediately. A legitimate spicy Jawnie haze should prevent her from having second thoughts. Trust me, I'm a guy. It works."

"Easy does it, Iggy." Jawnie's reference to Mack's buddy, who had lost money in an online romance scam, cracked them both up.

"What about Rosa and this insurance policy?" Rockfish said. "What do you make of that?"

"The first thing I thought of was Brick."

"Old fuck face himself. Everything circles back to him and his half-hearted extortion efforts."

"Remember his initial statement to the police? He swore there was a ton of evidence tying Fulsome to Marini and that 'she' had it secured?"

"Rosa."

"Exactly."

"We risk life and limb to come here, walking into God knows what. Hoping to come out with the slightest bit of intel and here you come up with the mother of all clues by making a trip to the can to fix your make-up."

Jawnie laughed and lightly punched Rockfish's shoulder.

"We're going to be all right," Rockfish said.

A fist bump sealed their agreement on the way forward and Rockfish started the car. The twenty-minute ride back to the condo was quiet. *If Rockfish's brain is thinking half as fast as mine, we'll be ahead of these num-nuts in no time. You got this. Send the picture, get access to whatever networks and information needed to bring this company down and shit on Annetta at the retrial. Let's go. It's your sole focus now.*

Rockfish pulled up in front of the building and the partners made plans to meet early the next morning for breakfast. Jawnie opened the door and stepped out of the car.

"Hey!" Rockfish said, leaning across the center console, repeating the word until Jawnie's eyes met his.

"Launch it. That's your lane. Concentrate and stay on it. I'll call Hasty. He's a damn good cop. With some forewarning, he'll be fine. Don't worry."

CHAPTER TWELVE

The next morning, in the middle of the morning rush hour, Rockfish pulled the Yaris into the parking lot behind Dot's Diner. No open spaces remained in the establishment's front, and he had spotted the Subaru to the left of the front door. Jawnie was inside. He pictured her tapping her nails on the table as she watched him circle the lot, looking for an empty spot. *Christ, what time did she get here to luck in getting that spot?*

The rental was smaller than Lana, and it made for easy parking. *Chalk that up as the one plus for driving this piece of shit. Fuck GEICO. Fuck the damn chip shortage.* The dealership had pushed his build order for the '23 version of Lana back twice. Angel had offered to get him a better car through the production company and didn't ask to recoup the cost, but Rockfish hated handouts. He vowed to drive this Yaris into the ground and make GEICO take it back in pieces before he would accept charity from a man who took a bullet for Jawnie.

Rockfish threw open the diner's door and Jawnie waved to him from a booth halfway down the left side. Chrome covered the inside of the diner except for the red vinyl booths and the matching stools at the old-fashioned lunch counter. It had been her idea to conduct what business they could in the great wide open. It had been his to choose a grease trap where she would probably have to settle for the vegan version of steak, bacon, extra sausage, and an egg on the side. He slid into the booth and hoped his poker face was up. No need to seem too anxious regarding her activities the previous evening.

"Dying to know, aren't you?" Jawnie said.

"No, I'm good."

"Steve, it's spilling out of every pore on your face."

She's got me pegged. Not literally. It's as if we're an old married couple. So much for keeping that itch under wraps.

"Alright then, how'd it go? Did Lynn get that thirst trap picture, as the kids say these days?"

"Mission accomplished," Jawnie said with a smirk. "We found one we both thought wasn't too risque but implied enough, if you know what I mean."

"I do. You good with it?" Rockfish said. He had concerns asking Jawnie to pull this off and hoped it wouldn't be a moment in his life that he'd regret or that she would hang over his head.

"Lynn did her best Annie Leibovitz and I'm comfortable with the picture, largely in part, if it lives on the internet forever. Because it will. That's what these things do. Women are only slightly better than men when it comes to forwarding pictures to their friends. But yeah, I'm sure it will get out at some point. I'm good with it."

"What if all those forwards click on it?"

"We're good. Once Rosa clicks, I'll shut the code down and any notifications I get will go straight into the trash."

Rockfish nodded and tried to see if his partner was putting up a front and telling him what he wanted to hear. In the end, he wasn't sure. He waited for her to continue.

"Once we settled on one, it wasn't too hard to compile and embed the code before hitting send. I've got it all tied to a Linux box in a closet at home. If the code executes, it emails my phone. I should know the minute she clicks. If she does. It's been almost ten hours."

"Nothing?" Rockfish questioned the picture Jawnie and Lynn had picked out. *I knew they should have run it past me. I could have told them if it was the correct, actionable image to send.*

"Nothing regarding clicking on the picture. We've exchanged a couple of chats since then. Some above-board, some flirty."

"Did she say anything important? Mention feedback from Grayson regarding the meeting?" Rockfish was grasping now. He could use some bit of positive information before the afternoon coordination meeting with Raffi. Those details were still unknown to Jawnie, and he wasn't sure he would let her know before the fact.

"Nothing of consequence. If she had, I would have already let you know," Jawnie said. Rockfish could read a tinge of annoyance in her tone and words.

Rockfish spotted their server walking past the order station. He headed straight for their booth with a coffeepot in hand. Rockfish picked up a menu and pretended to contemplate the intricacies of the Dot's menu.

"Hi, my name is James and I've taken over for Cassie. You were lucky to come in seconds before a shift change. I'll refill your coffees. What can I get for you this morning?"

Rockfish wasn't in a rush and there was a ton more conversation to get to without James walking by every three minutes to annoy the fuck out of him. The place wasn't half full. *Where the fuck did all those cars in the parking lot come from?*

"Keep the coffee coming. I'll wave you over when we're ready to order," Rockfish said. He could see the disappointment on Jawnie's face. *Maybe she found something she could eat here. After all, she and Lynn were regulars here during the Porbeagle case.*

"Enough with the offense. Any malicious payloads land in your inbox yet?"

"Yeah, not like I'm not starving or anything."

"Sorry, wave him over if you'd like."

"I can hold out a while longer. But no, nothing has come in and I've made sure all of our boxes are patched and updated. We should be good if we all follow what I've preached since I got you to purchase everything for our network."

"Maybe the pic spooked them? You know, the timing for both attempts is fucking uncanny."

"To say the least," Jawnie said. "But like you said, they're on the offensive. I'm betting no one there is thinking about playing some defense against this ragged twosome. Speaking of which. I gave Lynn a cyber safety education refresher in case they try to come in that door. She's good. I locked her laptop down, and she's a smart girl."

"That's why I, uh, I mean, we hired her."

"She took the news of working from her sister's house, effective immediately, better than I thought."

"Probably because she's tired of me hustling her over to my spare bedroom when shit gets hot here. Mack and Zippy can be a handful," Rockfish said with a laugh. "They both need an awful lot of attention."

"She needs to see her sister. It's been a while."

"Yeah, but time doesn't heal all wounds between the two of them," Rockfish said. "We've seen it firsthand."

"Their relationship is one thing, but we're both more concerned about her mental health. She, we, can't afford to have her involved to the point of another Porbeagle situation."

"Agreed," Rockfish said with a reaffirming nod. "Between going through that and watching Angel collapse in front of her desk, it's too much. No matter the type of work she does for us, we are to keep her off the front lines at all costs."

"You couldn't have prevented what happened to Angel. Lynn is safe, and that's all that matters. Not a damn thing she can't do from there with her laptop. I forwarded the phones to her cell. And I want to add, it wouldn't hurt for you to educate yourself on the same cyber security." Jawnie said.

"If you got the machines at work covered, I'm good. I do nothing official on my phone. Especially this fancy new one," Rockfish said.

He held up his new iPhone 13. "I still don't have all my shit copied over from the damn cloud. Maybe one day you'll take pity on a Luddite and help me out."

The partners shared a laugh and Jawnie waved their server over to take their breakfast order. Their conversation turned to mundane and monotonous topics until James swung by with a tray of steaming hot plates. He topped off their coffees and left for another table.

"Can we talk about the other thing?" Jawnie said, her eyebrows arched, and head slightly cocked to the side.

"The nuclear option? Your favorite, confidential informant, Raffi, and I discussed it at length over cocktails last night." Rockfish said. He immediately remembered the earlier promise to himself, not to mention his favorite burglar. A lecture would come, that much he knew. She was smart enough to put one and one together and immediately draw a negative conclusion.

"Raffi? He has a particular skill set that fucked us royally in the past. Those were your exact words. Need I remind you?"

"That was a unique case. Different circumstances." Rockfish said. "In our current adventures, he also rescued me from Conti's goons before they could turn me over to Provolone's shitbags. Then he got his ass whooped because of it. You saw his nose."

The furrowed brows staring back across the booth told him all he needed to know. She would not be a big fan of what he said or planned to do shortly. *She'd have to understand sometimes a senior partner veto override was necessary and this sure as fuck was one of those times. Fuck, I'm supposed to meet him as soon as the sun goes down. Guess it's too late to ask her to play lookout for us.*

"Yes, we considered getting the band back together, so to speak. It's been a long time since we combined our Wonder Twin powers to accomplish something nefarious. Seems to be a valuable piece of evidence if we can lay our hands on it. We went to the meeting to figure out or learn about some sort of game changer. I think this is it and it's an opportunity we, or I, shouldn't pass up." Rockfish stopped and took a deep breath. *Let's see if she adds to her disappointment in me and what I'm planning.* He watched as she pushed her food around her plate and then held up her mug for James to see.

"I bent to your will with the picture bomb. I went willingly after overhearing Warrington and Grayson speak yesterday. But I can't be part and parcel to breaking in and turning her house upside down. It's my newest line in the sand. But with an asterisk so that I can change my mind, based on future information."

"Noted. I'll miss your lookout skills. But this could be valuable in the right hands and I've got a righteous set. It has to be in her house. She wouldn't have taken it to her Mother's, would she?"

"Grayson said it's in a small safe," Jawnie said. "I doubt she'd have packed it, along with her clothes and any other essentials."

Rockfish raised his own eyebrows over that last part and Jawnie shot back a look to let him know now is not the time nor the place.

"Here's my last comment to you on the matter. We get our hands on whatever this is. I betcha it would also help with Provolone's upcoming retrial. I always said I'd respect your decision to testify again or not."

Jawnie nodded and lowered her head. "Yes. She needs to go back to jail. Rot there for the rest of her life. Toss in half-a-dozen types of cancer and not an ounce of dementia. I want her to feel each bit of pain, wish she could die, and then live another thirty years in that dirty cell. Foremost, if she goes after Hasty. Fuck, I forgot about him. See how fucked this is? How can I forget about him?"

"I spoke with him. Cell service is shit up in the Poconos," Rockfish said and reached across the table with his hand. "He's on a fishing vacation and not due back in the office for another week. Unless they followed him there, he's safe. He'll have his guard up when he gets back to the office. He's a good cop and can take care of himself."

"But what if they followed him up there and decide to do something?"

"I warned him, he'll keep an eye out even now. He said he'd call the US attorney's office and let them know of the threat."

"Won't that come back on us?" Jawnie said.

"No, he's a good cop, like I said. He knows how to build that Chinese wall to protect his source. Which, in this case, is me. Same as whoever we turn this forthcoming boatload of evidence over to. Now, if you'll excuse me, I have to hit the head."

Rockfish washed his hands afterwards and garnered a look at himself in the mirror. *You look like shit, my friend.* He splashed some water on his face and ran his hands through his hair. *Let's wrap this whole thing up and get moving.* He opened the heavy door and walked straight into Jawnie. His partner looked as if she had reluctantly won the Powerball.

"She clicked. We're in."

* * * * * * * * * *

Rockfish pulled the Yaris down Rosa Mangold's street and slowed to look for her house. She lived in an older neighborhood of middle-income housing built in the seventies. Split-levels ruled each street. The neighborhood was on the outskirts of Fort Meade, the home of the infamous National Security Agency. He wasn't too concerned about interference from the Feds in this case. *Way too much other shit going on in the world for them to scoop old Stevie's phone and wonder what he was doing casing Rosa's house. Now Raffi's another story.*

Rockfish had spoken with Raffi after leaving the diner and he quickly concluded he should be the one to check out the house and neighborhood in the daylight. The decision was easy and two-fold. First, Raffi continued to need the occasional pain pill and, to be honest, Rockfish didn't trust him out here doing surveillance. *I could see him now, standing out on the sidewalk talking to a neighbor, saying God knows what. Being just enough out of the ordinary to raise someone's hackles. My luck, the local PD would increase patrols in the area to get Karen to stop calling.* And the second was his friend's reaction to the house's physical location.

The conspiracy side of Raffi came out in full force, and it took Steve longer to convince his friend to accompany him in the evening. Raffi went on a long tin foil hat rant. He suggested they leave all electronics behind, to include Rockfish's current rental, because even cars are connected these days. Rockfish let him go on with all the 9/11 talk and get it out of his system. *I need him focused and on-scene tonight, ready to do his thing.*

Rockfish didn't slow as he passed Rosa's house. *Never know who's watching and what they'd deem out of the ordinary.* The recent Google satellite images were dead on. The neighborhood, to include Rosa's house, hadn't changed since the last pass over. Her split-level was dog-shit brown, with cement steps leading toward the door. Rosa, or a previous owner, had planted clumps of yellow forsythia along the property lines to give a feeling of privacy. These particular bushes weren't over five feet tall. None of the yellow flowers from the spring remained. *Nothing I haven't seen before and some half-assed seclusion for what we need to do.* A neighbor, across the street from Rosa's, moved a sprinkler from one side of her small front lawn to the other. Other than the woman in the housecoat with large pink curlers in her hair, the street was deserted.

Rockfish made one more lap around the block and noticed the sprinkler-moving, housecoat wearing neighbor from earlier had approached Rosa's house. He slowed and pulled the car against the curb and watched as she climbed the front steps.

All parts of the plan came to him in an instant. It would give him the up close and personal knowledge of Rosa's house and property the evening's crap shoot would need. Rockfish turned to the passenger seat. He had piled a ton of props, a couple of which would help him gain the information needed. He grabbed a pink cat collar with a small attached bell and the noisy bag of cat treats off the seat and exited the car. *Show time.*

Rockfish walked slowly down the street towards Rosa's house. He alternated from shaking the treat bag, then ringing the bell. In-between each action, he called out for an imaginary lost cat.

Shake shake shake

"Sir Arthur!"

Ding ding ding

He loitered in front of the two houses prior to Rosa's on the street. Then timed his arrival with the woman exiting Rosa's house. She bounded down the steps and Rockfish met her where the walkway met the sidewalk.

"Hi, ma'am, is this your house?" Rockfish said, continuing with his line of bullshit before she could answer. "I'm Jimmy Taggart, from over on West Hayden. My grandkid let the damn cat out the door and my daughter's on my case to find it. You ain't seen a tan and white tabby running through your yard, have you? I think I saw her sneak through that patch of forsythia." Rockfish wanted to hit her with enough words, so fast, the woman wouldn't be able to see through his story or think what's wrong with this picture. He rang the bell and shook the treat bag for added effect. "Her name is Sir Arthur. I know it makes little sense, but when little Chelsea throws one of her tantrums, my daughter doesn't have time for it. Enter Pop-pop. I've got to find this damn cat before the kid fills my afternoon with tantrums."

Rockfish stopped and assessed the situation. He thought he could see a slight window of confusion in her eyes and asked if he could take a quick lap around the house and see if he could spot Sir Arthur.

"Oh, I don't live here. I take care of Ms. Rosa's plants while she's away."

"I apologize. I assumed. If you've got permission to go inside, perhaps you could walk with me around the house? It will only take a couple of minutes and hopefully we can scare the damn thing out and I can grab her. Probably too fast for me, but I could always try to corral her back near the house. What do you say? Chelsea would be forever grateful. I would be too, for a little quiet this afternoon."

"I think I could spare the time, Mr. Taggart. I'm Martha, by the way."

"Thank you, Martha, you do not know how much I appreciate this." *Ha! You don't know how much!*

While they carried on with introductions, Rockfish looked over Martha's shoulder and up at the front door. This peek netted him two pieces of information. The front door had a modern biotech lock, the kind you would use a fingerprint to disengage the deadbolt, and there was no Ring doorbell anywhere that he could spot. With that lock, he knew they'd have to find another way in.

The newfound animal control tandem walked back towards the front steps and then veered to the right, Martha leading the way into the side yard. She took up calling out for Sir Arthur and Rockfish kept shaking the props for all he's worth, while taking in every inch of the house. There was no sign of Sir Arthur on the side yard, not to mention any signs of spotlights, motion detection or the old-fashioned kind. They turned the corner and Rockfish saw his in.

The basement Bilco doors were set at the far end of the back of the house. He assumed that portion of the lower level was unfinished. The furnace, water heater, and sump-pump were more than likely at the bottom of those steps. *Storage too? Might be the perfect place to hide something.*

Rockfish steered away from Martha and walked into the back of the yard. He brushed the clumps of forsythia, hoping to scare out an imaginary cat. Bent over, he gave the back of the house a good going over. Rosa had spotlights mounted on the corners, but they didn't seem upgraded to motion detectors. *But you never know. I'll have to be wary of that. Toss a stick or something into the backyard and see if she lights up.*

Martha had made her way over to the far corner and stood on the other side of the slanted basement storm doors. Rockfish heard a noise and looked over. Martha was tapping her foot against the bottom edge, where the metal door met the concrete base. *Haven't seen a set of these in a while. Back in my day, we called 'em Bilco Doors. Now, basement egresses are uncovered concrete stairs with a normal six-panel door at the bottom.*

He shot his eyes back in Martha's general direction. Her calls for Sir Arthur had become less enthusiastic as time went on and less frequent. *My time here is running out. I need to make the best of it before she blows the whistle on this charade. Get what I can on that damn door and get back to Raffi's. There's still a lot to do before nightfall.*

Rockfish picked up his fake pace, looking across the backyard for the imaginary Sir Arthur. Once he was sure of the neighbor's sight lines over the forsythia, he made a beeline towards where Martha stood, patiently waiting.

"Looks like we've come up empty, Martha," Rockfish said.

"That it does, Mr. Taggart," Martha said. "I'm sorry, but that cat is probably long gone. I need to get back to my yard and move that sprinkler again. The August sun has been hell on my grass."

"Do you think I could get a copycat from Petco? This kid, she ain't the brightest."

The frown on Martha's face let him know the woman left her sense of humor back with the sprinkler in her own yard. She shook her head and turned the corner, calling out for Sir Arthur one last time. *Probably humoring me now. But with her out of sight, I need to get a better look at this set of doors.*

The dual set of doors were a dark maroon in color. The right-hand door contained a single black handle close to the bottom. Rockfish spotted some other hardware on the corresponding spot on the left door, but wanted to believe beyond all odds, Rosa left the door unlocked. He pulled a handkerchief from his pocket, bent down, and grasped the handle. He then said a silent prayer to G.

Gordon Liddy, the Patron Saint of Break-ins, and gave a slight tug upward. The door only gave a smidge. Rosa had locked it from the other side. *Damn. But are you really surprised?*

He turned his attention to the door on the left. A silver cylinder cap and matching knob were located where the handle was on the other. He flipped open the cap and cracked a wide smile. *If Raffi's kept his tools sharp, we can blow through that lock in no time.* With the door unlocked, a turn of the knob would release the slide bar on the opposite side. The two men would be down the stairs and ready to face the next obstacle.

Rockfish stood back up and jogged around the corner, only to see Martha standing in the front yard, glaring back at him. He carried on the charade, shaking bushes and rattling the bag of treats for show. When he reached Martha, he gave her a story about thinking he saw Sir Arthur dart across one of the back corners. Rockfish didn't really care if she bought it or not. He needed to get moving. He gave her a fake address and number should she find the imaginary cat, before calmly walking back to the Yaris.

It's an old house with no new security features or upgrades on the outside. Could the outside be lulling my alertness into a false sense of security? Was the outside demeanor and blandness of the house a distraction only to set my mind at ease, while an alarm system was lying in wait at the bottom of the basement steps? Only one way to find out, buddy.

* * * * * * * * * *

The mental clock in Rockfish's mind determined the time to be a few minutes after 1am as he approached Rosa's house from the east. Twelve hours since the search for an imaginary Sir Arthur. The night was pitch black, with a lack of moonlight and only the occasional streetlight. There were no lights on in the house. *Not that there would be at this hour, but I hope she didn't unexpectedly decide to drive home and arrived after I left earlier.*

There would be no turning back, as he had no way to contact his accomplice. Raffi was coming in from the west and the plan was to meet in the backyard. *I can't even reach out to him. Stupid fucking conspiracy nut job.* When Rockfish met Raffi after scoping out Rosa's house, the man was still bent over a barrel about the NSA. It took Rockfish agreeing to leave his phone behind. Only then did Raffi pack his lock-pick-set. *As long as he meets me at the designated spot, he can believe in any off the wall shit he believes. Christ, I hope I don't regret this decision.*

They had taken Raffi's car, taking no chance someone noticed the Yaris driving around the streets for a second time. They had left it in the parking lot of a Chinese restaurant a half-mile away. The place had long closed a couple of hours ago, but there were a few cars remaining in the parking lot and Rockfish didn't think one more would draw any weird looks.

The two men had walked together until the halfway point. When Rosa's house was a quarter mile further, each man took a separate long sweeping arc to arrive at their designated entry spots. Each wore ball caps pulled down low that would hide any identifiable feature. While Rockfish couldn't spot a Ring doorbell on Rosa's front stoop, it didn't mean that every house he passed on the midnight stroll would not have some kind of outward-facing, streaming surveillance camera. A pair of thin tactical gloves stuffed into his back pocket. *Every PI should be buddies with the guy who runs the local police supply store.*

Rockfish kept his steps on the inner edge of the sidewalk, choosing to hug the fence or hedge line that each of Rosa's privacy conscious neighbors seemed to have. The streetlights, which were few, helped him stay in the shadows for much of his walk. As he drew closer to the house, his mind raced with questions. *Would the forsythia clumps and lack of moonlight give them ample cover? Had he missed some sort of security feature on the outside of Rosa's house? Trust your instincts, bud. This ain't your first rodeo.*

He had picked up a short stick, a little longer than a foot, from his front yard before heading out. It had been a recent favorite chew thing of Zippy's, but tonight, Rockfish felt he would make better use of it. Even with the small amount of pain remaining in his bicep area, he could toss the stick with his dominant arm to make sure it completed a high arc of flight into Rosa's backyard. If he had missed any type of motion detection spotlight, that should rectify the problem and most likely cause him to call the whole thing off.

When Rockfish reached the right side of the house, he launched Zippy's stick and waited. Nothing. He crouched down as far as his old bones would allow and slipped into the side yard to retrieve the stick. *Good boy.* He made his way to the corner of the house and said a silent prayer before tossing the stick one last time. The backyard remained covered in darkness. *Ok, we are good.*

Three minutes, or what seemed like several lifetimes later, Rockfish spotted a single flash of light from across the yard. *Raffi. Surprised at the pace he made, considering he had the longer route, but happy he made it and was ready to play ball.* Rockfish gave a reply flash from his own small light. The second signal told each man to make their way to the basement door. Rockfish had the longer distance to traverse and arrived to find Raffi on his stomach, flashlight in mouth, ready to work his magic.

"Like riding a bike, Stevie," Raffi said softly.

"Pedal faster and glove up."

Rockfish put his back against the house and crouched next to the raised door. He glanced around the backyard, his eyes moving right to left. He wasn't sure what he was on the lookout for, but had an idea his elevated heart rate and keen observation skills would know if he saw it. And he did.

A bright light lit up the neighbors' yard and illuminated half of Rosa's backyard at the same time. The men moved as two old pros, letting loose a string of profanities under their breath. Raffi rolled off the door to his right and hugged the ground. Rockfish fell forward, hidden behind the angled basement door. *Raffi had come through there. What the fuck? Why didn't it go off then?* The answer came with the sound of a back door opening.

"Goddamn you, Ranger."

The sound of a dog's nails traipsing across a deck and down a small set of stairs floated across the forsythias.

"That damn kid left the water bowl down again and you have the balls to come and wake me up?"

Rockfish held his breath, fearing what would happen next. *Zippy, or at least Ranger's best imitation. That's what would happen next.*

A volley of violent barks filled the night air. Rockfish turned his head to the left, expecting to see Ranger break through the privacy hedge.

"Fucking dog. Ranger. Get over here. Ranger. I ain't got all night. Now, boy!"

The barking stopped, and Rockfish could hear the obedient pooch head back up the stairs to the deck.

Fuck, I should stop by, knock on the door and see who trained that dog. Maybe they still have his card. Zippy could stand to learn a few things when someone other than Mack watches him.

The men waited for the door to shut and the light to turn off before they assumed their previous positions.

"Your heart still in your throat?" Raffi said in a whisper.

"Not a chance. I do shit like this for a living, minus the breaking and entering part," Rockfish said.

The next words out of Raffi's mouth were music to Rockfish's ears.

"Bingo," Raffi said, and moved to his knees. He reached and turned the knob. The slide bar on the opposite side released. He shuffled back to grab the handle on the right side of the dual doors and lifted. He held the door open only enough for Rockfish to slip underneath it and head down the concrete stairs. Raffi followed, gently closing the door behind him.

The men met up at the bottom of the stairs and turned on their flashlights. A wood entry door was the next obstacle the team faced. Rockfish moved closer and the beam of light moved through the glass panes into the room on the other side. The shadows he saw against the far cinderblock wall seemed to resemble a furnace and water heater.

"You good with that?" Rockfish said. He stepped back and giving his partner room to do his thing.

"Yup. Hold the light for me and let me get going."

Raffi approached the door and at first, used his own flashlight to inspect the door.

"No alarm. Nothing more than the simple knob lock. I'll be through it in a second."

Rockfish moved into position behind Raffi and shined his light over his partner's shoulder.

A minute later, Raffi pushed open the door. "Wa-Lah."

"It's voilà. Don't look for a light switch. Use your flashlight."

The twin beams of light crisscrossed the walls in a grid pattern. Rockfish estimated the room to be no larger than twenty-by-twenty. The walls were concrete block, and he confirmed the shadows against the back wall were the furnace and hot water heater. Boxes and shelves filled the rest of what was a storage room, running close to capacity.

"What about this other door?" Raffi said, shining his light on the door to their left, separating what was most likely the unfinished part of the basement and the rest of the lower level. Rockfish stepped closer and shined his light. A large recreation or living room stared back. A sectional, recliner, and treadmill filled the space.

"How about we finish with this one first, before we move on," Rockfish said. "Three minutes from now you'll be in the master bedroom opening drawers and hoping she doesn't notice a pair or two gone. I've been down this road with you before."

"And we agreed. No kink shaming."

"Cut the shit, Raffi. We're living on borrowed time down here. Get searching."

"You got nothing more than a small safe?"

"Yup, the description hasn't changed since the last half a dozen times I've told you," Rockfish said. "No idea if it's the size of a loaf of bread or a small mini-fridge."

The men started on opposite ends of the room and worked towards each other. Boxes were piled atop plastic bins and large totes. It wasn't long before Rockfish noticed Raffi's light constantly back on the rec room door.

"Enough with that. It has to be in here. I'd put money on it." Rockfish lifted two cardboard boxes off a brown plastic bin with a bright yellow lid. He held the small flashlight in one hand while the other sifted through the contents. "Honestly, if I were to hide something valuable, this room would be my first choice. Unless I've got one of those nifty safes behind a painting, but this is real life. And we're talking about a thirty-something female. She ain't exactly Ms. Home Improvement 2022. It's in here."

For the next fifteen minutes, they meticulously deconstructed piles of boxes, rummaged through said boxes and then put it all back where they found it. Rockfish waved his light and compared the two sides of the room. One partner was much better at the routine than the other. Silence and dancing beams of light filled the room.

"Stevie!" Raffi said at a decibel level Rockfish would have preferred to be a lot lower. "This what you're looking for?"

Raffi held something up in his right hand, and Rockfish pointed his flashlight in that direction. The beam paused for a second on Raffi's face. *Cat? Canary? Yeah, he swallowed it.* The light moved down, across his chest and to his outstretched arm. It looked to Rockfish like a decent sized hardback book. He stepped closer and could tell it was not the latest from Peter Straub. Raffi held the cover open and instead of a front page, Rockfish saw the combination lock securing what was inside. *Yeah, my copy of Koko didn't come with a three-wheel combo thingamajig.*

Rockfish snatched the apparent book safe out of Raffi's hand over his partner's objections and shined his light on it.

Cover looks legit. The Great American Conservative Bible, fourteenth edition. This damn thing looks more like a kid would hide his weed in it, or some porn, at the very least. Not the first steps to a large RICO case. Yet, anyone picking this up and not opening the cover would expect it to be as advertised. The weight of it did nothing to stir curiosity. Rockfish quickly did the math in his head. *Three wheels. Zero through nine. If you can repeat numbers, a thousand combinations. Of course, that is only if we're concerned with keeping the safe's structural integrity. Would we need to replace it back in its hidey hole at some point?*

Rockfish realized he was spinning his mental wheels and wasting time. He shoved the safe under his arm and turned to Raffi.

"I told you to stay away from that damn door. We're done. Let's re-stack this shit as best we can and get the fuck out of here."

"On it, Stevie."

"Can you re-lock the cellar door at the top of the steps?" Rockfish said. "No telling when she comes down here, but I don't want it to be that obvious."

"Piece of cake, boss. Gimme a second and we'll be back in the car before you know it."

"I've heard that one before. I remember your deal at Allison's. Can't afford to have a replay of that. Get it done so we can bolt."

As Raffi climbed the cellar steps, Rockfish locked the entry door behind him. *I can't believe this has gone off without a hitch. Finally, something in this damn case has swung in our favor. Soak it in, Steve, not sure when we'll get a repeat.*

Raffi reached the top of the stairwell and pushed up on the door. Bright, florescent light filled the small area, and he closed the door as quietly as he could, shrinking back down the steps.

I spoke too soon. Jinxed us.

They sat in the darkness weighing all options when a somewhat familiar voice reached their hiding spot.

"Ranger! Where the fuck did you run off to..."

Ah, fuck. It's gonna be awhile.

CHAPTER THIRTEEN

"Hey, Sonny, you got some company on the back deck." Mack's voice floated in from the kitchen.

The sunny Saturday morning, two and a half days removed from Rosa's basement, found Rockfish sitting in his living room. He had spent the past few hours trying to wrap his head around every aspect of this case, no matter the size or value assigned. With Mack's announcement, Rockfish tucked the pencil he was using to write behind his ear and laid the pad of paper on the coffee table. He had thought if he wrote it all out, put everything down in front of him, he could make sense of where this runaway train was headed. Maybe come up with a way to wrestle back control of it, at least more than he thought he had at the moment. But the pad was blank and the pencil as sharp as it was at sunrise.

He stood up and passed Mack in the kitchen.

"It's your partner. She had some playtime with Zippy and said she's ready to see you now."

He hadn't seen Jawnie since Thursday morning. After leaving Rosa's, he hadn't been able to sleep much and was waiting for her that morning at the office. She had gasped when she saw the mangled book safe and the small portable hard drive on Rockfish's desk. Over Raffi's objections, it had been his executive decision to tackle the book safe's structural integrity instead of wasting time trying combination after combination well into the next day.

From the moment he finished his tale of the break-in, and probably way before that, her body language let him know she wasn't happy. Not with his and Raffi's actions, nor his less of a request and more of an order for her to look and see what was on the hard drive. Arms crossed, the puss on her face and constant eye rolls let Rockfish know he was in for a lecture. And not the educational kind.

"Wasn't it you that taught me about the fruit of the poisonous tree and how Raffi almost fucked up the Porbeagle case for us?" She had said, with a stern voice. "If you get the evidence criminally, we're screwed in the same way. Nothing good is going to come of you skirting the truth about how this portable drive came into your possession."

"I, we, me, don't care, will cross that bridge when we come to it."

"Not to mention, Lynn will be the only one working on the document exploitation of all the files we exfiltrated from Rosa. That's going to slow things down to a crawl."

"Can we send Raffi over to help?" Rockfish had said.

Jawnie hadn't answered. She had closed her eyes and slowly shook her head. Rockfish got the message.

Now, he stared through the sliding glass door at Jawnie. She sat in a chair, her ever-present laptop on the small round table to the left. Zippy was curled up at her feet. *Sometimes that dog seems more hers than Mack's.* She stared out across the backyard, at the small inlet and out into the Chesapeake Bay. *I get it; the view is spectacular. It's why I dumped all that NikolaTV money on this place. Calming, more than spectacular. Alright, better get out there and see what she has to say. Tell me she found something on that drive that can wrap this puppy up in a nice bow.* He slid the door open and stepped out onto the deck.

"You know, if you want overnight visits with him, I know the owner. Zippy's food and water bowls are portable."

Jawnie turned and Rockfish knew her disdain for his actions hadn't subsided in the slightest. She had pulled the Phillies hat down low, and the sunglasses hid most of her emotional tells.

"Good morning, Steve. I know I should have called first, but I was in the neighborhood. I had a breakfast meeting with Andrist earlier. You remember our problem client?"

"Andrist? We wrapped that case a while ago. What's he bitch-moaning about?"

"No complaining. We had a casual conversation about him putting us on retainer for an upcoming issue he foresees. He thinks his new partner, that twenty-seven-year-old former dancer, might try to gain access to his bank accounts."

"No shit?" Rockfish said with a wide grin. "Everyone else saw that coming months ago."

His joke fell flat and Jawnie tilted her head at the empty chair on the other side of the table. Rockfish sat down and tried to put on his best business face. The air coming in off the bay might be the only enjoyment he would get out of this impromptu meeting.

"Things at our computer lab are moving slowly, now that we've had to divide the team and deal with the portable hard drive you brought me," Jawnie said. "Lynn's moving slowly through Rosa's files and emails."

"I also understand that she's working from her sister's house. While it's the best for her safety, I get she doesn't have you alongside her to help guide, teach, and troubleshoot her over any obstacles she encounters."

"At least you understand something I say," Jawnie said, tugging on the bill of her hat. "I'm still not over the stunt you and Raffi pulled the other night. We're partners. You ignored my advice and guidance. You threw it away and didn't think twice."

"I did not ignore it," Rockfish said. He wanted to keep this conversation moving and not dwell on the continuing disagreement. "I weighed your words and continued down that road. I always appreciated your input. But being old and stubborn, not to mention my experience, will sometimes trump common sense."

"To be honest, Steve, I'm not sure it was worth it in the end," Jawnie said. "You will not like what I say next."

"What do you mean?"

Jawnie sighed deeply. "Someone at Fulsome encrypted the drive. You know, like Stevie Wonder said. *I can't see shit.*"

"Ah Christ," Rockfish said. The thought had never crossed his mind. But it made total sense. If someone took the time to put it in a safe and tuck it away in a basement, then another level of protection shouldn't surprise him.

"That being said, I made a forensic copy of the drive and put the original in our safe. It should be safe unless someone gets through the plywood," Jawnie said with a grin.

"It's safe, trust me."

"I know, I was just busting your chops. Once the copy was ready, I hooked it up and started my examination. Got absolutely nowhere. Gonna need that encryption key if you want to know jack shit about this *insurance policy* of Grayson and Warrington." Jawnie spun the laptop screen so Rockfish could get a visual of what she was talking about.

Numbers and some colored graph lines filled the laptop's screen. None of which gave Rockfish the a-ha moment his partner hoped for. *I don't know what I'm looking at, but if she says it's encrypted, then we're fucked six ways till Sunday. Shit, that's tomorrow.*

"... And I took the opportunity last night to fill in Lynn on everything happening back here."

Rockfish shot a look of annoyance across the table before he could catch himself. *At least you didn't roll your eyes this time.*

"Look, I know you don't want the world to know about your breaking and entering exploits, but now she's the sole set of eyes looking through Rosa's laptop. She's part of the team. Like it or not."

"Like it," Rockfish said. He raised his eyebrows a tad, hoping to get across to his partner that he cared.

"Good. And if knowing what's going on here will cause her to look at something she would normally review and shitcan with a fresh set of eyes. Well, we need those eyes. This encryption key won't fall into our laps. I need her to keep an eye out if anyone at Fulsome ever sent it to Rosa."

"Never say never. You got us the info we needed to find this damn thing without risking life or limb. Lady luck is finally shining on us. You and Lynn are the key to this. I got faith."

"And if we never find it?"

"Let the Feds figure it out. Arrest Grayson and get him to flip. Not our problem. Or we hold the drive close to the chest. Use it as our get out of jail free card. Our insurance policy, if I may steal the bad guy's description."

Jawnie nodded, although Rockfish could tell a sympathy agreement when he saw it.

"That key has to be around somewhere," Rockfish said. "You would think with her clicking on the picture you sent and putting the evidence in a freakin' thirteen-dollar Amazon safe. This Rosa broad is dumb enough to save the key to a USB device and store it away alongside the hard drive."

"You checked, right?"

"Umm yeah," Steve said.

Jawnie's sarcasm hung in the air, and she looked across the table. Rockfish could picture her imagination replaying his *safe cracking* in her head. He took a hammer and crowbar to the book safe and, when it flung open, a small USB drive sailed across the room and fell behind a piece of furniture. Not to be found until the movers come across it many years down the line. Her version was far from the truth. He was there. There was no hidden USB drive.

"Yes, I'm sure."

Grayson and most of the executives at Fulsome wanted to dance with the devil and reap the benefits, while also having this so-called insurance policy in order to run to the authorities if the mob got too handsy. Then they trusted some glorified secretary to look after it. And she spent pennies on Amazon to hide it. You need to take full advantage of this situation and stop spinning your wheels, bud.

"I bet Grayson gave her a couple hundred or even a grand," Rockfish said. "She bought this POS and pocketed the rest. You'll find the key. I have faith. We're not battling rocket scientists here."

"Agreed, but the other half of the equation has a tendency to lean hard toward violence. Need I remind you of Angel, Raffi, and more importantly, Lana?"

"You don't."

"It's been great catching up, Steve, but seriously, I need to get back to the condo and do some network reconnaissance on her laptop. Make sure nothing has changed that would show in the slightest that they're on to us. That pencil behind your ear tells me you need to get back to the Sun's daily crossword."

"Classic McGee with that one. But a couple more questions before you bail. No incoming salvo from the infamous Freddie in IT?"

"Not a picture, not a link, or malicious attachment."

"That's a good thing," Rockfish said.

"Not exactly. It's the reason I want to check out her configuration. If they're on to us, then it explains the lack of an offensive volley on their part."

"Okay, last one, McGee. Anything you want to talk about, you know, get off your chest about the other half of that fiasco at Fulsome?"

"Annetta?"

"Yeah."

"You think anything I said scared the old bird?" Jawnie said with a wide grin.

"I think you walking out on her pissed her off to no end. But somewhere in the back of that brain of hers, she hopes you're scared. Enough not to come anywhere near the retrial. You've beat her once. Nothing to worry about again, kid."

"I always worry."

"I know, it comes standard on the Millennial base model."

The partners finished up, and Rockfish followed Jawnie down the stairs. They walked around the side yard to the front and said their goodbyes. When she pulled out of sight, Rockfish thought about going back inside. She was out of sight, but not out of mind. He was worried about her. More than normal.

* * * * * * * * * *

Rockfish leaned against the godforsaken Yaris and watched Jawnie's car crest the hill and disappear. One hundred and sixty miles to the Northeast, Annetta Provolone let fly with a string of curses.

"Damn it, fucking piece of shit knife!"

The butter knife had slipped from her hands, leaving her toasted tea biscuit partially smeared. The knife had skittered across the tiled floor and stopped half under the oven. Its thick handle prevented it from sliding completely under the appliance. She shook her head and stepped over to pick it up. The five second rule crossed her mind, but in the end, Annetta tossed the dirty knife in the sink and plucked a new one from the silverware drawer.

Someone's talking about me. That's what mom always said. The old wives' tale was the only option she'd accept this morning, because the other side of the argument was that her nerves were shot, and she knew that couldn't be true. *I'm fucking walking on sunshine! Not a goddamn care in the world about the upcoming retrial. I moved another step closer this morning towards the annexation of all Angelo oversees.*

Prior to the knife incident, Annetta had hung up a short, albeit productive janky tablet video conference call with the head of Baltimore's Marini Crime Family. Angelo had Ignazio by a dozen years, but the man handled technology like a six-year-old boy. Although his high-tech knowledge didn't prevent the old man from being played. *I pulled strings he didn't even know he had. I pulled this off without him having the slightest clue.*

Annetta had started the call on her end. The time had come for Conti's recent streak of clusterfucks to be brought to the attention of his boss. If for no other reason than accountability, but of course, Annetta knew there was much more behind her tattle. She played on Angelo's recent increased fear of law enforcement attention as the reasoning behind the call.

I know... It's not really my place to tell you your business but the more I heard, the more I felt this rise to the level where I needed to fill you in personally... yes, a crew of mine were working directly with him and when they told me of a run of screw-ups that are definitely costing you money... I know, I blame my men for not pushing that you or I be informed earlier of this joint effort... no; I don't know what he's thinking... you've got other capos who are watching and lord knows what they're thinking about the situation... leaders like us need to keep shit like this to a minimum... of course I think it's part of some greater power play by him... you've known him as long as I have... he's always had his eyes on the throne.

Annetta knew each word she spoke pushed Angelo closer and closer to issuing the order she wanted. The man listened attentively and the longer she talked, the more she felt him sway towards the position she hinted at, talked around, but never came out and said aloud. Annetta had chosen her words carefully and even worked off a notepad, out of camera range. She couldn't afford to fuck any of this up, or else the order would come for her. She continued her dance, alternating from a straight tap to a more complicated and faster one. If Angelo wavered, she'd wrap her arm around his waist and lead. The dance needed to end exactly how she had practiced.

"He's gotta go." Angelo said, almost in a whisper, although it was crystal clear to Annetta.

She could see the angst in his face. He had turned from the tablet's camera for a couple of seconds, but when he looked back, there was no mistaking how much this pained him. Annetta nodded and bit her bottom lip in solidarity. She knew there was a small piece of her—tiny, really—that regretted how things had turned out. She and Conti went way back, long before he was a Capo, and she was the boss in waiting. But for her very own manifest destiny to succeed, she'd have to bury some feelings deep down and keep the wagons moving. Annetta hated Westerns. Naturally, her mind flashed to a large tree and a handful of men in suits standing under its branches in the front yard. *This was strictly business.* Tessio had not only said it but knew the consequences of his actions. Conti, too, would understand when the time came.

The icing on the call came when Angelo asked if she would handle the problem. Personally, was how he put it. Annetta understood that there would be no subcontracting on this job. Indebted was another word Angelo used, and she knew the hook was set. This time, it was her turn to move away from the camera and play the emotional card. The grin was wide and stretched her cheek muscles to their limits. Annetta took a few seconds to revert to the caring, concerned friend before turning back.

"I'd be honored to do this favor to you. You are welcome, my friend." *Everything is according to plan. I am Goddamn Geppetto. And then some.*

The rest of their conversation dealt with the potential fallout, post-whack, so to speak. Annetta expected Angelo to deal with the anger or acceptance of the move by his own men. He mentioned compensation for her troubles. The least he could do was order the new Capo to kick up a sizable sum of the Fulsome cut directly to her. Angelo would see to it. Annetta was beholden and expressed her gratitude. But in the back of her mind, she knew it'd be only a matter of time before the king's cut would be hers. Conti's sacrifice would not be in vain, as the plan to nudge Angelo aside and absorb the Marinis into her family had moved into overdrive. The Fulsome cut, in the short term, was chicken feed on what she'd be collecting as soon as Giovanni was running things down south. She hoped to stay out of the can long enough to enjoy it.

The mention of prison brought her focus around to the other problem at hand. Jawnie McGee. And not only for the blatant disrespect shown six days ago during the meeting at Fulsome. The kid tried to put up a brave front, but Annetta knew the dyke was shaking on the inside. There was no way, after all this, despite Conti's and that damn Marshal's screw ups, she'd still testify. *Maybe not completely sold on the amnesia route to save her own skin, but close. One last push.* Jawnie'd be in Annetta's crosshairs soon enough, but the successful resolution of the Conti situation needed all her attention at the moment.

Annetta picked up the plate and paused. The tea biscuit was cold, the butter had melted and congealed. It no longer looked appetizing, but she picked it and the tablet up before heading for her study. The ocean view and its calming effect would aid when the call from Giovanni came, and she'd give the order.

Fifteen minutes and half an eaten tea biscuit later, the tablet vibrated on the couch cushion next to Annetta. Her right hand grabbed it before sliding off. She expected to see her consigliere's face. What stared back at the screen was a little lower than expected. His chest, a paisley tie, and a seatbelt fit squarely into the frame. Annetta could feel the rise in her blood pressure as the veins on each side of her head pulsed.

Madone! He knows not to use public internets for this. And this is the guy I want running the new Baltimore faction of my family? Am I the only one with any common sense around here? I'm surrounded by idiots.

"Call me back. You know the damn deal," Annetta said before Giovanni could get a word in.

"Wait, we're all good. I'm working off some new set-up from Chenzo. Uses some Russian satellite internet stuff. I don't know, but the kid knows his shit. Trust me. I'm headed out to the port of

Wilmington. Something came up about a load we're expecting, or else I'd be in the normal spot to call."

"Do I need to know or worry about it? Because I've got a shit-ton on my plate at the moment."

"No, I've got it," Bianchi said. "How'd the call go?"

"He ate it up."

"Our friend won't be a problem any longer."

"We're taking lead on it," Annetta said, and she heard him audibly gasp.

"Do tell."

Annetta recounted her conversation with Angelo and then took her own deep breath. She looked out across the sand dunes to the ocean before continuing.

"Reach out to both Grayson and Conti. Get them up here. On the boat."

"Wait. You wanna Big Pussy them?"

"Just our problem child. The other should be there and understand that fuck-ups have repercussions. Add to the leverage we'll need over him."

"That will not be so easy, boss. I think Conti's spooked as it is."

"Whether he is or isn't, make it happen," Annetta said. She could hear the aggravation building in her tone and assumed Giovanni did too. "Set up the sit-down for Oscar's and when they pull into the parking garage, do what you need to convince them there's been a change in plans. I don't know. The Feds are being pains in the ass and won't let me leave the house that day. You'll figure it out."

"No worries, boss. I'll go to the meet and celebrate route. Reach out and let them know the Ocean City Board of Supervisors will listen and, with the right amount of cash in their pockets, move forward with Fulsome's Amusement Pier Revitalization Project. A few minor details need to be worked out during the sit-down and then we'll pop some champagne."

"Don't fuck it up," Annetta said and hung up.

* * * * * * * * * *

Jawnie's Sunday night dinner remained cold on the plate, resting atop a pile of books, which teetered close to the coffee table's edge. The vegan broccoli mac-and-cheese had cooled and jelled into an impenetrable mass. *I'm probably going to run back into the kitchen and throw it in the microwave. Or grab a sharp knife and chisel off pieces to eat cold. I don't really want to get up at the moment.* Freddie from IT was doing his thing, or at least trying, and she had a front-row seat.

The email had come in as Jawnie removed the broccoli from the fridge and had washed and chopped up the florets. She stopped and pulled up the Gmail account from which she had previously sent her own malicious attachment. There was nothing in the inbox, but the spam folder had one unread message. Jawnie opened the folder and knew Freddie in IT had finally come through when she read the subject line and noticed the paperclip attachment icon right next to the date and time stamp. *Apparently, so did Google. Freddie, my friend, you are off to a horrible start.*

Despite the email's draw on her attention, Jawnie finished cooking dinner and then sat down and took in the show. She didn't want to seem too eager. After all, Rosa hadn't opened the picture the minute the thirst trap landed in her inbox. *Take your time. Don't mess this up because you're excited. Slow and steady wins the race.* She repeated that phrase as dinner cooked and then carried the plate to the coffee table. It balanced atop her pile of books.

Jawnie walked over to the coat closet and wheeled out the Linux box and brought it to a stop alongside her cooling dinner. Next, she pulled out and attached the keyboard, mouse, and monitor. Once the power cord met the socket, Jawnie was ready to open the email on what she hoped Freddie from IT and anyone else would think was the official Rockfish & McGee computer network.

Subject: Ellicott City's LGBTQ+ Hottest Night Spot! Now With Sunday Brunch!

Jawnie opened the message and ignored the text in the email's body, despite its multicolors, fonts and highlighted words screaming out for attention. *Freddie in IT either did his homework or Rosa did a decent job filling him in. I love a good brunch and champagne coolies.* She double clicked the attachment and sat back to enjoy the show.

Jawnie chiseled off cold pasta and rubbery broccoli for two hours while Freddie in IT slowly made his way across the network. His progress was slow and methodical, elevating his credentials, hoping to gain better access.

In her eyes, his fumbling skill set was the first honest to goodness belly laugh she's had in, well, she couldn't remember. He hadn't yet gained the administrator-level of access he or his bosses wanted. Jawnie had set it up that he wouldn't need root access to get at the juicy file folders that would entice his superiors. She had set plenty of roadblocks for him to encounter in order to see exactly what she was up against. She imagined if he was still struggling come the morning, maybe she would throw him a bone. *Maybe all he needs is a helping hand to earn that hacker merit badge. First Chenzo and now this nudnik.*

Jawnie's laughs on Freddie in IT's behalf eventually faded. They were replaced by a gravity blanket of guilt and sadness. She felt horrible for stooping to Rockfish's level of illegal stratagem. It was not the first time she had bowed to his wishes, but it did not make any of it easier to swallow. To dog pile on to the issues, Jawnie had, deep down, wanted to believe Rosa was an innocent bystander in this entire mess. Unfortunately, the ones and zeros that moved across her screen as someone mapped out her fake network told a different story. *Somehow, if, and I know, the odds are infinitesimal, Rosa wasn't involved in this, that she wouldn't do what Grayson asked, maybe she'd be in a position one day to forgive me for what I did. There was something there over Labor Day. Or am I trying to cover my ass and make myself feel better?*

The Freddie in IT & Rosa Show was a somewhat mental diversion from her own recent technology failures. She had given up that afternoon on ever cracking the encryption on the Fulsome portable hard drive. She didn't have the computing power or the tools necessary in-house or at the office. This wasn't an episode of *NCIS, Criminal Minds* or even that absolute pile of dog crap, *CSI: Cyber.* No matter how hard she hit the keyboards or projected some sort of 3D network modeling above her dining room table, she wasn't able to slip past the hard drive's front gate.

The same dining room table was where the offer from Fulsome lay, gathering dust. Jawnie had picked it up from Lynn's desk, where it had sat with other pieces of delivered unread mail. Rockfish had wanted nothing to do with it. He refused to open it, let alone have a lawyer review it. She had taken it home, hoping to have at least Pilar and Kara's lawyer, Susan Giacchino, give it the once over. Or better yet, why not call Angel? *He had high-powered lawyers on retainer and why shouldn't I ask a favor? Maybe because he's still going through hours of rehab because of you. Yeah, there's that.* It sat on the corner of the table, next to the stack of Orvis dog catalogs. *You buy one squeaky rubber chicken for Zippy and the next thing you know, you're inundated with junk mail.*

The opening notes of Tool's song Eulogy caught her attention and Jawnie looked up to find her cellphone. She squinted hard and gave her head a slight shake. *Time to focus on something other than this monitor.* She picked up the phone and saw the incoming call was from Lynn.

"I've got some good news and maybe great news," Lynn said, and Jawnie could almost feel the excitement ooze out of the phone's small speaker. "This is a day late and a dollar short, but the combination to that book safe is 814. I found a WordPad file buried in what first appeared to be a folder of vacation videos. It ended up being a list of what I think are passwords. All different formats and lengths, but get this, the last three characters of each are the same set of numerals. I know it's in pieces at the bottom of a landfill, but if you need a three-digit pin for her again, that's it."

"Nice one, Lynn!" Jawnie said. She was seriously happy for Lynn. Despite not needing the information any longer, the attaboy would go a long way. Or she hoped. The ones from Steve did for her. "I'll pass it along to Steve. And you said you might have something we can actually use?"

"Yup, and this one you might find useful. That same document detailed a file pathway, with the preceding text *Luther key*. I copied the file path and threw it in the virtual machine's explorer window. The file looks like an RSA private key. The file extension ends in .pem. Exactly like you told me."

Jawnie had to peel herself off the ceiling before responding to Lynn. *Maybe Steve was right. Someone is looking out for us now.* "Lynn, are you sure?"

"Absolutely."

Less than five minutes later, Jawnie downloaded the encryption key file from the firm's actual FTP server and onto her laptop. *Suck it Freddie in IT.* She used the key against the forensic copy of the drive she had unsuccessfully battled over the past couple of days. Now, the contents of the portable hard drive were at her fingertips. *Or touchpad clicks.*

She was excited. Even elated, but didn't realize how much so, until she spotted the cursor waiver on the laptop's screen. Her eyes glanced down, and her finger visibly shook against the track pad. Jawnie leaned back in her chair, pushed the laptop a few inches away, and took a deep breath. *Be happy. It's okay. You might have run across the motherland of all evidence stashes. Enough to build a RICO case from scratch, but think. Take your time. This is not the time for stupid, rushed mistakes.*

Despite the thrill of the chase and the feelings that rushed over her when the drive unlocked, that small piece of gray matter in her head, the devil's advocate, wouldn't let her totally enjoy the win.

How Steve and Raffi obtained the hard drive was still a sticking point with her. That he didn't take her advice seriously and broke into Rosa's house was huge. Jawnie would hold that grudge against Steve until someone, it didn't matter if it was the FBI in Baltimore or a United States Attorney in Philadelphia, told her the evidence was admissible. The fruit of the poisonous tree clause had hung over the firm's head since the Porbeagle case. The ruling was a lesson they had learned the hard way. *Yet Rockfish failed to consider risking life and limb to gather evidence a judge would only throw out before a jury hears it made no sense. But here we were. Again.*

When the anti-virus and malware program ended, showing zero infected files, Jawnie sorted the Finder window by date changed. One thousand and thirty-seven files, the most recent being from late July. The same timeframe when Pilar and Kara first approached her. The drive contained audio files, videos, scanned ledgers, spreadsheets, PDFs, and some image files. Jawnie randomly opened files, and it wasn't long before the excitement doubled, and she pushed the laptop away again.

Jesus Fucking Christ! No doubt this is the insurance policy Grayson and Warrington talked about! The audio files alone would hang Conti out to dry. The man should know better than to drink and tell stories. Someone at Fulsome realized they needed something to wield, if the mob got greedy. Smart in capturing this, yes. Dumb as a rock, asking a lower-level employee to secure it for you. A safe deposit box would have worked out better, but would that have been the first place one of Conti's soldiers or law enforcement would have looked for it?

Law Enforcement. The words flashed like a neon sign across her brain. The original drive plus a working copy would need to be handed over yesterday. Someone with a skill set above and beyond hers would need to exploit the data and start the damn investigation. But first, she had to reach out to Steve. He would need to know his felony burglary, in the first degree, was worth it. *This is going to absolutely wreck the Marini Crime Family.*

Jawnie picked up her phone. 9:37pm. *He could be up, or about to put Zippy out for the night.* She inserted a USB into the laptop and copied over a good sample of the files she had reviewed. With the drive in her pocket, she dialed his cell. *Voicemail. Can't say I'm surprised at this hour.*

"Steve, Lynn did it. I'm on my way, so when you get this, turn on the front lights. I don't really care if you're in your pajamas."

* * * * * * * * * *

A day and a half after Jawnie caught him in his skivvies and had spent several hours reviewing files from the Fulsome hard drive, Rockfish pulled into work. He parked next to Jawnie's car and took in the office's view from the front seat of the Yaris. Sheets of plywood still covered the front windows. He had doubts about the temporary door they had installed, too. The contractor was running into trouble with the county over permits. Each blamed the other for dragging their feet on completing the paperwork needed to get the construction started.

The explosion had done some damage but hadn't stopped the partners from continuing to take care of business each day. *For Christ's sake, it had been almost three weeks. When am I going to drive up and see something that doesn't look straight out of the Rodney King riots?*

Jawnie's Subaru out front wouldn't normally surprise Rockfish on an early Tuesday morning. Jawnie had beat him into the office pretty much every morning since they had cut the ribbon to open the place. What made him tilt his head in curiosity was that she had worked from the condo since the meeting at Fulsome, one week ago. They had agreed to it, for safety's sake. The same went for Lynn, working out of her old bedroom at her sister's place. He couldn't protect everyone, but with cars exploding and Hollywood producers being shot, the strip mall office probably wasn't the best place for any of them. *That damn low-grade plywood is only half a step better than wafer board. I'm shocked no one's taken a pair of scissors and cut their way in.*

With his extra-large coffee in one hand, Rockfish bit down on the grease lined bag that held a McDonald's breakfast meal numbers two and three, and used the now free hand to open the door. Rockfish set the bag and coffee down on Lynn's reception desk and looked around. The outer office was vacant and the noise from his keys hitting the desk echoed off the walls. *She must be in the back, tied to her desk, doing God knows what that couldn't be done at a safer location.*

"Steve, I'm in the back," Jawnie said.

Had she heard his keys or had the security system let her know the front door had opened? Wait, they didn't hook the security cameras up to the temporary door. Another job on the contractor's to-do list as soon as the city approved the permits. It didn't matter how she knew. He had more pressing matters to take up the little free space in his head. *No time for stupid thoughts. But was there any other kind?* He silently cursed the voice in the back of his head and walked past the conference table and down the hallway.

Rockfish stood in the doorway and looked down at Jawnie. He could see the lack of sleep in her eyes and the pressure of this case. *Is it really a case? Whatever it is, I need to get her to that retrial late next month and then make sure she takes a vacation. Doesn't matter what the current caseload is. We both need to get the fuck away from this strip mall for a couple of weeks and forget about all of this.*

"How long have you been here?"

"Good morning to you, too," Jawnie said. "I got tired of staring at the same four walls in that condo. Working from home doesn't make me feel like I'm accomplishing anything, so I came in. If I'm in the office, I must get work done, right? It's how my brain works."

"I'm not going to argue your point. You could have told me. I'd have come in with you. To tell you a secret, I really don't trust that wood out there to keep any of us safe."

"I've been here since a little after 4am," Jawnie said. She glossed over his concern for her safety, and he picked up on it. "I need to finish going through all these files from the portable hard drive. Categorize them and get some type of summary written about each. Then get it all into the hands of someone who can do something proactive with it."

"Find anything earth shattering?" Rockfish shifted his weight to the other leg and leaned against the doorjamb.

"It's all pertinent. But for your concern, it's all the same damning type of stuff I showed you on Sunday night. Just a ton more. The more of this I go through, the more clearly I see why Warrington referred to it as an insurance policy. If Conti ever got too greedy or wanted to push anyone at Fulsome to the side, any mention of this would give the mobster pause. The threat of turning this over to law enforcement would be enough to bring him back in line. Maybe Grayson, or any of the Avonlea Crossing group aren't as dumb as we think."

"I agree. An old school guy like me understands simple cover-your-ass. There might have been a hiccup in their working relationship in the past where Conti put the squeeze on for a bigger piece of the action. Grayson collects and records everything he can to prevent from being backed into the same corner again."

Jawnie nodded and pointed at the chair, a single, long stride in front of Rockfish.

"I'm good," Rockfish said.

"Steve, I want to get this done no later than tonight and then we have to give all this evidence to someone in law enforcement. The sooner the better. I feel it's our only option at this point."

"In that case, I better sit down," Rockfish said. He slid into the pleather chair and waited for the rest of Jawnie's suggested course of action.

"I want to give my copy, the notes, and the original to Agent Thomas. FBI Baltimore could launch a decent RICO case with all of this."

"Why your copy?" Rockfish didn't like where the conversation was going, but also understood there was most likely no way around the inevitable. He ran his hand through his hair and down to his neck. He could feel the tension.

"If I give them my notes and a copy, they can immediately begin their own forensic examination. Get the original in some sort of evidentiary chain of custody and lock it away until the defense's dream team asks for it in discovery. Not to mention they can begin figuring out how to get it admissible in court." Jawnie winked with a slight nod.

She's thawed a little towards my stunt. That's a good thing.

"Agreed. Where the heck did I put her card?"

"I've got one. With as many times as she's been here, I think there is probably a handful lying around. But Steve, while you're here, I wanted to fill you in on Rosa and Fulsome's attempt to turn the tables on us."

"Are they still pleasantly occupied, slinking around that fake PC you set up?"

"It's a real PC, but a fake network. I loaded the box up with a ton of bullshit. It should keep them and their eighth-grade computer skills busy for a while."

"Bullshit?" Rockfish tilted his head. He didn't follow. *Either there are files on the machine or there aren't. My middle school skills are confused.*

"Yes. Some real files. You remember the process we went through to digitize all your old paper files for the case management system we bought? They'll be spinning their wheels with those. Then there are the not-so-real-files. Also, some files they've exfiltrated are corrupted. They'll try to access but none will open."

"I like it," Rockfish said. "I think our next move after speaking with Agent Thomas—"

"Jawnie? Steve?"

Lynn! That voice is indistinguishable. What is she doing here?

Neither partner answered the shout, but each was out of their chairs in a heartbeat and headed for the front of the office.

They found Lynn standing in the front area of the office, between her desk and the bullpen area. Her arms were out, supporting her as she held on to the back of the couch. Rockfish's first thought was she looked better than the two of them. *Time with her sister had actually done her some good.* It re-emphasized the need for him to get away, even if it was for a Raven's away-game this fall.

"I found something... thought you should see it... right away." Lynn stopped and tried to catch her breath.

This is the suitable type of excitement. I'll take it in a heartbeat.

Jawnie led her around to the front of the couch while Rockfish retrieved a water bottle from behind the bar.

"Okay, breathe. Take your time." Rockfish cracked open the water and handed it to Lynn.

"They're all headed to New Jersey. Some big meeting," Lynn said after draining half the bottle.

"Fulsome?" Jawnie said. Rockfish agreed with the puzzled look on his partner's face.

"Yes. Grayson and Mangold. To meet with THE Lady."

"Provolone," the partners said in unison.

"That's what I thought too," Lynn said. She took another drink before continuing. "The email came in this morning, from Grayson to Mangold."

Rockfish turned to his partner, confused.

"Rosa. Rosa Mangold," Jawnie said, and Rockfish understood.

"Here, I printed off a couple of copies," Lynn said. "I didn't want you to go only on my interpretation of the contents."

Rockfish took the paper and skimmed. There wasn't much to it. A big meeting in New Jersey and with Rosa finally receiving a negative test, Grayson needed her to get back to Maryland ASAP. There were vague promises of a larger role in this future project and also, the request to make all the logistical reservations for the three of them.

"Thursday, that doesn't give us much time," Rockfish said.

"And the other guy?" Jawnie said.

"Probably Conti. He's going to broker the meeting between Grayson and the Provolone Crime Family. Just by making the introduction, he'd be in line for a kickback. Could be one time, or multi-payments."

Rockfish's attention turned back to the paper in his hands. He re-read it and stopped on the last paragraph. He had skipped it the first time in the avalanche of news regarding Fulsome angling to work with another mafia family.

And again, congrats on playing the dumb moulinyan like a fiddle. They'll be a little something extra in your check next week. Freddie says they have found nothing of value yet, but he's got tons more data to go through.

He looked over at Jawnie. Her face was flush and turning redder by the second. *It's a shot to the ego solar plexus. I might take advantage of the temporary rage...*

"Jawnie, don't let it get to you," Rockfish stood up and walked over to the end of the couch before putting his hand on her shoulder. "Can you toss some of those audio and video files you've been reviewing on your phone?"

Jawnie looked up and nodded. The redness didn't dissipate from her cheeks.

"Pick me some good ones. A few to get the point across clear enough so even those knuckle draggers can get the picture. Might let us play both ends against each other. Contrary to our earlier discussions, our options have doubled."

Jawnie looked up again. Confusion replaced some of the redness.

"We give the evidence to Thomas as planned," Rockfish said. "Then I hand the deed to the property back to Pilar and Kara and walk away. Wash our hands of the whole thing. Take a much needed vacation."

"You wouldn't," Jawnie said. Her eyes grew wide and Rockfish could see the concern.

"You're right. I wouldn't. Wanna go crash their party? I'll pack the extra-large monkey wrench bag."

"I would love to. The racist fucks."

CHAPTER FOURTEEN

Rockfish reached up and pulled down the driver's side visor. The glare from the sun blinded temporarily all the occupants as the Yaris crested the top of the Delaware Memorial Bridge and crossed into New Jersey. Jawnie rode shotgun and the man with vengeance on his mind, Raffi, man-spread across the back seat.

The team had gotten an early start and Rockfish had spent part of the drive pontificating aloud on how much better he would have felt making the trip with Lana. Jawnie had tried to play devil's advocate to get him to change the subject, but an hour and a half into the drive, it hadn't worked.

If we could kick Earl Porbeagle's ass and take down the grift of the Church of the Universal Nurturing II in an old mini-van, we'd be okay with a two-year-old Yaris. The man talks about that car like it was the love of his life. But she knew it was and Lana's memory would always be a topic of conversation between them. Even with Lana 2 arriving in a few months. *Fingers crossed for him.*

Jawnie stared at her phone. Eight hours remained before the term *evening* could be applied to the day. *Eight hours, a normal workday for some, but time's ticking away while we drive around. We need one more slight f-up by these clowns. Racist clowns. Damn, you sound like Rockfish now.* But the slur from Grayson's email had stuck in her craw. *Buried is a better word. That Rosa wasn't exactly Caucasian, and the man felt comfortable using it in a conversation with his Hispanic underling, only added insult to injury.*

The location of the meeting between the Fulsome employees and two of the larger mid-Atlantic crime families remained unknown to the team. Rockfish seemed nervous. She was even more so because they wouldn't learn of its location prior to it actually taking place. Lynn was firmly back at her sisters', observing Rosa's compromised laptop in real time, but had yet to learn any additional details regarding the meeting.

Earlier, Rockfish had said, "Maybe Rosa's back in town with Grayson. If she's now in-person, no need for email. Comms might only be by phone now."

Jawnie had nodded in agreement but kept trying to think of other ways, options that they could exploit. She had called her old friend Ned Hasty the previous day to learn some details and the conditions of Annetta's home confinement. An hour later, he called back.

"My source isn't one of the team sitting on her house, but he asked around and found out she cannot have visitors and the only approved trips outside those four walls are medical or consultations with her lawyer. Does this have anything to do with Rockfish's call the other day?"

Jawnie did her best Rockfish tap dance and gave her friend a line of bullshit. Not being honest with Hasty, after all they had been through, bothered Jawnie, but he was the chief of police for a small township, and she didn't want to get him involved or have him worrying about her.

Back in the Yaris, Jawnie made her best guess based on the information at hand.

"Based on what Hasty found out, my guess is Oscar Rosenthal's office. She's not going to the doctor to have a bunion checked around dinnertime."

"What do you think, Raffi?"

"Raffi smash!" Raffi said, and punched the back of the driver's seat. He was all about getting his hands around someone's throat.

Didn't care where, when, or how much pain he was still in. "Make it happen, Steve."

An hour and a half after stocking up on some key surveillance food stuffs, they arrived in Pleasantville. They located the small office building and Rockfish pulled down into the two-level parking garage.

"Twenty minutes from the old broad's McMansion," Rockfish said as he turned off the engine. "I like the way you think, McGee. Who's going upstairs to get this ticket validated?"

"I'm more concerned with a rent-a-cop doing his job and noticing us loitering here for the next five plus hours," Raffi said. "I didn't see any cameras when we drove around looking for a spot to park, but you can never be too sure."

"Good point, Raffi. We might need to pull out and come back a few times," Rockfish said. "Rotate levels, but one of us will always be with Jawnie." He looked at his partner to let her know he was serious. "But let's stick to the current plan until we see a uniform walking the concrete with a purpose. You think on your feet better than me. Spin a tale."

The team split up with Jawnie and Raffi watching the first level elevator banks and Rockfish taking the second. They agreed there was no way the group would park outside and risk the possibility of being seen entering the building around the same time as Annetta. The parking garage elevators would be their best bet. Three different hands had their fingers crossed, hoping to see a recognizable face. *The sooner the better. But then what?* Jawnie was concerned about the next part of Rockfish's plan. But before she could ask, Raffi spoke up.

"What then? Can I pounce on that fuck face, Conti?"

"If you can find an alcove away from any security camera, go for it. But in the meantime, I've got to think what our next step is going to be."

And there it was. The plan was fluid and still needed some serious work. *I got faith in ya, buddy. But in the end, I still feel once they're here, we call in the cops.* The last thing she wanted was a shootout at the Oscar Rosenthal Corral. Especially after both men informed her of their ankle holsters.

Much to Jawnie's liking, there were no guns pulled over the course of the next five very long and boring hours. Not even one case of the slightest of mistaken identity. *I had hoped for uneventful and successful, but even this has me wishing for a little action.*

The tap on Jawnie's shoulder surprised her. She looked up from the elevator door and there was Raffi, right where her attention span left him. He stood across on the other side of the silver sliding door. She wondered how Rockfish had snuck up on her without her knowing. *Fatigue, that's how. You lost focus.*

"Steve—" Her voice stopped. A very young security guard now stepped in front of Jawnie. She composed herself and noticed he looked as nervous as she did. His blue uniform, meant to obviously resemble law enforcement, was at least a size too big. His glasses were filthy. *I wonder if the sweat and grease from that hair was the culprit? And someone needs to buy him a belt.*

"Ma'am, I can't have you and your friend loiter here in the garage harassing our clients."

"Yo, Paul Blart. Over here," Raffi said and waved the young kid over. "Deal with me on this."

Jawnie stepped aside as she didn't want to hear the song and dance Raffi was about to lay on the security guard. *In a couple of minutes, that kid won't know which way is up. He'll go back to his chair and leave us alone for however long we're stuck down here.*

She felt her stomach rumble and unconsciously moved her hand over her abdomen. It made noise a second time before Jawnie realized it was the phone in her back pocket.

The notification came from Instagram. User RosaM4133 had uploaded a photo. Jawnie tapped the notification to be taken to the post. The post was a selfie, with a mandatory peace sign in front of a Range Rover with a wooden building with a large front porch in the background.

First business dinner as an executive. Can't wait to dive in at Momma Bruno's Trattoria #girlpower #womanstrong #empoweringwomen #womeninbusiness #mommabrunostrattoria #marinaresturant #madeit #workinghard #formymoney #neverunderestimate #nostoppingme #contentcreator #influencerinnewjersey

The location listed was Somers Point. Jawnie checked the distance. Sixteen minutes away. She hustled over between the security guard and Raffi.

"Officer, I couldn't agree more," Jawnie said, grabbing Raffi by the arm. "We're leaving right this instant. Go get Steve. We're in the wrong place."

* * * * * * * * * *

Thursday night rush hour traffic at the shore turned those sixteen minutes into twenty-five. Jawnie sat on the edge of the backseat, close to the edge, hoping they hadn't missed their window of opportunity. The men sitting in the front of the Yaris were silent most of the way. Rockfish had mentioned walking up to the table and playing a few of the audio files she brought. *He'll need a second camera so we can record the look on their faces. Rockfish, I bet, will want to watch that repeatedly for his own amusement.*

"Of course, that will only be a good monkey wrench to use, should Conti or anyone else from the Marini Family already be there." He had added.

What if that selfie was on the way out and they were now headed to the lawyer's office? I don't even want to go there. Her feet bounced on the floor, and she placed her hands on each knee to stop the fidgeting. Walking into the restaurant with no strategy, let alone a Plan B, wouldn't be the first time she followed Rockfish into the danger zone with her clueless meter pegged. But it wasn't the thing you got used to the more you did it. *Maybe there's a small part of me that hopes they caught the early bird special and are pulling into that parking garage right this minute. We'd be safe, but sorry.*

Rockfish killed the headlights as he pulled into the Dock-a-Jersey Marina.

"According to the map, we follow this road all the way back and it should dead-end at the restaurant."

"Thanks, Jawnie," Rockfish said.

"Out of sight of any prying eyes, I'm guessing." Raffi said.

"Let's do a lap around the place looking for that dark colored Range Rover behind her in the picture. If it's here, then so are they."

Two minutes later, the lights from the front of the restaurant came into view. The building was a single level wood structure, with a large front porch and hanging lights running all along the front. To Jawnie, the restaurant didn't come across like a place where business or mobsters would empty their expense accounts. *Looks like a damn converted Cracker Barrel to me. Now you sound like Rockfish. Don't judge until you see the inside.*

"Well, this place doesn't look all that," Rockfish said. Confirming his suspicions, aligned with Jawnie's. "Look at that cheap hanging string of lights along the front."

"I agree, Steve," Raffi said. "But I don't think any of these cars drive off the lot for under seventy-five thousand. Don't judge a rundown building by its cheap Amazon lights."

"Let's find that Range Rover and make sure we're in the right place and they're still here," Jawnie said. Her voice cracked with those last few words, but she hoped her partner didn't notice. *WWRD? Think damn it. Contribute. Ignore that pain in your stomach. Let it do flips through next Tuesday. Red-lining anxiety or not, you're part of the team. Offer something.*

Raffi spotted the Range Rover the second time through the lot. Someone had parked the vehicle in the second row, along the front, and Jawnie cursed herself for not noticing it on the first drive by. Rockfish kept driving and backed the car into the last row of parking. They had a clear view of the vehicle in question and the front door.

"What now, boss?" Raffi said.

"We go in," Rockfish said. The sureness in his voice settled over the inside of the car, but did nothing for Jawnie's gut.

"But what if they're not there, Steve?" she said. "What if Rosa stopped in front of that vehicle thinking it was the perfect backdrop? You know, despite every one of her followers knowing she drives a Honda CRV?"

"Won't know until we lay eyes on 'em."

WWRD? And she knew.

"I got this and whatever you do, don't move this car."

Before anyone in the car's front could answer, Jawnie threw open the back door and walked as fast as she could without looking suspiciously towards the front and then around the side of the wooden building. She listened for any shouts or orders to about face from Rockfish, but all that reached her ears were crickets.

She stood at the back of the restaurant and scanned the structure for the door she knew would be there. The door to the kitchen for employees and food deliveries was further down the right side. Jawnie approached it and tried the knob. It turned with ease. *Unlocked. Now act like you belong here and are late for your shift. Don't overthink it. Don't over analyze it. Self-confidence should get you a look at the dining room.*

Jawnie opened the door and slid inside. To her left was the walk-in freezer and in front of her, the busiest kitchen she had ever seen, including her summer working at the Ruby Tuesday's next to the retirement home. Flames danced, orders shouted, and servers slammed plates on countertops. Jawnie spotted a pile of aprons hung on hooks to her right, grabbed one, and slid it over her head. She moved across the kitchen space, trying to find the door that led out to the dining room.

She looked down and saw her clothes were clearly visible under the apron, not to mention not even close to the uniform the other employees wore. She caught movement out of her peripheral vision and saw the swinging door she had been looking for. Jawnie walked across the kitchen, dodging line chefs, waiters, and prep cooks as they did their own choreographed dance.

Jawnie ducked a server, returning a tray of empty plates to the kitchen and slid through the door. She stopped to take a breath and scanned the patrons without stepping too far into the dining space. Her adrenaline was pumping at a volume not seen by her veins since the Porbeagle case. It was half fear of not being questioned by anyone in the kitchen and half gratification when she spotted Rosa.

Rosa, her red dress standing out from the earth tones worn by almost every other diner, sat at a small table in a far corner to Jawnie's right. Luther Grayson, Ignazio Conti, and Giovanni Bianchi filled the other seats, and all leaned forward over their plates, trying to see who could leer down the front of her dress the best. A smile and toss of her hair let Jawnie know Rosa didn't mind the attention.

Jawnie took a mental snapshot of the table and reversed course straight back into the kitchen.

"Hey, who the fuck are you?"

The accusation greeted her before she stepped through the doorway. Jawnie kept her head down and pulled the apron over her head and let it drop to the floor as she picked up her pace towards the door.

"Anyone know who that is?"

The door to the back lot of the restaurant slammed shut behind her and all Jawnie wanted to do was stop, bend at the waist, and try to catch her breath. But she knew if she did that, with her luck, someone would have followed her out and grabbed her by the arm. Jawnie sped up and the loose dirt, sand and mashed seashells beneath her feet gave way. *Slow down before you fall and end up on your ass. You saw what you needed. Now get back to Steve in one piece.* Jawnie slowed to a jog and headed across the parking lot where her partners waited.

Jawnie slowed up as she approached the car and a loud flashing alarm went off in her head. Her eyes had readjusted to the dark and she could see the silhouette of a man leaning against the passenger side front door. Even from a few car lengths away, it was obvious. *That's not Steve or Raffi.*

She slammed on the brakes and pivoted on the balls of her feet one hundred and eighty degrees in the opposite direction. Jawnie hadn't taken two steps before her head slammed into the chest of another man. She staggered backwards, and the man raised a gun in his right hand. *Help. No one's coming. Gang's all here.* Jawnie breathed in deep, held it and tried to fight back the tears.

A moment later, the first man held the passenger rear door open.

"In," he said. Jawnie did as instructed. Rockfish and Raffi slid over to make room for their new cellmate. Her partners sat there, their heads down. All three felt failure, mixed with the humid night air rolling in off the salt water. Jawnie could see her cellphone. Someone had dumped it on the front seat along with the two others. She assumed her partners had also been searched and their ankle holsters, emptied.

"Maury, go let the boss know what we found," one man said. They had stepped away from the open window and into the darkness. Jawnie knew the two men were only feet away, but she couldn't make out any physical descriptions from her vantage point. "I told you, it wouldn't be long after we got word they headed up I-95."

They sat in silence, waiting for the other man to return. Sweat ran down the side of Jawnie's face and a glance to her left told her the others weren't dealing with the heat and tight space any better. *What's next? Would they try yet again to put the fear of God into us, or have we crossed a line this time? Who knows, we're here, other than Lynn? Hasty? How can I get word to anyone? Yell at the next car that pulls into this freakin' place?* Jawnie wrapped her arms around her waist, hoping it would calm the nerves that rattled her stomach. As for the tears, she didn't care anymore. *Who cares what anyone thinks? You need to size up this situation. Big brain this. You're part of this team, not a spectator.*

The door she leaned against opened suddenly. Jawnie's thought process was interrupted and she almost fell out. A hand caught her shoulder and pushed her back up. She turned, and Giovanni Bianchi stood next to the car. His right hand dropped over the open door. Annetta's consigliere had snuck up to what was now his captive audience.

"Great seeing you two again. I'm afraid I haven't had the pleasure of meeting your friend. But hang tight. I gotta finish my meal. We'll chat later." Bianchi grinned and shut the door. He stepped away from the car toward the other two and they continued their conversation.

Either oblivious to the fact the windows are down, or maybe they want us to hear. Probably don't give a shit either way. Jawnie looked to her left and nudged Rockfish with her shoulder. He turned and gently shook his head. She didn't like the defeated look in his eyes. *Not one bit.*

"Hey boss, with the added luggage, do you think we should call in Sally-B or one of his guys?"

"No, we should be good. Conti doesn't suspect a thing and by the time he does, it will be way too fucking late for that fucking dog. Guy's got old timer's disease or something. Or so she claims. Get 'em to the pier, tied up and below deck. We'll follow shortly. I'm not going to miss the lemon ricotta cake they have here."

* * * * * * * * * *

The boat engines roared to life and Rockfish lifted his head. He looked across the boat's small cabin at Jawnie and Raffi. He hoped they couldn't see the absolute fear in his eyes. Raffi's look of determined retribution had been replaced with a blank expression. Jawnie didn't look as bad, but he wondered if she knew exactly how hopeless their situation was. *I've half-assed my plan of attack one too many times. Think, you stupid shit. There's got to be a way out of here. For their sake. Not yours!*

Their car had stopped at the end of a long pier that jutted out into the canal. There was only one boat tied up and Rockfish had known that was their final destination. The henchmen had marched them down the pier at gunpoint, blocking the only dry means of escape.

The boat was a large hybrid. Part pleasure craft, part ocean fishing. Exactly the type Rockfish and Mack dreamed of having one day tied up off their back deck. Quick spins across the bay and out onto the ocean would be their drug of choice.

Rockfish, on the way down to the cabin, had stopped and glanced at the ladder leading to the flybridge. He craned his neck but couldn't see the upper portion where the captain would navigate from. A quick shove to his lower back had ended the sightseeing, and he followed Jawnie down the steps below deck.

The boat's small below deck cabin was cramped. The space wasn't as bad as the backseat of the Yaris, yet they still sat shoulder to shoulder on the floor, hands secured by zip ties and good old duct tape preventing any sounds from escaping. Rockfish noticed they had secured Jawnie's hands in front of her body, as opposed to behind, like he and Raffi. *I guess they didn't really consider her a threat, or someone got lazy. Probably a little from column A, a little from column B. These aren't the smartest group of imbeciles we've encountered. More lucky than anything to have us in this predicament. Goddamn you. How could you not think they weren't monitoring you? Fucking amateur hour and you missed it.* He hung his head, despite the message he knew it sent to the others.

Rockfish could hear the engines rev and felt the boat pull away from the pier. From here it would be a straight shot across Great Egg Harbor Bay, around Ocean City, and then nothing but deep ocean. *Damn it. Fuck. Fuck. Fuck.* Any hope he had for anything but the worst probable outcome just went up in flames. *Maybe I can still talk my way out of this. How? You gonna shout through the duct tape?*

Rockfish tried to make eye contact with their captor, but Guido... *Imma name you Guido...* was too busy checking out his hardware. The man dressed more for a day at the local social club than a quick jaunt out to the middle of nowhere. Rockfish looked to his right. Raffi's eyes were closed, and his chin touched his chest. Further down the line, Jawnie stared off into space. A single tear rolled down her cheek. Rockfish's shoulders sunk along with his head, and he grimaced. *There's not gonna be a heroic rescue. The mighty Rockfish has struck out.*

After moping for a while, Rockfish looked up at the Provolone soldier standing watch over them. *More like sitting.* He had deposited himself in the middle of a bench seat against the far wall. Far, being relative. Rockfish could reach out and touch the man if he wasn't bound.

That bench serves a dual purpose for storage. Like that will do me a lot of good now. The man stared down at the three captives with what seemed to Rockfish like contempt and a good heaping of I'd rather be anywhere else. The gun in his hand got as much attention as the three captives on the floor. *First day with the new piece, buddy?*

Rockfish's mind wandered with the rise and fall of each wave. Each thought kept him from accepting the ending that hung above all three of their heads. *Can I overtake this guy? When's my moment? It would be kinda hard with my hands tied behind my back. What am I going to do karate kick him to death? What was in the storage bench? A gaff?* Rockfish could picture sinking it into the man's neck and yanking hard to pull him off and to the ground. The fantasy ignored the fact Rockfish would have to unseat the man, open the lid, grab the gaff, and then sit the man back down before dispensing justice. *I'm not getting us out of this, am I?*

Muffled conversations from above filtered through the door and down the stairs. Rockfish couldn't make any of the words out, but the two prominent voices were Grayson and Conti. *Had Bianchi not made the trip after giving the order? What had he meant about Conti being blissfully ignorant of the endgame?* Rockfish didn't have to answer the voice in the back of his head. His father's voice filled his head instead.

You know damn well, Sonny. We've all seen this movie. Fuck, how many times have you seen The Godfather 2? Fredo is ready to start the Hail Mary. Or we can look to The Sopranos for a more recent example. You're about to be Big Pussy'd. Conti too.

Rockfish shook his head to evict the bad thoughts. He couldn't give up. There were two people, maybe more, depending on him. He hadn't tried keeping track of the boat, but assumed they had to be a mile or so out by now. The swells were getting larger and more frequent. The three of them rocked side to side, with only Jawnie able to keep herself upright. He had also noticed the captives weren't the only ones affected by the waves.

Guido had, at some point, got up and retrieved a metal soup pot from the small galley, while Rockfish was knee deep in his pity-party. It wasn't until the first violent heave into the pot that he caught on. *He's seasick. First day on boat duty. Enjoy, asshole.*

The scene repeated itself every so often. A series of retching noises. His free hand would wrap around the pot while the gun hand dropped to his side. Then the puke would fly. Guido would then stand, empty the pot into a trashcan and retake his watch position. The other thing Rockfish realized about the puke routine was Jawnie. She would rock forward with each puke session.

As if she was timing it. And there it was.

When the man's face next lowered into the pot, his gun dropped to his side. Jawnie leapt.

NO! Rockfish bit his tongue as to not give any warning and desperately wanted to close his eyes. But he didn't. He couldn't. All he could do was watch.

Jawnie threw her entire body weight at the side of the man and, with a little help from the seas, Guido fell to the floor. Jawnie landed next to him, her body weight holding down the arm with the gun. Before Rockfish could silently give her the attaboy she deserved, there was another blur to his right. Next was Raffi's turn, and he landed on the man's chest, knees first and knocked out what little wind the man had left. Rockfish could hear Guido sucking for air that wasn't there. Rockfish sat on the floor, in awe of his team, yet unable to move. Every muscle ignored his brain's commands. It didn't matter how loud the shouts were.

Jawnie rolled off the man's arm, picked up the pot and pounded his head until there was no noise or movement. Rockfish could see his chest rise and fall, so he wasn't dead. But that wind he so desperately needed a few seconds ago had refilled the man's lungs.

Rockfish remained frozen, watching his well-oiled team work effortlessly without him. Jawnie shoved her hands deep in Guido's pockets and found a small hunting knife. Once she freed Raffi's hands, he returned the favor before turning their attention toward their leader.

"Stevie, shake out of it, buddy," Raffi said. He cut through the zip-tie while Jawnie pulled the tape off his mouth. "We don't have the time for you to process all this shit. We need to act fast."

Raffi helped Rockfish to his feet. His first instinct was to grab the gun off the floor. His second was to point at the bench.

"Lift that lid. There's gotta be something we can use in there. We need to move. No telling how long this guy will be out for."

Raffi stepped over to the bench seat, and Jawnie took a step closer to Rockfish.

"Good to have you back, Steve." She held out her fist, and he bumped it.

"We hit the mother lode over here," Raffi said, and their attention turned. "Looks like this is the supply closet for when they make these types of charters."

"Wouldn't be a gaff in there, would it?" Rockfish said.

"Nope, but there's a decent sized fire axe and an aluminum bat," Raffi said. "I'm keeping the bat."

Rockfish liked the glow on his friend's face. *The revenge role is returning, full force.* He stepped over to the bench and reached in. He grabbed the roll of duct tape and two zip ties. "Let's make sure this mother fucker won't move or make a sound."

"Okay, what's next, Skipper?" Raffi said. With each minute, the boat moved further out into the ocean. Likewise, the odds increased for someone to come down and fit them for cement shoes.

"We can't go up the way we came down," Rockfish said. "Even with the element of surprise, it's tight quarters. Our bat and gat don't equal the two guns, maybe more, up there."

"What about that?" Raffi pointed towards a short ladder tacked against what would be the front of the boat. "Can only lead to one place."

Rockfish followed Raffi's finger across and up. *A hatch. Might be our only shot.*

Rockfish looked over at Jawnie and her death grip on the fire axe.

"Either way, kid, you're down here on prisoner duty," Rockfish said. "Be aware that when the shit hits the fan above, someone might beat feet down those steps."

"I'll be ready," Jawnie said.

"Good. Kick whoever it is in the nuts, then swing away. And if this clown moves an inch, don't dance. Swing hard. I don't care with what end."

Rockfish checked the handgun and looked at Raffi. "Full magazine and one in the chamber. Ready?"

"Fucking batter-up."

* * * * * * * * * *

Rockfish flipped the hatch up and raised his head enough to peer out. They would come out at the bow and work their way towards the back without setting off any alarms. He looked up at the flybridge. The boat was still moving at a pretty good clip, so someone was up there driving. *That's one and probably Conti, Grayson, and Bianchi in the back. Maybe the broad, but who the fuck knows?*

Rockfish lowered his head back down and nodded to Raffi. It was go time.

Rockfish scrambled up onto the bow, with Raffi right behind. The men separated, each moving to the side gunwales.

"Pincer attack," Rockfish had called it. "As long as the one in the flybridge doesn't spot us, surprise will be on our side, even if the numbers aren't. That's assuming we don't lose our grip and go over the rail." It would be a narrow path, but it was their only one. Rockfish worried about Raffi's safety. *Exactly how was he going to hold on and carry that damn bat at the same time? God, if you could ease up on the swells for a second, we'd be appreciative.*

Each man made it to their respective side and continued forward. Rockfish looked up and from this angle and some moonlight, it looked to him as if Bianchi was up in the flybridge. It was a guess, but whoever it was, was occupied, looking straight out over the bow. *No shouts, warning those in the back. We're still good.*

Rockfish took his first step onto the narrow gunwale. Navigating the narrow path would be a cinch compared to the chance Jawnie took below. *Eyes forward and go slow. Doesn't matter how long it takes, Raffi won't do a thing until you both are in place.* The surface beneath his Nikes was slippery as shit, and only a thin metal handrail prevented him from toppling over into the ocean. The gun firmly shoved in the back of his pants, he gripped the railing with one hand and placed his left flat against the boat's outer wall. His knees bent with the rolling of the hull against the waves.

He had lost track of time when he reached the back corner of the boat. With one hand on the rail, he grabbed the pistol and peeked around the back. The first thing he saw was Raffi's hair blowing in the wind. He had made it safely and was waiting for their signal. A signal they had never agreed upon.

Four people sat in the back cockpit area. Conti and Rosa faced the back of the boat. Grayson and Maury sat with their back to the swim platform. *I was right. For whatever reason, Bianchi is up in the flybridge. I can take this guy—*

The scream from Conti was louder than the boats inboard motors and Rockfish knew the sight of Conti had caused Raffi to go all vigilante. *Can't blame him.* Rosa screamed right along with the old man.

With all the attention focused on that side of the boat, Rockfish jumped down and shoved his gun into Maury's back.

"Drop it and kick it over to my friend."

Rockfish thought he heard a snicker and the man's arm shot out and the gun flew over the back of the boat and into the drink. Rockfish lowered his shoulder in retaliation and rammed the man with all he had. Maury skittered across the swim platform and fell ass over elbows into the ocean. *One down. He might be back. We'll see.* Rockfish turned back to his silver slugger partner.

Conti was down on the deck in the fetal position as the bat came down again and again. Grayson and Rosa froze in their seats. *It shouldn't surprise you. You signed up for this shit.*

"Raffi!" Rockfish said and at that moment, all hell broke out. The bat came down again on the old man's knee. Then Raffi's foot connected with the old man's head. *Attaboy, promise kept.* Rockfish knew the man's prognosis for walking off the boat wouldn't be good. *Somewhere I hope Gordon is smiling and enjoying—*

BAM

A shot rang out from above and ripped through the canvas tarp that served as a roof to the back area. Rockfish pressed his back hard against the cabin wall. Rosa leapt from her chair and grabbed for the door that led to the lower cabin. All Rockfish could do was yell.

"Jawnie! Incoming!"

A second shot rang out and Conti screamed louder. *Bianchi had missed, but had he really? Buried at sea, alive or dead. Did it really matter?*

Rockfish returned fire in the general direction of the flybridge. He didn't expect it to find flesh but wanted Bianchi to understand he wasn't the only one armed.

Then every sound became amplified, but there was no sound. Bianchi had cut the motors and to Rockfish, that meant one thing. He was coming down. Rockfish stepped back away from the ladder and up onto the gunwale. His feet slid and his right arm latched onto the railing for dear life.

BAM

The gunshot caused him to jump back down to the deck. He looked over to Raffi and received a thumbs up. *This canvas tarp won't give us the complete cover we need, but for the time being, until he comes down here or empties his clip into it, we should be okay. Lucky ass shots, not included.*

Raffi leaned against the wall on the opposite side of the ladder to the flybridge. Between it and him, Grayson remained in his seat, frozen in fear, while Conti lie on the deck bleeding and whimpering.

One left. Unless Grayson grows a pair to impress Bianchi. He looked over at Raffi and nodded. Raffi swung the bat hard and connected with the sitting man's chest. A second swing took out his left knee and Grayson crumpled off his chair and onto the deck. Raffi stepped over the man and stood next to the ladder.

BAM

"Raffi!" Rockfish watched as his partner grabbed his shoulder and dropped to his knees alongside the other two. The bat fell from his hands and rolled towards Rockfish. The shot had come from straight above and instinct had Rockfish stepping back up onto the gunwale. From this vantage point, he couldn't see shit above, but felt safer. *At least until the next shot.* He watched as Grayson dragged himself back to the swim platform to get out of harm's way. *Good luck, buddy.*

The minutes ticked by with the only sound coming from the wounded that littered the deck and the waves crashing against the hull as Rockfish hung on and waited. He leaned forward and looked around the corner. The coast was clear, but it didn't mean he was moving off the ledge.

The gun in his back made him step off the ledge yet again and plod over the wounded. *Where the fuck did he come from? Either way, that ladder must not have been the only way down. Dumbass. You let him drop down all Spiderman-like and come up behind you.*

"Drop it. Overboard."

Rockfish paused. The gun hung at his side. The equalizer in this fight. He couldn't sink it.

"Do it," and Bianchi pushed the barrel into his back a second time.

Rockfish waited for the hull to roll and swung his arm. The gun flew over Raffi's head and hit the railing on the other side of the boat. It bounced back onto the deck. Three sets of eyes stared at it. Only one was within arm's reach.

"Don't even think about it, Pérez," Bianchi said.

Rockfish could see the temptation in his friend's face. But each man knew it would be game over if he even twitched.

"It was an effort worthy of your shitty reputation, Rockfish," Bianchi said. He raised his arm with the gun. "After all this, she'll want to watch your demise in person."

Bianchi brought the gun down across the back of Rockfish's head. He dropped to his knees and the boat rolled right. Bianchi reached for anything to stop him from falling. The gunwales weren't the only slippery surface. Raffi saw his opportunity and dove.

Raffi picked up the gun. Rockfish, still on his knees, felt the blood pour down the back of his neck. He watched as Raffi mistimed the boat's next roll and pulled the trigger with his good hand. He missed wide left.

The same swell that screwed with Raffi's aim sent the aluminum bat rolling back towards Rockfish. Blood on his hands, he grabbed the handle tight. He twisted his back and swung for the fences. With a solid overhand swing, the bat's sweet spot connected with Bianchi's forearm. The man cried out in pain as the gun fell to the floor. *God, I hope it's broken.*

Rockfish frantically looked to the deck for Bianchi's gun, but it slid out of reach. He readjusted his bloody grip on the handle and worked back to his feet. He cocked the bat again. Swing and miss. Bianchi leaned away, seeing it coming from a mile away. The bat slammed against the guardrail. The reverberation shot up Rockfish's arms. His weapon fell harmlessly to the deck. He didn't have time to contemplate his next move when a shot to the jaw caught him off balance and he dropped back to his knees. *Hey dumbass, he's still got one good arm.*

Rockfish looked up to find Bianchi's arm was ready for the knockout blow when Raffi fired a round into the sky.

"Hey! We're done here!" Raffi said.

Rockfish turned and saw that Raffi had retrieved Bianchi's gun. He held both now, each barrel leveled at the consigliere.

The mobster didn't listen as he let his punch fly. Rockfish raised his forearms in front of his face and blocked it. Rockfish again struggled to his feet. He held his right palm out in Raffi's direction. He shook his head before looking back to Provolone's stooge. *You want to fucking go? Let's dance, motherfucker!*

Rockfish was woozy from the blow to the back of his head, but he still had two good arms. *Well, one good and one almost healed.* He made a couple of fists and waded into the fight.

The men stood and traded punches. Neither listened to Raffi as the wounded man yelled. Rockfish landed two punches to every one of his opponent's, but Bianchi kept coming back for more. The man bullied forward, relentless, pressing Rockfish with his broken arm guarding his face while his left hand swung wildly. Rockfish stepped backwards and tripped over the bat. He went down hard and could only watch as Bianchi stepped forward to close the gap, cocking his good fist.

BAM

Bianchi fell to the deck and Rockfish rolled to his left to prevent the mobster from landing on top of him.

"I told you two to cut the shit," Raffi said. "Ain't nobody got time for this."

"Is he dead?"

"Not unless his heart was in his hip."

* * * * * * * * * *

Rockfish pushed open the door to the lower cabin. He needed to make sure all was under control underneath, as it was topside.

"Jawnie, all good?"

"Aye aye, Captain," Jawnie said. "She's down here cowering next to our seasick friend."

"Nice job, kid."

"It wasn't my purse, but I knew her. She went down like a ton of bricks."

Rockfish chuckled to himself. The joke told him all was good in her brain as well. *We're going to have to sit down and watch that episode as soon as this shit show comes to a close.*

"Alright, send her up here. We've got restraints for everybody!"

Rockfish and Raffi made good use of the remaining zip ties and duct tape. Bianchi, Conti, Grayson and Rosa were bound securely and laid out across the deck like drum fish after a successful night angling. Jawnie remained downstairs, watching over the other henchman. With their combined injuries, there was no way they could get him up the stairs and alongside the others.

Rockfish looked out over the back end to see if Maury was within eyesight. He couldn't see anyone, but wasn't taking any chances.

"Raffi, can you drive this thing?"

"I'll fake it until I make it."

"I have no idea what that means, but can you drag your ass up there with one arm?"

Raffi nodded and turned to the ladder.

"Get it started and move us away from this area. I don't want this guy to come back at me like some bad Friday the 13th movie."

Rockfish watched over their captives, pistols in hand, as Raffi slowly made his way to the flybridge.

When the engines turned back over and began churning, Rockfish walked back to where Bianchi lie, on his back, his hands bound underneath him. Rockfish swung his foot back and connected with the man's broken arm. And then a second time.

"That's for your boss, since she's not here. I'm going to climb up and make sure we're headed in the right direction. You as much as try to roll over, I'll put one between your eyes. I'm not the shitty shot Raffi is."

Rockfish didn't expect an answer and didn't wait for one through the duct tape. He took each rung, one at a time, with a pistol pointed downward the entire way.

Raffi had increased the throttle when Rockfish reached the top.

"Just like a car, Stevie. This giant navigation screen doesn't hurt, either."

Rockfish looked at the screen and pointed with the barrel of the gun.

"We're here. She's there. Get me close."

* * * * * * * * * *

Annetta sat on her living room couch, calm, cool, and collected for the first time since the court overturned her verdict. She killed time, waiting for word from Giovanni, by watching Law & Order SVU. Ironic, she knew. But the woman loved a good police procedural. *Especially when the focus was on sexual predators and the slimy fucks who targeted children.*

When the episode ended, it bled straight into the next without a commercial break and Annetta reached for her water. How much longer would they be? She hadn't heard from her consigliere since

Giovanni had reached out and let her know the boat was pulling away from the marina and had entered the channel. *By this time, they should have motored out, deposited the trash and been well on their way back by now. What was his problem? Why hadn't he reached out? I'm the boss. Am I not allowed to celebrate with my men?* The other side of the coin? Concern and worry weren't something she would allow herself to address. The string of failures was to come to a glorified end this evening. *No more yips. Cement shoes for everyone!* And Annetta raised her glass of water and toasted herself.

She had paid little attention to the television, as the thoughts of Jawnie and Conti's demise danced in her head. *Two birds, one boat.* But when the notes from a strange theme wafted across the room and reached her ears, Annetta looked up. Christopher Meloni's mug flashed across the screen and her eyebrows shot to the top of her forehead. *This wasn't the old Stabler. Oh, hell no. It would be a cold day in hell when I let Law & Order: Organized Crime ever stream in this house. You should have stayed retired, little man.* Annetta reached for the remote and pressed the power button. The screen flashed and went black. *That's better.*

Without the sound of the television, noise from outside, muffled by the closed French doors, caught her attention. *Another fucking bonfire and underage kids drinking on the beach. Stupid kids.* While the local police would, in the past, have ignored it unless they got wildly out of hand, Annetta's current celebrity and home confinement had a more federal presence watching over this stretch of the boardwalk.

When the noise persisted, Annetta stood up and walked around the couch to the glass doors that overlooked her deck, the boardwalk, some sand dunes and finally the beach off in the distance. She turned on the spotlights for a better look, despite the light not reaching past the boardwalk railing. A crowd had gathered out past the sand dunes and was slowly moving towards the waterline as if being herded by unseen sheep dogs. The moonlight wasn't strong enough to give her a better view and she couldn't make out more than an enormous shadow towering over the individuals as they moved closer.

Annetta unlocked and threw open the doors. The cool September night breeze off the ocean came as a welcome smell, and she stepped out onto the deck. The noise from the beach was a different story. Having lived at the shore for as long as she had, it was obvious the roar of a revving inboard motor drew the crowd. She walked to the far end and leaned over the railing to get a better view. From this vantage point, along with the engine noise, the shadow resembled more of a large boat. While not beached proper, it seemed stuck twenty yards out past the waterline.

Annetta had no concern for the injured or survivors, having lived here for over twenty years and witnessed this kind of shit first-hand. *Of course, they pulled this shit more and more over the past two years. They never tried these damn beach landings when Trump was in office. Not the first time those dirty fucking Mexicans circumvented immigration and beached a boat full of illegals. Worse than the freaking border. Build that damn sea wall.*

What made matters worse, no one in Ocean City had a yard of any size that needed to be maintained. She expected the cops to show up at any minute and pulled up a chair. With all the commotion, it shouldn't be long until someone ran past on the boardwalk, a local cop a couple of strides behind and taser ready for action. Anyone, really. Annetta didn't care if it was a man, woman, or child. *I could watch those fucks be tased all day long.*

The engines soon sputtered and died out, leaving an eerie silence hanging over the beach. Shouts soon followed and Annetta got up from her chair to see what the new hubbub was about. She leaned against the railing at the far end of her deck and squinted. The crowd had parted, and a single individual emerged from the pack, walking away from the wreck. The man slowly trudged through the sand in the boardwalk's direction. He didn't walk in a straight line. Serpentine was more like it. Annetta wondered if he had a decent bump on his head from the wreck.

It wasn't until the silhouette cleared the last dune and approached the steps leading up to the boardwalk that she recognized her own personal nemesis.

Rockfish! What. The. Fuck?

The tablet slipped from her hands and landed face down on the deck. Annetta let it lie there, as there would be no call from her consigliere. No cracking open the bottle of Dom Perignon that sat chilled in the refrigerator waiting on a celebration. One a long time coming. *God. Damn. Fucking. Yips!*

She stepped back from the railing. Her mind scrambled to make sense of yet another failure on her men's part. *Speaking of those yahoos, where the fuck were they? No way this two-bit private eye and his band of halfwits overtook my men, but here he was. Please tell me at least Conti is a half mile or so beneath the surface. That bitch McGee, too!* Annetta watched in horror as Rockfish crested the stairs and strolled down the boardwalk towards her house.

Thunk

Thunk

Thunk

With each step, she made out more of the man. He dragged a bat behind him. It made an imposing noise as it slid between each wood plank on the boardwalk. Rockfish looked like someone had dismissed him from Fight Club for taking one too many beatings. Annetta wondered, if push came to shove, did the man have the energy to even lift the bat? At least her men had given him the what-for before succumbing to whatever happened. *That's one thing to be glad about. I guess.*

What about the gate? It's unlocked. If he comes down off the boardwalk... if he chooses... right, where the fuck do you think he's headed? The gate's waist high. It ain't stopping him and you know that.

Thunk

Thunk

Thunk

By the time Rockfish had reached her house, Annetta had backed away from the railing and stood in the center of her deck. A pair of barbecue tongs hung from the grill on her right. Not the weapon she needed at the moment, but the one she'd have to grab if Rockfish made a move down off the boardwalk.

He moved the bat to his side and then lifted it. The end pointed straight at Annetta. The motion answered her question regarding his ability to lift it and it also caused her to take a step backwards and reach for the tongs. *Even if Giovanni and his men are gone, I will not show fear.*

Thunk

Thunk

Thunk

Rockfish paced back and forth on the boardwalk, never moving further than the width of Annetta's deck.

"PROVOLONE!" Rockfish stopped his pacing and pointed the bat again.

Annetta held the tongs out in front, almost imitating her stalker, but conceded slightly and took another step backwards. In response, Rockfish took one forward and then another. He reached the first step, which led down from the boardwalk to the edge of her yard. The waist high gate remained unlocked. From there, it would be a dozen steps up to her deck.

Thunk

Thunk

Thunk

The noise from the bat became all Annetta heard. The crowd on the beach, the waves crashing upon the beach, all faded into the distance. She looked out over the deck and watched as Rockfish's head disappeared from view. But not his voice.

"PROVOLONE!"

Annetta stepped backwards again and found her back against the doors. *What was wrong with going back into the house, locking the doors and living to fight another day? Nothing, that's what.*

Thunk

Thunk

Thunk

He climbed the steps. Her steps. A minute later, the top of his head became visible, and Annetta dropped the brave face and slipped back into the house and locked the doors. Tongs still in hand, she contemplated what other weapon she could wield against this maniac. *A steak knife? Fucking feds had gone over this place with a fine-tooth comb before agreeing to my confinement. Fuck!*

She could only watch as Rockfish stepped onto her deck and raised the bat again.

"PROVOLONE! Your boys failed again. Now it's your turn. Like my bat? I named her Jawnie Two. She's going to enjoy this."

Rockfish swung the bat and a large clay pot of impatiens shattered. Flowers, potting soil, and bits of clay shards littered the deck. He moved methodically around the deck. More clay flower pots, her grill and a small glass patio table became victims of the one-man wrecking crew. When there was nothing left standing except two well-built chaise lounges, he turned and walked up to the French doors. Without realizing it, Annetta stepped back into the center of the living room and waved the tongs in the air.

"PROVOLONE. Jawnie and I have waited a long time for this, you goddamn bitch!"

Rockfish swung, and the glass cracked. An unfamiliar noise, off in the distance, appeared to give him pause, but then he swung again. And again.

For the first time in her life, she welcomed the sound of approaching sirens.

* * * * * * * * * *

Rockfish paused, took a step back. He admired his handy work. The hole in the French door was big enough to fit his head through, and a frightened old woman stared back from the other side. *Frozen scared? Doesn't matter. Swinging for the fences. Ain't gonna be pretty for you.*

Rockfish pointed the end of the bat through the gaping hole. "I'm coming for you, bitch!"

Consecutive blows knocked enough glass out to the point he could now step through. Yet Annetta hadn't moved.

"Pull up a chair, Provolone! You, me and the bat need to talk!"

The tongs dropped from her hand onto the carpet, but her feet didn't move. She stood and stared back. Her face was blank and Rockfish wondered if she even grasped what was about to go down. *Ain't so big and tough now, are you?* He could picture the bat connecting with the side of her face, and it warmed his heart. She needed to pay.

"Okay, have it your way. One more for good luck," Rockfish said and swung the bat back. He paused and grinned after their eyes locked. He went to swing, but the bat hesitated and he realized someone had come up from behind and grabbed the barrel. Rockfish whirled around, ready for a fight, with one hand on the handle and the other cocked.

Jawnie.

"Steve. Give me the bat." Jawnie said. She had come up behind him while all his attention had been focused on destruction. *Jesus Christ. What if it had been one of Provolone's men?*

Rockfish couldn't overlook the concern in her eyes and across her face, but he decided for that instant to ignore it.

"No. I've got our payback right here. We need this. You can help by staying out of the fucking way. Look at her. Scared to death. Don Chicken Shit. Now, let go." Rockfish tugged on the handle, but Jawnie didn't let go. She yanked back with vigor.

"Neither of us need it. Look at her. Look at me." Jawnie said. She locked eyes with Rockfish and let go of the bat. "We're not like them. Never have been. Hear those sirens? Let those with badges sort it out. I can't have you in a cell next to her."

Rockfish turned and looked through the hole in the door and then back at Jawnie. He shook his head.

"Steve, listen to me! We won. She knows it. That's payback enough."

Rockfish blinked as Jawnie's words spun in his head, looking to burrow further in. He understood everything she said. It took little for her words to knock down his wall of violence. He nodded in agreement and let the bat drop to the ground.

"Let's at least enjoy the show in comfort," Rockfish said. He led Jawnie over to the chaise lounges.

"If we only had some popcorn," Jawnie said.

"I can check inside," Rockfish said with a smile.

He never saw the punch to his shoulder coming.

EPILOGUE - GRAND OPENING

Rockfish glanced down at the clock on the dash and confirmed he and Raffi were arriving fashionably late. The launch party for the recently re-branded Guardian Angel's Mini Golf had started over an hour ago. *Mack won't let me live this down, especially after he hitched a ride with Jawnie and Lynn earlier to help with setup.*

Rockfish picked up Raffi on the way. Pilar and Kara had tasked the two of them with picking up the ingredients for a champagne punch, free to each adult with the purchase of a round. Unfortunately, neither man remembered it was New Year's Eve. The line stretched around the block with other procrastinators. By the time he had secured two cases of his preferred brand, Freixenet Brut Cordon Negro, in the trunk of Lana 2.0, the men were behind schedule.

Rockfish pulled around back of the Guardian Angel's club house and popped the trunk. Each man grabbed a case and hustled through the door.

The rebrand was Pilar and Kara's idea. Not long after Rockfish signed the property back over to them and recouped his dollar, the ladies shared their idea with Rockfish, Jawnie and Angel. They had witnessed firsthand the troubles and adversity those three had undergone on their behalf. Then read about the worst of it when the arrests of Conti, Grayson and a handful of Fulsome executives made papers. No one totally forgot Little Golf Big Tees in the rebranding. The sign, originally commissioned by Pilar and Kara, soon after their winning bid was accepted, hung proudly in the employee storage area as a reminder of all that had happened.

Rockfish found the large punch bowl and the bottles of mixers on a table directly under the old sign. The men put the cases down and got to work.

"Raffi, you get to mixing and I'll go find some sort of wheeled cart so we don't have to carry it and trip over God knows what."

Rockfish pushed open and walked through the employee's only door that separated the club house and Guardian Angel's pro shop. There he stumbled across one third of its namesake and ninety percent of the planning and funding.

"Angel, they put you right to work? I figured you'd be resting on your laurels and accepting kudos from some sort of reclining chair near the eighteenth green? After all, this baby is all thanks to you."

Angel smiled, and his body rocked with laughter. He sat on a tall stool; his cane leaned against the wall to his left. He collected tickets purchased at the front of the pro shop and exchanged them for a putter and colored ball of the golfer's choice.

Rockfish smiled. *The man was so much more than a checkbook to all of us. Good friend didn't tell the entire story. Who would have thought that two years ago? Even a couple of months ago?*

While the new name paid homage to the power of three, none of it would have been possible without Angel Davenport and his drive for revenge on his own terms. It started with VR nights in the parking lot and ended with an expedited schedule to program, design and build the courses, both actual and virtual. Each served as a huge Fuck You to Fulsome and its failed Avonlea Crossing project. Without the highway off ramp, the project ended up withering and dying on the vine. And watching Conti's perp walk in a wheelchair was icing on the cake. Angel still owed Raffi for that one.

Rockfish located the cart he needed and patted Angel on the back as he passed back into the clubhouse. He loaded Raffi's punch du jour and hoped the smoke emanating from the bowl was dry ice, but he was afraid to ask. And couldn't, as Raffi was nowhere in sight. *I did only ask him to mix it up.*

He slowly pushed the overfilled punch bowls out the back door and out to the waiting area around the first hole where Lynn was patiently waiting, along with some not so patient adults.

No matter how many times he stopped by during construction, Rockfish felt a sense of pride when he walked through the finished product. Trees dotted the physical course, each with their own set of Bluetooth lights that pulsed to the holiday music playing over the speakers. Heaters, the kind you would see on outside restaurant patios for Fall and Winter dining, lined the course. One sat next to each tee box and flag stick, with others strategically placed throughout the eighteen holes. And if the last day of December's cold was too much for you, VR headset rentals were available inside the pro shop to experience those same eighteen holes, but with warmth and a hotdog in hand. Angel out-did himself, making sure Guardian Angel's Mini Golf was now part of the Metaverse.

"Here ya go, Lynn, sorry about being late," Rockfish said. "Blame Raffi, if you run across him. I lost track of him. I got a sneaky feeling he's out somewhere on the course."

Lynn smiled and steered the cart over to the thirsty adults who thrusted their tickets at her, some more Karen-esque than others.

Once the threat level was reset to less than midnight, Lynn had packed up and returned to the condo with Jawnie and had felt more at ease at her desk with each day. Once the county approved the permits, construction moved fast. The new windows and door were made of some space age polymer shit. Rockfish forgot the actual name of it, but even Putin wouldn't be able to get through it.

"Hey Lynn, speaking of people disappearing, do you know where Jawnie got off to?" Rockfish said.

"She was hanging out with your dad but wandered off in that direction when her phone rang." Lynn pointed to her left, towards where the staff had all parked.

The jury was back. It had to be it. No other explanation. Well, she had other friends. But if it was the jury, Christ, that took long enough. Annetta Provolone's retrial had dragged through the late fall and the jury had only gotten the case a few days ago. What everyone expected to be a quick decision in the Government's favor had dragged on and everyone in the office had been on pins and needles the last couple of days.

He found her sitting in the Subaru with the engine running. *Most likely the heat was on full and the seat's heaters cranked up too.* Rockfish noticed she wasn't on the phone. He walked around the back of the car and tried the passenger door.

"You're missing an awesome party," Rockfish said as he settled into the passenger seat.

"Guilty on all counts," Jawnie said. "It might finally be over."

Her voice wasn't steady, and Rockfish hoped she wasn't rushing to any rose-colored assessment. None of it was over. It wouldn't be like he told her after the first time she testified. Somewhere, someone might get a thorn in their ass all over again.

"Jawnie—"

"I know, Boss. It's never over. The Marini RICO case is up next on our docket. It won't be next month or even in 2023, and we'll have to relive this entire shitstorm all over again. But you'll be on the witness list with me this time and not just in the gallery."

"One day someone's gonna write a book about how you single-handedly took down the South Jersey and Baltimore mob families."

"Yeah, and it's going to be Rosa Mangold after that sweetheart deal the US Attorney gave her to flip. Telling the Feds she told you where to find the hard drive still may come back to bite someone in the ass."

"Ain't gonna be us," Rockfish said.

"She kept such a straight face!" Jawnie said with her own shit-eating grin.

"Told ya, the Government would find a way to get it introduced. I mean, they're the good guys, but not all good guys work as cleanly as us."

They both laughed and Rockfish reached over and put his hand on Jawnie's shoulder.

"People out there having fun, because of all we accomplished. Tell you what. I need a vacation. You need one. Lynn too."

"Tell me something I don't know."

"Let's get out of this car," Rockfish said. "Grab a couple of balls and the winner picks the vacation location. All expenses paid by yours truly."

"Seriously?"

"Absolutely. You win, Mack and I will show up in Hawaiian shirts and will keep the complaining to a minimum."

"A little friendly partner competition. I love it." Jawnie said.

ACKNOWLEDGEMENTS

Each time I am lucky enough to have a book published, I must start by thanking my awesome and extremely patient wife, Nicolita. From reading printed out scenes and chapters to being handed a three hundred-page plus, three-ring binder, she was there to tell me what worked, what didn't, and when my inside jokes or witty dialogue fell flat. Lastly, her vision and hand-drawn sketches led directly to the awesome cover art of this 3rd in the series.

My editor Ben Eads, who for the third straight time showed me how to better my craft in a short time and had me realize how good a story this actually was.

Thanks also to my beta readers, Tim Paul, Jason Little, Tammi Westberg and Susan Niner. Your keen eye and input catches of all my screw-ups. The attention to detail is greatly appreciated.

Natalie Norlock and Rosalyn Rael for sticking with my morning Twitch streams and being a great help when it came to renaming two characters.

Speaking of Twitch, all the viewers, followers and even subscribers that tune in each morning with me to watch paint dry – You keep me motivated to bang these keys and create storylines and characters. Extreme introvert to Twitch streamer. Who'da thunk it?

Daniel Glavan for without your almost daily positive affirmations, I'm not sure this book would have turned out as amazing as it did. Glad you're back on the reading horse and I hope to keep you fully stocked with Rockfish for some time to come.

Lastly, I am grateful to Reagan Rothe and Black Rose Writing team for dealing with my dumb questions and for their support in allowing me to continue this wild ride. The opportunity to give life to these characters in a trilogy and then some is one thing I'll always cherish. Stay tuned, number four is on the way!

ABOUT THE AUTHOR

Ken Harris retired from the FBI, after thirty-two years, as a cybersecurity executive. With over three decades writing intelligence products for senior Government officials, Ken provides unique perspectives on the conventional fast-paced crime thriller. He is the author of the *From the Case Files of Steve Rockfish* series. He spends days with his wife Nicolita, and two Labradors, Shady and Chalupa Batman. Evenings are spent playing Walkabout Mini Golf and cheering on Philadelphia sports. Ken firmly believes Pink Floyd, Irish whiskey and a Montecristo cigar are the only muses necessary. He is a native of New Jersey and currently resides in Northern Virginia.

NOTE FROM THE AUTHOR

Word-of-mouth is crucial for any author to succeed. If you enjoyed *A Bad Bout of the Yips*, please leave a review online—anywhere you are able. Even if it's just a sentence or two. It would make all the difference and would be very much appreciated.

Thanks!
Ken Harris

We hope you enjoyed reading this title from:

BLACK ❦ ROSE
writing™

www.blackrosewriting.com

Subscribe to our mailing list – *The Rosevine* – and receive **FREE** books, daily deals, and stay current with news about upcoming releases and our hottest authors.
Scan the QR code below to sign up.

Already a subscriber? Please accept a sincere thank you for being a fan of Black Rose Writing authors.

View other Black Rose Writing titles at
www.blackrosewriting.com/books and use promo code
PRINT to receive a **20% discount** when purchasing.